MARION ZIMMER BRADLEY'S SWORD AND SORCERESS XXIII

Edited by Elisabeth Waters

Cover Painting:
"An Oriental Beauty" by Luis Ricardo Falero (1851-1896).

ISBN-13: 978-1-934648-78-0
ISBN-10: 1-934648-78-7

FIRST EDITION
Trade Paperback Edition

November 15, 2008

A Publication of
Norilana Books
P. O. Box 2188
Winnetka, CA 91396
www.norilana.com

Printed in the United States of America

ACKNOWLEDGMENTS

Introduction © 2008 by Elisabeth Waters
"A Morsel for the Plague Queen" © 2008 by Dave Smeds
"Daughter of Heaven" © 2008 by Michael Spence & Elisabeth Waters
"The Vessel" © 2008 by Gerri Leen
"Polish on, Polish off: A Dragon Tale" © 2008 by Tom Inister
"It's All in the Making" © 2008 by Patricia B. Cirone
"Daughters of Brightshield" © 2008 by Pauline J. Alama
"Undivided" © 2008 by Marian Allen
"The Fairest of Them All" © 2008 by Melissa Mead
"Deermouse" © 2008 by K.D. Wentworth
"Blood Moon" © 2008 by Catherine Mintz
"Stolen Ghosts" © 2008 by Jonathan Moeller
"The Frog's Princess" © 2008 by Kristin Noone
"Shalott's Inn" © 2008 by Leah Cypess
"Wolf Maiden" © 2008 by Linda L. Donahue
"Black Magic" © 2008 by Resa Nelson
"Remembering" © 2008 by Deborah J. Ross
"Squirrel Errant" © 2008 by Michael H. Payne
"Hope for the Dawn" © 2008 by Catherine Soto
"Scam Artistry" © 2008 by Mercedes Lackey & Elisabeth Waters

Marion Zimmer Bradley's
Sword and Sorceress XXIII

Norilana Books
Fantasy

www.norilana.com

Marion Zimmer Bradley's

Sword and Sorceress

XXIII

Edited by

Elisabeth Waters

CONTENTS

INTRODUCTION

by Elisabeth Waters

I was delighted to learn that *Sword & Sorceress 22* sold well enough to justify doing *Sword & Sorceress 23*, and I hope that this will continue. Not only do I enjoy editing these anthologies, but also I am happy that we are able to continue Marion Zimmer Bradley's work of discovering and encouraging new writers. It's gratifying to watch a writer go from submitting the sort of story that used to get MZB's "willing suspension of disbelief does not mean 'hang by the neck until dead'" rejection to a story that an editor would like to buy.

It's also great fun to see the next episode in some of the series that run through *Sword & Sorceress*. Mercedes Lackey's *Vows and Honor* series started with a story in *Sword & Sorceress 3*, continued with seven more stories in *Sword & Sorceress 4* through *10*, and then became a book. Catherine Soto's third *Temple Cats* story is in this volume, as is the fifth story in the *Treasures* series, which Michael Spence and I have been passing back and forth between us since *Sword & Sorceress 14*. Heather Rose Jones's *Skins* stories began appearing in *Sword & Sorceress 12*, and her most recent one was in *Sword & Sorceress 22*. Unfortunately, she didn't send me one this year, but maybe she will next year. We also have a couple of stories that are sequels to stories from earlier volumes, but it's too soon to know whether any of them will develop into a series or not.

Editors often hear two closely-related questions: "Why did you buy that story for the anthology?" and "Why didn't you buy my story?" Sometimes I'm asked the latter in person at a convention; ideally the questioner is a professional looking for more feedback, but sometimes he or she is an amateur who is out to convince me that I was *wrong* to reject his or her story. The most important thing to remember about rejection, whether you are just starting out or have been selling for decades (oh yes, rejection slips can still hurt, even then) is that the editor is rejecting the *story*, not you as a person.

Why, then, does an editor buy—or reject—a story?

In simplest terms, editors buy stories they like; what becomes complex are the reasons the editor likes a story. I have often thought that an editor is a collection of prejudices— certainly MZB was—but as long as what the editor likes matches what the readers of the publication like, this is probably a good thing.

There are a lot of other factors, of course: the story must fit the market (which is why reading the guidelines before submitting is essential) and must be the right length. The length desired changes over time, resulting in rejections such as "I really liked this story, but it's the maximum length the guidelines allow and you submitted it the day of the deadline, so I'd have to reject three other stories I've already put in the tentative final line-up to include this one." By the end of the reading period I am more apt to be looking for something short and funny; anything long has to be truly spectacular. Sometimes the length has to be the size of the current hole in the line-up, especially if the line-up is for a magazine, which has less flexibility than an anthology.

Then, at least for *Sword & Sorceress,* there's the issue of balance: Do the stories, taken together, emphasize the "swords," or the "sorcery"—or do they evenly mix the two? Have we included enough new writers? On the other hand, do we have enough writers who are well-known and whose names will help sell the anthology? (If you would like a more detailed explanation, see MZB's "Why Did My Story Get Rejected?" at www.mzbworks.com.)

What I personally tend to look for is a story that is both original and memorable. If I hold a story overnight and can't remember the next morning what it was about, I'm apt to reject it in favor of something I do still remember the next day, the next month, and beyond.

Once I have chosen the stories, the next question is what order to put them in. I've seen an anthology where the stories were in alphabetical order by the author's last name (the editor was a librarian by training), but I really don't think that's the ideal arrangement. Not that I know what the ideal arrangement is, or even if there *is* one, but I try to come up with one that I hope the reader will find satisfying.

Consider, as I have been lately, the book of Psalms. (For those not familiar with that portion of the Bible, it is a collection of 150 pieces ranging in length from 2 to 176 verses.) The first one can be taken as a keynote statement for the book: it praises the righteous man and condemns the ungodly, basically saying that keeping God's law is a right and proper thing and will make life good. The last several psalms end the book on a high note, with praises to God.

Similarly, *Sword & Sorceress* traditionally begins with a strong story representing a mix of the martial and magical arts, and ends with something short and funny. We want to leave our readers smiling. (I imagine that psalms praising God would have a similar effect.) Other than that, I try to alternate between short and long stories and between stories about swords, sorcery, or both.

So here are the stories I liked—for various reasons—this year. I hope you will like them too.

A MORSEL FOR THE PLAGUE QUEEN

by Dave Smeds

To paraphrase Shakespeare, some are born magic, some achieve magic, and some have magic thrust upon them. Verda, an extremely distant cousin of the king, never expected him to take any notice of her. When she became a pawn in his quest to save his kingdom, she didn't expect to live through the experience—but great things await a pawn who survives until the end.

Sword and sorcery works by Dave Smeds include his novels *The Sorcery Within* and *The Schemes of Dragons,* and shorter pieces in such anthologies as *Enchanted Forests* and *Return To Avalon,* as well as eight previous volumes of *Sword & Sorceress.* He writes in many genres, from science fiction to contemporary fantasy to horror to superhero and others, and has been a Nebula Award finalist. He lives in the Napa/Sonoma wine country of California with his wife and children. In addition to being an author, he has been a farmer, graphic artist, and karate instructor.

For a man with a wooden foot, Rayl moved with deceptive grace. Once again Verda failed to anticipate his thrust. The blunt at the end of his rapier struck her practice vest hard, adding to the bruises within her left breast. Too late, she sidestepped, deflecting away his weapon.

"Not good enough," he said.

Verda blew a sweaty strand of hair out of her face, wishing she had tied her braid tighter. She glared at Rayl. It was bad enough that he was so much better than she, but worse when he said it aloud.

He limped back to his spot. She tried to calm her mind, ignore distractions.

She saw he wasn't quite balanced. She charged.

He parried her. As she danced back to avoid his counterthrust, she stepped on the hem of her skirt and went sprawling on her rump.

Laughter came from the trees.

She bared her teeth. The two peasant boys, Gritt and Cauld, hooted at her from their perch on a thick oak bough. Or did until Rayl gagged them with his master-at-arms scrutiny.

At their various positions around the glade, the members of the squad worked hard to suppress their own signs of amusement.

Verda hated having to practice in a skirt. She was better in the boy's hose and tunic Rayl had allowed her to wear during the previous week's drills. But now he expected more. "An assassin will not wait for you to compose yourself," he had lectured. "You must be ready to fight at a moment's notice."

Lately he had taken to sneaking up while she was asleep and emitting a shout, and if she did not vault to her feet in an instant, knife in hand, prepared to meet an attack in nothing but her nightshirt, he would thwack her with his "learning stick" of bundled willow switches.

She stole a few moments of respite by staying on the ground. She didn't understand how Rayl could keep going without showing fatigue. He was ancient. Fifty, he had told her a fortnight after he had been assigned to lead her bodyguards. That was three times as old as she.

"Taking the offensive was the right move," he said. "Try it again."

"Must I?" she puffed.

Rayl sighed. "You are the last line of your own defense, girl. Do you want to be helpless?"

Groaning, she rolled onto her feet. But before straightening, she grabbed a handful of dirt. She flung it at Rayl's face.

He back-pedalled, belly-laughing with approval. She closed in. He cleared his eyes and tried to parry, but her sword blunt reached him, landing with enough force that, in a real engagement, he would have taken a serious wound in the mid-section.

"Better," he said. The other warriors murmured approvingly. In the tree, Gritt and Cauld grunted in astonishment.

Verda didn't let her guard down. That was one lesson she had learned well.

But Rayl did not test her further. When he saw that she was alert, he pulled the blunt off his rapier and sheathed the weapon.

"Catch your breath. Noon is nigh."

He stepped behind her and unlaced her practice vest. As the hardened leather casing fell off her body, and the breeze struck the sweat-drenched cloth of her blouse, the sharp, sudden coolness caused her bruises to throb.

She let herself dwell on the discomfort. Pain was a teacher, Rayl had said. It was also a distraction. She wondered if that might be the real reason Rayl had initiated her into a regimen of self-defense. All she knew was that at that moment, she would rather still be getting thumped with a sword and have boys laugh at her than move on to her next task.

∛❦√

As the sun filtered down through the leaves from almost directly above, heralding the interval when the magic she must wield was at its greatest potency—Verda strode from the woods onto the tilled part of the farm holding she and her escort of king's men had come to aid.

A small crowd of peasants was waiting expectantly at the edge of a barley field. Verda entered the enclosure of pavilion cloth they had erected for her privacy and removed all her clothes. She donned a knee-length frock of rough burlap and reemerged into the open.

Rayl handed her a spear. He had made it earlier this morning from a sapling he had cut down. It was a thoroughly primitive article, its point nothing more than a whittled tip. There was no reason to craft anything better.

She set off into the field.

The squad had taken up sentry positions at regular intervals around the entire parcel. If an attack came, the men would protect her as best they could, but only from threats that came from beyond. The threat within the field was hers alone to deal with.

Her calves brushed against stalks of ripening grain. A good harvest had been shaping up here—enough to cover the king's taxes and still leave the serfs with a bounty for their toil. But up ahead, nearly half the field had been transformed. The crop had sickened and collapsed, leaving a matted terrain of spongy, blackened compost. It stank of sewage. Midges and flies spun in lethargic spirals above the area.

The outline of the sick zone was amorphous. Tendrils threaded outward like mangrove roots. What Verda was confronting was a tumor of the land.

Her prey was the spore from which the ugliness sprouted. The cyst. Strong and well-armed as the twenty warriors surrounding her were, they could not locate it for her, nor survive the encounter.

Her gait faltered as she approached the boundary of the infection. A sulphurous plume wafted over her, making her snort. She forced herself to take a step, then another and another, propelled by the knowledge that her only hope of success was to spend as little time as possible in the blighted zone.

As she crossed the threshold, the air clenched around her, dank in spite of the arid summer day. At noon, the effect was as weak as it got, but it was still enough to force sweat from her pores. Her frock began to cling to her sides below the armpits. Her feet sank in with each step, first only a toe's height, then nearly to the ankles. Only the lightness of her body, the lack of heavy gear or armor, and the interlaced net of fallen grain stalks prevented her from becoming bogged down.

Her throat constricted. Her lungs did not want to fill with the putrid air. She made them do so. The inhalation made her feel as though foulness were taking root inside her chest, but if she didn't breathe, she would pass out, and the blight would claim her.

Now that she was within the boundary, the enchantment that had been placed upon her became active, revealing the proximity and direction of her goal. The cyst lay to her left. It was not in the center of the vileness—that would have been too easy. Too symmetrical. Less evil.

She struggled through the rest of her approach, reaching a place where the earth was slightly mounded, though this was only apparent now that she was close. As she took the last few steps, insects harassed her eyes, tried to crawl into her ears, into her nostrils. The stench increased.

Finally she was close enough. In a swift, sure motion, she thrust into the mound with the spear.

A shriek overwhelmed the buzz of the insects. The spear bucked. She pulled it free before she lost her grip.

A viscous mass, greatly resembling a ball of mucus, emerged from the soil. It oozed a puslike discharge from the wound Verda had made.

She thrust again, this time right at the center.

Another shriek set her eardrums to ringing. Knowing what was coming, Verda threw up her free arm to shield her eyes. The cyst . . . popped. Sticky, clinging matter expoded in all directions, spattering Verda from head to foot.

Around her on the field, the substance began sizzling, eating into the matted stalks and soil like acid. Both her spear and her frock began to decompose. But the anointment did nothing to her skin and hair save hang there. It revolted her with its texture, its heat, and its odor, but it had no destructive effect.

The shreds of the cyst collapsed. Verda poked the larger flaps of membrane several more times, but did not get a living reaction. She discarded the spear.

Already the flies and midges were drifting away in the wind. The stench was fading. The grain, of course, would continue to rot, but in a natural way, fertilizing the soil. In three or four years, the patch would seem normal to look at, to tread upon, to smell. In a decade, people could safely eat food grown in its soil.

Most important, the area would no longer expand until it consumed the entire holding and those next to it.

Verda wobbled away from the thing she had killed. At first, the droplets that fell from her bubbled and fumed as soon as they hit the ground, then even this lingering element of sorcery ceased. Her frock, which was holding together only because half of it had been shielded from the spray by her body, stopped disintegrating.

Finally she reached the pristine zone. Rayl was waiting there.

"Well done," he said.

Beside him stood the peasants, whose field this was. They included the boys, Gritt and Cauld. The latter did not appear ready to mock her now. Verda almost wished they would, rather than see them cringe in disgust at the spectacle of her.

"Great Lady," said Mott, the landholder, "on behalf of myself, my kin, and all my neighbors, I thank you."

Verda acknowledged him with a nod. It was all she could manage.

"Let's get you cleaned up," said Wreena, Mott's wife.

Verda returned to the enclosure, this time accompanied by Wreena and her teenaged daughter Brigg, a sister of Gritt and Cauld. Verda slipped out of the remnant of the frock. Wreena handed her a block of soap, and then she and Brigg took turns pouring ladlefuls of warm water over Verda. The water came from a cauldron the family had transported to the site on their hay wain.

Viscous strands of ichor and greyish suds flowed off her. She stepped clear of the resultant muck and the procedure was repeated.

Verda appreciated the peasant women's trouble, to heat water for her and bring it out so far from their hearth. The last time she had destroyed a cyst, she had bathed in cold well water. "More," she murmured as soon as the third round of rinsing was done.

Pampering was not something Verda was used to. She would not waste the experience.

ઝઉ૨ઠ૭

She was still light-headed when the peasants and her bodyguards gathered for supper, but at least she was clean. The aroma of the food even awakened her appetite—just a little.

The meal was served outdoors around a bonfire in the farmyard, for none of the buildings would have accommodated so many visitors. The holding was home to three large families, but their dwellings were hovels clustered against the half-collapsed remains of a watchtower left over from the Forgotten Age. The peasants did not even have a barn, only a pigsty and goat pen. Their grain was stored in root cellars, their hay in stacks in the open fields.

Their hosts proudly served skewers of roast chevon along with brimming bowls of porridge. Verda realized they must have slaughtered a pair of goats for the feast, and wondered how many months it would be until they had meat again, aside from whatever small game might succumb to snares or to the boys' slings.

Many gazes were upon her. She made sure to eat as heartily as she could manage to honor their hospitality—their only material way of showing their gratitude. Much as her bony form needed a little fattening, it was not an easy task. Every time she encountered a cyst, she had to re-learn the desire to thrive.

When everyone had eaten and beer had been served, Mott raised his cup in salute. "To King Takk and his cousin, the noble Verda, a true daughter of Ommero."

A cheer went up.

"Where will you go next, My Lady?" Mott asked. "How long until you return to the palace?"

Verda knew the serf was trying his best to be an amiable host and engage her in as much conversation as someone of his low station could dare, had she been who he thought she was. She could not answer him.

Rayl responded for her, before the pause grew uncomfortably long. "Alas, the Plague Queen is determined to reclaim her realm. She has roamed far and wide, spewing out the sort of abomination you saw destroyed today. Tomorrow we must move on to aid your neighbors at Heather Bluff. From there, we cannot yet know how many more places we must visit."

"May you fare well," Mott said.

"The old tales say Prince Ommero killed the Plague Queen. Is this *another* one?"

The speaker was young Cauld. His mother twisted his ear for his lack of etiquette.

Rayl held up his hand, granting pardon.

"It is a fair question. One that is on the minds of many in the realm, I am sure." Rayl's tone became grim. "What we face is indeed the same being. Evra, the Plague Queen, who ruled these lands until two centuries ago, when nearly all of this great valley was the Fever Swamp, and our people were little more than shepherds and olive growers in the hills. She is one of the bloodwraiths who was unleashed in our world during the Sorcerers' War. It is not possible to truly slay a bloodwraith. Ommero destroyed the suit of flesh she wore. It caused her great agony. It made her unable to wield most of her power, so that when Ommero assumed the kingship and commanded his engineers and laborers to drain the swamp, the effort succeeded, giving us our fine, fertile croplands and noble estates. But it did not kill her. For generations our people described Evra as dead because it was assumed her essence had been sucked back to her dimension, where she could bother us no more. Now we know she hid away somewhere, perhaps in the deepest part of the delta where men never go. She has manifested again. With a corporeal body, her sorcery has its old potency back. So for these past four years, she has laid her hideous spores, trying to turn our realm back into the Fever Swamp."

"Is it true she has killed two of King Takk's sons?"

"It is," Rayl replied.

The peasants murmured apprehensively. A small child hid behind his mother's skirts.

"Evra has a special enmity for the House of Ommero," Rayl continued. "First, to have revenge. Second, because anyone who carries the blood of the man who defeated her is immune to the full effect of her magic, and this enrages her. The princes are only two of the victims. Outside the king's own household, a score of other descendants have fallen. Evra is powerful and she is resourceful."

"But King Takk can kill her, can't he?" asked Gritt. "The way she was killed before?"

It was an even bolder question than his brother's had been. Rayl frowned at Gritt, the way he had frowned at him back in the tree during the sword practice. Gritt cowered.

"The Plague Queen's day of reckoning will come. The king hunts her as we speak. Meanwhile, he has arranged to send his lesser kinsfolk—even fourth cousins, fifth cousins—to such places as this, to destroy the cysts before the land is rendered too sick to be worth saving."

Verda saw the serfs glance at her with new insight, understanding now why they had never heard her name before. They had been too intimidated by the escort of twenty king's guards to confess their ignorance, fearing they would cause insult.

She knew they didn't suspect the rest. Undoubtedly they still assumed she was a figure at court. The truth was, she had never seen the palace, much less been welcomed inside. Long ago, Ommero's youngest daughter had been given in marriage to the first Duke of Riverbend, who gave his own youngest daughter to a favorite vassal, a knight beloved far and wide, but only a marchwarden in terms of rank. Later the warden had needed money, so he made a rich merchant into a son-in-law. The merchant had been a commoner, and so Verda, his granddaughter, was a commoner as well.

Her ancestry had never been significant until those with even a drop of the blood of Ommero in their veins had been conscripted into the war against the Plague Queen.

"Excuse me," she said, standing up. "I am very tired. I would like to sleep now."

Wreena leaped up to show her the way to her accommodations—Wreena and Mott's own straw tick in the loft of their hovel. A cheer followed her away from the bonfire. To Verda, it was an assault on her ears when she only wanted silence and solitude.

Rayl studied her as she passed by him. She avoided his gaze.

ରେଷ୍ଠିର

S he burst awake to find Rayl with his hands on her shoulders. He was shaking her.

The nightmare—the usual one of drowning in a stagnant, scum-coated pool deep in a swamp—lost its grip on her. Her eyes focussed, recognizing the loft. A rooster was crowing, but it was still full dark, the only illumination coming from the lantern Rayl must have re-lit.

Furrows were etched deep in Rayl's forehead. "Breathe deep. Let it pass," he said. He let go of her, letting her sink back onto the mattress.

She tried to let go of the tension. But her heart kept hammering the inside of her ribcage. Muscles ached all over her body. And her left arm itched in a maddening way. It was the worst episode yet.

"I don't know how much longer I can do this," she said.

He raised a finger to his lips. She caught the mouse-stirs from below—cookfires being stoked up, bed pallets being removed from the floor to be stored away for the day. The peasants were awake, and might overhear.

She kept the silence he wanted, but it was harder than it had ever been. She wanted to shout until her outcry echoed from the thatch above her head: *The king cowers in his palace under triple guard. He sends cousins he has never met out to save his lands, to become targets for his nemesis.*

"I'm just a girl," she murmured. "How did it come down to me?"

"If you don't do it, who will?" Rayl whispered.

CR

It was a mark of her exhaustion that she managed to go back to sleep, if only for one more hour. She awoke to the sound of eggs frying and the aroma of porridge as it bubbled in Wreena's kettle. She stayed still and kept her eyes closed, trying to hoard her strength. She was sure the squad already had their bedrolls packed and would be ready to depart for Heather Bluff as soon as breakfast was over. The prospect of fighting another cyst at noon was unbearable.

Unfortunately the itch on her arm tormented too much to let her linger further. She gave up, threw on her clothes, and climbed down the ladder.

The peasant family curtsied and bowed. "Good morning," she said in as friendly a tone as she could manage given her unsettled mood.

She lifted the door flap and stepped out. The east had buttered, but the sun was not yet peeking above the horizon. The air was refreshingly brisk.

Rayl, as she could have predicted, was the guard stationed closest to the door. "What's wrong with your arm?" he asked in place of a greeting.

Verda realized she had been scratching even while she walked. She turned the arm outward. Now that she was in the light, she saw just how large the irritated area was at the inner elbow, and spotted the pinprick of red.

Rayl's face went pale. "She has found you," he told Verda. He tossed away the mug of tea he had been drinking and shouted to his men: "Battle ready! The Plague Queen comes!"

As always, a third of the squad were stationed at intervals around the holding; they had only to stay as they were in order to do as Rayl commanded. The rest began donning armor, lacing up boots, stringing bows, buckling on scabbards.

Verda vomited the remains of her supper onto the ground in front of her.

All three peasant families burst from their hovels. Rayl held up a hand to quiet their cacophony. "The Plague Queen will be upon us at any moment. Gather everyone inside the watchtower. We will try to fend her off, but you should bring anything that can serve as a weapon. Bring your dogs."

Men and boys rushed to do as he said, while mothers snatched babies from cribs, and girls rounded up toddlers.

Rayl helped Verda straighten up. He held out her rapier and sword belt. "Remember all we've spoken of. Hope is not gone."

She spat out a final bit of vomit. "Yes it is. You know it is. Hope is for the king in his castle."

"Then be brave." He made her close her hand around the sword hilt.

"I'm not ready to die, Rayl. I've barely lived."

"All the more reason to cling to hope," he said. "Now, please, get into the tower."

He assisted her to the place in the ruined wall where the barbican had once been. These days only a gap remained, but most of the rest of the wall was eight or ten or even twelve feet high, a nearly unbroken ring that made it a credible place to attempt a last stand.

Suddenly the northernmost sentry cried out, "Mindless ones!"

Men were shambling out of the woods where Verda and Rayl had sparred with blunted rapiers the previous morning. The newcomers marched straight into the blighted area where she had killed the cyst, the still-repugnant part of the holding that any sane man would avoid.

But these were not sane men. The first rays of day revealed their blank countenances. They were the Plague Queen's slaves—men who had succumbed to her snares, and now had no will of their own.

The sunshine also revealed the swords and axes and pikes in their grips. And one other, far worse thing. The bloodwraith herself hovered in the air, personally directing her army.

Verda screamed.

Rayl covered her eyes and pressed her through the gap, taking her to a spot against the wall opposite the opening, the place that would be farthest from the point of attack.

"No," Verda pleaded.

Rayl stood up to leave. Verda clutched him by the leg.

"I have to command the defense," he said gently. "If I could, I would stay. It has been an honor to know you, Verda of Weaver Crossroads."

"Don't say that. Don't go. Don't die."

Rayl beckoned Mott, who had just appeared with a bundle of long sticks to make into torches. "Keep her close. Protect her as long as you can."

Mott nodded. Rayl hurried away.

"Nooooo . . . " Verda wept.

The watchtower filled with the rest of the locals. Verda's moans were drowned out by the wails of the children. Rayl ordered archers to the tops of piles of fallen tower stones. It seemed like only a moment had passed before they were nocking and releasing their arrows; the enemy was already that close. It was only a moment more before the first of them fell dead, shot through the eye as he stood above the level of the wall to shoot a second time. Evra's army had its own archers.

The bulk of Rayl's squad gathered just inside the opening, forcing the mindless ones to come at them one at a time. The first attacker flung himself onto the points of the defenders' swords, heedless of his own safety. Before the swords could be pulled from the body, more mindless ones surged forward, and just that quickly, the front two of Rayl's men were speared in their midsections, struck so violently that their chain-link armor gave way.

An insectlike whine rose in pitch and volume. It was maddening in a preternatural way, making the guardsmen stagger and shake their heads, breaking their concentration.

Verda huddled in her spot between two pickle barrels, trembling. Suddenly Mott knelt down beside her. He was holding a lit torch.

"I did not have time to tell the captain . . . "

"Tell him what?"

Mott handed her the torch and moved the barrel beside her out of the way. Beneath it was a trap door. Mott lifted it, revealing a tunnel.

"The people who built the tower made this. It leads through the hill to a hidden spot in the woods. We will send the children through. But you go first. Your survival matters most."

Verda seized the torch and, rapier clutched in her other hand, plunged into the opening.

The walls hugged close. Diminutive as she was, she had to stoop in order to avoid hitting her head on the roof. The air was stale with the musk of earth and grubs. The torch gave off only enough light to make it seem as though she were vanishing down the gullet of some giant creature.

The screams of men dying faded, replaced by the echoes of her own panting and, somewhere far behind her, the muffled shrieks of small children who did not want to be forced into the passageway.

Only then, in headlong flight, did guilt swell. Rayl and the others were facing death. According to the plan, she was to be with them to the end. But now that she had the unexpected chance, she couldn't stop running.

A gleam of daylight appeared ahead. She threw down the torch, letting it snuff out in the dust. She put on a burst of speed that made her trip and skin her knees, but she was up and going again even before the blood could ooze from the scraped spots.

She burst through the veil of scrub ivy and into the open.

In front of her, a creek babbled. Trees and leaves shaded her. She was so far from the battle she could only hear a faint clang of metal striking metal. She couldn't hear the awful insect whine at all.

She darted across the stream and ran along the far bank. It did not take her perfectly away from the holding, but it kept her under cover of brush and trees. Her other choice was to cut across an open field.

She ran like a hare flushed from its burrow. She might lack girth and strength and training, but speed was one attribute she was blessed with.

She was daring to believe that she might actually be getting away when a sharp blow to her upper back sent her sprawling into a patch of bracken. She landed so hard the wind was knocked from her.

Breathless, she forced herself to spin onto her back. She swung her rapier in a wide arc.

Above her, the Plague Queen flitted back. The sword stroke missed.

Verda would have screamed again if she'd had air in her lungs. Rayl had told her the Plague Queen's current form was nightmarish, but he had spared her the details. The bloodwraith was a monstrous mosquito, its body as long as her own, its wingspan greater than the largest eagle. A swamp mosquito, its abdomen oily and red, the bristles on its legs dripping with greyish scum.

Verda held her sword at the ready. The Plague Queen . . . laughed. "Spawn of Ommero. You only had the one chance." The mirth and the taunt were decipherable in spite of being rendered in a mosquito-like burr.

All too soon Verda understood what her attacker meant. A numbness claimed her neck, and began spreading down into her body. She reached behind her head and found an oozing place at her nape. Evra had not merely knocked her down; she had stung her.

Verda became so weak the rapier fell from her grip. Soon her arm itself plopped to the crushed bracken. She tried to wriggle away—anything to put more distance between her and the bloodwraith—but her legs were so leaden she could barely divot the loam with her heels.

Evra descended, landing right atop Verda, flicking away the sword with a middle foot.

Verda thrashed as frantically as she could manage, but Evra was barely jostled. At her leisure, she took aim with her proboscis, and thrust it into Verda's neck.

As her blood was siphoned away, Verda grew faint, but not so much that she was graced with unconsciousness. She felt the sharp pinch of the wound, the weight of Evra's body atop her. She could see the giant mosquito abdomen swelling and reddening from the meal.

Evra lifted her head back, pausing at her feast. "Your blood is sweet. I will savor it. I may keep you alive for days, child of Ommero, and snack upon you when the mood strikes me."

From farther down the creek came high-pitched human cries of terror. The peasant children had emerged from the tunnel. Gritt and Cauld were yelling at their juniors to be quiet and run. Verda moaned, realizing that the youngsters were heading to the spot where she lay, unaware of Evra's presence.

Evra rose into a hover, scanning through the trees. "Oh, good," she said. "My slaves needed some fresh meat for their supper." And she began to laugh again.

The laugh transformed into a screech. Abruptly the bloodwraith began thrashing in midair. She spun in a circle, then crashed to the earth an arms-length from Verda. She writhed there, her movement quickly becoming feeble.

"Your . . . your blood was *sweet*."

"It had a little something extra in it for you," Verda said. As Rayl had so often told her, she was the last line of her own defense. How she wished he could have been there. She had not played her part quite the way they had pictured, but the goal had been accomplished nonetheless.

Evra crumpled. Her new body, that had taken her two centuries to shape and to inhabit with her essence, twitched a final three or four times, then it moved no more.

CRSO

Verda slid into a state of hazy consciousness. She remained aware of pain, of the heaviness of her limbs, of the metallic scent of clotted blood wafting up from her neck. A twig snapped. Gritt and Cauld and a bevy of small children were staring at her and the dead bloodwraith in the crushed bracken. They ran off shrieking.

Eventually—she could not calculate how soon—she heard heavier footsteps. Figures loomed over her. To her astonishment, she recognized Rayl and two other members of the squad. They were bloody and all three moved gingerly, but they did not seem to be mortally injured. At Rayl's command, one of the younger men chopped the giant mosquito body in half with his battle axe.

Rayl knelt down at Verda's side.

"You live. You live," she murmured. Tears welled on her eyelashes and let go, dribbling down her cheeks.

"I do," he said.

"I'm . . . sorry. I'm sorry I ran."

"Had you not, I would not be here now." His tone held no reproach. Suddenly the pain, the numbness, the certainty of her own death, did not trouble her as they had.

Rayl cradled her head, hissing as his fingers touched the oozing bite at the back of her neck. As he gazed at the other puncture, the crease in his brow grew so deep it stretched from the top of his nose nearly to his hairline.

"It's bad," she said. "I killed her, but she killed me."

"Hope is not lost," he said.

"You always say that, even when you don't believe it."

"I *always* believe it," he replied.

The delirium deepened. Time did not flow; it skipped. At one point, gentle hands were cleaning her wounds with a moist cloth. In the next moment, so it seemed, the surface beneath her was jostling and bumping, and she realized she was being transported on a wagon. Her flesh felt so hot and waxen she felt sure it was melting off her bones.

A blanket was draped over the wagon, screening her from the sun. The coolness and the dimness appealed to her so much she surrendered to them.

❦

The next she knew, she was lying in a bed softer than any she had ever before felt.

She opened her eyes. The bed was immense, its posts made of finest rosewood, its canopy draped in fine Southern blue silk. Cut fresh flowers filled Ayr porcelain vases on matching nightstands on either side. The walls were draped in tapestries of superb craftsmanship, depicting key events in the lives of leading members of the House of Ommero.

And in a plush chair, his hair combed, dressed in fine court livery, his face and hands more pristinely clean than she had ever seen, his weapons absent, sat Rayl. His eyes were closed. His head rested on the cushioning. His chest was rising and falling at a steady rate.

She tried to speak. It came out as a cough.

Rayl was instantly and fully awake. He sat up sharply, a warrior ready to deal with whatever he must. As he became oriented, he relaxed and grinned at Verda.

He *grinned*. Verda had never seen him do that before. He picked up a crystal bell from the small table by his chair and rang it. The tone reverberated enchantingly off the ceiling's great wooden beams and panels.

She coughed again. He poured her a cup of water from her nightstand pitcher. She drank without stopping until it was gone.

"There. You look better already," Rayl said.

"I thought I would die."

"It was a near thing. Such a fever you had. It took the skill of the queen's best healers to pull you through."

"What happened back at the holding? How did *you* survive?"

He held up his left arm. Verda saw a partially healed slice that ran halfway from wrist to elbow. It would leave him with another battle scar for his collection. "The attack ceased the moment Evra died. Deprived of her influence, the mindless ones lowered their weapons and simply stood where they were. I am afraid we killed several without need before we realized what had transpired."

"And the peasants?"

"All were saved. We shielded the adults from the horde. The children made it through the tunnel unscathed."

"I saw Gritt and Cauld. I think."

"They found you. You are their heroine, you know. They wanted to run to every holding and shepherd's hut in their whole shire to tell what they had seen. They only gave up the idea when I told them they could help escort your litter to the palace. It's only been three days since they returned to their farm."

"Three . . . days?"

"You were ill more than a fortnight, and it has been another day since your fever broke."

The wonder of being alive was replaced with something less sweet. "Why did you tell Gritt and Cauld not to tell everyone what I did?"

"Because they would not have told the right tale."

The speaker was a woman. She had already reached the foot of the bed—Verda had paid only minimal attention to the subtle sounds of a door opening and closing. Her attire, though clearly meant as casual parlor wear, was so resplendent Verda had no doubt of the woman's identity.

Verda deliberately did not make any attempt at an obeisance. "What tale do they tell instead?" she demanded.

"That the king laid a trap for the demon," said the queen, "and when Evra fell into it, Takk was at last able to confront her. He slew her with his own axe, showing himself to be a true heir of Ommero."

"Of course," Verda said bitterly. "And what tale do they tell of me?"

"That you were among the cousins sent into the provinces to kill the cysts. That you did more than that? I suppose there will always be rumors that the king was not present when the Plague Queen perished. There are rumors noted in the old histories that say Prince Ommero was not there when she was killed the first time. But you will tell whoever asks that they should not believe rumors. Nor will you ever speak of Evra dying by means of poison, or of you and the others being sent out as bait, at the risk of your lives, while the king remained hidden in his stronghold."

Verda gritted her teeth so firmly her jaw hurt.

"You want to tell the truth."

"Should I wish to further lies?"

"Lies will be furthered, whether you wish it or not. It is for the best. My husband is like any king; he does not wish to lose face. The people are like any people. They want to believe their leader is mighty. Even as we speak, His Majesty and his retinue are visiting every corner of the kingdom, displaying the body of Evra for all to see. You cannot imagine the rapture and relief his visits bring. You would not wish to see how fearful those same people would be, were they to know the real story, and understand how near the bloodwraith was to success, and how impotent we were against her these four years."

Verda could not understand how the queen could gaze at her so steadily, so unabashed. "Did the king do anything? Was he even the one who came up with the *plan*?"

"No. It was my plan." Yet even that confession did not cause the queen to drop her gaze. "But it was a king's magician who altered your blood. Those were king's men who escorted you, enough of a guard that Evra did not suspect you were bait. Does it matter who takes credit, as long as the realm is saved?"

Verda sighed. "I see. So I am to go back to my fief, and keep my tongue." The last three words burned her throat on the way out.

"Your silence is necessary, but going back to your village? That won't do at all. I need you here."

Verda blinked. "What do you mean?"

"You are a young lady of proven ability and bravery, who wishes to do what is best for her land. You want your contribution to matter. I can give you that chance."

The conversation had taken a direction Verda had not expected. She didn't trust it yet, but Rayl's quiet smile made her willing to hear more. "What is it you're proposing?" she asked the queen.

"As you have seen, there are things the king cannot do, that nevertheless must be done if the realm is to thrive. The real work does not happen in the throne room or out on the parade grounds. It happens quietly, in rooms such as this. Think what you will of Takk, but he understands this. He could have failed to follow my advice of how to lay a trap for Evra, but he heeded what I said. He consulted his magicians. He listened to old comrades such as Rayl. And success was achieved."

The queen took Verda's hand. "The right advice, given discreetly and at the right time, means everything. I want to add another voice to the cause. I am getting on in years. It is time I took on another lady-in-waiting, to learn what must be learned, to ensure when my son comes to the throne, and when *his* son comes to the throne, the administration of the kingdom will go on as it should. Will you accept this honor, Verda of Weaver Crossroads?"

"Me? Live in the palace?"

"Yes."

"What of my family?"

"You may visit them when you like, and they visit you. But I think your mother and father will be well occupied arranging their new estate. And your eldest brother busy with his handsome new merchant vessel. But perhaps your sister will agree to join you here. You will need an aide, if you take on as much responsibility as I hope you will."

Verda looked for hints in the queen's demeanor that would indicate insincerity, but did not see any.

"All I have to do is agree, and this will happen?"

"The estates and the ship will happen regardless, as a reward for what you have done already. And the money, of course."

"The money?"

"We will not mention how much coin you will have to spend as you like. That would be gauche."

Verda felt the urge to cough, and hurriedly sipped more water.

"I wish you to understand. I do not demand that you stay. I offer it. Along with whatever other rewards are within my power to grant. So what do you say? Do you wish to make a difference?"

Verda's glance darted to Rayl, then back to the queen.

Rayl began laughing.

"What's so funny?" the queen asked.

"Hope is stirring. She isn't used to it."

Was that the feeling? All Verda knew was what was awakening inside her was strange and vivid, and she wanted to learn its nature.

"I will answer you in the morning," she told the queen.

DAUGHTER OF HEAVEN

by *Michael Spence & Elisabeth Waters*

I don't know what it is—the upcoming Olympics in China, perhaps—but this year I got enough Oriental stories that I could have done an entire anthology of them. There are some stories I expect to be set in China (I don't think Catherine Soto is going to be dragged out of the Tang Dynasty anytime soon), but I didn't expect it from Michael. Of course, I didn't know that he and his wife, Ramona, are, as he put it, "recent Sinophiles. Not that we support the mainland government; but China existed long before the Party and will exist after it." In this story Laurel, who is still working in the Customs House, finds something in a batch of documents for a shipment from China that will change her life forever.

      Michael Spence and I have been collaborating on and off since we were in high school. Our first joint published story (and the second story in the *Treasures* series) was "Salt and Sorcery" in *Sword & Sorceress 16* in 1999. Nine years—and four stories—later, we're still trying to get Stephen to pass his mastery exams (fourth time's the charm), but Michael has finished his PhD and is discovering the joys of hunting for a job that will use it. He has continued his Harlan Ellison scholarship with an article in *Sci Phi: The Journal Of Science Fiction And Philosophy,* and his writing and acting credits now include audio drama also (for the shows *The Astral Audio Experience, One Eighteen: Migration,* and *Star Wars—Codename: Starkeeper,* all available through the Internet). For more of his writings, see http://www.michaelspence.us.

Work at the Customs House was much more interesting these days. Laurel hadn't realized how bored she had been getting, but things were different now. She barely had time to think, and, when she did, there were lots of wonderful new things to think about.

To celebrate an extremely complicated alliance/trade deal between their country and China, the Museum of Albion was assembling a special exhibit called "Power and Glory." In addition to the treasures on loan from the King's collection, the Emperor of China was graciously allowing some of the "lesser treasures" from the Forbidden City to be shipped halfway around the world to be displayed. With these "lesser treasures" came guards, servants (they even brought their own cooks—and food), and paperwork. Much paperwork. Mind-boggling amounts of paperwork.

Despite being the youngest person ever to pass her Senior Ordeal and become a full-fledged mage, Laurel was still stuck at the University's College of Wizardry. Her older brother had been dithering for years, rather than even attempt his Senior Ordeal, so when Laurel passed hers, their grandmother had put a *geas* on both of them. Until Stephen passed *his* Ordeal, Laurel had to live on campus with him and his wife Melisande. The original idea was that she could tutor and encourage Stephen— or perhaps be enough of a pest so that he'd pass the Ordeal just to get rid of her. Unfortunately Laurel, who was only seventeen at the time, had fancied herself in love with a young man called Edward, who, while he liked Laurel, turned out to be more concerned for his own career. In an attempt to win a scholarship for which Stephen was more qualified, Edward sabotaged Stephen's magic during his Ordeal, causing Stephen serious injury in the process. As part of Edward's punishment, he was working on Stephen's long-term—very long-term—therapy. They had been at it for two years now, but Stephen was still unable to use magic and thus unable to pass his Ordeal. So

Laurel, despite having long since graduated, still lived on campus.

Laurel, however reluctantly, had to give Edward credit. Even though his work with her brother had been mandated by a Wizards' Tribunal, he pursued it with the fervor of a dedicated researcher. While Stephen provided the theoretical underpinnings, it was Edward who worked out and field-tested the procedures that turned theory into applied magic. Some of their collaborations had been not only published but acclaimed by several thaumaturgical societies. The University's Board of Elders had been impressed and were now talking about starting a joint program between the Colleges of Wizardry and Medicine, and hiring Edward and Stephen as program faculty—as soon as Stephen passed his Ordeal.

Having no desire to teach, Laurel's choices of employment were severely limited by Stephen's perpetual student status and her consequent inability to leave the city— thank you *ever* so much, Grandmother. When Stephen was injured and she realized that she might be stuck for a time, Laurel had gone to work at the Customs House. Now, two years later, she was the most senior of the Imports Clerks. This—along with the fact that she had studied Mandarin and could both speak *and* read it—meant that all the documentation for the Chinese treasures passed through her hands.

"It would be more interesting if the treasures themselves passed through my hands," Laurel muttered, looking up from the pile of papers in front of her to see a new and very junior clerk who had just brought her a cup of tea. "Oh, bless you! I really need that!"

They both studied the desk, looking for a safe place to put a cup of liquid. Laurel shifted some papers from where the side of the desk met the wall, and said, "Put it there; that's the place where I'm least likely to knock it over." He managed to put the cup down without toppling or sloshing anything, then smiled shyly at her before leaving her office.

She took a couple of sips of the tea, then turned back to the papers. An hour later she finished that batch, took another few sips of what was now cold tea (at least it was wet), and opened the next crate of documents. As she started to pull out the first bundle of papers bound together with red silk ribbon, she saw a glint of silver at the bottom of the box. She pulled all of the papers out, stacked them all neatly to one side of her desk, and then examined the object. Its form was simple: a straight, cylindrical piece of silver about five inches long with a loop at one end. Laurel examined it briefly, wondering what it was, then set it in the cleared space next to her teacup and reached for the next batch of documents.

Easter was a full month past, and the weather was getting warmer. Laurel didn't dare to open the windows in her office lest the stacks of paper be disturbed, so she was getting hot, sticky, and tired. Pulling her hair back from her face and off her neck, she coiled it and looked for something to hold it in place. Her gaze fell upon the silver whatever-it-was, and she picked it up and shoved it into her hair. It held, and Laurel took another sip of cold tea and turned back to the paperwork.

By the time the workday ended, Laurel had completely forgotten her hair (it wasn't anything she paid much attention to at the best of times), so the pin was still holding it more or less in place when she got home to the College.

Melisande, who was a Sensitive, was pacing across the parlor when Laurel came through the front door of the cottage assigned to Stephen and Melisande as resident advisors. Melisande whirled to look at Laurel with a look Laurel hadn't seen in two years and didn't want to see now—or ever again.

"It's you, Laurel," Melisande said. "That's what I've been feeling this afternoon. Dear God, what have you done now?"

∽⳨⳨∾

Laurel blinked at her sister-in-law. "Um . . . good evening to you, too," she said. "You know, if I were . . . oh, I don't know, still a *teenager*, instead of a mature, working professional, I could get the impression that you were actually *accusing* me of something. Am I that much of a menace to the world?"

Melisande started, shook her head as if to clear it, and sank into an armchair. Looking Laurel in the eye, she said, "Oh, Laurel, I'm so sorry. Please forgive me. Of course you're not. I just—"

"Just saw me as 'annoying kid sister' again. Melisande, I love you dearly, but when is this going to end? I really am a capable person, you know. Senior Mage and all that, just like you, and—" Suddenly she thought she knew what this was about, and her eyes moistened. "—as much as I'd like to be helping Stephen pass his Ordeal, I really can't be of much help until he's cured of this whatever-it-is that's taken away his magic, so yes, I'm stuck here by Grandmother's infinite wisdom but it isn't my fault and *I don't like it any more than you do!*"

Before Laurel could pull away, Melisande leapt from the chair and held her in a tight embrace, while she fought, and failed, to hold back the tears that seemed to come from out of nowhere. After a moment, Melisande relaxed her grip and, holding the weeping younger woman's head against her shoulder, said softly, "You're fine, Laurel, really, it's all right. You *are* a capable adult, and I apologize for not treating you like one. It's my fault, really it is. I've had this unsettling feeling all day, like things were just *wrong* with the world, and I had no idea why. It's not the usual sort of 'out of sorts' feeling; this one seems especially bad, as if something has broken apart and if it isn't put right we're all in trouble. And then you came in, and suddenly the feeling seemed to coalesce around you somehow. I have no—"

She fell silent and moved her hand away from Laurel's head about twelve inches. Melisande stepped back and circled Laurel at a cautious distance, holding her open palm about a foot away from Laurel's body. "Your hair," she said finally, frowning in bewilderment. "It's your hair. There's a . . . feeling about it that's different. But that doesn't make sense. What have you done to it?"

"N-nothing," said Laurel, struggling for a degree of calm. She took a fold of her sleeve and blotted her cheek. "I've been working in my office all afternoon." She waved a hand. "Oh, I'm planning to color my hair black for the opening of the exhibition next week, but I'll do that with a glamour. Today's been just paper pushing. No magic at all."

For some reason Melisande was turning pale. Slowly she said, "Why would you be coloring it black?"

Laurel smiled weakly. "It seems appropriate. Black hair, red silk dress with mandarin collar, fan, you know. Call it playing dress-up, call it being culturally cooperative, whatever; I just thought it might be something nice to do."

"Um." Her sister-in-law put an index finger to her lip, pensive, and gazed at Laurel.

After a moment of silence, Laurel's curiosity finally overcame the last remnants of her emotional outburst earlier. "Okay, what? Is there a problem with the idea?" Her sister-in-law shook her head, and she continued. "Then what are you staring at?"

"Your hair," Melisande answered. "It turned black just now—while you were talking about it."

ങᘓᘏᘔഌ

"You're joking!" Laurel said, and went to the mirror in the cottage's entryway. Sure enough, she was no longer the blonde that she had been that morning. "But how?"

The door opened behind her, and she felt strong arms encircling her and lips nuzzling her ear as a voice whispered, "Hello, beloved. I've missed you so much today!"

Well, now, *this* was something new. "I've missed you too, brother dear. But your wife is over there."

Stephen stiffened and released Laurel as if she had suddenly sprouted porcupine quills. "Wha—?" He stared across the room at Melisande, who giggled and waved at him. "My word. It appears we have two raven-haired beauties in the family. How did this come about?"

"We have no idea," his wife replied. "It happened just a few minutes ago."

"I . . . see," Stephen said, hanging up his cloak. "No, I don't. Not a bit. That *is* peculiar." He deposited his portfolio on a side table. "As much as I'd like to look into it, though, might it wait until after dinner? Frankly, I'm starved—and class went overtime again this morning, so I didn't make it to the dining commons."

Melisande humphed. "And whose fault is that? It's your class; if you don't dismiss it, what do you expect? I should make you cook dinner yourself as punishment." When Stephen said nothing, she relented. "Oh, all right. I'd just have to throw away what I already made, and that would be a waste."

As they made their way to the dining area, she added, "Don't worry, Laurel, we'll figure out what's going on, one way or another. Maybe it's something that can be fixed easily."

⋘⋙

The day of the Exhibition's opening arrived, and the crowds were every bit as large as its organizers had hoped. Stephen, Melisande, Laurel, and Edward roamed the mammoth exhibition hall, awestruck at the finery before them. Laurel had seen the likeness of each item included with the import documents, of course, but the images couldn't do justice to the reality. Perhaps it was merely the exotic nature of the pieces—after all, armor was armor and a sword was a sword, no matter what style they might be made in—and perhaps if she saw an everyday version of the same thing she wouldn't be nearly so impressed. As it was, though, every one of these artifacts proclaimed that it was the property of an Emperor.

Laurel had not managed to convince any of the others to go along with her in imitating Chinese dress; nonetheless, they had to admit that hers suited her quite well. "You'll have to be careful," Stephen had said. "When the exhibits return home they might take you back with them!"

While Stephen and Edward examined a case containing a scroll written by a court magician from the Ch'in Dynasty, Laurel and Melisande admired a terra cotta warrior sculpture from the same era. As they marveled at the detail of the soldier's facial features—indeed, he seemed to be an actual warrior who had been transformed into earthenware—a voice behind them said in Mandarin, "Excuse me. May I ask who you are?"

They turned around to see a middle-aged Chinese woman in western garb, accompanied by two men who were rather more massive than the typical Chinese male. When she saw their faces, she said in surprised English, "I beg your pardon! I had not realized—Please forgive me. I had thought you were of our homeland rather than of Albion. I did not mean offense."

Laurel answered in Mandarin, "Please do not be concerned. No offense was taken." For Melisande's benefit, she continued in English. "I am Laurel, Senior Import Clerk, and this is my sister-in-law, Melisande. How might we assist you?"

The other woman's fluster receded somewhat, but her confusion remained. "I am Nianying, if you please, assistant to the curator of the Emperor's Treasures. I could not help but wonder, how is it that you have a blue halo around your head?"

Laurel and Melisande were both taken aback. "A what?"

"A halo, is that the correct word? A nimbus, a cloud of light? I am a Perceptive; I see things about people that others do not. And I see your head surrounded by a glow."

Melisande looked at Laurel and chuckled. "A halo, eh?"

Laurel laughed as well. "This is the closest anyone's ever come to accusing me of being angelic."

Melisande turned back to Nianying. "If I understand you correctly, I have the same gift as you—we use the term 'Sensitive.' But I don't see this halo you speak of."

Nianying paused to consider this. "Perhaps it is because you are unfamiliar with the phenomenon and thus do not know what to see. Would you take my hand, please?" Melisande did, and Nianying continued, "Now, please, look again."

"Hmm. I still don't—Wait. There is a difference." Melisande continued studying the bemused Laurel, and said, "Goodness!"

"You see it, then?"

"I certainly do," Melisande answered. Then to Laurel, she said, "Like a bright cloud of robin's-egg blue, hovering behind your head, or maybe around it, I can't tell for sure. Perhaps you'd better get measured for wings after all."

"Wait," said Laurel. "Nianying, you said we were unfamiliar with this. Does that mean you *do* know what's causing it?"

The other woman replied slowly, "I . . . know one thing that *could* cause it . . . but I did not expect to see it outside of our homeland. Tell me, please: have you been chosen to be a Servant?"

Laurel and Melisande looked at each other and shrugged. "Er . . . at the College we learn that we are chosen servants," Melisande said slowly. "We do what we can to fill that role. Is that what you mean?"

"I do not know," Nianying said. She paused, and then, as if deciding to try again, she said, "You see here," waving her arm at all the exhibits, "the Lesser Treasures of our Emperor, the Son of Heaven. But there are also the Greater Treasures, which do not leave China. Each is attended by a Servant, who helps it to fulfill its proper task. The Servant is blessed with long life by the gods, and holds a special place in the hearts of the Emperor and his people."

Melisande thought about that. "I see. No, that's not what I meant. But we do have the sort of people you speak of; we call them Guardians. My husband and I have three of them as mentors."

"Wait a second," said Laurel. "Are you saying that I'm a Guardian?"

"Not yet," said Nianying. "If that is what I see, then you have been chosen to be a Servant but have not submitted to that choice. If you have Greater Treasures in Albion, which of them has chosen you?"

Again Laurel and Melisande looked at each other. "All the ones we know of have Guardians already," said Melisande. "And as far as I know, they're all in good health—the Guardians, that is. The treasures are well taken care of."

At this, Nianying seemed troubled. "There is one possibility, but it seems unlikely. Twenty-six days ago, in the Forbidden City, the servant of the—I suppose the best translation is 'Scholar's Pin'—died after a millennium of life. The Emperor chose a young woman to replace her, but she has not yet submitted to the choice. She was engaged to marry a young man of her province, and did not wish to enter that union knowing that they would not live and grow old together. When I left to come here with the exhibits, she still had not submitted."

Melisande chuckled. "'Submitted.' Huh. It sounds as though becoming a 'servant' is tantamount to a marriage."

"It has been compared to such, yes. That is another reason she is reluctant."

"I see. But that doesn't sound like anything that affects us—"

"Wait," said Laurel. "Nianying, this 'Scholar's Pin'— what does it look like?"

"It is the counterpart of the Warrior's Pin: a hairpin, made of silver. From the end it appears round. There is an inscription along its length, and a loop at one end—"

"I think," said Laurel, looking at Melisande, "we have our answer." She reached back and removed the pin from her hair, which fell haphazardly to her shoulders. Showing the pin to Nianying, she said, "Is this it?"

Nianying's eyes grew wide, and before Laurel and Melisande knew what was happening, she and her two attendants were bowing deeply to Laurel. "Please accept our reverence, O Daughter of Heaven! We did not know—"

"Hey, hold it right there!" said Laurel. "I'm not an angel and I'm certainly not God! Stand up!"

"But this is appropriate," said Nianying with a hint of sternness to her tone. "When you are trained in the Forbidden City, you will learn what is done and what is not done—"

"Trained? In the Forbid—Do you mean I have to go to China for the rest of my life?" Laurel was thunderstruck.

Nianying was puzzled. "Of course you will. That is what is done."

"And I'm going to live for a thousand years, and never see home again? *No!*"

"I do not understand," said Nianying. "This is a supreme honor. The gods surely know your mind, that you are a great scholar, and they have given you this gift."

"I know, but—wait a minute. Great scholar? I may be precocious, but that's hardly the same thing."

Melisande interjected, "Laurel, don't be silly. You're an excellent student. We know it even if you don't. And this is not only an honor, it's an opportunity. You've enjoyed your Chinese studies, right? Here's a chance to—"

She stopped suddenly. "Oh, no. Stephen. The Ordeal."

Laurel blanched. "The *geas!* I couldn't go to China if I wanted to."

Melisande fixed her with a look. "Do you really not want to? At all?"

"Well . . . " She paused. "Look, if anyone had told me at any other time that I could find a good job in China, let alone an Imperial post, I'd be all over it. Yes. But . . . but not if I can't ever come home again! How would you like it if someone decided *you* couldn't ever see Stephen again?"

"That's different—but okay, I see what you mean."

Nianying asked, "What is this 'gayas'?"

Laurel explained the College's course of study, the final Ordeal, and the magical bond that kept Laurel in the capital city until Stephen should pass his—which at the moment appeared unlikely.

"That will not do," said Nianying. "You must live in the Forbidden City. The Pin must return home. So must its Servant."

"Can no one leave the City?" Melisande asked thoughtfully. "Can the Pin's Guardian never travel?"

"It has never been done before. The Treasure . . . "

"Our Treasures are kept safe, but their Guardians are free to move about if necessary. Lord Logas and Lady Sarras are out of the city even now, looking into a matter in the north country, and their Treasures are well taken care of. Again, I ask: Can this not be the case in China?"

Nianying spluttered, "In four thousand years it has never—"

"In four thousand years things can change. We have travel options that we did not have a century ago, and Laurel need not be separated from the Pin for very long. Might this not work?"

This time Nianying paused. "I shall ask those who know."

Melisande turned to Laurel. "And we too can travel, don't forget." To Nianying she asked, "Unless the Forbidden City is forbidden to the Guardian's family also?"

The other woman reflected. "I truly do not know. It is forbidden to most. But the Servant is held in high esteem, not far from that of the Son of Heaven himself. This may not be impossible."

Laurel broke in, "But the *geas!* How—?"

"Do you think Grandmother would lift it for this?" Melisande asked.

Laurel snorted. "Not for all the tea in—uh, sorry. There is no way she would do that. She's decided that Stephen has to have his Senior rank, and that means the Ordeal. There's no getting around it."

"I didn't think so," Melisande said. "Nianying, we need to talk."

❧❦❧❦

"And that's the story," Laurel said to Stephen and Edward. Along with Melisande and Nianying, they sat on benches placed in the center of the room, provided so that people could rest their aching feet between studying the exhibits. "It seems the Guardian-designate doesn't want the job, so she hid the Pin in one of the crates headed for Albion, probably thinking that it would delay the situation. Which might also have happened because the influences that govern the Pin didn't want her anyway. The Pin wants me."

Stephen frowned. "But what about the *geas*?"

"That's the problem. It has to be broken, and quickly. And you know Grandmother will never lift it, so you have to pass the Ordeal."

"But that's impossible," Stephen said. "I can't do magic, so I can't do the practicum."

"Look," Laurel said. "Lord Logas and the Order of Saint Luke took care of the physical damage Edward did. That's history. We just have to figure out the *para*-physical factors that are blocking your magic. And we need to do it fast."

Edward protested, "But that's what we've been trying to do for almost a year now! Diet, classroom environment, possible counteragents—we've even looked at the *weather* patterns around the University, and nothing has worked yet!"

Nianying broke in. "This is nonsense. The Servant must return to China with the Pin. Everything else is of lesser importance."

Stephen fixed her with a hard glare. "Look, lady. I'm sorry you haven't been able to hold on to your Treasure, but this is a family matter!"

"It is an *Imperial* matter. The Servant is part of the Emperor's family now."

Edward murmured, "Uh, Stephen, you're talking to a representative of the Emperor here. Are you sure you want to start an international incident?"

Stephen turned to Melisande. "What do *you* say in all this?"

She took his hand and smiled at him. "Whatever you decide, I'm with you. All the way."

Laurel broke in. "Look, Stephen. We have to decide this, and we have to decide it *now!*"

At that moment several things happened, so quickly that in the blur of motion no one could tell which came first and which followed, even though afterwards the logical order was quite clear.

A siren's wail ripped through the hum of conversation in the hall.

Those who were looking in the proper direction saw that the case that had held the terra cotta warrior was now empty.

As everyone looked around them, wondering what had gone wrong, Melisande let go of Stephen's hand, rose to her feet, and backed away from the group.

A roar echoed throughout the hall, bouncing off the walls and terrifying the attendees to within an inch of their lives.

Through a doorway charged the earthen statue, no longer standing at attention but running as if to battle, swinging a sword over its head and heading straight for Melisande.

Stephen reached over and behind his head, made a peculiar movement with his thumb and third and fourth fingers, shouted a phrase in Hebrew, and, like a Colonial pitcher firing a fastball, flung his hand out toward the rampaging warrior, which exploded into a thousand shards of pottery.

The siren stopped. Silence blanketed the room. Everyone looked around them, wondering just what in the world had happened. One by one, bits of puzzled conversation commenced. Stephen, Melisande, and Edward stared at the pile of terra cotta fragments that had been a charging soldier.

"Ooooh boy," said Edward. "*You* get to tell the Emperor you broke his doll."

Stephen said nothing.

Melisande grabbed him around the waist and held him tight. He turned and clasped her in a fervent embrace.

Behind him, Laurel commented, "Well, brother dear. It looks like the Goliath Maneuver still works."

Edward turned to stare at Stephen. "What was *that?*"

Stephen slowly shook his head. "I . . . don't know. A freak weather pattern?"

"Horse feathers," said Laurel. "You have your magic back and didn't admit it even to yourself."

"Pegasus," said Stephen absently.

"What?" said Laurel, nonplussed.

"Pegasus had horse feathers."

Laurel punched him in the arm. "I'll Pegasus you! So when's the Ordeal?"

Stephen let go of his wife. "Wait a minute." Going over to the remains of the fallen soldier, he said, "From what I saw, this thing blew up. So why aren't the pieces all over the room?"

He looked at Melisande, who grinned and nodded to Laurel. The latter shrugged and gestured; the terra cotta soldier reappeared in its display case, and on the floor sat one of Nianying's attendants, slowly picking himself up, rubbing his chest, and giving Stephen a not-too-friendly look.

"Because I can only cover so much space at once," Laurel replied.

"Well, there you are," said Edward. "They don't call her the 'glamour queen' for nothing."

Stephen glared at his sister. "I suppose I should be grateful to you. But frankly, I'm ready to spit nails. Just *what* on God's green earth did you think you were doing?"

His sister glared right back. "If you're really asking—" She ticked them off on her fingers. "One, we verbally knocked you around so you wouldn't have time to think. Two, we scripted it so that Melisande would support you and then get attacked, so you'd be sure to defend her, *Prince Charming.* Three, we had the siren go off to stir up the chaos even more. Four, we were sure your daily magic form exercises would kick in, and you'd go through the proper motions. And five, we made the attacker nonhuman so you wouldn't hit it with something lethal!" She smiled sweetly. "Any questions?"

"Yeah! When's the next slow boat to China?"

"Depends," she shot back. "When's the Ordeal?"

"It's next Wednesday," said Melisande. Stephen looked at her incredulously. "Well, it will be when I talk to Lord Logas. He gets back the day after tomorrow." To Nianying she explained, "Don't ask my husband to schedule a test when he thinks he's ready. He'll *never* think he's ready."

Stephen's scowl turned into something halfway to a smile. "*Touché.*"

 recognition mark

Three weeks later, the sun shone above the docks and a stiff breeze blew, as a Chinese ship prepared to depart with the Scholar's Pin and its new Guardian, the Eyes of Heaven.

"Well, Lady Laurel. I can't say I ever expected to be calling you that." Logas beamed, like a proud father on graduation day.

"It's not something I expected either, I must admit," she said. "No matter what everyone says, I still keep thinking I'm the young idiot who's going to mess things up when nobody's looking."

He laughed. "And you think you're the only one who's ever felt that way?"

"Well, no . . . Actually, yes! I don't know what everyone else is thinking, so of course I assume I'm the only one who thinks the way I do."

He chuckled. "I cannot fault your reasoning. But keep this in mind: As you grow in your Guardianship, you will come to know many people and observe many others. You will notice common patterns, to the point that you may indeed know what they think."

"Yes, in time . . . " She looked beyond Logas to where Melisande, Stephen, Edward, Nianying, and others waited who had come to see her off. The exhibition would run for four months, but for the sake of the Scholar's Pin the ship was leaving early, and would return. "Lord Logas—"

"Just 'Logas' will do," he said with a chuckle. "You are part of the fraternity now. A rather exclusive one at that."

"I'm not sure whether 'May you live a thousand years' is a blessing or a curse. That's one of the two things that's bothering me."

"How so?" His expression might be that of a father or a physician; she couldn't tell which.

"I'm something they're not," she said, indicating the others. "They will grow old, and for a very long time I won't. So that's a wall between us. And from what they've been saying, I know they're thinking about it."

"Go on. You said there was a second thing."

She tried to find the right words. "There's a wall on the other side of me, too. I'm going to spend the rest of my . . . life . . . in a country where they don't know Resurrection, or the Risen One. And that's what my magic is based on, and . . . what I'm based on, too, I guess. It's like, 'how shall we sing the Lord's song in a foreign land?' I don't know if I'm saying this right—"

Logas's voice was warm. "You say it quite well, child. Perhaps this will help. As one who is well past his first millennium of life, I can tell you that dealing with different life spans is a challenge at first, but one does learn to live with it. And with familiarity, neither you nor the people you deal with will find it quite as hard as you feared. No matter how many days each of us is allotted, we all find ourselves taking them the same way: one at a time.

"As for the second matter—When the Chancellor and I made arrangements with the Imperial court, we added one non-negotiable stipulation: that since your being there has opened the door between our two countries and cultures, there will be a team of scholars from our University there in the capital, and a similar team from China here in Albion. I intend to see to it that our team includes a substantial number from the College of Wizardry. And if the program in thaumaphysiology is enacted, that team may well include Stephen and Edward. They'll find the Asian perspective helpful, I'm sure."

He smiled and placed a kiss on her forehead. "So be sure of this: You may travel far, and you will learn and understand much, but you will never, ever be alone. You will come to know and appreciate the people among whom you live, and you will continue to sing, knowing that others are singing with you."

The signal came to prepare for departure, and Logas cleared his throat. "Even if some of us aren't as melodic as others." He placed a hand on her head in blessing. "Go in peace, Laurel. We all hope to visit you before too long, and you will show us magic untold. Make us even prouder of you than we already are."

Laurel could manage to say no more, and so didn't try. She simply gave everyone a final embrace—especially Senior Thaumaturges Stephen and Melisande—and boarded.

As all on the dock cheered, the ship rose majestically into the air, its sails filled, its keel clove the winds, and it glided with increasing speed toward the East.

THE VESSEL

by Gerri Leen

You can tell a story is good when you finish it and then wonder what will happen to the characters next. Namali, the warrior of the god Settet, needs to get to his temple. Her way is blocked by enemies, and she can make the journey only by taking up temporary residence in the body of a disgustingly pretty doll belonging to the pampered daughter of a wealthy merchant. It's an interesting journey, with an end that nobody involved would ever have expected.

Gerri Leen lives in Northern Virginia and originally hails from Seattle. She came to fiction writing late in life and writes stories in many genres, including fantasy—often centered around mythology—science fiction, horror, crime fiction, and romance. She dabbles in poetry and has one poem published. In addition to *Sword & Sorceress 23*, look for her stories in the following anthologies: *Sails & Sorcery*, *Ruins Metropolis*, *Triangulation: Taking Flight*, *Desolate Places*, *One Step Beyond*, and *GlassFire*. A complete list of her published and accepted work can be found at her website www.gerrileen.com.

Namali moved soundlessly through the forest, until her knee creaked, giving her away to anyone waiting. Fortunately, the only ones waiting for her were the priests of the warrior god Settet.

"Great One," they said, falling to their knees in front of her.

She envied them the mobility. Her knees and hips were aching so badly she was not sure she could walk any farther. This time she may have waited too long to call them to her. "Get up."

They looked disappointed in her lack of formality. They always did, life after life. She wasn't a diplomat—or a goddess. She was a warrior who never died, moving from one willing host to another. Namali couldn't remember what this host's name had been or even how long ago she had taken her body. She'd stopped counting once she hit eighty.

"Have you found me a way home?" This body was old and tired. It was time to move on. But Settet's enemies had blocked all the ways back to the ancient temple in Dahlinia where the rite had to be performed—not because it couldn't be performed elsewhere, but because the warrior who had been training since childhood to be Namali's next vessel was trapped there, cut off.

The priests looked uncomfortable. "We have found a way, yes." They didn't meet her eyes.

"I'm not going to like this idea, am I?"

"No, Great One."

Namali sighed. She didn't have much time left. Arguing with the priests was pointless. "Tell me."

"There is a noblewoman traveling in the right direction. A somewhat . . . empty headed girl, but with a doll collection."

Namali could feel her features freeze. "A . . . doll?"

"Your spirit has traveled in statues before on the way home."

"Statues of Settet's warrior woman, yes. Dolls, no."

"All of Settet's statues are being destroyed at the checkpoints. And . . . it is no doubt a very nice doll."

She sighed. The number of Settet's faithful were growing smaller by the year. Soon, there would be no one to support her.

Of course, that was immaterial. She was here to do one thing until she no longer had the strength to do it: protect the land. Not any political boundaries—those had changed too many times for her to try to keep track. But her homeland, keep it safe from those who would commit atrocities to take over some part of it.

It was up to her to interpret exactly what that meant. And to her, it was a simple mandate. One she could not do in this aging, soon to be decrepit, body.

A doll it was.

ಜಂಲ್ಜಿ

Leanna lazed on the silk cushions as her women packed her clothing. "Throw in the gold robe. I may be invited to dinner with someone important."

One of her women held up the robe in question. "I anticipated your need, my lady."

"That's excellent, Sella."

"I am Fanel."

"I knew that." She hadn't actually. Her father was always switching the servants around. "Who is packing my dolls?"

"I am, my lady."

She was pretty sure this one was Sella but decided not to risk it. She didn't want to lose face in front of her servants and besides, who was the boss here? "I need to decide which ones to take."

Her father didn't understand why she had to travel with so many dolls. It wasn't that they comforted her as they had when she was a child—when her mother died, and all her father had to give her was things instead of love. Well, some of it was that, but also it was that they were expensive and exotic and having them was a luxury.

They made her special.

She studied the gorgeous dolls, purchased from all corners of the world—her father had spared no expense.

"This one," she said pointing to a black-haired beauty with dark brown eyes, a doll so delicate she always seemed on the verge of breaking. "And this one."

Sella handed her a dark-skinned doll, thin and elegant with amber eyes and gold jewelry as fine as anything Leanna owned.

One more. Which one?

"Perhaps . . . this one?" Sella was holding up the warrior doll Leanna normally pushed to the back of the collection. There was nothing beautiful or elegant about her. The only thing interesting was the shiny sword she carried—it had a gorgeous red stone stuck in the handle of the sword.

"I don't think so." She picked up the most recent addition to her collection. A blonde-haired, blue-eyed doll in a gossamer dress of silver and lilac. Her hair was done in an elaborate style; her silver sandals and jewelry shone with the care of the finest craftsmanship. She was bigger than the other dolls, almost the size of a toddler.

"The warrior might be different." Sella put the other two in the waiting chest, then tried to take the blonde from Leanna. "Some variety?"

"Uh, no." She slapped Sella's hand away and cradled the blonde. "I haven't gotten to know this one yet. Traveling will be a perfect opportunity."

Sella shot her a look of what had to be pity. Leanna tried not to think that if she had any real friends, she might not have to get to know her dolls. But her father didn't consider the other girls in town quite suitable for her to spend time with.

"As you wish, my lady."

"Yes," Leanna said, as she eased the blonde into the chest. "As I wish."

⠀⠀⠀⠀⠀⠀⠀⠀ಜ෪ഔ൸

Namali followed the two priests to the outer gate of the house. Their contact was waiting.

"Great One," the woman was about to fall to her knees, but Namali stopped her. "I am Sella and I pledge my life to your serv—"

"Just take me to the dolls." Namali was not enamored of this plan. It was, however, the only plan in sight—short of fighting her way to the temple, and the various pings and creaks from her body told her how well that stratagem would work.

"I tried to get her to choose a warrior doll," Sella said as she opened a chest finer than anything Namali had owned in all her lives, "but she resisted. I was able to throw in the sword." She reached in and pulled out a remarkably well made little weapon. The stone gleaming in its pommel had to be real.

Namali took it from her, testing how strong it was. It would do. "Good work."

Sella beamed, then her smile faded as she set the dolls up so Namali could see them. "I know they are not quite what you would want but . . . "

"I cannot work with this." They were all so . . . pretty.

She glared at the priests, saw them shuffle and look down, mumbling something about the vagaries of young women. Sella shook her head, as if trading the dolls that had been chosen would be more difficult than changing heads of state.

"Fine." With a sigh, Namali studied the dolls. One of them was much bigger than the others. She looked sturdier, too. "This one," she said, pointing to the blonde with the silly hairdo.

The priests seemed relieved. Sella bowed deeply and held the doll out with both hands.

Namali looked up at the sky, taking in the stars for the last time with these eyes. It had been a good body; it had served her well. "Thank you," she said to the woman who had willingly let herself be pushed out of her body so that Namali could have absolute control.

Then she closed her eyes and let go. She felt her spirit slide out of her old body, felt the uncomfortable constriction of a much smaller vessel as she slipped into the doll. Opening her eyes, she felt the heaviness of the lids, the awkwardness of the limited joints. There was no life energy from this body, no connection to Settet. Even one of his statues was better than this.

The priests were covering her old body with rough fabric; they would burn it in one of the many guild furnaces.

Namali tried to speak. The doll's mouth didn't move, so some of her words came out indistinct. She tried again, working at it until she got a reasonable facsimile of her normal speech, if not her voice—the doll's was annoyingly dulcet.

"Do you want me to try to convince her to change her mind about the warrior?" Sella asked.

"No," one of the priests said before Namali could tell her to do it. "They will be looking for such things. But not for this." He waved his hand toward Namali's new body and seemed to be trying not to laugh.

Namali took the sword Sella held out and lifted it as high as she could. "I can still cut that tongue out of you." The movement was jerky and in her new voice, the threat sounded more like a come-on.

Would fighting her way through a blockade have been such a bad way to go?

"Sacred duty," she muttered as she climbed gracelessly back into the chest. "Sacred damn duty."

಄ଞଵୈ

Leanna reclined in her litter, the chiffon curtains blowing in the light breeze as the men carried her down the crowded road. She ignored their huffing breaths, the sounds of other travelers, the whinnying of horses and lowing of oxen. Ignoring the smells around her was less easy, and she dabbed more perfume around the litter.

Leanna had napped. She'd read. She'd eaten some of the figs and cheese the servants had packed. Now, she was bored. If it wasn't so low born to walk, she'd ask the men to stop and let her out, so she could stretch her legs and at least see some of the countryside she was passing through. What she could make out through the curtains looked hazy but inviting.

Reaching behind her, she dragged the doll chest to her and opened it. Arranging the three dolls in front of her, she admired them for a few minutes, checking the workmanship, straightening their clothes, and making sure their chains were hanging right and their hair was in place.

They were beautiful. So feminine and—

Why was the blonde holding a sword?

She tried to pry it out of the doll's hand, but the fingers seemed glued around the handle of the sword. "I'm going to kill Sella," she said, as she considered beating the doll upon the pillows to try to loosen the sword. But that would probably ruin the doll's hairdo and could tear its fine, expensive clothes.

She sat the doll back down, pulled its arm back so the sword was at least behind it, where she wouldn't have to see it. It seemed to serve as a stabilizer as well. The other dolls kept falling over as the litter pitched in the normal movement of six— or was it eight?—tired men. But the blonde stayed upright the whole way.

"So, my friends, here we are."

The other two dolls fell over again, so she popped them back into the chest. "Okay, honey, it's just you and me."

She called all her dolls "honey." Naming them was just a little too pathetic, too much like they were her friends.

"Here we are, on the way to Dahlinia, probably so that Father can entertain his latest mistress without me in the way." She'd heard the servants muttering about some new woman in the long line of female companionship her father had used to replace her mother.

"I'm supposed to make nice with Abbel, the son of my father's best friend. Abbel's shorter than I am, dumpy, and his breath smells like my cats' nether regions." Not that she made a habit of smelling those, but cats being how they were, she was often presented with their backsides whether she liked it or not.

She picked up the doll and let it peek out of the curtains with her. The countryside had changed from forest to low hills. Dahlinia was in the high desert; they had another day or two of this to go.

"Gods help me, but I'm sick to death of my life." She lay back and ran her hand over her beautiful dress, could feel the warmth of the beads that wrapped around her neck, the reassuring clink of the bangles she wore around her ankles and wrists. It was all so predictable. So safe.

An adventure. That was what she needed. She could go hunting in the forest, or fly hawks across the desert, or seek the great white cats of the upper reaches. She could go into battle and—

She heard a strange zing, then two more, and felt the litter lurch to one side. Then it began to fall, hitting with a strange crunch that she realized was probably because the litter-bearers were under it. She glanced out, saw arrows sticking out of what she could see of the men, and began to hyperventilate.

The litter fell again, and she heard the sound of running feet—had the other men abandoned her? Then she felt something push her toward that side of the litter, and she fell through the chiffon, landing on the carry pole and then onto the hard-packed dirt.

A soft, sweet voice said, "Run, you nitwit."

She ran.

ଓ🙰🙰ଓ

Running in a doll body was difficult. Namali glanced back— handy to have a head that could turn all the way around—

and saw that the men were gaining on her.

Then she felt herself being lifted, heard her fancy dress tear as it caught on a shrub as the girl she'd been forced to share the litter with grabbed her and took off running.

Namali had to give her credit. For a pampered thing, she could run like the wind. And in fragile house sandals, no less.

Namali turned her head, fighting her way through the girl's long brown hair, and her voluminous veils and layers until she could see behind them. "It's okay. We're clear. Slow down before you fall down."

The girl slowed slightly.

"I said—"

"Shut up"—the girl sounded less winded than Namali expected—"or I'll drop you."

Namali decided to shut up. She let the girl run, occasionally closing her eyes when it seemed a crash was imminent, but fear kept the girl on her feet. Fear was an excellent motivator for some; for others, it just made them freeze.

The girl finally stopped, and she dropped Namali to the ground rather than setting her down carefully as she expected. "Okay, what are you?"

"I'm a doll." Namali was not supposed to divulge the secrets of Settet. The fact that she changed bodies over and over was known to very few: the priests of Settet, the rival sect, and the few outsiders deemed critical and who had proven themselves trustworthy. This girl fell into none of those groups.

"A talking doll?"

"I am . . . unique." In her lilting voice, Namali sounded nothing like a scary warrior. She tried to hide the sword she'd held onto throughout the chase behind her back.

"A talking doll with a sharp weapon."

"A novelty. And magical."

"Or evil." The girl backed away. "Are you evil?"

"I saved your life, you ninny."

"Quit talking to me that way. No one talks to me that way."

It was obviously high time someone did. But Namali could see this was getting her nowhere, so she decided not to be the one to start the trend. "I need your help." The girl had said she'd wanted an adventure. Here was the biggest one of her life.

"*My* help?" The girl looked around the grove of trees they'd stopped in. "I saved your life, too. So I think that my assistance to you has come to an end." She looked around. "I'll just be going."

"Good luck, then. I'm sure you know exactly where you're headed." Namali sort of fell down instead of sitting down; her knees weren't hinged and her legs stuck out in front of her. "Don't walk right into the arms of the killers while you're on your way home."

Home: a place it didn't sound like the girl was particularly wanted.

"You could tell me which way to go."

Namali tried to shrug; it didn't work. "I could. But I'm an evil doll, remember?"

The girl strode back, kicking dust—on purpose, Namali suspected—up around her. It would have been annoying if dolls had to breathe.

"What do you need help with? Not that I'm saying I'm going to help you. But go ahead and tell me your situation."

"My situation is that I need to get to Dahlinia. It is urgent. I cannot tell you why. I need you to get me there and drop me off at a certain place and then leave."

"That's it?"

"Well, you will have to hoof it, not ride in the lap of luxury."

"Very funny." The girl looked up. "I've never had an adventure."

"Yes. You were saying that."

"Oh, so you were listening?"

"I talk, ergo I listen."

The girl laughed, and it was a sweet sound, almost self-deprecating. "It's not been my experience that the one necessarily follows the other."

Namali wanted to grin, but when she tried, the doll's face stayed in the same insipid little "O" it was always in. "I, too, have noticed that."

"Okay. An adventure will be fun." The girl picked her up, not gently, and held her upside down. "Does that bother you?"

"No."

"You could be lying. I bet it does bother you. I hope it does." She tightened her grip. "Which way, evil doll-thing?"

"That way," Namali tried to point to the side, but her arm only went on an up-down track. "Toward the tree with the bark stripped off by deer."

"They all look the same to me."

Namali sighed. The sound came out languid rather than exasperated. "Turn right and then go straight. And hurry. They haven't given up, you know."

"Let's talk about them."

"Walk now. Talk later."

The girl didn't seem to like that, so Namali refused to answer her questions, and eventually she stopped talking and just walked.

CRSO

Leanna got tired of looking at the doll's feet and flipped her around so she could see her face. The pretty blonde hair was all over the place, her dress was torn, and one of her silver sandals had fallen off during their flight. "You ready to talk?"

The doll made a spasmodic gesture that Leanna guessed was a nod.

"So, what's your name?"

"That's not for you to know."

They were just getting close to a gently moving stream. Gently moving if you were human sized. Not so soothing if you were the size of the doll. Leanna held the doll over it by one arm. "I'm sorry but I didn't quite catch your name the first time."

The doll looked as placid as ever, and her voice was her normal sweet tone as she said, "Namali," but Leanna had the distinct impression the little thing was angry.

She pulled her back up to her original position. "Pleasure to meet you, Namali. I'm—although I know you don't care—Leanna. Of the house of Frador."

The doll didn't disappoint her by saying anything nice in return.

"What I can't figure out," she said, pretending that Namali and she had been deep in conversation rather than on a forced march, "is why anyone would have attacked us."

"They were robbers. You're obviously rich."

"This road is very safe or my father would have rented guards. I'm worth a lot to him, being so pretty and marriageable." The last part came out bitter.

"Perhaps they were desperate." But the doll's voice lacked conviction

"Why would desperate robbers pick on a litter with six men? Aren't they usually opportunistic types? You know, prey on the weak or something?"

"Maybe the litter-bearers looked very tired. The litter was, after all, heavy."

"I know you're not implying I'm fat. I'm pleasingly curved. And tall. Men look at me all the time." When she was allowed to leave the house, anyway.

"I meant with all your clothes. And the doll chest."

All her pretty things. Lost now. "But . . . " She pulled the doll around so she could see her face. "Why would they be chasing us, then? All my stuff is back there." She'd heard of women being attacked, of course. But not on that road. And not by robbers confronted with all the luxuries she'd had with her.

"Perhaps they are assassins?"

"My father's not political. He has no enemies—I've heard him tell people that a good businessman keeps friends on all sides and enemies on none. And I'm . . . nobody." It hurt to say it, but it was the truth. She was nobody, but not nothing. She was worth something to her father for what she could bring him, not for who she was.

"I believe they were robbers."

It still didn't make sense. She'd traveled that road often and never had a bit of trouble. Not until now. "Wait a minute. You're the new thing here. I think they were after *you*." She dropped the doll and backed away. "Did you kill someone? Are they hunting you?"

The doll pushed herself up. She'd fallen with her head turned nearly all the way around: it was not a comforting pose. "And they said you were empty headed."

Leanna stomped closer, hands on hips. "Well, they were wrong, weren't they? And, who's 'they'?"

"I am sworn to secrecy."

Leanna laughed at her. "Well, let me know how you like Dahlinia. You should be there in, oh, a month or so with those little legs. Hope you don't melt in the desert."

"It appears I must trust you." The doll looked this way and that—another very creepy thing to watch—and then leaned in. "I am . . . not a doll."

"No? Really?" Leanna glared at her.

"I am the Warrior of Settet. Have you heard of me?"

"Can't say I have." She knew who Settet was, of course, but he wasn't a god her father worshipped, so by default he wasn't one she worshipped.

"My spirit moves across the centuries, from body to body. This doll is a temporary vessel. I can only stay in it for a short time before the lack of life energy begins to deplete my spirit." The doll sighed. "I am on my way to the temple to meet my new vessel. But Settet's enemies block my way at every turn. As you saw back there."

"So you want me to get you to the temple so you can take over your vessel. The vessel's alive, I take it?"

Again the jerky nod thing.

"So, what will you become? A great cat? Maybe a wolf? A hunter, right? So not a deer or a—"

"I am human. Just as you are. Or I will be as soon as I get to the vessel."

Leanna frowned. "Human? So you possess a human the same way you possessed the doll?"

"I do not possess. I take possession. It is a slightly different thing."

"What happens to the person who was in the body to begin with?"

"She will be no more. It is a choice she has made. She will have been trained to be a warrior from the time she could walk, but the choice is made once she is old enough to understand the consequences."

"So . . . you kill her?"

"She will give up her life so I might live."

"Right. Like I said."

The doll seemed to be fidgeting. "It is her choice. An honor."

"Yeah, some honor." Leanna suddenly wanted to get rid of the doll as soon as possible. She scooped her up, trying not to hold her too close, and began to lope across the countryside.

"You will tire yourself out."

"Little late to start thinking of others, isn't it?"

"Coming from you . . . ?"

"Look, I may be selfish and pampered—and maybe a little vain. But at least I'm not a murderer."

The doll turned her head away sharply. Leanna was glad not to have her dead blue eyes on her.

"**P**ut me down," Namali said, turning her head this way and that, scanning the countryside around them. "I thought I saw something just now."

Leanna had stopped loping some time back. She was subdued, not meeting Namali's eyes anymore—also not doing anything to antagonize her. Namali had admired the spunk of the girl, was almost sad to see that she was now afraid of her.

Leanna set her down carefully, and then looked around. "What is it?"

Namali saw it then. The flash of the sun on metal on a hillside about three over from their position. "Get down."

Leanna didn't question, just crumpled and stared at her in alarm.

"They've found us."

"Wonderful." Leanna swallowed hard. "And if I left you here, would they leave me alone?"

"Probably."

"But I'd be a murderer, then, wouldn't I?" Obviously the girl had been thinking about this option. "A murderer of a murderer, so does that make it all right?"

"I cannot tell you that." Nor did Leanna look like she wanted her to. "You must do what you think is right."

"Is there a safe way to run?"

Namali felt a surge of disappointment. More in Leanna than in her imminent demise—she would comport herself well, might take a few of her killers with her. But this girl had seemed to hold, perhaps, some promise. "That way," she said, the direction one her useless doll arm could point to.

"I want you to know that I really hate you," Leanna said as she scooped Namali up and ran, covering the ground as fleetly as a fox.

"You are a very good runner."

"When my father is gone I run through the house. It helps me work off excess energy. Also keeps my curves pleasant since we tend to eat a lot."

Namali kept an eye on the flashes; they were gaining ground. "Leanna, I believe they are on horses."

The girl slowed.

"You tried. You must always remember that. You acted with honor." She struggled to get down. "Now, go."

Leanna put her down, but she didn't go. "They know you're in the doll, right?"

"Yes, they appear to know."

"Can you—I can't believe I'm even asking this. Can you possess without taking possession?" She crouched down. "If I let you in, could you share this body for a while, until we got to your vessel?"

"I don't know. I could try."

"Try is the best you can come up with? As assurances go . . . "

"I understand, Leanna. You don't have to do this. I have lived many lifetimes. Avoided death for centuries. Maybe . . . maybe it is my time to go?"

"Maybe it is." The girl sounded like she was trying to convince herself.

Namali touched her on the cheek. "You have a life of your own to lead. This was never supposed to happen. I was only seeking safe transport."

Leanna stared at her for a long moment, her brown eyes boring into Namali's. "What are the odds that you'll win if I let you in?"

"When I first met you, I would have said very slim. But you are agile and stronger than you look. And very stubborn. Also not stupid."

"So pretty good odds?"

Namali tried to nod. It was frustratingly difficult with a head meant to go around, but not up and down.

"Then do it." Leanna sat down cross-legged. "What do I need to do?"

"You need to be sure of this. I cannot guarantee that you will survive."

"I understood that the first time you said it." She shook her arm, making the bangles tinkle prettily. "This, Namali, this is the extent of my life. Look beautiful. Smell good. Make pretty sounds when I walk." She met Namali's eyes, looked resolved.

"Hold out your hands to me."

They touched and Namali felt herself drawn into Leanna; she began to expand, began to take control even though she didn't want to this time.

Hold it right there.

Namali felt her expansion stop.

My body. My life, too. We share.

They would share. It was good, or at least preferable to dying in the doll. Leanna had a surprisingly strong energy to her. Namali drew it in and felt her old strength returning.

If you want them to believe you're gone, then you should let me do the talking.

"I need to be in control of this."

I knew you'd say that.

Namali heard the sound of pounding hooves, saw the men come over the hillside. She backed away from the doll, trying to look scared.

The men dismounted, one of them coming up to her. "Why did you run?"

"It's my favorite doll and I've lost everything else." She aimed for a vacuous smile, tried to bat her eyelashes at him.

She knew she wasn't good at it, but Leanna was beautiful enough to convince him of anything.

"Go home, miss. This never happened." He grabbed the doll and started to mount his horse.

"Wait." From the back of the group of horsemen, another man got down. He wore a black traveling robe but underneath she could see glimpses of grass-green satin.

A priest of the rival sect. He would know that—

"The doll is empty."

Now what?

Namali reached down and snatched the sword that had fallen from the doll's grasp as soon as she'd vacated. She ignored the priest and went for the man who'd fallen for Leanna's wiles.

Wait, he's kind of cute.

Namali did not wait. She chucked the tiny weapon into his chest, and as he fell, grabbed his sword and twisted, swinging it and taking the priest's head with her.

Okay, that's disgusting.

Namali worried that she—they were going to throw up. "Try to control yourself."

Sort of the problem, isn't it?

But Leanna shut up and let Namali work with no interference. Only, it wasn't work. Not in this young, lithe body. She'd been old for so long; to be this agile and strong again was delightful. She parried and struck, taking men from the ground or from their horses. The animals she spared—they were creatures with no choice on whose side they fought. But she slaughtered every one of the humans.

When it was over she stood bent over with her hands on her knees, breathing hard, her skin stinging from many small wounds.

If those scar, we are going to have words.

Namali laughed and took the scabbards off two of the men, buckling them so the swords would hang on opposite hips. Grabbing another sword, she jammed it and the one she carried into the scabbards. Then she swung up on one of the horses.

Now, there's a look that goes well with this gown. You haven't done much accessorizing, have you?

It was going to be a long ride to Dahlinia.

⊱✦⊰

Leanna heaved a sigh of relief when they reached Dahlinia with no further incident. Feeling Namali take control had been nauseating—not as nauseating as the massacre that followed, but still high on the "not to be repeated" list.

She'd let the horse go just outside of town. Namali had said someone might recognize it, ask too many questions. Which would no doubt lead to Namali hacking off their head, and Leanna could go the rest of her life without seeing that again.

The temple is just ahead, on the right.

"Doesn't look like much."

It's very old.

"And I stand by my original assessment. A little embellishment never goes wrong." As they got to the door, she saw blood smeared on the door. Not the embellishment she had in mind.

Be careful.

"Strangely, I knew that. The blood was a big clue." She felt Namali's desire to not go in through the front and headed back the way she'd come, to a side street where she could connect up with the small alley that ran behind the buildings. There was no blood on the back door.

She eased the door open, waited a moment and listened hard.

Go. Namali seemed to be feeding her a layout of the temple, so she darted inside and then took cover in an alcove.

"Oh, no." She could smell it from where she was standing. Not just blood: death. Organs and waste and all the things that came out of bodies when you killed a whole bunch of people in a messy way. It was a smell she'd never experienced before today.

Keep going.

"I am. Just give me a moment." She forced her feet to move; the smell grew stronger and more horrible as she went.

It was worse to look at than to smell. Four priests were dead, and a girl was pinned to the altar by six daggers with bright green hilts.

No. Namali sounded broken, and Leanna knew the girl was the vessel. For a moment, she was overwhelmed with the despair.

"Isn't there a back up?"

Yes. Yes, of course, there is. Not here, though.

They ran. Leanna didn't try to take control from Namali, but the warrior was too upset to fully lead them. So *they* ran together and it was a feeling unlike any Leanna had ever known. She could feel so much more of Namali, as if the woman had let all her barriers down. Life after life teased at her, she got glimpses into battles, into mayhem and vengeance and all the things the Warrior of Settet was called to do.

But no love. Never any love.

Love is for others.

They rounded a corner and Namali groaned again.

The building was nothing but ashes and smoldering bits of wood. An onlooker saw her, seemed confused at her fine dress and swords, but moved closer to her.

Are they gone?

"Did they suffer?" Leanna asked instead.

The man looked down. "We tried to get them out. Someone had locked the doors. We couldn't break through." He took a deep breath. "I heard them screaming."

She touched his arm, gulped hard but somehow this scene wasn't as bad as what she'd seen earlier—smoke smelled clean, at least compared to innards.

"They were such nice girls. Always training. Dedicated. You don't see that anymore."

How many of them? How many? Namali seized control. "How many of them died?"

"All of them."

The answer hit Namali like a wave, causing Leanna to nearly fall down. She wrested control back just to stay on her feet. Then she ran, far away from the building and the temple, until she found a secluded spot that seemed safe. "Now what? These were all the vessels?"

They were brought here when it was known that I was nearly ready to move on. So that in case the chosen one did not please me, there would be others.

"So there aren't any more vessels?"

No.

"That's great." She thought furiously. "You know, I think there's a warrior training camp in the next town over. Maybe one of them worships Settet and will help you."

There are priests of Settet there, too. They can . . . end this partnership.

"If the warriors won't work, there may be other options. I didn't say you had to get out of my body."

That is not what I meant.

It took a minute for the words to sink in, and the tone in Namali's mind-voice sent chills down Leanna's spine. She heard regret—and utter resolve. "What? You think I'm getting out?"

I can tell you don't want to.

"It's my body."

You will be reborn.

"How do you know?"

I am.

"Technically, you never die—you just jump from body to body. So you really don't know what will happen." She wondered if there was a way to get Namali out of her head—or wherever she'd taken up residence. "Anyway, it's my body and I'm not leaving. And it's not as if you can force me." She felt something—a guilty twinge sort of. "You can't force me, can you?"

The priests can excise you.

"Excise?"

It has not been done in centuries.

Leanna felt as if she couldn't get enough air. Her heart was racing, and sweat ran down her back and between her breasts.

Please, don't panic. It will not hurt.

"You're asking me to give up my life just when it's getting interesting."

I know what I'm asking you to do. Please, you showed such honor before. Show it again.

"Honor? It's my life and I have a right to live it." And by gods, she wanted to live it. "If you force me out, then you really are a murderer."

There was no reply and Namali seemed to go quiet inside her. Leanna tried to still her shaking hands. Could she walk one way if Namali wanted to go another? Could she refuse to go to Settet's temple? Could she fight off his chosen warrior for long?

I have never had to share a body.

"Well, me either. I've never even had to share a room. So I think it's going to be an adjustment on both sides."

There is no precedent for this.

Something in Namali's voice told her she wanted to be convinced.

"Okay, sure, no precedent. But think about it. We could learn from each other. You could obviously teach me a lot about fighting and honor and well, smoky taverns filled with men with bad teeth and last year's pants. And I could . . . " A vision of her host's house filled her, the dances, the elaborate dinners. "And I could teach you what fork to use." She could tell that wasn't the strongest argument. "How to blend, Namali. How to get into places you've never had access to. Someone betrayed you—they knew exactly where to look for you—and I bet that it was someone high up. Don't you want to have *every* opportunity to find that person?"

She felt something relax inside her, a moment of surrender. A rush of happiness filled her, and she wasn't sure if it was coming from herself or from Namali.

What you say makes sense. We will try it.

"Oh, good." She wondered if Namali would consider it bad form to vomit in relief.

Are you all right?

"I will be." She could tell Namali was nervous just sitting around, not killing anything, so she got up unsteadily and made her way to the stable. "Why walk? We can afford to ride, after all."

We could just steal the horse.

"I am the daughter of one of the richest merchants around. We will buy the damn horse."

As you wish.

"So, what do you wear most of the time?"

Leathers. Armor. Metal shod boots.

She tried picturing herself in that. "I don't think so."

It is for your own protection.

"Prudence is no excuse for poor fashion sense. You teach me to fight; I'll teach you to dress, how's that?"

I need no lessons on how to dress, you dim girl.

"Aww, you haven't insulted me since we met. I have to say, wasn't missing it."

You are making me reconsider my decision.

"Decision's made. Honor demands you abide by it." She waited, hoping she was right. She could tell by the way Namali was fidgeting inside her, which made her a little dizzy, that she was on the mark. "And just for the record, if you had been able to take your vessel over, I would have missed you. I've enjoyed the company."

I am the warrior of Settet, not your houseguest.

"You are too my houseguest. Inviting you in was pretty hospitable. And are you saying you didn't enjoy the company?"

I respect the bravery you have shown.

"But nothing more than that? You'll come around. I know it doesn't compare with hacking up evildoers, but eventually, you'll admit how much I mean to—" Her attention was diverted by a cobbler who was setting out a table of samples in front of his shop. "Oooh, shoes!"

POLISH ON, POLISH OFF: A DRAGON TALE

by Tom Inister

I've often heard the phrase "a knight in shining armor," but I never really considered its implications until I read this story. This is Tom Inister's first fiction sale, although he's had a fair amount of non-fiction published.

Tom can often be found at his church, on a wrestling mat, or wherever there are lots of books. He has been a pastor since an otherwise-sensible church asked him to. He has wrestled since discovering that it's okay to throw people so long as a mat and a referee are involved. He has written the occasional article, column, or story ever since he supposedly recovered from doing those research papers in seminary. The writing is therapeutic. So is the throwing people.

In the hilly part of Brittany where the dread dragon Biggun ravaged the countryside and the koi in his pond swam in solemn patterns, a knight and a maid met on a trail.

George the Greathearted had the most polished armor in Brittany. Madeleine the farmer's daughter possessed more radiant beauty than even the three maidens locked in towers around the countryside. Thus, it should have been he who went to face the dragon and she who warned him of the danger. This being a fairy tale, he would have nobly ignored her warnings and gone on to perform deeds worthy of his nickname, and everyone but the dragon would have lived happily ever after. But this is not that sort of fairy tale.

Madeleine met George on her way up the mountain toward the lair of the dread dragon Biggun. Behind her, she dragged the sword she had surreptitiously borrowed from above the hearth of the village chieftain. George sat beside the road, using more force than necessary to polish scorch marks from the steel of his greaves.

Upon hearing the scraping of the scabbard of the chieftain's sword on the trail, George looked up. Seeing Madeleine, he stood and put on his most gleaming smile. "Where are you going, my pretty maid?"

Madeleine paused to lean on the hilt of the sword, which reached from the ground to her breastbone. Though she much preferred warmth over shine in smiles, the knight on the path gave her a good excuse to rest a moment on her mission of deliverance. "I'm going to slay the dread dragon Biggun," she said.

To laugh at a beautiful maiden upon first making her acquaintance, however deranged she may sound, is terrible knightly etiquette, so George turned his guffaws into a coughing spell. When he recovered, he replied, "I'm sorry, pretty maid, I had some smoke in my throat. You mean you were taking that sword to one of the men who set out to slay Biggun?" He eyed the magnificent sword. As the last survivor of said group of men, it ought surely to devolve upon him.

"No. None of the men of my village dare to oppose him. But he has taken my sister, so I am going to slay him. Though if you wish to accompany me, I'm sure you have more experience with this sort of thing than I do."

"But pretty maid, I have just come from the lair of the dread dragon Biggun. I am the only survivor of nine who went.

We hoped to take for ourselves the dragon's great hoard of gir . . . that is, of his gold."

Madeleine looked at him askance, for she thought this not at all the proper motivation for knightly deeds. Seeing her look, he continued hastily, "and to rescue any prisoners, of course, and to, um, deliver the countryside from his ravages. But he had the mastery of us. No one can stand against him."

"Well, I will not let him have my sister." She nodded her head and turned to go.

George hated to see anything beautiful wasted. And he believed that allowing Madeleine to go up to the dragon's lair would be a terrible waste. "Wait, fair maiden! Would losing your own life make any better the loss of your sister?"

"I don't intend to lose my life. I intend for Biggun to lose his."

This time, when she started back up the trail dragging the sword, George could think of nothing more effectual to say than, "But . . . " In spite of her beauty, her clothing declared her to be a poor farmer's daughter. He couldn't tie himself to some pretty face with no money to support him while he went knighting about.

George returned to polishing his armor. It wouldn't do at all to arrive back at court with smudges on his greaves. The sound of the dragging sword receded up the trail, along with its pretty bearer. Such a shame for a girl like that to be burnt to a crisp.

A thought struck George like a flash of sunlight off a burnished shield. Just because the girl would be burnt alive or enslaved by a dragon didn't mean the sword had to be lost. If he was going to lose his comrades and his chance at the gold and the girls, at least he could come out of this venture with a big sword. None of the knights he knew had a sword as big as that one—it would take hours just to sharpen it, much less shine it properly. His greaves almost forgotten, George slipped up the trail behind Madeleine's scraping passage, glad for all the oil he used biweekly on his armor joints.

When Madeleine reached the pool at the mouth of the dragon's cave, she could hear her sister inside beginning to go hoarse from wailing. Her sister had always wailed far better than she cooked or cleaned. Although her chief talent, it had not yet been adequate to find her a husband. It had, however, preserved Madeleine from having to marry Peter of the pigpen, who had worried that this tendency might run in the family. Since marriage to Peter of the pigpen would have been slightly more horrible than death by the pox, Madeleine felt she owed her sister the effort of a rescue. At worst, Madeleine would end up burnt to death, which would still put her ahead of being married to Peter, a far longer-lasting and smellier torment.

Madeleine examined the entrance to Biggun's lair. Heaps of armor displaying the smoky signs of having been recently inhabited lay crumpled near the cave mouth. A puff of the smoke wafted over to Madeleine, making her gag. Perhaps marriage to Peter wouldn't have been all that smelly, after all. She considered a moment. At least if she were burnt to death, she wouldn't have to live with the smell.

With renewed determination, Madeleine surveyed the clearing around the dragon's cave. A steep slope rose above the cave mouth, and a ledge above it actually overhung the cavern's entrance. With a sigh for her tired legs, she slung the sword over her shoulder and clambered to the ledge as silently as she could, having learned from her skirmishes with mice in the kitchen that being higher than the enemy is of at least mental comfort, if not actual advantage.

George crept up in the brush surrounding the dragon's pool in time to observe Madeleine climb to the ledge. He enjoyed watching her ascent, but decided she was lucky some girl was screaming inside. If it weren't for all that racket, surely Biggun would have heard her climbing. So far as George knew, there was no way into the cave but through the entrance beneath her; he began to wonder what Madeleine would do from the ledge.

Madeleine was pondering the same problem. Every element for her plan was in place—she had a massive sword, she had arrived at the dragon's lair, and wisps of smoke from the entrance showed that the dragon was puffing away inside. Now, she just needed the plan. Preferably one that didn't result in her body smoking and stinking like the ones in the suits of armor below.

She eased the sword from its sheath. What would a knight like the one she had met on the trail do with such a sword, a sword long enough and probably heavy enough to smite completely through a dragon's neck? She looked again at the heaps of armor and roast knight. Ah. She decided she should try something different than whatever the current knightly strategy for dragon slaying was. It had probably involved a courageous charge and shouting of mighty battle cries. Right. No charging, and certainly no battle cries. Her sister was doing enough crying inside the cave to suffice for several battles, anyhow.

Madeleine hefted the sword, trying to get a feel for it, and nearly dropped it off the ledge. George, watching from the bushes, smirked. She'd probably give up soon and go back, in which case, he'd meet her on the trail and tell her he'd changed his mind and would gladly go smite Biggun if she'd just give him the sword. That, or she'd go down to the cave waiving the sword around like a twenty-pound spatula, and Biggun would fry her before she stepped inside. Then, under cover of that amazingly perpetual wailing, George could just stroll over and walk away with the sword. He eased closer, right up to the edge of the brush.

The near loss of the sword, however, had given Madeleine an idea. Why not drop the sword? Wait until the dragon began to emerge, then drop it on his head or neck? It certainly was heavy enough to cut into Biggun if she dropped it, and the point gave up little in sharpness to her best sewing needle. The problem lay in getting Biggun to come out slowly enough that she could time dropping the sword right. If she missed, not even her sister's wailing could get her out of the mess she'd be in.

What could she do that would encourage the dragon to creep out to investigate rather than rush out to incinerate? Her eyes fell on the pool near the cave entrance. If she could make something splash in the pool, perhaps the dragon would come out to take a look. Madeleine positioned herself on the ledge with the sword propped awkwardly against her hip, took a deep breath, and tossed a stone into the pool.

An event that completely satisfies one person may leave another quite disturbed. Though Madeleine was pleased with the splash produced by her stone-throw, George was horrified. The stone landed no more than ten feet from where he crouched in the brush, and he thought for a moment that she had spotted him and thrown it at him. This, he decided, was the problem with taking novices dragon-hunting. At least his fellow knights only managed to get themselves killed—they had felt no need to drag him down with them. He crouched in the bushes, hoping the dragon wouldn't notice his motionless form in the brush when it came out to roast Madeleine.

Biggun, meanwhile, was lying in the shadows near the entrance of his cave. He was rather beginning to like the notion of eating this latest prisoner instead of keeping her, in spite of the oily taste. At least the others had eventually learned to just whimper. This one wouldn't even have any trading value if she wouldn't quiet down. He'd been hoping to swap her for that redhead Belchor had grabbed; good redheads were so hard to come by, and he needed one to fill out his collection. A splash from his pond drew his attention. Normally, his koi didn't jump about like a lot of unmannerly mullet.

One of the problems with making something so shiny that no one can miss seeing it is that someone might see it when you wish they wouldn't. George had spent the last ten years perfecting his polishing skills. And now the sun gleamed off that almost perfectly shined suit of armor.

Biggun saw the flash of sunlight and heaved himself to his feet. Maybe one of those knights was still hanging around. It was one thing to charge his cave with all the battle-crying and sword-waving, but it was something else if some oaf of a knight disturbed his koi pond. Those fish had cost him a blonde and two brunettes in trade with Sheng Fui. If a knight had hurt one of his koi, he'd slow-roast him for sure.

He wondered for a moment if he could chase the knight far enough to get out of earshot of that wailing. Just on principle, he decided to cook the next three women he saw unless they happened to be redheads. The other dragons would all make fun of him if he torched part of his own collection, but no one would know the difference if he just happened to accidentally fry a few women bystanders.

Biggun shook his head from side to side, but it didn't clear the ringing in his skull. The gleam still came from the bushes, so he ambled from the mouth of his cave, hoping the knight would lead him a good chase into a few bystanders.

Madeleine, standing above the cave holding the sword, was far happier to see Biggun emerge than George was. As the dragon's head emerged from the cave, she hurled the enormous sword down from the ledge. The point struck Biggun at the base of his skull, and he reeled out of the cave, thrashing and randomly belching flame.

George, however, hadn't waited to see this. When Biggun poked his head out of the cave looking directly at him, George renounced such worldly pleasures as the acquisition of giant swords and immediately fled temptation. He was hastened along by one of the first random bursts of fire curling around his lumbering ankles, igniting nearby small bushes. Madeleine missed George's second retreat down Dragon Mountain, being too occupied with evading the landslide triggered by the death throes of Biggun and distracted by the change in pitch of the wailing from the cave inside.

Madeleine's sister finally ceased howling when Madeleine entered the cave, much to the relief of the other women within. For a few minutes, Madeleine thought she might have to protect her sister from them next. However, when they realized they were free to leave the cave without being obligated to marry, or even kiss, some smelly, pompous knight, their moods improved considerably. The discovery of the dragon's hoard of gold pleased them as well.

When Madeleine's party came back down the mountain, George was back on his rock beside the trail, gloomily finishing the polish on his helm. He hated losing swords, he hated losing women, and he hated losing to dragons. When he saw the women coming back down the trail, he was so astonished he dropped the helm in a mud puddle.

Muttering imprecations, he picked it up and began to clean it. When the women drew near, he addressed Madeleine, who had replaced the sword with fantastic gold ornaments. He struggled to keep sheer disbelief from coloring his tone as he spoke to her. "You have slain the dread dragon Biggun, fair maiden?"

"I have." She smiled, walking by him.

"Then where are you going, my pretty maid?"

"I am taking my sister back to my father's house."

George fell in with the women. "May I go with you, my pretty maid?"

"You may go to my father's house if you wish, though it is only my sister," here she gestured at a girl hardly less beautiful than herself, "who will be staying there."

"Then may I go with you wherever you are bound?"

Her laughter was the sound of silver bells on a summer breeze. "If you'll not go with me to the dragon's lair, you'll not go with me from my father's house, sir knight. In fact, if you are going with her, there is no need for me even to go that far."

George looked at the sister again. She also had her arms full of treasure, an adornment which set off her beauty to him as nothing else could. "May I accompany you to your father, fair maid?"

Madeleine's sister smiled and replied in a voice made soft by hoarseness, "Why certainly, good knight."

George determined to marry her before she could spend any of the money on her own. The perfect wife—she was pretty, rich, and seemed hardly able to speak. Surely the village priest would be available for a wedding this afternoon.

And so in the hilly part of Brittany, where the dread dragon Biggun once ravaged the countryside and his koi still swim in solemn patterns in their lonely pond, a knight and a maid parted company on a trail.

George the Greathearted, who put polish on his armor so well, bound himself to his destiny, which was both what he thought he wanted and what he truly deserved. Madeleine, who polished off the dragon, freed herself from hers, which was neither.

IT'S ALL IN THE MAKING

by Patricia B. Cirone

Culture changes with time and distance, and different talents are valued in different societies. Desi had been taught that her ability to *feel* the metal when mending or making things was evil, but when a foreign Guardswoman brought her an enchanted sword to mend, it was going to be difficult to keep her talent hidden.

Patricia B. Cirone has been writing for a number of years, and has sold more than a dozen short stories, some of which were published by Marion Zimmer Bradley. One of her greatest joys is that she got to meet Marion several times and talk to her about writing, life, and writing some more. In her day job as a librarian, she spends more time talking about books than reading or writing them, but she is currently working on a novel which she hopes to finish before the characters in it get so frustrated they stop talking to her. She lives in New England with her husband and two cats.

"It's all in the making . . . " Askread's unctuous voice penetrated the thick oilcloth that separated the front of the shop from the utilitarian work area.

That was for sure, Desi thought, silencing a snort as she hunched over the fine filigree of the brooch she was working on. *Not that dear Uncle Askread had anything to DO with said making . . .* She reached over and wiped her right hand on the heavy linen cloth to remove even the faintest moisture of sweat, and stretched it open and shut several times before picking up her tool again. The voices from the other side of the curtain continued to pick at her attention. Whoever her uncle was talking to had an unusual accent.

"Your shop came highly recommended," the stranger was saying.

"Oh, I'm sure. The best in the city, my dear," purred Askread.

Desi's head jerked up. *My DEAR???* Hadn't the stranger been asking about repair on a sword hilt?

"I'd like to talk to the craftsman who will work on it," the husky tenor insisted.

"Oh, I hardly think that is necessary . . . "

"I do," the stranger interrupted firmly. "I never deal through intermediaries in matters as important as this. Through here?" the stranger asked.

Desi heard Askread sputter as the curtain was flung aside and booted feet entered her domain. "Really, really . . . " Askread protested as he trailed helplessly after the . . . yes, a woman.

Definitely a *her,* Desi thought, goggling at the stranger, all pretence of being busy at work forgotten in her lax hands. The boots that encased the stranger's feet stretched all the way to her knees. Not town boots then, but riding boots. Or possibly Guard . . . but these boots were not polished, but scratched and dusty. Breeches and a smooth brown jerkin with the insignia of a crown over crossed swords covered a muscular but obviously feminine figure. Her hair was cut short—no, not cut, but *hacked* as if style or appearance was of no concern. Desi's eyes rose to the stranger's face. Amused, vivid green eyes stared straight back at her.

"Hallo," the stranger said politely.

"H . . . hello," Desi squeaked in reply. Uncle *never* let anyone know she was the one who made some of the jewelry and all of the sword hilts the shop was famous for. He was *not* going to be pleased, she thought, and glanced at his face. His face was mottled red, and his throat quivered as if about to explode.

"Are you the one who repairs sword hilts?" the stranger asked in that husky voice that was almost, but not quite, a tenor.

"No, of course not," Uncle Askread grated out, striving to maintain his oily politeness with this unruly customer. "My niece is only cleaning up in the shop, right, Desi?" he demanded.

Desi, obviously perched on the high stool at the work bench, her jeweler's guard on her left hand, tool in her right, and oil on her face where her hand had brushed against it while shoving her hair out of the way, sat there frozen, not knowing what to say.

"I think not," the stranger said confidently. She turned abruptly to confront Uncle Askread. "Don't try to play me for a fool, sir. This is obviously the craftswoman who fashions your wares."

Askread gobbled ineffectively for a moment, then flapped his hand at Desi, his mouth twisting as if he had swallowed a particularly bitter prune.

"What can I do for you?" Desi asked softly, her mind racing. Who could this woman be? That insignia on her breast had a small embroidered crown over it, and so was obviously a royal emblem; she couldn't be just some caravan guard. And then Desi's mind made the connection between the rumors of a royal wedding that had been flying around the city for two months and the recent overwhelming demand for fine jewelry and sword hilts so decorated they would hurt even a calloused hand. Could Prince Trakear be getting betrothed to someone so foreign she had *women* for guards?

The stranger drew her sword out of its sheath. "Here," she said, pointing to an area on the hilt which had obviously sustained damage.

Desi reached forward and touched the hilt with her fingertips. She traced the design that was part of the grip and ran her fingers over the harsh break where something—another sword?—had scored and dented it. She let her fingers linger, letting her *other* sense reach out to the hilt. Each piece of work had its own soul, its own spirit that was a blend of its materials and a touch of the craftsman's own soul, and Desi liked to get the *feel* of a piece before working on repairing it. It was this ability that made her so good at repairing all sorts of metalwork and had brought her uncle prosperity ever since he had taken her in. But when she reached out with that hidden, inner sense she saw not metal or the forge of a fire, but bright runes that blazed like fire in front of her eyes.

Desi gasped, her eyes widening. This sword was more than a mere crafting of metal. She felt the Guardswoman tense and look more closely at her. Desi swiftly dropped both her hands and her eyes. Arts such as hers were considered dangerous to possess. Her mother had warned her again and again and had swatted her hand whenever she caught her "adjusting" a tear in her clothes or "coaxing" a daisy chain to stay together.

"I feel sure we can repair this . . . " Desi's voice trailed off awkwardly. *What did one call a female Guard?*

"Can you truly *repair* it?" the Guard asked in a strange manner, her eyes seeking Desi's.

Did this Guardswoman *know* her sword was spelled? And also . . . know *Desi* could work with such arts? No, she couldn't! No one living, not even her uncle, knew Desi possessed such witch's craft. She had to be imagining the intensity of the stranger's words. She was just overreacting to having a woman Guard just barge into the back room and worrying about what her uncle would do and say to her later about it. As if it had been her fault. And she was overtired from all the extra work they had been having lately. Yes, that was it. It was just a sword hilt. And this stranger was just a Guard.

"Yes, of course, Madam," Desi said firmly, tucking all thoughts of her extra art away. "We've been having quite a bit of extra work, but I feel sure we could have this repaired in . . . "

she glanced at her uncle, "three days?" Askread nodded. "Three days," Desi said to the customer.

"All right," the stranger said. "I'll leave it here, then. Here's a surety against the work," she said, pulling a gold coin out of her pouch. Askread's eyes gleamed, the pruned twist to his mouth easing somewhat.

"Of course, of course," he said soothingly, and drew the Guard back out into the outer portion of the shop. Desi didn't listen to the closing murmurs of her uncle's arrangements with the Guardswoman, but instead stared at the bespelled sword and wondered what she had gotten herself into.

Only once before had she felt such a making in an object. That had been when a distraught acolyte had brought in a temple chalice she had dropped and dented. Nervously she had scurried into the shop on a day when Desi had been minding the counter. The young woman had looked frantically about before dragging the precious object out from beneath her cloak and asking if their craftsman could repair it so well no one would ever know the difference. And . . . would they do it without asking for payment? For the church . . . ? Desi had agreed to try, feeling sorry for the young woman who tearfully thanked her and hurriedly stumbled out of the shop with breathless promises to pray for her in lieu of coin.

The opportunity to work with such a beautiful object had been payment enough for Desi, who would never have seen any of the coin anyway. Her uncle made sure of that. She worked for her meals and a roof over her head and was supposed to feel grateful for that. And sometimes, she admitted grudgingly, she was. It had been good of her uncle, she reminded herself, to take her in when her mother had died. He wasn't even a blood relation, but the husband of an aunt who had died before she had even been born. Desi sighed. If only. . . .

But wishes didn't get work done. She picked her tools back up and returned to working on the brooch that was promised for tomorrow. Another one of the gewgaws that had been in such demand recently. Her eyes kept straying to the sword hilt.

She remembered working with that golden chalice, and the peace she had felt when the spells interwoven in the gold had swirled around her, like the chimes of the temple bells. She had spent hours working on that chalice, staying up late when her uncle thought her abed. It wasn't just the delicate beating out of the dent until it was invisible; it was tapping it until those inner bells sounded pure and sweet. It wasn't merely retracing the intricate pattern on the outside of the chalice; it was weaving the pattern so it fit precisely with the pattern she saw glowing in her head, so both the pattern on the outside and the pattern that glowed behind her eyes swirled as one.

It had been working with the chalice that had made her more fully aware of her powers, and made her wonder why her mother had said they were evil. What could be evil about making or mending things of beauty?

It hadn't been the acolyte, she remembered, who had returned to fetch the chalice, but a stern-faced temple mistress. The woman had handed over coin and thanked Desi for their "attempt" to mend the temple chalice. "Such things are not repairable," she had said, "but thank you for making the attempt. It was very good of you to agree to do such work for free. The Goddess will surely note your generosity,"

She lifted the chalice to put it into a wooden box she had brought, then paused and looked sharply at it. She had turned it slowly, round and then around again, staring at the flawless pattern, and Desi thought she could hear the faint echo of the chimes she had heard when working with the object.

"This is repaired quite well," the woman said, staring at Desi.

"My uncle is careful to employ the finest craftsman," Desi replied innocently, trying not to gulp down the lump in her throat.

"Hmm . . . " the woman said, before placing the chalice firmly into the box. She had given Desi one more keen look before departing, her sure steps taking her swiftly from the shop.

Now, sitting in the shop next to the sword hilt, Desi suddenly remembered the terror she had felt then, the fear that someone would accuse her of witch powers and burn her, like she'd heard they'd done to a man up in the hills where she had grown up. But she knew she wouldn't let her fear stop her from working on the sword hilt. She would just be careful. She wouldn't let Uncle Askread know how long she would have to work on it; longer than merely fixing a physical dent would take.

She wondered if working on this would feel different than the chalice. She had thought maybe the spells on the chalice had come from years of being used in a temple. Or perhaps . . . well, there were rumors that "witch" powers were welcome when someone was dedicated to the temple. But this was no object of worship, soaking up prayers or quietly being "dedicated" by a priestess. It was a weapon of destruction. Those spells had been placed there. And she would get to work with them, feel them weave about her and dance out her fingers. Her fingers itched to work on it right away, but she forced herself to continue working on the brooch. *Soon* she promised herself.

"Don't you have that finished, yet?" Askread demanded, suddenly looming over her shoulder, a few hours later. Desi gritted her teeth.

"The brooch for Lord Urstar is finished, Uncle. This is the one for Lady Demaetrede."

"Well you'd better work swiftly. No dawdling. We've lots of demand, you know."

Desi swallowed a sigh and only trusted herself to nod. When did she *not* work swiftly?

"I'm closing the shop as soon as it's full twilight," Askread remarked. "Have that piece finished by then."

Desi glance out the window and her mouth tightened. Yes, she *would* have to work swiftly, to meet this unnecessary demand. But she had learned from experience that it was no use arguing with Uncle Askread or pointing out that this piece wasn't due to be picked up until the late afternoon of the following day. She'd had bruises from such arguments when he had first taken her in and taught her the basics of jewelry making. She made sure the second brooch was finished and the work area cleaned up by the time Askread closed the shop.

As usual, Askread left to enjoy a convivial supper at one of the local eateries, while Desi turned and trudged up the outside stairs to the upper floor over the shop, her daily housekeeping chores, and a meager dinner she had to make for herself.

She passed old Nossie sweeping the stairway landing on the outside of the next house, which crowded up, practically nudging their own.

"Good even, Nossie," she said politely, too tired and distracted to stop for conversation. But Nossie had other ideas.

"Lots of business these days with all the goings on at the palace," she said, a gleam in her eye.

"Yes," said Desi tiredly. "Near run off our feet with orders for brooches and cloak pins and other fine stuff."

"Hmmm. Lots of doings. Mornings, noons and nights," she said suggestively.

Desi smiled tiredly. "Well, best be going," she said and trudged on up the rest of the length of staircase. Dinner revived her, and after washing the dishes and setting the morning's bread to rise by the side of the small kitchen stove, she curled up in the comfortable chair by the other side of the fire to read for a bit. Askread had picked up a new book with eastern designs in it from some caravan dealer. He always seemed to know everybody, and to be getting some tidbit from here or there: books of designs, small nuggets of different shades of gold, silver wire pulled finer than they had time to do in the shop, even the odd lot of gemstones.

Desi yawned widely. It did make the shop stand above most of the competition, and helped pay for all those dinners on the town which Uncle Askread said were so important for business. "Contacts," he would say wisely, waggling his eyebrows. "Can't expect a mere girl to understand, but it's contacts that makes a business."

Desi woke suddenly with a snort, her neck stiff and uncomfortable from falling asleep in the chair. She strained, listening for the sound that had woken her, and then realized, as it slithered the rest of the way, that it had been the book falling from her lap. She laughed nervously to herself and stretched the kinks free from her neck and back. The fire had died down, and the sky outside the heavily leaded window was pitch black. She peered out, trying to see any stars or either of the two moons, but it must have clouded up while she slept. Uncle was late—very late. That usually meant he had stopped for the night at some bawdy house and wouldn't be home until nearly time for the shop to open.

Carefully she banked the remains of the fire, let herself back out of the upper story, and crept down the stairs, lighting her way with a glowing piece of tinder she had lit from the fire. She eased the heavy iron key to the shop into the side door, careful not to let it clank against the iron of the lock and wake Nossie, who was surely as nosy as her name. Cautiously she opened the door to the shop and slipped inside, locking the door behind her. Swiftly she crossed the outer room of the shop and entered the back portion, lighting the fat candle on the work table at the far end with the piece of tinder. Then she tossed the tinder into the small pot-bellied stove that served as both heat for the shop and for warming the more malleable metals. She moved back towards the outer room and pulled the oilcloth tightly closed, clamping it against the frame so that no chink of light crept out. She jerked closed the small heavy curtains on the high windows at the back of the work area, as well. Uncle Askread had always impressed upon her that it was dangerous for a jeweler to show light at night for fear of tempting a thief to break in, knowing you were alone in a shop full of treasure. Desi had the added reason of not wanting Uncle Askread to know she was in here, should he come home unexpectedly. Not that he would mind her putting in extra work . . . but she didn't want him coming in on her and maybe guessing that she was doing more than simple mending on the sword hilt.

Desi soon became lost in her art. The difficult part wasn't the metalworking, it was matching the inner pattern, drawing its energy into a continuous flow, soothing the jangle of its cry of hurt. She became lost in time, lost in the beauty of those runes and light.

It was the cold that jarred her loose from her trance. The small pot-bellied stove had gone out, and outside the high window birds were starting their morning calls in anticipation of the sun. Desi yawned and stretched the kinks out of her body. It had felt good to work with so difficult a project. It wasn't that she was *bored* with metalworking; she loved making new things. But it wasn't the challenge it used to be, even when surreptitiously adding a delicate charm to make the piece gleam more, or give the wearer added grace. Working on the hilt brought sweat to her brow and made her feel as exhilarated as if she had walked briskly up a steep hill. A few more sessions like this one and she would have it finished. If Uncle Askread cooperated and stayed away another night, he would never know how much more time she had invested in the piece than a simple repair would take.

Desi carefully put away her work and lit a small candle from the fat worktable candle before snuffing the latter out. Then she unhooked the heavy oilcloth and walked toward the side door of the shop, shielding the candle with her hand. Suddenly she was stumbling forward, trying to catch herself with her hand as the candle flew free in a dangerous arc onto the floor. She landed with an "Ooof!" her fall broken by something large and soft, the something she had tripped over. She crawled awkwardly over it and snatched her sputtering candle up before it either went out or set the shop alight. She held it over the bundle on the floor and gasped in horror.

Uncle Askread lay dead on the floor, blood staining his tunic in a large splotch around the hilt of a knife, his eyes staring, horribly open, glistening a sickly white in the gleam of the candle. Desi gulped and hesitantly leaned forward to touch him, shaking him slightly, just in case.

"U . . . uncle?" she stuttered. But his arm was cold and strangely stiff. She shook so hard the wax from her candle dripped and splattered on his chest. She sobbed aloud and ran for the side door. She ran out, wild-eyed and ran for the street.

"Watch! Watch!" she called. Within moments shutters were opening and curious faces were peering out of the upper stories. It seemed forever, but it was probably just minutes before the overweight watchman puffed up the street towards her. After that, everything seemed to blur.

Desi answered questions as more and more people crowded into the shop. Nothing really penetrated until a sergeant of the watch grasped her arm and said: "Come along now. Got to lock you up."

"Lock me up? I can lock up the shop if you're through. But shouldn't something be done about my uncle's body? We can't just leave him here like this!"

The sergeant looked at her, exasperated. "Should have thought about that before ya murdered 'im."

"Me!" Desi exclaimed in astonishment. "*I* didn't murder him!!"

"Right. Ya were just ten feet away working on some frill while someone *else* got into a locked shop and stabbed him wi'out you hearin' a thing. And the blood on yer clothes just leapt there. I weren't born yestiday, ya know. Come along, girlie."

He grabbed her by the arm and started moving toward the door. He turned back to say to one of his men: "Better get the sniffers here, just in case. Don' wan' anyone sayin' we didn't do our job."

Desi stumbled a bit in terror, and masked it by pretending she had tripped over the raised doorjamb. *Sniffers.* Would they sense the working she had been doing with the sword hilt and burn her for sorcery as well as murder? She couldn't imagine they would find any sorcery in her Uncle's death; he had clearly died of being stabbed by that knife. But she knew that sniffers were often brought in for any unusual death. And it *was* odd she hadn't heard anything from just feet away on the other side of the oilcloth. At least at night. In the day, she knew, twenty customers could come in and out of the shop without her hearing them when she was concentrating on a piece of jewelry . . . *especially when she was using just a bit of her powers to tweak that extra bit of sparkle or strength into a piece*, as she had done increasingly after working with the chalice and discovering how much more fulfilling it was to work with metal instead of daisy chains or the heaps of mending her mother used to assign to her.

She stumbled along beside the sergeant of the guard, and dawn found her locked in a cell. A clean, very nice cell, but a cell all the same. Exhausted, she sat down on the cot and, without intending to, fell asleep.

The sound of a clanking outside her cell woke her abruptly. Confused, she knocked her knee trying to get out of the side of the cot that was against the wall. She sat up in the cot and peered dazedly as the heavy door to the cell opened. Outside was the female guard that had dropped off her sword hilt to be mended. What was *she* doing here???

"Come along now, this woman's paid yer surety," the jail keeper said.

Desi found herself bundled up and outside the jail before she could stutter out a question. "I don't understand," she said, finally, as they were walking down the street. *Where were they going, anyway?*

"Well, I figured if I wanted my sword hilt properly repaired in this benighted place, I had better get you out of that jail," the woman said with a grim, but amused, smile.

"How did you even know I . . . ? And why . . . ?"

"The sniffers," the woman said succinctly.

Desi shuddered. *Oh Goddess, they had been able to track her spells. Did they burn witches here in the city like they did in the hills?* She'd heard some places merely drowned spell casters, but had never had the courage to ask what was done here in Cascara. It might have started questions about why she wanted to know.

"Will I . . . ?" Desi started to ask shakily, and then stopped at the quick frown and slight negative shake of the other's head.

"The sniffers tracked my sword hilt," she continued conversationally, "and a look at your Uncle's books quickly gave them my name. That's how I found out they had incarcerated you . . . *idiots,*" she added beneath her breath. "I need that hilt repaired, so I've paid your surety and promised you would remain in our custody, while you repair my weapon for me. I'm Sanat, by the way."

"Good meet, Sanat," Desi said automatically, feeling silly. "My name . . . "

"Desi. I know."

Of course she would know, you idiot, Desi thought. She just paid surety for you!

"Hope you won't mind our quarters. They're a bit Spartan."

"Better than a cell," muttered Desi.

The woman gave a sudden crack of laughter. "They are, at that!"

"Won't you get in trouble for having a . . . for your sword hilt?" Desi finally asked the question that had been on the tip of her tongue since the woman had admitted the sniffers had identified her sword as enchanted.

"I'd be in trouble if it *weren't* 'enchanted,' as you call it," she replied. "I'm a lieutenant in Princess Majari's guard."

As if *that* explained anything, Desi thought.

It did, though, she found, when they had reached the guard's quarters, above a wing of the stables on the palace grounds. She had been right in her surmise that a betrothal was being arranged for the Prince with a foreign Princess, namely Sanat's Princess Majari. She was from Tuorum, half way across the world, on the edge of the true sea. There, she was told by several others of the guard, "enchantments" and "witches' powers" were prized beyond measure. Only those who were rich or employed by the rich could afford them. Sanat, as a lieutenant in the force that protected one of their royal Princesses, was *required* to have spells woven into her sword and into the armor she wore when on the road. Protecting the lives of the guards who guarded her was considered part of protecting the life of the Princess.

"*Evil!?* " was the response her tentative questions gained. "How could the gifts of the Goddess be considered evil??"

"We lost Tsari, our unit's Protector, fighting off some bandits at Outreacher's Pass," Sanat said grimly. "That is why I had to come to you to repair my hilt. I was worried sick I wouldn't be able to find anyone to repair this here, knowing the local believers are still influenced by the old hill superstitions."

"Why did you?" Desi asked. "Come to me, I mean? How did you know . . . ?" By then she had confessed her powers to the others of the guard, not that they hadn't already known, apparently.

"The Goddess's temple quietly tracks those they suspect might have powers, and intervenes if possible, if it looks they might be in danger. The Goddess's servants know that any gifts She gives aren't evil, but they don't seem to be able to change your people's beliefs. I asked if they knew of anyone who might help me, and was told you were a Mender. That you had mended one of their chalices as well as one of their own Menders could have."

"A Mender?"

"Someone who can sense the patterns another has spelled, and repeat them. It's almost as difficult as casting the spell in the first place. In Tuorum you'd be paid in gold for such talents."

Desi shook her head, feeling as if its insides had been turned upside down. Female guards—and they told her there were female merchants and craftswomen who worked out in the open, as well—spell casters that were prized instead of killed? Was there truly a land in which such existed or were they telling her tall tales?

Over the next few days, while Desi worked on repairing the sword hilt to the best of her ability, she got to know most of the Princess's guards by their first names, and blossomed within their camaraderie. She had never had friends her own age, and even though these young women wore breeches and spoke with accents, she felt more at home with them than with the girls of Cascara that had come into the shop giggling and whispering of boys. Maybe it was because the guards had a job to do, and were proud of doing it well. All too soon, the sword hilt was mended, and it was just days before she was to appear before the magistrate.

"We're going to ask your neighbor a few questions," Sanat said firmly.

"Nossie?" Desi asked incredulously. "You think she had something to do with this?"

"No, but she might know something about it, just the same. She's been watching out some window or door of hers every time I've been to your shop."

"Oh. But it was in the middle of the night!"

"Old folks don't always sleep as soundly, or as long, as young folks."

They questioned Nossie, and the old woman had eyed Desi's escort carefully, before finally revealing she had seen a man enter the shop with Askread and leave hurriedly just a few moments later, blood splattered on his clothes.

"Why didn't you tell the watch!?" Desi asked.

"They never asked," Nossie said huffily.

"Too busy locking *you* up," Sanat said to Desi wryly. Sanat, with the influence of the Princess behind her, soon had the Cascara city watch scurrying in circles, doing the investigation they should have done in the first place. Nossie's description of the man's clothing made it sound like he might be from the court and not a merchant, and the magistrate, instead of ordering Desi's execution, ordered the Watch to ask questions in the bars and eateries Askread had frequented to see if they could identify who the real murderer could have been.

Now that she wasn't remanded to the custody of the Princess's guards, Desi went back to living in the quarters above her Uncle's shop. It felt strange to know her Uncle would never appear at the top of the stairs, blustering and demanding. It wasn't as much a relief as she had thought it would be, when she had daydreamed about the shop and apartment above it belonging to her, with no Uncle Askread to contend with. In fact she found herself starting at noises that never bothered her before, when she had often been alone in the evenings and even through most of the night.

She chided herself for her foolishness and kept busy with the work that was still pouring into the shop. She wouldn't know whom Askread had left the shop to until the Jewelers Guild officials processed the request to dig his will out of their files— for a fee, of course. In the meantime, it was her only source of livelihood.

A scant two days later, she was putting away an assortment of sleeve pins two customers had spent almost an hour examining, before deciding not to buy anything, when the chime by the front door of the shop sounded. She looked up, smiling politely at the man who entered. He was richly dressed, his chin sporting the narrow goatee that was considered fashionable at court and laughable everywhere else. A pale pink jewel the size of a robin's egg adorned the elaborate pendant that hung around his neck. Desi wished she could get a closer look at the silver curlicues that wove around the edges of the jewel and held it in place.

The man walked swiftly over to where she was standing and grabbed her, wrenching her arm up behind her back and clapping a hand over her mouth.

Desi fought to get loose as he dragged her behind the oilcloth curtain into the work area of the shop. "Mmmmpph!" She tried to scream. She tried to bite his hand or stomp on his foot, but for all his affectation of a goatee, he was strong and had taken her by surprise.

"Thought you'd blackmail me like your blessed Uncle did, huh?" he was muttering. "Well, I'll silence you like I did him!"

Desi was terrified now. This wasn't some robber . . . or even rapist, like she had imagined. This was her Uncle's murderer. He was going to try and kill her unless she did something!

"So you saw me that night, and now you're sending out a description of me to let me know you're going to take up right where your Uncle left off, huh? Well, I can kill two fools as easily as I did one!"

She heard the shop chime sound, and tried harder to get away.

The man panted, but held onto her. She heard the customer walking around the shop, calling: "Hello?"

Her foot connected with part of the worktable and she kicked out as hard as she could. One of her sharp tools fell to the ground, but the man ground it under his heel and dragged her further toward the back of the shop. Desi could feel his pendant digging into her back.

She could *feel* his pendant . . .

Desi let her senses run out through her shoulder blades instead of her fingers. The silver in the pendant came alive and writhed into tendrils that lashed up to the man's neck, choking him. Another set of tendrils leapt forth and bound themselves around the wrists that held her mouth and held her arm. With a choked cry of pain, the man let her go as he tumbled backward, and she fell, gasping, to the floor.

Quickly she scrambled up, and turned, but the man was helpless, his wrists bound to his chest with solid bands of silver. Silver ran around his chest and anchored him to the floor. His fingers scrabbled weakly, trying to reach for the tendrils of silver that wrapped his neck, slowly choking him. Desi reached out with her senses only, not risking letting her hands get anywhere near the man, and eased the silver bands around his neck enough that they wouldn't actually kill the man. He glared silently at her, his eyes gleaming wildly with hatred, and tried to kick her with his feet.

Desi backed away, then turned and ran out through the oilcloth.

"What's wrong?" asked Sanat.

Desi could only stare at her and gasp, then pointed to the back of the shop. The woman went swiftly back and gave an exclamation of astonishment. Desi found her voice. "He . . . he was going to murder me. He . . . he said that Uncle was blackmailing him. He thought it was *me* who saw him that night, and he was going to kill me . . . "

"Hmm . . . " Sanat's eyes gleamed as she took in the sight of the silver tendrils imprisoning the man's wrists and neck, arcing between them as if they were an elaborate new form of jewelry. "Well, you sure took care of that, didn't you!" she said appreciatively.

"What should I do?!" Desi wailed. Anyone seeing the man would know that she had enchanted the silver.

"Can you get that back off of him?" Sanat asked.

"Yes," Desi whispered. "But then . . . "

"Don't worry." She walked up behind him and grasped his head by the hair, ruining the carefully arranged hair. She took a knife from a sheath by her waist and held it ready. "Go ahead," she said to Desi.

Carefully Desi crept forward and touched the edge of the silver nearest her. It coiled as if it were alive and flowed away from the man and into her fingers. The pink jewel it had originally embraced fell to the floor and rolled away. Sanat swiftly hauled the man to his feet, *his* arm held behind his back now, her knife at his throat. "Summon the watch," she said.

Desi put the lump of silver down onto the workbench and ran out into the street.

When the watch came, Sanat told them she had overpowered the murderer, and they took the man's ravings for that of a madman. Weakly, Desi sat down on her work stool after they had hauled him away. She looked about the shop.

"What should I do?" she asked Sanat. "*Someone* might believe him. Besides, I'm not sure I want to live here anymore. First Uncle Askread's murder, now this . . . "

"Just as well. The Princess Majari has taken an interest in you and asked Prince Trakear to get the Jewelers Guild to move faster than a glacier in unearthing your Uncle's will. He left the shop and all its contents to a nephew on his side of the family."

Desi looked around and gave a short, bitter laugh. Her work, all of it, left to someone else. "So what *do* I do?" she asked the other woman.

"Desi, you are not just a Mender, as I thought, but a *Maker*. You *have* to be to do what you did . . . to make silver do that, to create that . . . and without even tools! . . . and with no training! Come back with us, when Princess Majari leaves Cascara and goes back to Tuorum to prepare for the wedding. We need a Protector; we'll hire you. Once you are in Tuorum, and you get training, you will be able to do almost *anything!* You have incredible power to be able to do what you did. In my land your gifts will be valued. Indeed, I beg you to come back with us. You have no idea . . . Makers are *rare*, sometimes only a few in a generation! You . . . you *have* to use these gifts. You are *wasted* here, mending bits of frippery, when your talents could change worlds!"

Desi looked around the familiar confines of the work area that had been both a delight and a prison. A home . . . and yet never a Home.

Could she go to a strange land, where she wouldn't know the language, where everything from her looks to her clothes would be different? . . . *but where her talents would be trained instead of hidden* . . . Where the food would be strange, and the stars different in the sky? . . . *but where she wouldn't risk her life every time she did what felt as natural, and as right, as breathing . . . ?*

"It's all in the making," her Uncle had loved to say, while selling her work to his customers. Maybe it was time to *make* herself, to let her own patterns spring free and create who she was meant to be.

"All right," she said.

DAUGHTERS OF BRIGHTSHIELD

by Pauline J. Alama

I have never quite understood why women are called the weaker sex, particularly when we generally outlive men. Perhaps some women in the past found it advantageous to foster this belief, so that men would underestimate us. Certainly the raiders in this story underestimated a village of "defenseless" women.

       Pauline J. Alama is the author of the fantasy novel *The Eye Of Night* and winner of a second-place Sapphire Award for the short story "Raven Wings on the Snow" in *Sword & Sorceress 18*. Her work also appears in the anthologies *Rotten Relations, Mystery Date,* and *Witch High*. Between day jobs as part-time grant proposal writer, full-time mom, and overtime cat-slave, she finds time to work on two new novels: *The Ghost-Bearers,* a heroic fantasy of war and peacemaking; and a comic fantasy about a cursed actor and a bear, provisionally titled *Dancing With Zita*.

I was born a chieftain's daughter, but for a time I was a slave. It was then that I learned of my heritage.

       I was twelve years old when the Scathan raiders landed at Salthaven on the Corholm coast. Their long, narrow ships cut the water like arrows, but before they reached the shore, they made shallow dives from the decks and swam with their swords strapped to their backs, rather than landing their boats like fishermen, like our men. Inexorably, like some drowned man's dying curse coming up from the deeps, they clambered up the boat-wrecking rocks at Seal's Cove, where we had believed no human boatman could land.

They found our town undefended. I was the first to see them from afar, so I rushed into the Great House and told the news. "Where's Father?" I demanded, almost too angry to be afraid. "Where are the fighting men?"

My mother's lips pressed tightly; she was as furious as I. "Either they're still in their boats, waiting for those pirates to make for the harbor, or—" She did not say, but shook her head, and I knew what dreadful thing "or" meant. "I told him he should have stayed to defend Salthaven, rather than taking the fleet out to challenge them at sea. As if honest fishermen could beat pirates in a sea-battle!"

"I should have been with them," I muttered. "I can wield a sword. Seahawk showed me."

"Hush, Linden," my mother said. "Let me think what to do."

"I'll get Grandfather's sword," I volunteered.

"You'll do what I tell you!" Mother snapped.

My sister Darkshield cut in, "As if you could beat them back single-handedly with one rusty blade. Get yourself killed, and others with you, more likely."

Of all the hard things I had to do that day, not striking Darkshield just then was the hardest. Instead I said, "Why couldn't I? Aren't we descended from Brightshield, the bold headwoman who single-handedly defended Salthaven against an army?" Mother had told us the story many times, and I would not fail to draw a lesson from it.

But Grandmother, who sat nearby with her drop spindle, said, "Not single-handedly. You don't know the whole story, Linden. There's more to defending a village than flashing a sword."

"So what are we to do? Surrender our homes, our herds, our honor to these brigands?"

"Unless you will be quiet and let me think, that may be the only way of saving all our lives," my mother said. "Great Mother of All! They'll want to gloat over the chieftain's household most of all. They'll want us to bake them bread, serve them beer, wait on them, dance for their pleasure—" She ran her hands through her hair, distraught.

But my grandmother calmly let her spindle twirl, spinning out a long yarn. "So be it," she said. "All those things can be spun into a cord to bind them."

Mother turned to meet Grandmother's eyes. "A binding—?"

"The knots of mystery," Grandmother said, and all the other women, even Darkshield, nodded, as if this explained everything. And perhaps, to them, it did; they'd all been initiated and learned the sacred stories. At twelve years old, two years shy of initiation, I only knew the tales told to children.

"What's that?" I said.

"No time to explain," said Mother. "Darkshield, get the priestess and the brewster. Bid them greet the strangers and lead them here. Tell everyone you meet to offer no resistance and take no risks. My man left our village undefended, so I and my kin will shoulder the burden.

"Linden, stay here and spin with your grandmother, while I knead. Say nothing, but watch everything. Do you hear me?"

I heard, but I did not understand. Sit and spin while the raiders overran Salthaven? Knead dough? Offer no resistance? I had heard what Scathans had done to unlucky towns along the Corholm coast: kill all the men; burn the houses; steal anything of value, even from the House of the Hallows itself; keep the women in chains, or sell them like cattle—or slaughter them like cattle if they no longer deemed them useful.

Still, Darkshield was right: I could not kill them all, not by myself. Mother and Grandmother had some plot brewing. From the corner where Gran sat, I would be best positioned to see all, and find out what blow I could strike for the defense of Salthaven.

Heart hammering, I sat silent beside Gran and took out my spindle. She smiled at me and whispered in my ear. "Watch my spindle dance, and do as I do. When your time comes, you must follow the spindle's path."

She sang softly as she spun the wool, words that sounded like nonsense but were probably old words, strong words. I watched her spindle whirl and bob in time with her song, and it seemed to dance indeed, till my fear receded as the rhythmic motion sent me half into a dream.

As we spun, as my mother and her women started kneading the dough for bread, in came the Scathan captain, surrounded by a pack of warriors with swords bared.

Taller and broader than Corholm men, the Scathans seemed to fill the Great House to bursting, even when most of their force was left outside. Their gleaming helmets, adorned with sidepieces shaped like boars' tusks, made them look like strange half-metal beasts, savage and invulnerable. More than that, it frightened me to think how strong they must be to swim with such a weight upon them. Bushy beards the color of wheat or fox-fur bristled out between the tusks of their helmets. Their pale eyes glinted with malice. The swords they carried did not gleam, dulled by old bloodstains, battered by cruel use, but these most of all drew our eyes. Beside the Scathans, Gladstar the Priestess and Coldbrook the Brewster cringed like slaves, not daring to look in their faces.

My mother, her hands deep in the dough, bowed her head reverently, as if to the Hallows. "Mighty conquerors, you find none here but women and children. We are no threat to you. As Headwoman of Salthaven, I welcome you to my house. You have caught us in the midst of making bread; we have none left baked to adorn a feast fitting for you. Rest until the baking is done, and Coldbrook will refresh you with beer while we prepare a feast for you, my lords."

The Scathan captain scowled. "Understand this: you offer me nothing that is not already mine to take. This village is mine. This house is mine. You are mine. You do not welcome me here as headwoman. As my slave, you welcome me to *my* home. Anyone who challenges my right to anything in this village dies."

My mother bowed her head, while I wished fervently that my spindle were a lethal weapon I could wield against the captain. I comforted myself with the thought that perhaps it was: my grandmother had not ceased chanting under her breath, and I felt the rhythm of that chant in the rhythm of our spinning. I stared intently at my thread, willing it to wind around the Scathans' throats, to grip them tighter than bindweed on a rotting tree.

But my mother spoke meekly. "We are at your mercy, Lord. If it please you, I will go on kneading the dough, and my daughters will dance for you." My face flamed as my grandmother thrust me forward to stand before the Scathans.

"Gods, yes," the captain said, glancing from me to Darkshield, his eyes sweeping down her night-black hair to her shapely feet. "Yes, let them dance, bare-headed and bare-legged as they are, the brazen Corholm sluts."

This remark mystified me almost as much as it stung me. Of course we were bare-legged and bare-headed: it was a humid, warm day in late spring, with a hint of summer thunder in the air. But the way the captain looked at us, I felt naked, and might almost have reached for my winter leggings and head-shawl to hide myself. The last thing I wanted to do was dance under those leering eyes. But my grandmother hissed, "Dance! You know how!" and shoved me between the shoulder blades—and as she did so, I felt her slip a length of yarn down the back of my smock.

The thread tickled my back, tingling with Gran's spell, and I found that I did indeed know how to dance. As Gran's muttered chant became a full-throated song, I spun my young body in the same figures her spindle had shown me. Just far enough away so that our outflung arms did not collide, my sister danced the same figures, as though she, too, felt the spellbound thread. A dab of my mother's bread dough stuck to her arm, but she did not trouble herself to brush it off, dancing with abandon, as if it were the greatest pleasure to show off her grace to these raiders who might, for all we know, have killed our father and all his men at sea. She danced in ecstasy, but I danced in fury.

If the Scathan captain noticed my scowl, he did not seem troubled by it. He watched us both with greedy eyes. Around him, his men also gathered to stare. Whenever another raider came into the Great House, he joined the circle around us. None who saw us went off again on their errands; all stayed, captivated. The brewster brought them beer, but they seemed already drunk on what their eyes took in.

Our skirts swirled up as we danced, baring more of our legs to the raiders' lascivious eyes. As they muttered lewd comments to each other, I calmed myself by imagining how my grandmother's spell would twist this dance against them. Were we spinning the rope to hang the raiders? Would my dancing arms grow blades to cut them down?

My mother and her women finished the kneading, and joined in the singing as they waited for the bread to rise. The young maids began to dance with me. We dancers and our audience overflowed the Great House into the square, till it seemed all the young women in Salthaven whirled in unison, our rhythms echoed in the creaking of the spit that the children turned, the scrape of the spoon an old woman used to stir the pot on the hearth, the thumping of the churn: all the preparations for the promised feast were part of the dance.

Bread takes long to rise; it was a long dance. Did I tire? I must have, but I don't remember weariness. I remember my fear and my fury and my impatience for the spell to be complete so I could strike my blow against our enemies.

At last my mother and her women left the dance and returned to their dough. They shaped it into loaves—braids, whorls, and knots of dough—and carried it to the great oven in the village square. We danced along with them, and the raiders followed as if on a halter-rope. The scent of baking filled the village and a hot wind blew from the landward side, just at the time of day when I would have expected a wet, cool wind from the sea.

At last the bread was drawn from the oven, hot and fragrant. The butter was taken from the churn, the roast meat from the spit, and all the feast was ready on the table. My grandmother spun out the last wool on her spindle, and my sister and I collapsed, giddy with fatigue, in each other's arms.

My mother proclaimed to the Scathans, "Come feast, my lords, and celebrate your homecoming." She offered the captain my father's seat, the hero's portion of the roast meat, and the most beautiful golden-brown loaf of bread. Into the braided loaf, I knew, was woven the curse we had spun all day in thread and chant and dance.

But the Captain said, "You taste first, woman, lest you think to poison me."

Before she could answer him, I sprang forward. "I will taste it, Mother!" In this, I thought, I could be as brave as Brightshield of old, though there was no sword in my hand. Let my willingness fool the brigands, even if I too must die for it.

The captain looked shrewdly into my mother's face. "Well, woman?"

"Very well," my mother said calmly. "Go on, child. Eat."

I took a mouthful of everything offered to the captain: a swig of beer, a sip of broth, a bite of roast meat, and last of all, a fragrant morsel of the beautiful, deceptive bread.

As I tasted the bread on my tongue, warmth and ease spread through me. Would death, indeed, be so gentle? I could not resist a second taste, though I had not been offered one. "Mother, this is the best bread you've ever made!"

I hoped they would eat soon, before the fatal effects were apparent. The captain watched me anxiously for a time, and I found, to my surprise, that it was no labor to smile at him. *What a fearful man*, I thought. I felt almost sorry for him, hungry, with a feast before him that he would not let himself touch.

But at last he fell to it, he and all his men. I watched them as avidly as the captain had watched me, waiting to see what the bread would do to them, to me. I noticed for the first time how hungry most of them seemed. So many weary days at sea, they had not tasted fresh bread for too long. Many of them were mere boys who smiled gratefully at the women who served them, as if they half expected to see their own mothers passing the warm bread and fresh butter. Some of the older ones bore terrible scars. Harsh need had driven them to the raiding life. I found I could no longer hate them. This rush of fellow-feeling caught me by surprise—though perhaps it was fitting that I should feel compassion for those who would share my death.

And yet we did not die. Every man tasted the bread and praised it above the meat, even above Coldbrook's best beer. And they smiled, even on the women they had conquered, and made way at the table for all to sit, conquerors and slaves together, conquerors and slaves no longer. By the feast's end, they had brought out their Scathan flutes and begun playing music for us. By morning, they had bundled up all their swords and sunk them in the sea.

My father did come home with some of his men, though a storm had sunk some of the fishing-boats on their ill-conceived expedition to challenge the Scathans at sea. We met the survivors with jugs of beer and loaves of fragrant bread braided in the patterns of the spindle dance, in which the people of Salthaven and the Scathan raiders were bound together.

The captain married one of the women widowed by the storm. As for me, when I came of age, I married his son, one of the youngest of the Scathans who came to raid us, and stayed to take the places of the drowned men of our village. It seems strange to think I once hoped to kill him and all his companions. He tells me it seems strange to him that he ever wanted to loot our pleasant village.

It is in the nature of such spells to make themselves forgettable. People explain away the magic as an ordinary thing, a misunderstanding: surely the raiders never meant to conquer us, but only to settle among us, lacking land in their own country. But I was at the center of the spinning, and I know the truth: we women of Salthaven defended our village, not by a single heroine's might, but all together. We all are daughters of Brightshield.

UNDIVIDED

by *Marian Allen*

There are legends of people (generally wicked sorcerers) who hid their hearts outside of their bodies so that they could not be killed. The warrior in this story purchased *two* charms that would let her do this, but what she did with them might not have been quite what her enemies expected.

Marian Allen's stories have appeared in on-line and print publications, on coffee cans and the wall of an Indian restaurant in Louisville, Kentucky. She writes a food history column for the electronic recipe magazine *Worldwide Recipes* and blogs on Marian Allen's Weblog (http://marianallen.wordpress.com) and the group mystery/food blog Fatal Foodies (http://fatalfoodies.blogspot.com). She is a member of the Short Mystery Fiction Society and of the Southern Indiana Writers Group, and is a regular contributor to the SIW's annual anthology. For free stories, surrealist poetry, recipes and more, please visit her at Marian Allen's Fiction Site (http://MarianAllen.com).

Pimchan's Female did the unthinkable—she burst through the workout room doorway, knocking over the rosewood filigree screen, and entered her Mistress' practice arena uninvited.

Pimchan, ripped from battle meditation, whirled from her knees to her feet and grasped the girl in a double-handed grip designed to tear soul from body. With a brief quiver of muscle, she stopped herself on the very brink of harm.

Through clenched teeth, she said, softly, "Give thanks, my Female, to Chaos, who has granted me control. Now you know why I must not be interrupted."

"Mistress, come!"

The lack of repentance rang alarms. Pimchan released her gently, registering the panic of her female slave, a dark-haired and dark-eyed child of twelve, padded with baby fat. When the girl turned back toward the doorway, Pimchan grabbed her arm.

"Talk first."

"We have to hurry!"

"Talk quickly."

"It's your Male. They took him! They came over the back wall right into the garden. They tried to take me, too, but I was farther from the wall. They're gone—he's gone."

Pimchan threw the girl across her shoulder and ran, talking as she went, the girl answering as best she could between bounces.

"How many?"

"Two."

"Dressed how?"

"Like . . . house servants. One m-male and . . . one female. Brown . . . trousers—and—tunics, short boots . . . of cracked red leather."

Pimchan felt the girl shudder as they reached the back wall and the Female craned around to share Pimchan's view of the bloodied bricks.

"Is he dead?" her Female asked.

"If he were dead, would they have taken him?" She put the girl down, ignoring the child's agitated fidgeting.

"Go on," she prompted her Female. "You got away."

"The male stopped chasing me when I got close to the door. When I got in, I looked back. Your Male nearly got loose, but the woman swung him against the wall. I heard a thunk. The man went back and boosted her over the wall, then picked up your Male and went after them. It all took less than a minute. It's only been a couple of minutes now."

Pimchan heard the unspoken sentence: *You can catch them if you hurry!*

She replied aloud, "A Warrior moves quickly, but never hurries."

She inspected the blood on the wall, rubbing the runes tattooed on her own shaven head to help sharpen her vision.

"A few hairs in the blood, but not many. Probably hurt but probably not badly."

She inspected the boot prints, pressed deep into the dirt, where the invaders dropped into the garden.

"Anything else?"

"The female was not as tall as you, but she was big—" Pimchan's Female held her hands out in front of her own flat chest, "—here. Her skin was yellow like mine, only more brown. The male was taller than you and his skin was dark, almost the color of the good garden dirt. I didn't see the color of their eyes. I was running by the time they hit the ground."

"Did either of you strike a blow?"

"Your Male may have. I just ran."

"Well done. Now go inside and stay there. Tell Tyana to lock you in the keeping room, but to give you wash water, food, drink and fresh clothes."

"Y-yes, Mistress." Pimchan's Female only hesitated a second as the enormity of her trespass into the Warrior's arena hit her, then she returned to the house to prepare for her warranted punishment.

Pimchan drew her serpentine blue-steel dagger and lifted it high.

"Let there be steel between me and mine. Let there be a sharp edge." She gave way to anger at the unexpected trespass, to resentment at having to set protections appropriate to the wilds but—usually—unheard of in a Warrior's home. "Let my Male and my Female, my Overseer and myself pass unharmed, but let all the unprotected feel the full power of my arm."

The curling runes near the dagger's tip darkened, then faded again.

Pimchan sheathed the weapon, willing her emotion to go with it.

She climbed the garden wall so quickly she seemed to levitate, and stood atop it, surveying the paths around what was supposed to be her inviolable sanctuary. Invasion was bad enough—Warriors had been attacked in their safeholds before— but kidnapping a Warrior's attendant slaves was even more perilous a gamble. Who would be so stupid? Who would have so much more to gain than to lose?

She looked down, focusing her eyes to see what was no longer there. Finally, a vague shape coalesced into two shadows, one carrying a smaller shadow. They clarified into a man and a woman, the man carrying Pimchan's Male. They climbed into an oxcart; the woman mounted the driver's seat and picked up the reins, the man clambered into a hollow in the middle of a stack of bulging grain sacks, lay down there with the unconscious child, and flipped a cloth over the hiding place.

The wagon pulled away to the north, toward the market.

Pimchan jumped from the wall, landing lightly, and followed. She bore no weapons except her dagger, but a Warrior *was* a weapon, capable of turning anything to destructive or defensive use against clubs, blades—even, with luck, spears and the new foreign firearms.

The phantoms became more difficult to see as they passed through real carts and real people. Pimchan raised a hand, palm out, at belly level and muttered a string of syllables she had been taught by a very old man in a cold desert cave. The shapes she followed took on a yellow nimbus. She growled—dark blue would have been better in this bright sunlight, but the Glow colored itself arbitrarily. One of the drawbacks of accepting someone else's spell in payment instead of cash.

The second-hand spell fizzled and died in the sunlight and high traffic of the marketplace. Just before the glowing cart entered the turbulence of buyers and sellers, the driver looked back and Pimchan caught the gleam of spectral teeth, as if the shade expected her to try to follow and expected her to fail.

Her quarry gone, she became more than peripherally aware of her surroundings.

Lek, the chestnut seller, with his bags and brazier and bamboo fan, hunkered down at the corner. In a moment, she stood beside him.

Lek raised a heavily wrinkled face and squinted at her as she described the invaders and the generalities of their vehicle. Lek had once served in a Warrior's household, and had no more fear of a Warrior than he did of any of the many other people more powerful than he was.

"I saw a woman in clothes like that with a scratch on her chin driving an old wagon down this street and into the market." He pointed with his fan. "This wagon was painted black, but the paint was peeling. Is that the one you mean?"

"It could be. Tell me more."

"Well. . . ." He scratched his thin beard with his fan. "The grain sacks were white with red catfish on them. The oilcloth was brown, but not the same brown as her clothes. Her clothes were like. . . . Like your skin, if you forgive the familiarity."

Pimchan glanced at her bare arms: the red-brown of roasted fowl. A difficult color to reproduce in dyed goods. That and the red leather boots pointed to a wealthy household. The disrepair of the wagon and age of the boots pointed to bad times.

Lek went on. "The oilcloth was the color of this dust. Pale."

"Have you seen her before? Or the wagon or the clothing? Or the symbol on the grain sacks?"

Lek shook his head. "But there are a lot of farms and estates and enclaves tucked back in the passes and down in the foothills. They don't always send the same people to town, or the same carrier."

Pimchan bowed her thanks.

"Did they take anything?" Lek's voice sounded concerned, but Pimchan knew he was eager for details. Even the priests' quarters were more open than Warriors' compounds, and any crumb of information would be worth a free drink or even a bowl of rice.

"A purple orchid blossom. They tried to take a white one, as well, but they were stung and gave it up."

"A precious blossom?"

Pimchan shook her head. "One of many. They just wanted a trophy, I think, to prove they won a dare. I hope it was worth it to them."

Even if this had been the harmless prank she had invented, the taboo against entering a Warrior's domain without permission could not be broken without punishment. The outrage that had actually been committed demanded worse than death, and only a Warrior's domestic impenetrability would keep the revenge from being as public as possible. Instead, it would be an open secret, communicated by whispers and facial expressions and nodded understandings, unspoken horrors that would enforce the taboo on impressionable young minds so it would be less likely to happen again.

This was not a prank. It was not even a crime. It was a gambit—a move in a game that had yet to be announced.

கௐன

Tyana, the Overseer, stood at the back door of the small house that extruded like an afterthought on the workout arena. Pimchan could have lived happily in the arena, cooking for herself and sleeping in the open. But two years ago she had saved the All-Father from an ambush when her mercenary wandering crossed one of his not-as-clandestine-as-he-thought travels. The cost of that service—meant to be a reward—was this small town nestled in the Circling Sisters mountains.

But Warriors made townspeople nervous, even Warriors bound to the town by the All-Father's decree. Town Warriors were given walled enclaves with workout arenas built to their specifications in the hope they would be content to practice there and not on innocent townsfolk. Town Warriors were given a male and a female slave—unwanted and unnamed orphans, trained from birth for a life of service. Someone had to oversee and train the children to care for a Warrior and a Warrior's equipment—an Overseer, usually a former Male or Female who had been freed and named by his or her Warrior.

Three dependents, so now a Town Warrior needed a house and a garden and a chicken run and a goat or two to supplement the townspeople's grudging tribute which was not always sufficient for four appetites, two of them young and bottomless.

"You didn't find him?" Tyana's sun-browned face was stained with tears.

Pimchan shook her head. "He was taken for a purpose. They wanted both the children, but one will serve their design. I'll be hearing from whoever sent them. Is my Female safe?"

"Safe and waiting."

"Bring the Discipline."

Pimchan removed the carved bar that held a screen of woven rattan across the keeping room doorway and folded the screen to one side. Her Female kow-towed, body trembling in fear. Pimchan knew that rumors told of slaves killed for what this Female had done. Judging from some of her fellow Warriors, she believed the rumors. Her own chest pounded and she rubbed the white scar just below her right collarbone.

Tyana entered the room and Pimchan accepted the Discipline from her: a small leather whip, half a meter from butt to lash.

"Stand," Tyana said.

Pimchan's Female scrambled to her feet.

"Turn."

The Female presented her cringing shoulders.

The Warrior laid one blow, calculated to sting but not cut, across the small back. With the butt of the whip, she lightly bumped the girl's skull—well-padded with unruly black hair.

"Honor is satisfied," Pimchan stated, and handed the Discipline back to the Overseer. "You did well today."

The girl flashed a smile of surprised gratification and dropped into another kow-tow.

"I'm going back to my meditation," the Warrior said. "I will not be interrupted."

ೞ◌ಃ೮ಀ

After meditation, Pimchan worked out physically, barehanded and barefoot, then in boots and with weapons.

When she crossed into her living quarters and called for water and fresh clothes, Tyana said, "You have a visitor."

"Where?"

"In the shelter outside the gate, of course. Do you think I'm so stupid I would invite someone in past your wards? I passed him rice cakes and tea through the window. He hasn't touched them. He didn't say what he wants, but we can guess."

"Does my Female recognize anything about him?"

Tyana shook her head. "He isn't the one."

Pimchan took her time over washing and had her Female dress her in blue steelcloth woven with protective runes.

"Tell Tyana to bring more tea and rice cakes to the Chaos garden. I'll unbar the screen to our visitor."

The screen to the outside world was solid mahogany hung with a hundred tiny brass bells. The bar was hinged so even the children could swing it up out of the way, and the screen balanced on bearings that made it slide easily—if noisily—aside.

The man who stood to face her shone even in the shelter's gloom. His trousers and tunic of red-brown silk were trimmed in gold, and his red leather boots shone with polish. He dipped the shallow bow of the highest caste, then seemed to force himself a little lower in honor of her.

"Come in," Pimchan said, leaving out the inflection that would have added, "and welcome."

He stood half a head taller than she did, black braids slithering against his silk tunic like twin snakes. Pimchan felt a thrill of terror at the sight of those braids, and knew it was a terror her Male had been made to feel.

She moved back so the man could pass, then closed and barred the screen without taking her eyes off him.

"Take the red path," she told him, and followed him as red tile curved away from the blue tile that led to the living quarters' door.

The low table in the center of the Chaos garden's gazebo was already set. Pimchan knew the tea was cold and the cakes were stale—Tyana wasn't one to waste good food and tea on a meeting where nothing would be consumed—but the form was acceptably observed.

They knelt on either side of the table and listened to bees buzzing in the garden's wildflowers while each waited for the other to speak first.

Pimchan was certain he was the wealthy man fallen on hard times whose peeling wagon and threadbare slaves had carried off her Male. He would be accustomed to speaking first, so the pressure of the silence would weigh more heavily on him.

It wasn't long before he shifted his weight and said, "I have a problem. I think you can help me."

She nodded, her gaze never leaving his face but her wide range of vision missing nothing of his body language.

The man fingered his empty teacup and said, "Something was stolen from you. Something important. You want it back. Your heart is set on it."

His gaze seemed to harden and sharpen as he said the last sentence.

Pimchan remained still, but knew that her visitor knew the shaft had struck home.

The man smiled. "There's only one sorcerer around here capable of making a heartsafe charm. He admitted to making two, of a power suitable for use with children. For you." He shook a finger at the Warrior, which would have earned him a broken hand under other circumstances. "It's selfish enough to hide your heart in the body of one child, but to divide it and make two children suffer your adult emotions—your Warrior's rage and remorse. . . ."

Not her whole heart, obviously—everyone knew the heart was the seat of thought as well as emotion, and was also a muscle that pumped blood through a body's veins. But there was one part of the heart—a part no one could see—that held the life force. That part could be removed by sorcery and hidden in a person or a thing. Warriors sometimes did it, as did royalty and merchants—even courtesans—anyone wealthy enough to pay the price.

"We wanted both pieces, but half is enough," the man assured her. "Better, in fact."

"You must be very persuasive, to make that sorcerer betray a client."

"We are persuasive. We are."

Pimchan imagined her Male at the mercy of this man and his associates and understood the terror the sight of him had inspired. She felt an ache in the purple scar below her left collarbone, but gave no sign of it.

"You want something from me," she said. "What is it?"

"Very little. Tomorrow morning, go for a walk. A long walk. Leave your door unguarded by might or magic. Take your Female, if you like, and your Overseer. Go through the Karashi pass and spend the day." He shrugged. "Spend the night, if you like, or a week, but at any rate don't come back here before dusk tomorrow." He shrugged again. "That's all. When you come back, you'll find your Male here, safe and sound, as well as a chest of gold coins—a fortune."

"Why do you want this?"

He shook his head. "If you refuse, or agree but don't leave, or leave and come back, your Male will die, and half your heart with him. Half your courage, half your strength, half your wit, half your will, half your connection to life."

It was a living death. It would leave the sufferer with insufficient resolve even to end an insupportable existence. Yes, taking half her life was an infinitely more frightening threat than taking it all.

Looking into this man's eyes, Pimchan could see his willingness to murder a child, to leave a Warrior helpless, with full remembrance of the might that had been lost.

"Do we have a bargain?" he asked.

"There is no question. I have no choice."

ೞ ೮ Ⴝ ೞ

She gave orders for the next day's expedition and ate what meat and bread and fruit her Female put before her. Instead of finishing her day in the arena, where she ordinarily followed a final battle meditation by wrapping herself in a cloak and sleeping on the sand, she had her Female bring the cloak to her in the Chaos garden. She would spend this night between the outside world and her sanctuary.

She would spend the night, but sleep little. She sat at the tea table and studied her memory of the day's visitor.

A wealthy man in rich clothes. The clothes were newly made, but the man had the air of one accustomed to fine things. The invaders wore his color, but they were shabby, as was his oxcart. Fallen on hard times, with a fresh infusion of money, possibly a first payment for his usefulness? And he had said "we," yet he delivered the threat and the demand himself, so he was the servant in this enterprise—whatever it was. Again, she saw a man restoring his resources by selling his honor.

Very well, then—selling it to whom? Obviously, to someone with great wealth. Someone of power and position, or a man of her visitor's caste would take the money and report the bribe to the All-Father's Warrior, Pimchan.

The All-Father sat at the edge of her thoughts like a Primus figure on the corner of a carto board. Pimchan left him there and continued her musings.

They wanted her out of town for the day. No, not out of town: they could have demanded she stay within her walls and not respond to any calls for help. They didn't want her out of town; they wanted her out of her enclave. They wanted to use it for something. They wanted to use her—use her absence—for something.

In her mind, the All-Father slid along the edge of the carto board and she remembered the ambush she'd saved him from during one of his unattended meanderings. Had he learned nothing? The Primus figure clicked into place at the board's near corner and, in her mind's eye, the All-Father sat in the center of her arena.

No. He had learned nothing.

The All-Father was coming to visit his Warrior here in this remote village. Someone in his confidence knew it—someone who knew his most secret plans and knew enough about Pimchan to tell the man with the braids where he might look for Pimchan's weakness. They were setting a trap for the All-Father, and they were using Pimchan for bait.

The rest of the night alternated between rehearsing possible courses of action and resting in a deep meditation that was more refreshing than sleep.

⋯ ❧❦❧ ⋯

They left before dawn, Tyana and Pimchan's Female swathed in lengths of woolen cloth and Pimchan dressed in black leather armor reinforced with blue steel, rectangular arm shields of red leather strapped to her forearms, twin swords crossed on her back.

No one was visible, but Pimchan had no doubt their movements were observed. Tyana led the way with Pimchan's Female behind her, both laden with sacks of necessities and luxuries for the Warrior's jaunt. Pimchan followed, instincts tuned to their highest pitch.

Yes, they were being followed, but it didn't take a Warrior to know it. The follower seemed unused to the rough trail leading to and through the pass. The occasional suppressed curse floated to them across the rocks and, when they reached the meadow pass, green and yellow with the wild mustard that bloomed there, the occasional smothered sneeze.

Before the day was half gone, they had reached a tidy stone hut that overlooked the south side of the gap. It had one narrow doorway and no windows. Snuggled under an overhang, its entrance could only be seen from one angle. Pimchan entered first, to make certain no unpleasant surprises waited inside.

She came out and let her Female and her Overseer light the candles they had brought with them and sweep grit and pollen from the floor and benches. Pimchan stood, facing the valley below but concentrating on her peripheral awareness, looking at what was not before her, listening beyond the sounds closest to her. When the hibachi was burning and the tea was brewing and the rice with dried vegetables and smoked meat was cooking, she went in.

"Just the one," she said.

"Where?" Tyana asked.

"Up by the spring, in the mouth of the cave. Shade—water—the most obvious place."

Tyana snorted.

Pimchan's Female served the three of them chrysanthemum tea, her hands trembling in spite of herself.

Pimchan patted the girl's head. "Try not to fret. When I chose you and the boy, I promised you I would keep you safe and bring you through your bondage skilled and healthy—and certainly alive. I gave you a Warrior's word. I suppose the word of a Warrior is good enough for you?"

Pimchan's Female, a worried frown lingering on her brow, said, "I know you'll do your best."

Tyana laughed, slapping her knees for emphasis. "Spoken like a true companion! Two years ago, she was a mouse. Now, she's a mongoose, dragging truth into the light whether you want her to or not. That's my training of her."

"Oh, yes," said the Warrior, lips thinned but eyes crinkled in humor. "I'm very well served. What luck." She tossed the dregs of her tea onto the hibachi's coals and stood. "This won't take long."

She slipped out the door and darted across the meadow, directly toward the cave. The watcher, unable to leave without losing sight of the quarry, would be pinned in place until Pimchan reached the broad ledge where the shallow cave overlooked the pass.

The Warrior crossed the stream, drawing both swords as she did.

"Come out," she said.

There was no answer.

"You *will* come out. The only question is: in how many pieces?"

The movement was so sudden, Pimchan nearly struck. A woman flopped into the sunlight, kow-towing so vigorously her head made little clonks against the stone.

"Forgive me, Mighty One! Forgive me! I didn't mean to hurt your Male—it was an accident. He woke up later, and ate and drank. He's a very brave boy—"

"Stand. Stand now."

The woman stood. Small and big-bosomed, with a scratch on her chin, she fit the description Pimchan's Female and Lek had given and wore a threadbare version of the red-brown clothing of yesterday's visitor.

"Who do you work for?" Pimchan demanded. "Why was I sent from my home?"

"I don't know, Sun of Strength. I mean, I don't know why. I work for Master Aroon Kama, whose land is in the valley to the north. He made us rob you, Mighty One, and he made me follow you. If we disobey, he swears he'll give us to the monster."

"What 'monster'? All the monsters were driven out of our land by Kuhn Pane, long ago."

The woman shook her head.

"Come, then," Pimchan said. "We're going to that hut you've been watching."

The woman scrambled before her, clearly terrified even after Pimchan sheathed her swords. All the way across the meadow, she cringed as if expecting a kick and twice she whined, "Will you protect me from the monster, Sun of Splendor?"

Inside the hut, Tyana and Pimchan's Female waited on either side of the door, each holding a teakwood club, in case Pimchan needed backup. The captive, utterly cowed, gave them no excuse to use their weapons.

"That's her!" Pimchan's Female said, and raised her club.

"Ah-ah!" Tyana blocked the blow. "Wait for the Warrior's orders."

"Tie her up," Pimchan said. "She hurt my Male by accident, and he's safe and well. I'm going back, now, to make sure he stays that way. My Female, I leave you in charge of her."

And if she thought a Warrior was frightening, or a monster, Pimchan reflected, as she headed back to her enclave at a kilometer-eating lope, wait until she spent some time as the prisoner of a twelve-year-old girl with a grudge.

ೞಀಽಀ

Pimchan crouched in the brush on the far side of the path that circled her wall. She watched as a man wearing scruffy red-brown trousers and tunic passed, then waited until he passed again. She wasn't surprised to find such lackadaisical security: Aroon Kama was obviously running this operation on the cheap, keeping as much of his payment as possible for his own use.

The third time the man came around, she confronted him, both swords drawn.

"Not a move. Not a sound," she said.

His face turned a sickly gray-yellow and his eyes darted back and forth like minnows in a koi pond.

"The woman is safe and out of the way. Wouldn't you like to be safe, too?"

The man nodded.

"Answer, then: How many inside?"

"My master and the monster and your Male, and I let in a vagabond—a flute player—and then I was sent out on patrol."

The "vagabond" would be the All-Father, in one of his go-among-the-people disguises. But "the monster"?

"What sort of monster?"

The man nodded, quivering. "It gives the master gold and tells him what to do. The master isn't afraid of it, but it told me it would eat me if I failed . . . ." His trembling grew more violent, then his eyes rolled up in his head and, with a sigh, he collapsed in a faint.

Pimchan sheathed her swords, dragged him into the bushes and bound and gagged him with sections of his own sash.

A monster? Intuition tripped a series of switches in Pimchan's mind, and she rose and ran, vaulting the wall and landing soundlessly in the garden. Swords again drawn, she eased up to the house door, listened intently, and slipped past the painted bamboo screen inside the doorway. She heard voices coming from her arena, and one of them belonged to the All-Father.

"I fail to see how The Blessed Land would benefit," he said querulously.

She slid closer to the rosewood screen in the arena doorway and peered through the filigree. The All-Father knelt in the center of the arena, as she had seen him in her mind the night before, but dressed in shabby clothes and with a long flute tucked into the sash at his waist. Before him was a tea table and on it was a piece of paper—paper of a snowy whiteness covered in even lines of black symbols. Aroon Kama knelt beside him, holding an inkpot and a quill pen. Her Male was bound, his hands high above his head, to the empty rack that usually held the swords now in her hands. Seated on her meditation altar, legs stretched in front of him and crossed at the black-booted ankles, was "the monster".

His skin was pink-tinged brown; his eyes were as green as a spring frog and his hair was the color of a fresh egg yolk. His nose was long and pointed, like a beak, and one of his teeth flashed gold. No wonder he had terrorized the servants, who would never have seen or heard of such a creature. Pimchan, the All-Father, and the no-doubt well-traveled Aroon Kama recognized him as a Fahr-ang—a foreign Barbarian from across the Endless Sea (apparently not endless, after all).

When the Fahr-ang spoke, he spoke clearly, but with the words of a child. He had been expertly taught and had learned

The Beautiful Language well, and was intelligent enough not to over-reach his abilities.

"I have told you. Twice. The Blessed Land needs to grow up and work with the rest of the world. You and your old nobles hold it back. Some of your young nobles are tired of the past. They are right. Sign this and make your young nobles glad. You will see it's best. Trade is good. We have bright goods to sell you. You have some things we might want to buy."

"There are Fahr-ang in and out of my court daily," the All-Father said. "I've heard many presentations of trade agreements. My advisors and I consider all of them. We will draft a comprehensive policy on this subject soon."

The Fahr-ang shook his head.

"Those ones from other lands lie to you. They want to rob you. Only my land can be trusted. That's why I had to see you like this, where they can't tell you lies. Sign."

Aroon Kama thrust the inkpot closer. "Do as he says, Blessed One."

The All-Father reached for the quill, then drew back his hand and tapped the paper. Ignoring Aroon Kama, he spoke to the Fahr-ang:

"This is written in your language. I can read it, but not well. There are some things I don't understand. I need—"

"Sign!" The Fahr-ang pushed himself to his feet as he shouted. He loomed over the All-Father, who quailed back toward Aroon Kama. "Sign!"

The All-Father flinched, knocking the inkpot up and splashing the liquid into Aroon Kama's face.

Pimchan kicked aside the screen and erupted into the room.

The Fahr-ang drew an object Pimchan knew to be a firearm—a "gun"—and pointed it at her. Something exploded in it, and she dropped her left-hand sword and reeled back, struck by an invisible blow. He threw the spent firearm aside and drew another, striding to the All-Father's side. Kicking Aroon Kama out of his way, he held the gun to the All-Father's head.

"Oh!" said the All-Father, eyes wide with surprise. "If you shoot me, who will sign your paper? Pimchan, who will sign their paper?" He picked up the quill from the table, where Aroon Kama had dropped it. "Pimchan, I have no ink."

What was wrong with the man? He wasn't old enough to wander in his mind. Had they knocked him on the head? Had terror chased away his sense?

"You fool!" Aroon Kama shouted, wiping sand and ink out of his eyes. "Warriors are sworn to let the All-Father die, rather than give in to Fahr-angs or other bandits. Here's what will stop her." He wrenched a spear from its place on the wall and drove it with all his weight into Pimchan's Male. The child didn't even have time to cry out, but sagged against his bonds, the spear piercing the red rune just below his breastbone.

Aroon Kama laughed, his ink-smeared face a purple mask as Pimchan turned blankly to the All-Father.

The Fahr-ang, his attention on Pimchan, failed to see the All-Father's hand move, failed to see the quill become a small knife. The All-Father somersaulted over the tea table, using his momentum to drive the knife into the Fahr-ang's forearm. The gun discharged into the air.

The Fahr-ang drew his sword and backed to one of Pimchan's many weapons racks and pulled down a small red shield worked with silver runes of defense. He couldn't have chosen better.

The All-Father ripped the flute from his waistband, put it into Pimchan's empty hand, and stepped aside.

Aroon Kama gasped, "No . . . ," and was quiet.

The All-Father's placid voice said, "Proceed, Warrior."

Pimchan became a blue-steel whirlwind. She could feel the runes carved into the All-Father's flute, carefully rubbed full of ink from the soot of holy candles. Time after time, the flute blocked the other's assaults, and even struck him once on the tip of his over-reaching nose.

The "monster" fought well, but his pale blade was no match for the blue steel forged in The Blessed Land, which cut through the Fahr-ang sword like fire through straw. Only the shield he had taken from the wall saved him, and gave him the chance to unrack one of Pimchan's swords and meet her with an equal weapon.

He was good, he was disciplined, he was strong, and he was fighting for his life. But Pimchan was a Warrior, so enraged that only the self-command learned in battle meditation kept her from losing control. He tired before she did. She saw his death reflected in his eyes, and his death was herself.

Two blows, and he sprawled face down on the sand, his blood mingling with the ink to make a richer purple.

Pimchan dropped her sword and the All-Father's flute and turned, barehanded, to the man who had put a spear into the body of a child she had sworn to protect.

He lay, eyes wide, mouth gaping, in a heap near the wall. The All-Father was lowering Pimchan's Male to the floor, having cut his bonds.

"What happened to Aroon Kama?" Pimchan asked.

"Hmmm? Who? —Oh, he killed himself. Strangled himself with his own braids. Or took poison. Something or other. Are you all right?"

Pimchan inspected herself. Cuts on her hands and face, chest deeply bruised where the lead ball of the Fahr-ang's gun had hit her steel-reinforced armor with the steelcloth beneath, weary and sick at soul, but all in one piece. Alive.

"Even with half a heart," the All-Father said, "you fight like an angel."

"You know I don't have half a heart."

"Go fetch the other half. Go."

Pimchan kow-towed, retrieved her swords and left.

Aroon Kama's male servant was right where she'd hidden him. She freed his feet but kept his hands tied and his mouth muffled. She wanted no trouble from him and she wanted no talk. There were three dead bodies in her arena, and the fact that two of them were Aroon Kama and his monster instead of the All-Father and herself only lightened that burden but didn't eliminate it. The third body was still that of her Male, the beating of his heart silenced by steel.

At the stone hut, all she said was, "The men who ordered these two to take my Male are dead."

"The monster is dead?" cried Aroon Kama's Female. "You killed it?"

"Go away," Pimchan said. "Both of you. Down this side of the mountain and through that valley. If I see you again within three days' walk of here, I'll kill you, and honor be damned."

"Names—our names!" said the woman.

"You don't want any names I would give you. Name yourselves after the first creatures you see when you leave here. But don't leave until we've gone. I don't want to see you walk away alive."

She left the hut and took a deep breath, calming her spirit as best she could.

When Tyana and Pimchan's Female joined the Warrior, the girl said, "I hope the first things they see are a spider and a toad."

Tyana shook her head at the girl, and then followed the silent Pimchan through the afternoon light back to the enclave.

The "vagabond" had set the screen back in the doorway of the arena and draped it with a woven cloth to hide what lay inside. Pimchan's Male lay on the floor of the common room, washed and shirtless. A pot of unguent and a roll of linen were arranged beside him. The shaft and part of the head of the spear protruded from his thin chest, too small to engulf so large a weapon.

Tyana cried out, but Pimchan's Female walked calmly to him, knelt by his side and took his hand.

"I thought you should do the honors," said the All-Father.

Pimchan grasped the spear and, gritting her teeth, tugged it out cleanly and cast it through the doorway into the garden beyond. From now on, it would be a beanpole and never again a Warrior's valued ally.

"Tend his wound," she said. "Bind it tightly, before his heart goes back to work." She stepped away and Tyana knelt by his other side, packing the gash with unguent and folding some of the linen into a pad.

"Help me lift him up," she ordered Pimchan's Female, "and we'll use the other strips to tie this on."

Pimchan waited until the color came back into her Male's flesh, then followed the All-Father out into the Chaos garden. They sat in the soft shadows of the gazebo until Pimchan had recovered her serenity.

The All-Father, as was proper, spoke first.

"I'm not a fool."

"Of course not, All-Father. Anyone might have a councilor who betrayed him."

"Any fool might. I would not have a councilor who was not above betrayal." He sniffed in disdain. "Some of the Fahrangs think I'm a fool. The man you killed was one of the worst. The rest will reconsider their opinions, now."

"All-Father. . . ."

"Yes, my Warrior?"

" . . . Did you arrange this yourself?"

"A dear, straightforward gentleman like me?"

"Who else knew about the heartsafe charm?"

"How unfortunate for Aroon Kama that he judges others by himself. He assumed that two heartsafe charms meant you had divided your heart in two to protect yourself. It never occurred to him that you hid the children's hearts in your own bosom to keep the children safe."

"My Male. . . ." Pimchan bit back the words of chastisement that would have dishonored her.

The All-Father spoke them himself: "I miscalculated. The Fahr-angs think the heartsafe charm is superstitious nonsense. That yellow-hair only intended to use your belief in it to force you to do what he wanted. He wouldn't have tried to disturb your spirit by frightening the child, and he wouldn't have thought he could harm you by killing the boy. Aroon Kama was a danger I failed to foresee." He inclined his body a noticeable degree—an unheard-of abasement, and one neither of them would ever mention to anyone.

The clop and rattle of oxcarts stopped outside the compound. An official fist thumped at the screen, making the bells fixed to it jump and jingle.

"Ah," said the All-Father. "My conveyance back to the capital, I think. We'll drop off your unwanted visitors somewhere along the way. Let my bodyguards in, my Warrior."

"Of course, All-Father." Pimchan kow-towed but rose with an impudent smile. "A poor weak noble dare not go anywhere without them these days."

THE FAIREST OF THEM ALL

by Melissa Mead

Marion used to reject stories submitted to *Marion Zimmer Bradley's FANTASY Magazine* for being "re-written fairy tales." Personally, I like taking a fairy tale and playing with it. I'm not the only one; Mercedes Lackey has written several novels that used a fairy tale as a jumping-off point—in fact, she has two series that do this: the *Elemental Mages* series and the *Godmother* series. One can, however, have too much of a good thing. The first version of this story was twice as long and had every fairy tale reference possible. I sent it back for a rewrite, and this is the result.

Melissa Mead published her first short story at The First Line in 1999. That got her hooked on writing, but it wasn't until she attended her first convention (Albacon 2002) and joined the Carpe Libris writing group that things really took off. Her first novel, *Between Worlds,* is available as an e-book from Double Dragon Publishing. To find the book, links to more stories, and updates on what Melissa and the other writers of Carpe Libris are up to, go to http://carpelibris.wordpress.com/melissa-mead.

"Snow White?" That was just an alias. Good queens don't name their daughters for "skin white as snow, lips red as blood, and hair black as ebony wood." My mother didn't, anyhow. Everyone called her Constance the Fair. I try to be fair, too.

She died trying to negotiate with a sheep-stealing dragon. She'd heard the villagers' story (which would've ended, in their version, with the dragon's severed head adorning the village hall) and felt the dragon should have its say. Unfortunately, the Dragon words for "emissary" and "hors d'oeuvre" are identical.

I missed her terribly. Father did too, but he claimed Mother'd gotten killed because she insisted on dealing with the dragon herself.

"Talking to monsters. In my day we whacked their heads off. My sainted mother, Lady Aletheia . . . she never tried talking to dragons! Proper lady, she was. Embroidered, dressed well . . . none of this "justice and diplomacy" nonsense. My poor Constance. Crisped by a dragon. Such a lovely woman, too."

He gave me a regretful look. I wished I wasn't wearing my oldest dress, pitted with holes from experimenting with my Little Enchantress alchemy set.

"You need proper feminine role models, child."

"What about Jayel, Abby, Irene, Tracy, Christina, Jackie . . . " I reeled off the names of the maidservants.

"A gentlewoman, child! Someone refined. With that certain Jeanie Sayquoy."

"*Je ne sais quoi*," I corrected, unheard.

⚜

L ady Sable arrived within a month. I'd barely changed my muddy clothes before Father summoned me to meet her. He wore a disturbing expression—equal parts awe, glee, confusion and terror. The newcomer ran to me and caught my chin in her hand.

"Such perfect bone structure!" she gasped. "Those cheekbones, that glorious black hair, that snow-white complexion . . . which face powder do you use, child?"

She turned my face back and forth, scrutinizing me from under eyelids painted like storm clouds. I felt like a bug pinned inside a collector's box.

"None, Ma'am," I said when she released my bruised chin.

"What?" Her eyes narrowed. Her scarlet mouth thinned. That carefully-painted face looked about to crack.

"Lady Sable, this is my daughter . . ." Father began.

"It's natural? No powder, no rouge?"

"Bethanie takes after her mother," said my father. "Quite the fair young lady."

Lady Sable glared at me. "Indeed."

ಞ⊂ଽୡ⊃ಐ

Lady Sable's squadron of servants included a dancing-master, a lady's maid, Cherie, and teachers in elocution and deportment. To my horror, I learned that these last were for my benefit.

"Your education's been lopsided," my father said. "Sable will set you right. Quite the beauty, Sable. Knows all that feminine fol-de-rol. Answer to a prayer." The besotted look faded for a moment. "Not that she's Constance. But as Constance herself used to say, 'For the greater good,' hey?"

The besotted look returned. Lady Sable's army descended with tapes and shears, and strapped me into a whalebone restraint called a "fashionable corset." They wrapped me in gilded crimson velvet, and braided my hair into a Medusa's tangle. Then Sable painted me with white lead and crushed beetles. My cheeks swelled. My eyes watered. I scrubbed the stuff off while Lady Sable cackled.

"It really is natural. Pray it lasts, young lady. Once age sinks its claws into you you'll be a mummified crone, with no way to lessen the blow."

"Lady Sable," I wheezed.

"You look like you've been stung by a wasp . . ."

"Lady Sable . . ."

"Like someone's blacked your eyes . . ."

"Lady Sable, I can't breathe!" I staggered against the cosmetics box, spattering everyone with eyeliner and clots of rouge. Powder billowed in choking clouds. The hairdresser cut the corset strings just before I blacked out. Lady Sable threw a tirade and banished me to my room until after the wedding. Looking back, I wonder if she arranged the whole fiasco so I couldn't disrupt the ceremony.

She dragged me out to show off her favorite wedding present—a full-length mirror, the frame beautifully carved with leaves and vines. While Sable preened before it, I examined the back.

"It's by the WNDFTFT!" I exclaimed.

"The what?" said Queen Sable.

"The Homunculi Brothers. WNDFTFT stands for "We're Not Dwarves, for the Fortieth Time!" I explained. "People call them the Eight Dwarves. They make the best enchanted products."

"My mirror's enchanted? Make it work!"

She shook the mirror. I flipped the switch on the back.

A starburst of light radiated from the glass. I blinked away the pink afterimage, and a worried spectral face peered from the frame.

"Too melodramatic? Sorry, I'll tone it down. Ahem. I am Fred, the Servant in the Mirror, bound in this vitreous state to serve the owner of this mirror . . . "

"Fred?" I said. "Just Fred?"

"Just Fred, fair maiden."

"I'm your owner, slave!" Queen Sable interrupted. "Address me as Your Majesty."

The spirit's face fell. "Well, technically you own the mirror, not me."

"I also own a large, heavy scepter."

The glass was sweating now. "Yes, Ma'am. Your Majesty. Um, I'm required to state that the owner of this mirror shall agree to hold the crafters blameless in the event of malfunction, breakage . . ."

"Enough! What are you enchanted to do?"

"Er, talk," said the mirror-spirit. Sable frowned.

"That is, I can praise Your Majesty's charms in fulsome and extravagant terms . . ."

She leaned forward. "Go on."

I left poor Fred stammering odes to Sable's every feature from earlobes to toenails. I wanted to find my father. No one had seen him since the ceremony.

He was in bed, feverish. I ran back to the hall. Poor Fred looked relieved to be interrupted. Queen Sable, furious, banished me from the hall. I set to work with my alchemy set.

I developed a floor wax, six varieties of hot sauce, and a lotion that de-warted toads, but no fever cures. Father got steadily worse. Lady Sable discovered my experiments, and confiscated the set.

ଔଓଃ୪ଠ

After Father died, Queen Sable kept me running after ingredients for new beauty potions. When I objected, she threatened me with a loaded blush-brush. Fortunately, she never noticed my substitutions: well water for dragon tears, or crushed eggshells for powdered unicorn horn.

I was pondering a plausible substitute for fairy gold when Fred hailed me from his mirror.

"Fred? You look glassy-eyed."

"I'm inside a mirror! I always look glassy eyed!" he shouted. "Sorry . . . Princess, I tried to object, but the sadist has a glass-cutter—"

"Object to what?"

The tapping of Queen Sable's six-inch stilettos echoed through the marble hallways. "Find the Speaking Oak," Fred whispered.

Lady Sable spotted me and beamed. "Ah, there you are! I've splendid news. I've discovered the Elixir of Youth! It just needs the heart's blood of a fair maiden."

I started to protest that I wouldn't murder some poor girl just so she could make wrinkle cream. When she summoned our Master Huntsman, I realized she meant me.

Wulfgar had faced charging boars, but he would've preferred rabid wolverines to Queen Sable. If he'd had a tail, it would've been tucked between his legs.

"Remove her heart, Huntsman," said Queen Sable. "But not over the carpet! Outside."

"Woooods . . ." Fred moaned. "Harness the power of the Woooods!"

With no idea what Fred was doing, I played along. "Not the Enchanted Forest!"

Queen Sable's face lit up. "Perfect! That infuses the elixir with Arcane Mystical Forces. Wonderful exfoliant. Do it there."

Poor Wolfie looked nauseated. I acted like he was forcing me out the door. Once we'd crossed the bridge, he cried, "I won't kill you, Princess! Even if that witch has me tortured. Which she'd enjoy."

I could've hugged him. "Trick her. I do it all the time. Just point me toward the Speaking Oak, please."

Wolfie obliged, looking savagely gleeful about hunting something edible instead. I ran the other way.

The Speaking Oak dominated its clearing. When I approached, the limbs waved as though storm-tossed. Verdant eyes opened below the crown. A mouthlike crack split the bark.

"Yoohoo, boys!" the tree bellowed. "Company!"

Wizened faces peered from behind trunks. I'd never seen anyone like those people—stick-thin, their skin patterned like wood grain. The tallest was barely my height, yet they weren't children. They glanced toward the tree, green eyes wide.

"Don't be bashful! She's that nice princess Fred talks about. Come say hello."

"You know Fred?" Compared to talking trees and silent tree-men, the disembodied mirror-spirit seemed comfortingly familiar.

"Honey, they MADE Fred!" the Speaking Oak boomed. "I'm Donna. These are my boys: Orrery, Astrolabe, Ratchet, Kerf, Mortise, Bevel, and Chris. The best crafters in the Enchanted Forest."

"Chris?"

The smallest crafter blushed, looking polished.

Recognition dawned. "You're the WNDFTFT! Aren't there eight of you?"

Mortise looked at his feet. "Tenon said he wanted to put down roots. So he did. Deep ones. We can't dig him up."

My head spun. "Donna? The Homunculi Brothers are your children?"

Donna nodded her crown. "The Forest respects them, because they never cut living wood. You'll be safe with them."

The little men led me deeper into the woods. No one spoke but Chris, who talked enough for all seven.

"You're the meat people's princess? Shouldn't you be Queen? You know we're not dwarves, right? Dwarves are meat people. We're not. Why does the Queen want you chopped down? Because Fred says you're pretty? Fred says you know Alchemy. Do you know LaVerre's Transformation? I think . . ."

"Chris, stuff a knot in it," said Orrery, and the smallest Crafter fell silent.

ଔଔଡ଼ଫ଼ୡ

We reached a clearing. Orrery stumped over to a nearby thicket to argue with a sapling.

"Tenon says she's to stay in the workshop," he reported. "And Fred's so upset he's about to crack."

"Fred? Fred's in the castle!" I said.

"I thought you knew alchemy!" Chris chided. "Fred's a mirror-spirit, not a mirror. C'mon." He wrapped twiggy fingers around my hand and pulled me through the thicket into an open space. Towering trees formed a living fence around us, branches twining overhead. The dirt floor had been planed smooth. I turned in slow circles, awed. The place melded an alchemist's laboratory, woodworker's shop, forge, and greenhouse. The forge had its own stone-shielded corner. Workbenches lined one wall. Plants sprouted from tabletops. Flasks and beakers dangled from branches growing through walls. A spring bubbled through a hole in the floor, and streamed out between the tree trunks. There was only one true door in the workshop, flanked by pines.

"Flesh people aren't supposed to see this," said Chris. "But Tenon says you'll need a roof and a fire, and the forge is the only fire we allow near the living trees. You won't tell, will you, Princess?"

"Of course not."

"Tenon, we've got a crisis here!" shouted a familiar voice from behind the door.

"Fred!"

Chris nodded. On the other side of the door was a gatehouse, lit with alchemical lamps that switched on and off like Fred's mirror.

"Tenon?" said Fred's voice from behind a curtain on the opposite wall.

"Don't crack yourself. We're here," said Chris.

The curtain hid a mirror, plainer than Sable's, with Fred's anxious face peering from it. If color could've rushed back to his face when he saw me, it would've. I'd considered him a sort of two-dimensional court jester. He wasn't joking now.

"Princess! Thank goodness. Wolfie brought back this dripping . . . anyway, you're alive!"

"Did Queen Paintbox really eat something's heart?" said Chris, with nauseated glee.

"Yes, you twisted little rootstock. Raw. She couldn't bully anyone into cooking it."

"Ewww!"

"Enough of that," said Orrery from behind us. "Fred, what's up?"

"Everyone's mourning the princess. Sable's bought a black mink cloak for the occasion, and created a new Blush Tax to pay for it." Fred flickered nervously. "And Wolfie wants out. I don't blame him. Anyway, he wants you to perform LaVerre's Transformation on him."

Orrery frowned. "I'll consider it."

"I think we should Transform YOU, Fred!" Chris piped up.

"Chris," said the mirror-spirit, "Shut up. Go find the nice lady some food. Like fruit and nuts. No dirt. And something soft to sleep on."

"Flesh people are so delicate!" Chris scampered off, shedding leaves.

"It's so good to see you, Princess!" Fred was beaming, but I was too bewildered to be polite.

"Start explaining or I'll soap you."

"Er, yes. I suppose I should introduce myself properly: Alfred Glass, Homunculi Brothers Prints and Images Division, mirror-spirit, and W+DFTFP agent. At your service, Princess."

"WNDFTFT agent?"

He smiled and spelled it out properly. "Wild and Domestic Faerie-Tale Forest Protectors," he explained. "Although the mixed-up version's wonderful for our cover."

"Cover? You're a spy?"

He shook his head. "A counselor to the Royal Family. I was with your lady mother when she faced the dragon. Reflected in her shield. But the smoke dulled the polish . . . there was nothing to hold. I failed her. I'm sorry, Princess."

I swallowed. "Why serve Sable, then?"

He winced. "I watch Sable. We need eyes in the castle, and I can go places Wolfie can't. A mirror, a basin of water, polished silver—all windows, to me."

"Peeping Tom."

"Princess! I swear by my silver backing, I'm a gentleman. And mirrors don't lie."

I believed him. I realized that he could've been spying for Queen Sable, but I doubted it. Sable was too unpredictable to win the loyalty of someone she could shatter in a fit of temper.

"Anyway, what's this LaVerre's Transformation that Wolfie wants? Why does Chris think you should do it too?"

He grimaced. "A shapechanging spell. Excruciatingly painful, but effective. Wolfie wants the Brothers to change him into a real wolf, so Sable can't find him."

"Why does Chris want you to transform?"

"The little troublemaker thinks it would be funny to turn me into a human man," said Fred shortly. "Never mind that it would hurt worse than cracking one of my mirrors would. Ah— the Royal Face-Powder Keg is calling me to tell her she's the "fairest of all" again. Fortunately, since 'fair' can mean 'light-complexioned' and she's wearing inch-thick white talc, I'm safe. Pardon me . . ."

He vanished. I grew accustomed to that, living in the gatehouse.

The brothers were uncomfortable having me around until I started helping with experiments. Fred's latest news gave me an incentive to learn: Sable, with the help of my old alchemy kit, was fast becoming a competent alchemisorceress.

So was I. Turning lead into gold was easy (and purified the local drinking water). Wolfie's Transformation was hard both to assist with and to watch. By the end the poor wolf was panting and exhausted, hoarse from howling. I could see why Fred didn't want to put himself through such an ordeal.

Within a year I was "Snow White," a full-fledged sorceress and W+DFTFP agent. The kingdom was in chaos. Queen Sable passed sumptuary laws banning cosmetics for commoners. Her Vanity Police flogged anyone wearing so much as lipstick.

"We have to distract Sable." I told the W+DFTFP. We'd all crowded into the gatehouse for Fred's latest report. "Get her attention off the people long enough for them to rebel."

"And onto what?" said Ratchet.

I grinned. "Snow White."

"No!" Fred vanished, but I was a certified Alchemisorceress now. I knew how his mirrors worked. I flicked the switch on and off, turning the lights on and off with it, until he returned.

"Stop! You're making me dizzy."

"Will you help?"

"No."

"You owe it to the kingdom."

"No."

"You owe it to my mother."

He looked like I'd threatened him with a sledgehammer. "Not fair!"

"What do you want Fred to do?" Chris piped up.

"I want him to help me make the Queen so jealous of 'Snow White' that she'll forget everything else," I said, still staring down Fred. "All he has to do, the next time Queen Sable comes to him for reassurance, is to say that Snow White's the fairest woman in the kingdom, not her."

"So why won't he? 'Snow White's' just a made-up name. Or does that mean that Fred would have to lie? Cause he can't."

"Because Sable will look for her, you knothead!" For an image, Fred looked quite solidly stubborn. "Snow White's a fiction, but Bethanie isn't!"

"Fine," I said. "I'll distract her myself. In person."

"NO! I'll do it. But promise me that you won't leave the workshop alone. Please."

I sighed. "Fair enough."

ଔ⃝ଓ

Fred did his work well. Soon Queen Sable was spending days at her mirror, skeletal and hollow-eyed from forgetting to eat and sleep.

"You're a genius, Princess," said Orrery. "Half the Queen's Guard's quit because she forgets to pay them. She doesn't ride around the kingdom scrubbing pretty girls' faces with cold cream any more. Snow White's becoming a legend."

"Snow White's becoming an obsession," said Fred. He didn't sleep, but he was developing a nervous flicker in his reflection. "Sable knows, Princess! She talks to her reflection. She knows you're alive. It's driving her mad that she doesn't know where or how."

I'd never seen Fred so terrified. "It's not like she knows where I am," I pointed out.

"You don't understand!" Fred wailed. "I can't lie! If she asks me how to find you, straight out with no room for misinterpretation, I'll have to tell her. I've told her where to find the Fairest of Awls, the Forest of Owls, and the Failed List of Ales. Soon she'll realize that I can't be hard of hearing, because I don't have ears!"

The little room was suddenly full of the sound of eight mortals not breathing.

"She'll remember eventually," said Orrery.

"She'll realize that Fred's been toying with her," said Astrolabe.

"She'll be furious," said Ratchet.

"She'll probably break Fred's mirror," said Kerf.

"Which would be excruciating for him," said Mortise.

"And then she'll come here," said Bevel.

"I don't want her to come here!" Chris wailed. "I don't want her to break Fred. Stop her, Princess!"

"She'll do worse than break Fred," said Tenon from the doorway, his voice like wind in branches. "She'll chop down Mother and burn the Forest. The W+DFTFP will have nothing left to protect."

"If she'll find me eventually, let's make it on our terms," I said. "Fred, tell the Queen that she'll find Snow White at the Speaking Oak."

"And what will she find?" said Fred, immediately suspicious.

"Me. With Donna. Nothing short of an axe can break Donna's grip."

Fred objected, but the Brothers were confident that Donna could easily overpower the Queen. After all, she was solid oak.

Sable showed up with an axe. Fortunately, Donna's a quick thinker. Acorns rained down. Queen Sable screamed. The barrage of falling acorns and a few unladylike kicks from me forced her to retreat, stumbling over nuts.

"You look beautiful, Princess!" said Chris when I went to conjure up some ice.

"I do?"

"Yeah! You've got all these pretty knots and burls on your head. And you're turning more colors than Autumn."

I gave him a pained smile and went to talk to Fred. Well, first to get yelled at by Fred for endangering myself. Eventually he agreed that since the queen knew roughly where I was, we had to try again.

"A Reflective Reversal!" Fred said. "I'll goad her into trying an enchantment on you, but reverse it with my mirror. The boys will be in the workshop if anything goes wrong."

Chris peeked in from the workshop. "Let's make 'Crabby's Deadly Apples!' They put flesh people asleep until they die or a prince kisses 'em, and they smell like cinnamon."

"Chris, you're one warped little man. Go back to work," said Fred.

"A sleep spell's not a bad idea, though. Sandalwood Slumber would make her drowsy and suggestible."

"Plus it sounds like an eyeshadow. Brilliant." Fred grinned. "Want to watch?"

"How?"

"Second switch on the back up, others down. Sable won't see or hear you. Go ahead."

It was unnerving to have Queen Sable staring at me, through Fred, close enough to see every crack in her pancake makeup. I had to remind myself that she couldn't see me.

"Mirror, mirror, on the wall, who's the fairest of them all?" she demanded.

"Lousy poet, isn't she?" I muttered.

"Ready for worse?" Fred whispered back.

"Stop mumbling, Mirror!" Queen Sable shouted. "Answer me!"

"My humblest apologies, your Majesty. Um . . . My Queen/I'm sworn to tell the truth/It cannot be ignored, thus/Upon my oath, I have to say/'Snow White' is drop-dead gorgeous!"

I giggled. Then I remembered that Fred couldn't lie, and blushed.

Queen Sable hefted a heavy jewelry box.

"Seven years bad luck!" Fred shouted. "Your Majesty, if I might suggest something less drastic . . ."

With admirable calm, Fred mollified her and talked her through creating a sandalwood comb that would induce sleep upon contact with the wearer's head. Then, looking innocent, he proposed a costume that would make Queen Sable look as gnarled, ugly, and ancient as possible. "What better way to ensure that 'Snow White' won't recognize you, O Queen?"

Fred couldn't lie, but he could act.

ଔଔଔ

Queen Sable arrived at the gatehouse looking crone-like and disgruntled. I welcomed her with the enthusiasm of someone desperate for company, and offered her tea. She refused, although she eyed the teapot with the look of someone parched from a long and thirsty hike through the Enchanted Forest. I admired the comb, holding it up as though to study it better. Really, I wanted it in Fred's line of sight. I slid it into my hair— and heard a click and Fred's anguished cry as the lights went out.

I came partially awake in cinnamon-scented darkness.

"Smells like pie," I mumbled.

"Apple pie, princess," said a voice I really should've recognized. "The best you'll ever taste. Take a bite."

I did. Crabby's Deadly Apples really do taste like apple pie.

ଔଔଔ

The next thing I knew, something was pressing on my lips. I slapped whatever-it-was.

"Ow! I think it worked," said a familiar voice. "Princess? Wake up, please. Mind the broken glass."

I opened my eyes and sat up. That seemed to please the young man beside me. He was remarkably pale, except for my handprint on his cheek. His white-blond hair looked like he'd survived a hurricane, but he radiated joy.

"Pardon me, Princess, but there's only one cure for Crabby's Deadly Apples. I was prepared for the comb, but not those."

"Fred? But you're not a prince."

"Prints and Images Division," he reminded me. "I was an image. Now . . ." He shrugged.

"But . . ." I took in the shattered glass, the empty mirror-frame on the wall, him. "LaVerre's Transformation?"

He nodded. "You can't kiss if you don't have a mouth."

"And boy does he!" put in Chris, sticking his head through the door. "Screaming, swearing . . ."

"Chris," Fred and I chorused, "Shut up."

"Aw." He closed the door again.

"Sable?" I asked Fred.

"You were right. Once you were unconscious, she drank the tea. She's out cold."

"We tied her up really good!" said Chris, popping in again. "Come see!"

The Brothers had bound Sable in roots and were watching, rapt, as squirrels made a nest in her hair.

Chris twisted his twiggy fingers together. "Let's put red-hot iron shoes on her feet and make her dance until she falls down dead!"

Everyone stared at him. "No!"

"Stuff her in a spiked barrel and roll it downhill?"

"No! Honestly, Chris! Where do you get these ideas?"

He shrugged. "Fairy tales."

"She does deserve a harsh punishment, though," said Fred. "I know just the thing."

ଔଔଔ

You guessed right. LaVerre's Transformation, reversed. Sometimes the people who suffered the most under Queen Sable beg us to let them break one of her mirrors. We just point out that they'd get seven years of bad luck. Which just wouldn't be fair.

DEERMOUSE

by *K.D. Wentworth*

She knew that the guide job was risky when she took it, but Spark didn't expect it to lead her into the one place she was forbidden to return. Even less did she expect to get herself or her charge out alive. What you expect, however, may be very different from what you get.

K.D. Wentworth has sold more than seventy pieces of short fiction to such markets as *F&SF*, *Hitchcock's*, *Realms of Fantasy*, *Weird Tales*, and *Marion Zimmer Bradley's FANTASY Magazine*. She has been a three-time Nebula Finalist for Short Fiction. Currently, she has seven novels in print, the most recent being *The Course Of Empire*, written with Eric Flint and published by Baen. She lives in Tulsa with her husband and a combined total of one hundred sixty pounds of dog (Akita + Siberian Husky) and is working on several new novels with Flint. Her website is www.kdwentworth.com.

Spark sat on her heels beside the steaming mudpots, steadying herself with her scabbard, and wrinkled her nose at the fierce stench. Though the day had been cool up until now with early spring, the thick mud was on the boil, a sure sign that what lived in the valley ahead was paying attention. Her wealthy client had engaged her services as a guide only because no one else would venture this close, with very good reason.

The massive bubbles pop-popped, whispering to her in hot wet voices that she took great care not to heed lest they ensnare her thoughts. The Tamraire who inhabited these parts understood the wild presence down there, though outsiders, to their peril, did not. For a heartbeat, she flashed back to that long-ago day when she'd first blundered into the valley herself and how Jorn had found her drowning in the black waters of a swamp, trapped in writhing tree roots and down to her last gasp of air.

"This means what's up ahead is listening," she said over her shoulder to Franz-Wallace Garth, Fifth in his line of that noted name. "It's as I told you—we must go around, work our way through the foothills."

"Don't be a superstitious oaf," her client said, wiping his face with a red silk scarf. He dismounted to peer over her shoulder. "I have to reach my uncle's holdings in three days. The Duke is investing me as a member of his court." Garth had gleaming black hair drawn tight into a fashionable club and a heavy brow that made him look far more formidable than he actually was. She supposed he was a good enough fellow, well suited for the indoors sort of life he was meant to lead, but certainly not for the wider wild world.

"These things never boil without *something* paying them mindful attention," Spark said, straightening. Her gray mare snorted uneasily, shuffling her hooves. Small and shaggy, the beast had come of the wild herds that ran these parts and most likely had a notion what that smell signified. "They're a warning, to them as has half a brain."

He edged around her, him in his fine black riding boots, to peer down at the roiling mudpots. His brown eyes widened. He swayed and would have fallen into the pit if she hadn't snatched him back by his belt. "Don't listen, you idiot!"

He sat down hard on the verge and then stared up at her, breathing shallowly. "Goblets of—diamond," he said dazedly. "Just ahead. Alabaster combs, opal—"

Heart racing, she slapped him. "I told you—don't listen!"

His head rocked back, then sagged forward. He rubbed his jaw. "You struck me!"

"And I'll do it again," she said evenly, "if you don't heed what I say." She jerked her chin back toward the stinking mudpots. "The land is alive in these parts. That's why we can't barge straight through. It schemes and plans, and I can promise you that what's down there wants your liver. You want to give it over without a fight?"

He shuddered. "No, of course not."

"Then don't listen to those things," she said. "They'll burn the thoughts right out of your head, suck up your will, and leave you hollow. In the end, you'll go to your death laughing."

His eyes narrowed, and she knew what he saw: an unmarried, sun-hardened woman clad in worn buckskin, with no connections, carrying at least fifteen more years than he had achieved, and who owned little more than a sturdy horse and a sword. In his father's massive house, she would not have been considered fit to scrub the flagstones.

But she had been bonded, once, to one of the Tamraire who lived down there, beautiful, leggy Jorn with her cornsilk hair and gray eyes. Though the Tamraire had cast Spark out after Jorn's death, she knew the valley's tricks all too well, and these mudpots were only the least of them. *Something* sinister lived down there. For Jorn's sake, she had dwelled in its shadow for almost twelve years, but in all that time she'd never slept easy as it whispered and gibbered in her dreams.

"Mount up," she said, then swung back into her worn saddle. It creaked under her weight.

Scowling, he did likewise.

ଔଔଛଉ୬

They skirted the valley, gradually climbing the pine-studded foothills that rose into forbidding granite-topped mountains in the distance. Riding in her wake, Franz-Wallace Garth, Fifth of his name, kept silent, doubtless glowering, though she took no notice. She'd helped raise Jorn's two Tamraire sons by an earlier liaison, who had both started out far more ill-mannered than this hot-house flower, and she'd had to slap sense into them when the need arose. They'd turned out all right, at least up until the day she'd left, and she could certainly handle this sulking bit of male business.

They were working their way around a stand of thick pines when her sturdy mare threw her head back, nostrils flaring. She leaned over the shaggy mane. "What?" she whispered as though the beast could answer. The nape of her neck prickled. She could feel *its* presence, strange and mean and oh-so-deadly.

It was late afternoon, and the light lay golden on the valley below and its meandering river. Down there, the Tamraire conducted their lives, and none of it an outsider's concern. She remembered the wild stories of the land's sense of humor told in Jorn's honor on the night she and Spark had officially bonded, the elaborate patterns worked onto tunics they had worn that made your head swim when you looked at them too closely, the shell and onyx necklaces that brought wonderfully vivid dreams when you slept wearing them. All gone now.

They had allied themselves with power, the Tamraire, and they wielded it to keep intruders out. She had been tolerated among them only for Jorn's sake and not a second longer than required. None would speak for her after that last terrible night. She had been Jorn's partner and that was finished now. Jorn's relations made that abundantly clear when they drove her out of the valley.

Garth rode up beside her on his flighty bay gelding. The nervous beast danced in place, hooves muffled by the thick mat of fallen needles. The cool tang of pine filled the air, so much more bracing than the air of any keep. "Do you see something?"

"No," she said, straining forward, "but I sure enough *feel* it, very close."

"A pox on your damned feelings!" he said. "At this pace, I'm going to be late—"

"Shut up!" They were too close, and the *something* had suddenly noticed them. She could feel how its attention had turned this way. "Ride!" She put her heels to the mare and leaned over the shaggy neck, urging the beast higher into the rugged foothills where they would be safe. Hoofbeats clattered over rock as Garth followed.

Listen, the *something* was saying, twining through her mind, seeking her tender, unprotected places. *I have stories to tell.*

"Don't listen!" she called over her shoulder, trying to shut it out. The hoofbeats behind her slowed. "Keep going!"

Such wonderful stories, the *something* said. *Ones you have been waiting all your life to hear.*

"It's lying!" she said, glancing back, but the bay gelding and the young man, her client and therefore her responsibility, disappeared into the blue-black shade of the pines.

Nothing will ever be the same once you hear what I have to say, the *something* continued, but more faintly now.

Blood thundered in her ears. He had gone to it, the fool! She reined in the mare and then slipped off and sat on a boulder, heart pounding, staring down into the valley until the light failed and darkness settled into every hollow, nerving herself for what she must do.

She would have to go after him, into the heart of that place where she was forbidden to ever again set foot.

ଷେ(ରେ)ഇ

Spark checked her sword and dagger, then rode the hardy little mare down toward the broad dish of the valley, trusting the beast's night vision more than her own. She should have seized Garth's reins and not trusted him to follow. It wasn't his fault he was an idiot. He'd never had a chance to be anything else, raised in that high-living court with its silks and blood-red wines and silver cutlery. It only made sense that those who grew up soft would be soft in the head as well. Jorn would have seen straight through him from the start.

Jorn. The thought of her partner with her pale-gold hair still made her heart ache. The valley's strangeness had run through Jorn's veins, so that her gray eyes were opalescent in the sunlight and luminous moonlight in the dark. She had been so strong, so fearless, so alive, Spark had found herself but a faithful shadow, content to bask in her lover's presence.

Listen! the *something* said as she rode, skirting a fumarole that steamed out of the side of a hill. Off to the left, she spotted the still waters of a marsh, similar to the one that had almost swallowed her life years before.

Leave me alone! she told it. *I listened to all your blamed stories and then you still killed Jorn and cast me out!*

I know more, it said.

Lies, she said. *All lies. No one knows that better than I do.*

Beneath her, the sturdy mare trembled, sweating and snorting at every step, ears flicking back and forth. She patted the shaggy neck. "Don't listen," she told the beast.

They reached the main valley floor just after moonrise so that silver limned the trees and streams and meadows of long grass bending in the breeze. Sometimes, as she rode, a bear kept pace with them, its eyes gleaming, sometimes a wolf or fox.

Such stories you have missed, the *something* said. *Such goings-on! And of course Jorn waits for you still.*

White-hot anger surged through her, so intense, that for a breath she could not even see. Her fingers clenched on the reins and her face heated. *Do not speak her name to me!*

So you no longer love her?

I'll kill you! Though she did not know how. No one did. Even the Tamraire only made pacts with the fierce wildness that abided here. They didn't rule it.

I was never alive, the *something* said slyly. *But you know that.*

ଔଓୡ

The Tamraire watched as she drew closer, passing boulders that had crashed down from the mountains long ago, moon-silvered ponds and beaver dams, and meandering weed-choked streams in no hurry to lose themselves in the rushing white-water heart of the river. Some of Jorn's people she saw, their eyes glittering in the darkness, others she only felt. Perhaps they would slay her for returning when she had been cast out. Or, perhaps they would only kill Franz-William Garth, Fifth of his name, slowly, with great attention to detail, as was their way, and compel her to watch.

She was angry at Garth for forcing her to come back, and yet it was not his fault. She was his guide, and so should have found better words to make him understand what listening to the wild *something* cost. Words, though, had never been easy with her. She and Jorn, well, they had done best without words in the deep silences of the night.

The moon's pale quarter was just setting behind the western mountains when she arrived at the hot spring terraces where the Tamraire kept their main camp. The *something* lived very close to the earth's surface here, so they considered this place sacred.

Her mare stopped, hanging her head, nostrils flaring. The air reeked of sulfur as hot water bubbled down a hillside of white mineral-coated rocks into a broad steaming pool.

A woman emerged from one of the tents off to the side. "You were never to come back here," she said, her eyes gleaming moon-pale as Jorn's once had. Her voice identified her—Matda, one of the elders.

"My client was lured down here, so I have come after him," Spark said. She drew her sword and held it ready.

"If the *something* wants him, then he is ours," Matda said. She was a tall woman, taller than even Jorn had been. Her plaited hair, once close to the same shade of gold, was now silver. "You lived among us long enough to understand that."

"I gave my word to deliver him safely to his uncle," Spark said, knowing full well they would not care. What was the honor of outsiders to a Tamraire? She slid down the mare's sweaty side and then dropped the reins.

"Then this—uncle—will be disappointed," Matda said. "The *something* finds him amusing."

"Where is he?" Spark said. The short sword felt entirely inadequate in her hand, but it was all she had.

The darkness stirred, then a group of Tamraire, male and female emerged from behind a line of hide tents. Garth was among them, walking stiff-legged as though dazed.

"We have to go," she said steadily to him, though her heartbeat hammered in her ears. She felt dizzy as again the *something* probed her defenses.

Mine, it whispered. At the top of the steaming white terraces, a massive geyser erupted into the night air.

"I never understood why Jorn wanted you," Matda said. She wore one of the wildly decorated Tamraire hides cut into an overshirt and leggings.

"Nor did I." The old unwanted tears scalded her eyes, but Spark fiercely refused to spill them. Jorn had hated tears.

"That must be why the *something* possessed her in the end," Matda said. "She had given herself over to someone unworthy. It was the only way to redeem her."

It had been a night much like this, fine, with only a hint of late spring's chilly edge. They had lain together in the privacy of their tent, twined in one another's arms, then the *something* had called Jorn outside.

At first, Spark was too deeply asleep to hear its voice, but then, becoming aware of the cooling emptiness in the furs beside her, rolled over and went to find Jorn. Out in the night, beyond the scattered tents, her partner stood at the top of the terraces, staring down into the broad thermal pool below. Her pale-gold hair shimmered in the scant starlight. She looked more beautiful than Spark had ever seen her, as though she were made of moonbeams.

"It wants me," Jorn said, wonder in her voice. "After all these years, I finally interest it."

"No!" Spark scrambled up the trail toward the top, slipping and falling in the darkness, skinning hands and knees. "Don't listen!"

"I am Tamraire," Jorn said. "How can I not listen? It is the bargain we made long ago when we came to this sacred place. We belong to it."

"No!" Spark cried. "You belong to me!"

Jorn's sons, both almost man-grown, had emerged from their tents and were following Spark now, racing to the top. They caught up with her and trapped her arms, holding her back. She fought them savagely until Brod, the oldest, clouted her on the head with his fist, sending her to her knees. Her vision fuzzed.

There was a splash, then, when she could see again, Jorn had cast herself into the steaming pool at the foot of the mineral-coated terraces, the one that had no bottom if you ventured close enough to the torrid water to gaze down. Spark staggered to her feet and tried to follow, but Jorn's sons held her back. That was not to be permitted either.

Did you think I wanted you? the *something* had said then, and in its terrible voice, there had been a hint of Jorn's beloved timbre, her cadence of speaking. *Jorn should have left you to the swamp where at least you could have made yourself useful feeding my trees.*

She blinked and came back to the present time, the night with all its unfeeling stars, and the terrible wild *something's* amusement.

Matda gestured and two hulking men came to stand beside her, Jorn's sons, grown well into their manhood. The angles of their cheekbones, the paleness of their hair, and the cast of their eyes, all reminiscent of her lost love.

"For Jorn's sake, we only drove you away that night," Matda said. "By returning, you end any obligation for leniency on our part."

Then Garth lurched forward with none of his usual careless grace. His tunic was torn and there was a darkening bruise over one eye. "Fight!" he said in a strained voice and drew his fine sword with a great ringing hiss.

"No," she said, keeping her weapon down at her side. "Put the sword away and come with me." Her throat was constricted. "You don't want to be late for your investiture."

He cocked his head in a way she'd seen before, just such an angle, on someone else's body. Ice enclosed her heart. "Spark, what are you doing here?" his voice said, but the words were not his.

The hot tears were back, dammit. "Jorn?"

"You should not have returned."

"It is a matter of honor," Spark said, "along with not much caring what happens to me, since you—" She could not finish.

"Deermouse, it was always going to be this way," Garth's borrowed voice said. "I can see that plainly from this side of things. It was ordained."

The old endearment cut. "Not by me!" She would not shed the stupid, useless tears, she—would—not!

"It allowed me to have you, so that I would be happy for a time," Garth's voice said.

The breath caught in her throat. "And now?"

"I am happier."

That was a blow more solid than any she had ever received over the entire course of her life. "No!" Her answer was but a hoarse whisper.

"You should not have followed him here, worm," Garth's voice said and now it was the wild *something,* not Jorn.

"Then strike me down," Spark said. She whirled, looking into face after Tamraire face, all impassive in the starlight, eyes glimmering with *its* presence. "Make me nothing. I have been full ready since that night!" She raised her old sword with all its nicks and scratches.

Garth's blade swung toward her, but his stance was still awkward, unbalanced, as though he had never trained in the weapon's use. Sweat ran down her neck, soaked the length of her back. She couldn't kill the mush-brained wretch. He was her responsibility, but perhaps she could knock him senseless, just long enough to throw his body over her saddle and lead the mare back out of the valley. If she could get him up into the hills again, he would come to his proper senses.

Garth's body lunged at her, taller by a full head with a correspondingly greater reach. She shuffled aside, feeling the steaming terraces and that dreadful pool all too close at her back. Who was she fooling, thinking she had any sort of chance to succeed? Even if she knocked him out, the Tamraire would never let her just walk away. Not unless the *something* said to let her go.

Garth swung again, as clumsy as a boy wielding his first wooden sword, stumbling as he threw himself off balance.

"What in the name of all Creation do you want?" she shouted at the *something.* "I've never understood!"

Garth stopped, and again his body took up one of Jorn's achingly familiar postures, free hand on its hip, eyes narrowed.

"You have everything," Spark said, "this valley and the Tamraire, every deer and bear and spider that makes its home here, even Jorn, who was the sun and the moon to me. What more do you want?"

Freedom, the *something* said, disdaining to use Garth's voice this time. *I have been trapped here since long before your kind walked the earth. I want to go back out into the world again.*

"Then why don't you just leave?" she said.

The *something* laughed and it was a broken, painful sound, like the grinding of rock against rock, even inside her head. *I am bound.*

"By what?" she said, even as Garth took another awkward swing at her. She edged back again and then almost stumbled on the stones bordering the thermal pool. She could feel the moist heat rising off its surface, smell the noisome sulfur of its waters. She'd always hated living next to that reek, but Jorn had insisted.

I—

She waited, steam droplets condensing in her hair.

I—have forgotten.

Matda closed in on her then, and Jorn's looming sons, whom she'd help raise, and the rest of the Tamraire, their eyes gleaming in the star-riddled darkness. "I am not afraid," she said, though in truth, she was. "You've already stolen the only thing I ever cared about, the only thing I will ever care about!"

Yes, I did, and there was satisfaction in its tone.

"And you would do it again, given the chance," Spark said. "You're vain and wicked! Whatever imprisoned you here was right to do it. You don't deserve to be part of the wide world!"

Up on the crest of the mineral terraces, the geyser erupted again in a fury of superheated water and steam. Flying drops of hot water stung her cheeks and neck and the reek of sulfur thickened. The Tamraire, caught in their trance, did not seem to feel the water's savage heat on their skin.

"Do your worst!" Spark said as their hands seized her and dragged her to the trail leading upward. "You can't kill me twice!"

I can trap you here forever with me, the *something* said.

But it had already done that, she realized. A large part of her had leapt into that bottomless pool with Jorn. Only the merest shell of a person had ridden back out of the valley the next day. Briefly, she struggled free of the imprisoning hands. "How long?" she said as they closed in again and held her even tighter.

I do not understand.

"How long has it been since you tried to leave?" She glanced down into the simmering pool, which looked black and oily under the stars. "Or do you just swoon about the valley, using the Tamraire for playthings while bemoaning your fate?"

I—do not remember that either.

"Not much good to anyone then, not even yourself!" she said as the Tamraire with their strong hands forced her closer and closer to the geyser. The spray was so hot, she could feel blisters rising on her face and arms. They would throw her in! she thought with rising panic, fighting with the last dregs of her strength. No comparatively kinder plunge into the steaming pool for her.

How would I go? the *something* said. *I have no form.*

"A Tamraire could carry you," she said, digging her heels in to little purpose.

They cannot leave the valley, the *something* said. *I have bred that into them, bone and blood, down through the centuries.*

"A bear then, or a wolf?" The column of superheated steam was so close now. Each drop stung like liquid fire.

The same, it said. *I do not allow what is mine to stray.*

She closed her eyes against the terrible heat as her captors strained to throw her in.

But you could leave.

The hands fell away and she stumbled back from the deadly spray.

Or your ungainly companion.

Yes, Garth, she thought wildly. If it had to be one of the two of them, let it be him!

Garth loomed down below, sword in hand, still and silent in the darkness, seemingly unaware that Spark was up here bargaining his life away. What would he become if the *something* took him? There would be no investiture in his uncle's court, no marriage to the properly brought up young lady who most certainly had already been selected by his family, no children of his own to turn out equally self-assured and insufferable. The *something* would take it all away and pour itself into what was left.

And it would be her fault, the back of her mind whispered. She had known the full measure of what lived down here, though he had not. She had pledged her honor for his safety. "No, take me," she said, though her flesh crawled at the thought.

I prefer the youth. His body has more years left than your pathetic carcass.

Garth's head raised. His hand jerked up and starlight gleamed along his expensive sword.

"He is well known!" she said, darting back down the path. "His people will come looking for him! You'll never have a moment's peace!" As she ran, she visualized the companies of armed men who would surely be sent to find the rich man's son, the ducal uncle dispatching his troops to join the search, the fiance's family—

Very well.

The night exploded behind her eyes. She fell to her knees, filled with opalescent white fire, cold *cold* flames searing a hollow inside her head where the *something* could fit at least a portion of itself. Memory after memory burned in a flash like sawdust put to the flame. In the space of one breath, she lost her childhood, the next, her youth. Then the flames hesitated. "Take the rest!" she said. "Take it all! I don't want to remember!"

Not even me?

It was Jorn's beloved voice.

"Stop—that!" She felt broken. "I'm giving you everything! There's no need to torment me with what I can never have!"

I'm still here.

"You're dead!" Spark said, though the words still hurt as much now as ever they had.

I gave myself to it, Jorn said, *much as you have just now, and you are still here.*

Or at least some portion of Spark was. She wasn't sure how much the *something* had burned away. The opaline flames still scintillated inside her head and it was difficult to see out of her own eyes.

Poor Deermouse, Jorn said. *I'm sorry it has been so hard.*

"Is it really you, love?" Spark whispered.

It is.

⊗⊙⊗⊙⊗⊙

In the gray reaches of morning, when the light was thin-edged and painfully new, the Tamraire watched the two of them, Spark and Garth, saddle their horses and ride into the dew-drenched grass. An eagle soared overhead for a time, frogs hopped along in their wake, and several long green snakes kept pace for as long as they could, finally disappearing as the little party approached the foothills.

The *something* held itself back for the most part, letting Spark hold the reins and teach it how to sit in the saddle without falling off. Jorn was so silent, Spark worried that her partner was no longer present. Or had her seeming survival been just another vicious trick after all?

Garth stared ahead as his nervous bay picked its way through scattered rocks, across streams, around fumaroles and ponds, never once deigning to look aside at her. He seemed unaware of how close he had come to losing all that he was and had once again focused upon reaching his uncle's court.

She held her breath as they climbed into the forest that surrounded the valley. Would the *something* be able to cross the invisible boundary, and if not, would she die too?

They were just entering the trees when she felt a growing feeling of constriction, like a band stretched tighter and tighter, pulling them back. The mare rode on, unconcerned, but Spark had to fight to remain in the saddle.

I—cannot! the *something* said, throwing off white-hot flashes of pain inside her head. *Turn—around!*

If they went back, she would be trapped in that valley with it for the rest of her life. Though she was afraid, Spark leaned forward, throwing her arms around the gray's shaggy neck, and dug her heels in. "Run!" she said, though her teeth were clenched with pain. The mare's head came up, her ears flickering uncertainly. Spark kicked her again. "Run, damn you!"

The gray lurched into a lope, then flattened out into full gallop, weaving sure-footed through the pines and hemlocks. Spark heard Garth shout as she left him and the bay behind.

The constriction dragged, sucking the breath out of her body, the very life out of her heart. A roaring whiteness filled her head. It was like being gutted as everything vital was drawn back to the valley. The *something* had been right. Her head lolled and she tasted blood. It—and she—could never—never—

The bond snapped, and then she was breathing again in great heaving gasps. Tears ran down her cheeks and she didn't know whose they were or even why she was crying. She pulled the mare up with shaking hands that blessedly once again answered to her own will. *Jorn?* she said inside her head.

Here, love.

Then she felt for the *something's* presence. *I remain, too*, it said, but the power behind its words was vastly lessened. It now possessed but a shadow of its former strength. Most of its substance had been left behind in the valley with the Tamraire, but enough lingered, she thought, to ride with her and Jorn and experience the wide outside world.

Franz-William Garth, Fifth of that illustrious name, caught up with her, standing in his stirrups. His elegant bay courser looked wild-eyed and his own cheeks were quite flushed. Pine needles were stuck in his black hair. "What was that all about?"

"We—" She gazed at his strong-boned face, handsome in spite of the bruises and so very sure of himself, exactly as the world had made him. Not his fault, she told herself, and there was always the possibility of future improvement, a chance he had nearly lost, though he seemed to have no memory of those moments. "We have to hurry," she said. "I don't want you to arrive late at your uncle's court."

"Oh," he said with an arrogant twist of his head. He flicked at a speck on his fine sleeve. "Which way then, woman?"

Yes, which way? demanded the *something.*

She knows, Jorn said. *This is her territory. Let my Deermouse take the lead.*

Spark smiled to herself. She glanced back over her shoulder down at the valley with its roiling mudpots, hot springs, and fumaroles, then urged her gray mare west.

Muttering under his breath, Garth followed.

BLOOD MOON

by Catherine Mintz

When I first read this story, I found it intriguing but totally baffling, and I wondered if the long hours—and late nights—were scrambling my brain. I wrote back to Catherine and said that I liked the story, but I didn't quite understand it. It turned out that I wasn't the only one working too late at night; the version I had was missing a scene near the end. As Catherine said, "One should not send email after midnight." Unless, presumably, you're a night person. I'm strictly diurnal, and I suspect that Catherine is also.

Catherine Mintz' work has appeared in a number of publications, including *Interzone*, *Asimov's*, *Weird Tales*, and the anthologies *Whitley Strieber's Aliens* and *Warrior Wisewoman*. Often it reflects her interest in languages, anthropology, and the history of genre literature. She also owns the Copper Penny Press, which publishes genre literature.

The Dame sat on her balcony, hands folded, white lap pelt in place. Every day, all day, she kept watch on what happened within the Fastness. At night, the watchdogs were unchained. Now they slept in their kennel near the gate, heaps of russet, ash, and charcoal fur. By day, the Dame kept watch within the keep.

It was Blood Moon, halfway between the winter solstice and the spring equinox. Nearly a hundred seasons ago, the stone circle that marked the eight festivals had been pulled down, so no one could be sure of the exact day. Soon, the Dame was sure.

Now, although the high pastures were green, cold rain pelted down. Hail had rattled on the courtyard paving earlier. The old took the long way around, under the porticos, to stay dry and warm. The young were indoors, set to work. The Dame sighed. It had been a dull day with nothing to do but worry.

Children tried to evade her keen eye. Adolescents saw the Dame as an old busybody. Older people had a better understanding of her worth. Her contemporaries were envious or wary, depending on how wise they were themselves.

Knowledge is power. Secrets more powerful still. The Dame knew many. Hammett, Wenna's son, was not her husband's boy, but his brother's. Three of the kitchen staff were pilfering from the storerooms. The captain of the guard slipped down to the gate after dark every seventh night and stood, listening. Sometimes he spoke a word or two.

Since there was no cure for a sterile husband but a discreet agreement, the first was probably laudable. There were so few babies. Because food might be short this year, the second was not yet important but could be. The fields were too muddy to plant, even if the cold broke. However, given that there was no good reason anyone talked with anything that lived beyond the walls of the Fastness, the last was important. There were things outside that wanted in.

The Mother and the Maiden must know. *I have delayed,* the Dame thought and stroked the white fur. The other two would want to act. She sighed, thinking, *I have waited long enough. "Such matters are not for you alone,"* a voice long dead reminded her.

It was early, but no one was abroad. Best to get on with it. The Dame wrapped her pelt about her and rose, stiff with long sitting. Aided by her cane, she hobbled into her sitting room. A hot tisane would be welcome, even if her evening meal had not been brought up.

Elowin was a marvel, for although there was no supper yet, there were three thick slices of bread under an overturned bowl on a plate, a toasting fork, and a pot of honey. Raspberry tea was in her caddy on the mantle piece. Her jug was full of spring water. The hearth glowed.

The Dame sat the kettle on the hob and barred the door. She went to her privy chamber and stripped off. One hand on the back of a heavy chair, she worked slowly until her muscles were supple and she could work free standing. Then she did thrusts and blocks with her cane.

She washed and anointed herself with rosemary oil. Rinsing everything so that no scent of sweat remained she emptied the basin down the shaft. The Dame's personal privy was a necessary luxury. Just how capable she was physically was something she didn't share.

In fresh-aired clothes, she unbarred the door, settled to brewing tea and toasting bread. Putting the last slice onto the hearth-warmed plate, she heard Elowin on the stairs. "Butter," said the serving girl as she came in. "Dinner will be late. The salt beef's still tough."

The Dame smiled.

Elowin grinned. "If he'd just set it to simmer early. It's a bad season for game." The girl looked sober. "It's a bad season to be out of the Fastness, if you ask me. People talk about how old and thick the walls are. To me, that says they worry about them."

Yes. The Dame nodded and reached for the butter crock, thinking, *Now she will tell me.* Elowin was thoughtful, but she could just as well have left the butter on her first trip up the spiral stair. She'd wanted a few minutes with the Dame.

"The cows wouldn't go out to graze this morning."

"Why was that? Tea?"

"No," said the girl. "Thank you. I had buttermilk in the kitchen. I've been at the churning. It's a good batch. You can taste the early clover is up."

The Dame poured a cup for herself. Its steam formed restless ghosts. She asked again, "Why wouldn't the cows go out?"

"No one knew."

The Dame looked up from her cup, alert. The girl was not yet old enough to be a dairymaid, but she helped cut the curds and turn the cheeses. Elowin was perceptive and more inclined to listen than to talk: reasons the Dame favored her.

"They were frightened. At first the herd master decided to bring them into the stone folds when they wouldn't let down. Even with the calves right with them, they were hard to milk. Now he's bringing them home."

The click as the Dame put down her cup seemed loud, even against the steady drumming of the rain. The night was going to be wet and windy. *Blood Moon*, she thought, *when dormant things wake.*

"The herders and the dogs had all they could do to keep them on the road." The girl's eyes were cloudy with fear. "They got them into the fold at Second Switchback. There wasn't time to send for food. They drank what the calves didn't want, stripped the rest into the dirt."

"Why wasn't there time?"

"No one will travel in the dark. They'll bring the goats down the day after tomorrow, if they can."

"Why didn't the herd master send word?" That she, the Dame, not know there was trouble in the high pastures was as worrying as the news itself. Herders were used to lonely pastures and the cows' instincts were sound. The goats, half-wild, couldn't be gathered in haste, but the Fastness could not afford to lose them.

Elowin looked away. "There was howling. Far away and then near. Eyes said he saw tracks. Like a wolf's. Bigger than his hand." She looked back. "The herders argued a lot. Then they took that for a bad sign."

Wolves. There hasn't been a wolf here for a generation. "If Kenver saw something, it was there. Why didn't they move the herd?"

"They moved from South Peak to West, two days ago, without sending word. Drove the cows and the goats across the Neck. Then they rebuilt the Gate of Sarsens." She looked into the scarlet coals, finding the truth there. "Well, they pulled four stones into place and closed the road. Now they're coming *home*." The girl's voice shook on the last word.

The Gate of Sarsens. The stones held power. A hundred years ago the people of Fastness had broken the circle to use its sarcens to close the road from the peaks. When that need passed they had pulled the stones aside but had not rebuilt the circle. It took ox teams to move sarsens. The Fastness had fewer oxen every year.

Indeed, there were fewer people now than there had been when the circle was broken. Fields were fallow from lack of plowmen and teams. If the herdsmen had moved four of the "silent giants," whatever they feared was more than a matter of a stray wolf and the dairy herds. The Dame asked, "When did you hear this?"

"This afternoon." The girl gestured at the food. "I thought—"

"Yes. Well done." The Dame lifted her tea, paused, then put it down. "Tell the war master I'd like to see him. Don't let anyone hear you. Before full night is soon enough."

The girl went: quick and silent.

War Master Tremain was past active duty, but he would understand there was no time to explain, to argue, to reach a consensus. People would have to be swept into action.

I was not worried enough, thought the Dame, and stroked the white pelt in her lap, soothing herself. Once darkness had fallen, there would be much to do. She could only hope that the war master had been receiving news she had not.

Tremain was prompt, if out of breath. Stout and smelling of the stables, he sat without invitation and listened. "No," he said. "I hadn't heard." He frowned but did not speculate. "The walls are sound. The people trained. We are the Fastness; we can defend. That much I have made sure of. But we need more."

"Then there will be more," said the Dame. Between them, they outlined a plan. Then War Master Tremain rose. "I'll send the other two, separately."

The Dame nodded.

Well after dark, what might have been three huge wolves—a black, a red, and a white—met at the gate of the Fastness. They nosed around and loped into the shadows near the kennel. All the guard dogs whined, once. The patter of the rain rose and fell. Once a spurt of sleet rattled on paving. Torches burned down and fell, hissing in the puddles.

The Fastness was always dark and still at night. People who rise at dawn go to bed not long after sundown. They let walls protect them, not sentinels. Midnight, and the captain appeared, walking as though there were no rain. He went to the gate, lifted its three massive bolts, and slid back its bar. Then he waited, empty-eyed, his sodden clothes black by waning torchlight.

Alert, the three crouched. Like wolves, they bared their teeth when something began to open the gate. Without bothering to glance over his shoulder, the captain of the guard slipped out. There was an odd noise, then nothing.

The three rose and padded to the gap in the Fastness defenses. Something, roused from its eating, snarled at them. Dog-like, the three quietly backed away. Unlike dogs, once inside they stood on their hind legs, pushed the gate closed, and took off their pelts.

Swiftly and silently, the three women rebarred it and dropped the bolts. The captain would not be coming home. They gathered their pelts around them, ready to go their ways. Then the oak panel creaked as something heavy hit it from the outside. The bolts groaned and the bar shuddered.

The Dame handed her white fur to the Mother, the Mother handed her red pelt to the Maiden, who draped it over her own black one. The Dame, clothed in nothing but shadows and light, drew her cane from hiding. The other two fled to call the guard and wake the keep.

Every dog in the Fastness howled as the Dame opened the gate and stood in the opening. In her left hand was a sword and in her right the cane-sheath. *It's been a good beginning*, she thought. *If it must be, let it be a good end.* "See me!" she shouted.

Seeing her, the thing reared back. It dripped the red of blood over the white of bone and the black of dung. "Sister," it hissed at her, "do you not know me?"

"I do," said the Dame. "You are the one who came before me."

"I can name you!" it said.

"So you can," said the Dame, "for you knew me as Maiden and Mother."

"I am the many in one," it cried, in a different voice. The wailing of the guard dogs was terrible.

"Sister, you may have me," said the Dame. The guard dogs' silence was more terrible still.

The thing billowed like flames, although the rain fell straight down.

"You may have me," said the Dame, and sheathed her sword cane. "I come." She cast the cane behind her.

"No!" said the figure, in yet another voice. "It will be too many!"

"You may have me!"

"No! We will die the real death!" cried many voices, all together.

"*You must take me!*" said the Dame and strode into the other. There was a vast silence. Something stood there, flickering uncertainly. It drew in on itself with a sound like fire eating wood. Livid lightning leaped from earth to sky. Thunder smote the smoking earth and echoed everywhere.

The Mother held the Maiden and both wept, but they were the only ones who mourned. They, and the wailing dogs, who did not know what had happened, but knew a creature akin to them was gone. The people of the Fastness shouted as one for joy.

In the courtyard the air was still, but high above the clouds fled on a swift wind, and the night's pale eye looked down. In moonlight the new Dame took her place on her balcony. In moonlight the new Mother spoke to the people, choosing the father-to-be of her first child. In moonlight there were beginnings and an ending.

Softly at first, then more loudly, women's fingers brushed drumheads, and the men did the slow dances that mark the passing of someone rich in years. Then the men tapped the drums, and the women danced the fast dances that celebrate a new Dame and a new Mother.

At dawn there came the cry of a newborn girl. She was wrapped in the pelt of the Maiden and so sanctified it. They took the black fur, shook it out, warmed it before the fire, and wrapped startled Elowin in it. You won't forget me, said a voice deep in her mind. No, answered the Maiden, knowing the other would whisper in her dreams. On her shoulders, her pelt shivered.

STOLEN GHOSTS

by Jonathan Moeller

This story is a sequel to "Black Ghost, Red Ghost" in *Sword & Sorceress 22*. Caina slew a necromancer and stopped his murderous experiments. Now, however, she will learn that her past mistakes carry grim consequences.

Jonathan Moeller writes mostly fantasy—his novel *Demonsouled* was published in 2005—in addition to some science fiction and freelance non-fiction. He says that if you wish to argue with him over the Internet, visit him at www.jonathanmoeller.com. Presumably you can also go there even if you don't want to argue with him.

W hen Lord Governor Anabas of Marsis kicked down the door and stormed into her room, Caina was astonished.

After all, the Emperor had sent her to kill him.

"Lord Governor," said Caina, smoothing her skirts and performing a quick curtsy, the fabric rich and soft beneath her fingers. As part of her disguise, she had taken a room at the city's finest inn. A fortune's worth of fine furniture and expensive carpets separated her from Anabas. "My father and I were to show you our wares on the morrow, but . . . ."

"You," Anabas said, drawing his sword. "I know you."
He looked drunk, his face pale, his bloodshot eyes glittering.
"Yes, I know you very well."

"My lord?" said Caina, her mind racing. She took a step
closer to the bed. "We met this morning, my lord, of course you
know me. I am Anna Callenius, and my father and I are jewel
merchants. I hope you have come to view our wares, for your
lordship would find them most . . ."

"Oh, I know your wares," said Anabas. "But you deal not
in jewels, but in treachery and murder." An ugly rictus of a grin
twisted his mouth. "I know you. Spy. Deceiver. Murderess. A
Ghost of the Empire."

Only years of hard training kept Caina from flinching.

"Surprised?" said Anabas, stepping closer. "I am not. I
knew that the Emperor would learn of my plots with the magi.
He's sent one of his pet Ghosts to kill me, hasn't he? Probably
two or three of them, at that." He laughed, and no longer looked
drunk but stark mad.

"My lord," said Caina, taking another step towards the
bed, and what lay beneath the plump pillows, "I know not of
what you speak, I . . ."

"You do," said Anabas. "In fact, you're probably
thinking of killing me right now." He laughed again. "Though
little good it will do you."

"My lord," said Caina, "please, you must be mistaken."
How had he seen past her disguise? Well, Anabas was a traitor
to the Empire, and whether he died here or in Marsis's grim
citadel made no matter. Unless, of course, Anabas had a host of
armed men waiting outside the door. "I am but a merchant's
daughter and nothing . . ."

"Wretched little Ghost," hissed Anabas. "How I weary of
your lies."

He lunged at her, the sword blurring. Caina dodged, and
the blade ripped into the mattress. Her hand darted under the
pillow, and came up holding a long dagger. She sidestepped his

next swing, raised her arm, and plunged the dagger into his chest. Anabas stumbled back with a groan of pain.

And then he smiled.

The Lord Governor fell out the broken door and onto the balcony overlooking the spacious common room. The city's wealthy and powerful looked up in sudden surprise. Anabas sagged against the railing, coughing blood.

"Murder!" he shrieked before Caina could reach him. "The jewel merchant's daughter has slain me! Anna Callenius! Anna Callenius!"

And he looked back, winked at her, and shoved himself over the railing.

The Lord Governor landed on a table and shattered it beneath him, expensive wine and food spraying in all directions. A hundred pairs of shocked eyes turned up to stare at Caina, among them two men in the livery of Anabas's personal guards.

Only two?

"She's killed the Governor!" someone shouted. "Take her!"

Caina leapt back into her room and reached under the bed. Her hand came up holding a leather belt of sheathed knives. She flung it over her shoulder and snatched an oil lantern from the desk just as the first bodyguard hurtled through the door. He lunged at her, and Caina threw the lantern into his face. The glass shattered, oil spraying over his head and chest, and the man shrieked as his clothes burst into flame. He bounced off the wall, setting a tapestry on fire, and tumbled down the stairs.

She raced onto the balcony, saw the guests fleeing into the streets, saw the flames spreading. Another bodyguard reached for her, and Caina ducked under his arm and leapt down the stairs. Men shouted, women screamed, and Caina heard people calling for the city's guard.

She had to get out now.

Caina turned towards the kitchen, intending to escape out the back, and caught one last glimpse of Anabas's corpse. The strange madness had vanished from his eyes, his expression frozen into a mask of bewildered shock. As if he could not understand what had happened to him.

She did not understand, either.

Caina fled through the kitchen as the flames devoured the inn.

☘

I ron bells filled the night.

Caina hurried from shadow to shadow, wrapped in a stolen cloak to cover her rich clothes. She had kicked off her cumbersome heeled boots, and the cobblestones felt cool and damp against her bare feet. Shouts echoed through the alleys. She saw companies of armed men moving to seal the city's gates, others moving from house to house, all intent on hunting down the Lord Governor's murderer.

How had things gone so bad?

A Ghost circle had been hidden in Marsis for years, but how could a fool like Anabas have uncovered them? Why had he confronted her with only two bodyguards, instead of sending a hundred armed men? And why had he flung himself off that balcony? Suicidal madness? Sheer spite?

And that final, damnable wink.

Caina shoved aside her doubts. Distractions would kill her. If she lived through this night, she could unravel the mystery later. Anabas was dead, as the Emperor had desired, and with any luck no one would connect the jewel merchant's daughter to the Ghosts. Now she had to warn her circlemaster. If Anabas had breached their secrecy, the Ghost circle in Marsis was in terrible danger, and they had to flee at once.

At last she came to the rambling, reeking docks, a hodgepodge of quays, warehouses, and cheap inns. Caina slipped through a narrow alley, knocked at a splintered door, and waited. The door parted a crack, and then swung open all the way.

A hulking man stood in the doorway, a crossbow cradled in his arms. Sweat beaded his grizzled face, and strands of lank gray hair covered his eyes. He stared at her for a moment, then lowered the weapon. "It sounds as if the entire garrison has been roused. Why do I suspect that you were involved somehow?"

"Halfdan," said Caina, relief flooding her. Halfdan had been her circlemaster for years, had brought her into the Ghosts as a child, had taught her almost everything she knew. He would know what to do.

She loved the old man.

Halfdan beckoned her inside with a jerk of his head. Caina followed him into a cluttered sitting room lit by a crimson glow from the fireplace. A few pieces of battered furniture leaned against the rickety walls. Here Halfdan masqueraded as a pawnbroker, listening to the rumors and passing everything he learned to the Ghosts.

"Well," said Halfdan, staring at the dying fire, "out with it. What happened?"

"Anabas learned I was a Ghost, I know not how," said Caina. "He attacked me at the inn and I fought him off. But he named me his murderer before witnesses. I scarce escaped with my life, and made my way here at once."

Halfdan grunted. "Foolish of you."

Caina flinched, hesitated, and kept talking. "Perhaps. But our secrecy has been broken. Anabas learned of us, and he might have told others. He is dead as the Emperor commanded. But we must leave at once, before his soldiers find us."

Halfdan still gazed into the fire and said nothing. There was a grim tightness in his jaw. Caina hesitated again, and touched his arm.

"We have faced trials more dire than this, surely," said Caina. "But if we act at once . . ."

Halfdan snarled, whirled, and backhanded her across the face.

Caina fell back with a cry, clutching at her cheek. For a moment she could not think through the shock. In the dozen years she had known Halfdan, he had shouted at her, screamed at her, and lost his temper more than once. But he never had hit her.

"Stupid child," hissed Halfdan, his mouth clenched. "Do you have any idea how much you disgust me?"

Caina stared at him, too stunned for words.

"You have wasted too much of my time," he spat. His breath rasped through his nose, his chest heaving. "You contemptible little fool." He laughed, hard and cruel. "You remain blind even as death closes around you."

"But," said Caina, her voice cracking, "you took me in, you taught me everything . . ."

"An egregious mistake, clearly," said Halfdan, scooping up the crossbow. He crossed the room and flung open the far door. "See what your folly has wrought!"

A scream caught in Caina's throat.

Besides her and Halfdan, four other Ghosts had been stationed in Marsis. All four of them lay dead and piled in the back room, their clothes stiff with dried blood, their dead faces frozen with shock. Crossbow quarrels jutted from their flesh.

She looked up to see Halfdan's mouth twist in a hideous grin, his bloodshot eyes shining red with the fire's glow. "Wretched little Ghost. I should have killed you when I first laid eyes on you. Well, hindsight is ever clear. But let's rectify that little error right now."

He leveled the crossbow at her, and Caina's reflexes, reflexes that Halfdan had drilled into her, took over. She kicked out, and the side of her foot smacked into the bow. The quarrel hissed past her chest and buried itself in the wall. Halfdan flung aside the crossbow and yanked a dagger from his belt.

"Stop!" shouted Caina.

He stabbed at her face, and again Caina's reflexes took over. She sidestepped his clumsy lunge and yanked a pair of knives from her belt. His arm pumped, driving the blade at her, and Caina blocked his stabs again and again.

"Stop it!" she said. "By all the gods, stop it! Stop it!"

He laughed at her and came in a bull rush. His forehead cracked against her nose, and she stumbled back. His dagger swept past her face, and Caina's hands moved of their own accord. She beat aside his thrust, and drove one blade between his ribs and buried another in his neck.

Only when the old man sagged to his knees before her did she realize what she had done.

"No," she said, letting go of the knives, "no . . ."

Halfdan sneered at her, and spat blood into her face. And then his expression cleared, and he gaped at her in confusion. "Caina?" he whispered. "But . . . why? Why . . ."

He sagged to the floor, dead.

Caina stared at the corpse, her mind reeling, hands and knees trembling. A single sob burst from her lips, and she fled into the night, heedless of who might catch her.

When her senses returned she found herself huddled in a doorway, tears streaming down her face, her breath hitching in her throat.

How could this have happened?

Halfdan would have told her to think it through. The mind was a blade sharper than any dagger, he always said. But Caina had buried her blade in his neck, had stilled his mind forever.

She sobbed again, looked at the blood drying on her fingers.

But Halfdan still would have told her to think it through.

Caina scrubbed her eyes dry and glared into the night. Why would Halfdan have turned against her? Had the Emperor ordered her killed? Perhaps, but Halfdan would never have done something so inelegant. Some poison in a glass, or a quick slip of the knife between the ribs, nothing so brutish. For that matter, why kill the rest of the circle? Halfdan had not even acted like himself. In fact, he had acted a lot like . . .

Caina blinked.

Halfdan had acted, and sounded, a lot like Anabas.

Wretched little Ghost. Both men had called her that. Such an insult might have slipped Anabas's lips, but Halfdan had been a Ghost circlemaster. Why would both men use the same turn of phrase? Why had Halfdan fought so ineptly? Caina never would have thought she could best her teacher.

It was as if both Anabas and Halfdan had wanted her to kill them.

Caina's hands curled into fists, dried blood crackling between her fingers.

There was a power, she knew, that could twist men's minds. That could make them act in suicidal ways. That could transform a man into a puppet in the hands of a cold and heartless master.

Sorcery. Wielded by a magus of the Imperial Magisterium. And Anabas had been plotting with the magi.

Caina had killed magi in the past, but knew little of their arts.

But others might know more.

•◦◦•

She came to a decaying house at the end of a narrow lane.

The docks were a crowded, raucous place, even at night, but no one, save for the most desperate, ever came here. The house sagged over the lane like a rotting tree. No light came from the shuttered windows, and the air here stank of strange chemicals and rotten meat.

Caina hurried to the door and hammered on it. Nothing happened, and she glanced over her shoulder. She glimpsed torchlight moving through the streets, heard the tramp of marching boots, and kept pounding on the door.

At last it opened a crack. "You dare to disturb my rest?" snarled a rasping, bubbling voice. "Leave me! If you have need of my arts, return tomorrow. If you can meet my price."

"I will have your aid now," said Caina.

"Leave at once," said the voice, "or I shall show you the pain my arts can . . ."

Caina flung back her hood. "Remember me, Nicorus?"

There was a horrified gasp.

Caina shoved her way into a dim-lit room. Shelves covered the walls, lined with jars, vials, books, scrolls, and bones. The only light came from a corroded bronze brazier. A squat man clad in dirty brown robes stood near the door, his head pale, misshapen, and hairless, like a ball of kneaded dough. He had once been a rising master of the Magisterium, until he had enspelled a concubine favored by the First Magus. The First Magus's wrath had been fierce, and Nicorus's downfall sudden. Now he eked out an existence selling love potions and petty charms to the rabble of Marsis.

And selling his arts to the Ghosts from time to time.

"Nicorus," said Caina. The floorboards felt soft and greasy beneath her bare feet. "So you do remember me."

"You must leave!" There was no rage in Nicorus's voice, only terror. "I have aided your brethren too often. If the Magisterium learns that I aided a Ghost yet again . . . I dare not risk it. Not now. The city is in an uproar. Some jewel merchant's brat stabbed the Lord Governor to death in a jealous fit . . ."

Caina stared at him.

Nicorus's face, already slack, fell further. "You? Oh, gods. No. No! I will not aid you. I dare not draw the wrath of the Magisterium down upon me again. I have already paid too dear."

Caina didn't know what form the First Magus's vengeance had taken, but Nicorus had lost both his hair and his eyebrows, and seemed unable to grow a beard.

"You will help me," said Caina. "I might die before this night is over, but if you turn me away now, I swear the vengeance of the Ghosts will find you one day."

Nicorus sighed, and gave a curt nod. "Then speak quickly."

"I require only the answers to my questions," said Caina. She told him of the night's terrible events, of Anabas's bizarre behavior, and managed to keep her voice steady as she told him of Halfdan and the circle. Nicorus's face changed as she spoke, the fear draining away, replaced with something else.

Dread.

"So?" said Caina. "What spell can do this?"

"A spell?" whispered Nicorus. He began pacing, his hands kneading the filthy skirts of his robe. "You think a spell did this?"

"If not a spell, then what?" said Caina. "Do you mean to say that both Anabas and Halfdan went mad on the same night?"

He turned to face her, lip curled with contempt. "Tell me, Ghost. Have you ever slain a magus? Or any other worker of sorcery?"

Caina nodded. "Thrice."

"Recently?"

"Yes. Not a year past, in Varia Province."

His pale face managed to grow whiter. "And this magus you slew. Did he practice necromancy?"

"He used murder and the blood of children to power his spells. Why do you think I killed him?"

"And after you slew him," said Nicorus, "did you chop off his head? Cut out his heart? Burn his body, mix the ashes with salt, and scatter them into the sea?"

"Of course not," said Caina. "He was wicked, but a mortal man. Not a devil."

"Oh, no, of course not," said Nicorus. Beads of sweat stood out on his white brow. "But such measures are appropriate, if you wish to slay a man who studied the necromantic sciences."

"You mean to tell me that he has returned?" said Caina. "Absurd. I killed him myself. He was dead. I would swear to it."

"I'm sure," sneered Nicorus. "But . . . there is a spell. A great spell of the highest necromantic science. *Metempsychosis*, the wizards of old called it. The body is slain . . . but the spiritual essence lives on, anchored to the dead heart. And that essence can inhabit the bodies of the living, usurping living flesh from its rightful soul. And if the stolen flesh is slain, the essence can claim another body, and another, and another."

"Impossible," said Caina. But her heart hammered against her ribs.

"All things are possible to the master of arcane sciences," said Nicorus. He laughed, lips slithering over his yellowed teeth. "Can you not see? You slew that magus, but he transcended death, and now he is coming for you. He possessed Anabas to ruin you. He possessed Halfdan to wound your heart. Think of what he will do when at last he lays hands upon you."

"Not if I kill him first," said Caina.

Nicorus shook his head. "You already killed him. Little good it did. Have you sorcery to fight his sorcery? Better to just lie down and die. Or to cut your own throat. It will certainly be kinder than what he will do to you."

"Even the mightiest spell can be broken," said Caina. "His essence is anchored to his heart, you said? What happens if his heart is destroyed?"

Nicorus shrugged. "The spell will end, I presume. Though the magic will render his dead heart impervious to weapons of steel."

"How, then?" said Caina.

"A spell of sufficient power could do it," said Nicorus. "That is beyond your reach, though. Exposing the heart to sunlight will destroy it, but presumably he has taken precautions against that." He picked up a tarnished knife from the shelves, glanced at it, and put it aside. "A knife of pure silver would pierce the spells. And silver causes agony to the undead, besides."

"Then I know what I must do," said Caina, turning to go.

"Fool of a Ghost," said Nicorus. "You will never find the heart. Not before he kills you."

Caina glared at him. "He slew Halfdan. I will make him pay for what he has done, or die trying."

She turned again to go.

Nicorus snarled and gestured with his right hand. There was a gust of wind, and the door slammed shut. Caina whirled, knives in hand.

He smiled at her. "Your foe is a magus of great power. Power enough, perhaps, to restore my lost manhood in exchange for a gift. And perhaps he will even teach me the secrets of immortality . . ."

Caina whipped a knife at his face. The blade struck his cheek and bounced away, leaving the skin untouched.

"A wardspell," said Nicorus. "Did you think I would take no precautions?"

He gestured again, and an invisible force seized Caina and slammed her against the wall. The breath exploded from her lungs, the knives falling from her hands. She felt her ribs trembling beneath the weight of Nicorus's will.

Nicorus walked past the brazier and retrieved an axe from the shelves. "I can't have you escaping. Your foe wants you alive . . . but I doubt he'll mind if you're missing your fingers. And eyes." He thrust the axe into the smoldering coals, heating its edge.

Caina could not free herself from the crushing force of Nicorus's spell, but she could move her right arm. She seized a heavy book from the shelf and flung it as hard as he could. It missed Nicorus and slammed into the brazier.

The brazier wobbled, tipped, and spilled a wave of hot coals onto Nicorus's legs.

The former master of the Magisterium shrieked as his greasy robes caught flame. The pressure on Caina's chest vanished, and she fell to the floor with a gasp. Nicorus pawed frantically at the flames, and Caina grabbed a jar from the shelves and ripped off the lid.

"You were right," she shouted, "I should have burned his corpse!"

She threw the jar at him. It shattered against his temple, and the clear fluid within erupted into blinding white flames. Nicorus's wails sharpened into agonized screams, and the floor beneath him caught fire. Caina grabbed the tarnished silver knife from the burning shelf, went out the door, and ran as fast as her legs could carry her.

She looked back just in time to see flames erupt from the roof.

Two buildings burned down in one night. The Ghosts were supposed to remain secret. Gods, how Halfdan would have scolded her.

Halfdan. Another wave of grief and rage roared through Caina, and drove her into the night.

ଔଓରେଚ୍ଚ

Nicorus might have betrayed her, but he had told Caina what she needed to know.

There was one place in Marsis where sunlight never came. The city had been conquered and reconquered a dozen times over the centuries, but the grim citadel at its heart still stood. Dark vaults honeycombed the earth below the citadel's courts, and only the Lord Governor held the keys to those lightless dungeons.

But Anabas had been possessed.

The Ghosts knew of a secret way into the citadel through the vaults. Caina had hoped to use it to quietly rid the Empire of Anabas. Now she glided down the dark tunnel, a hooded lantern in one hand, her bare feet making no sound against the damp stone. Soon she came to the vaults. Glistening pillars reflected the lantern's glow, spotted with dark patches of mold. Rusting iron doors stood open in the stone walls, but all of the cells looked empty. Caina heard nothing but dripping water and the rapid throb of her own heart.

Leather rasped against stone.

A young man in a guard's livery stepped from the leftmost cell, a sword in hand. He was unshaven, his mail spotted with rust, his tabard torn and stained. His mouth curled into a rictus grin, and his bloodshot eyes glittered, seeming to glow with their own inner fire.

He raised the sword and began walking towards her.

"I know you," said Caina.

The guard stopped, staring at her.

"Your name was Ryther. You were a magus, a brother of the Magisterium, and you murdered children to fuel your necromancy. I slew you once, but by all the gods it seems that your crimes have earned you another death."

Laughter burst from the guard's lips, the same mad laughter she had heard from Anabas and Halfdan.

"Wretched, clever little Ghost. I had hoped to tell you the truth as I cut the flesh from your bones, but you are clever, aren't you? I've been waiting for you. I thought you might find your way down here."

Caina drew a knife, pulling back her arm to throw.

"Go ahead," said Ryther. "Cut down this flesh. Just as you slew poor drunken Anabas. Just as you butchered that old fool. But I will live again." He laughed at her. "Perhaps I should thank you. I have transcended the flesh, transcended death itself." The rictus grin widened. "But I still owe you a death. You can kill me a dozen, a hundred times, and you will still die in torment at my hand."

"I know you for what you are now," said Caina, "and I will stop you." Kill his stolen flesh, find the enspelled heart, and Ryther would pay for the last time.

"No," said Ryther. "You won't."

He spun his free hand in a circle, and a harsh crimson light burst from his fingers.

The pain struck Caina at once, waves of icy cold flooding into her flesh and bones. She fell to her knees with a trembling shriek. The stone floor felt cold, so cold, and she saw waves of glittering frost creeping across the ceiling and pillars. Caina threw the knife at Ryther, but her shivering wrist sent the blade spinning into the darkness.

"Strange," said Ryther, strolling towards her. "I thought death would strip me of my magical powers. A small price to pay for immortality, of course. But it seems that death only enhances sorcery. Especially the necromantic sciences." He gestured again, and unseen force picked Caina up, floated her through the air towards Ryther.

She tried to curse him, but her teeth chattered too badly.

"This," said Ryther, "is going to be very special." He tossed aside the sword and wrapped his arm around her waist, pulling her close.

"Let . . . let . . . me go . . ." spat Caina, forcing the words through shuddering lips.

"Oh," said Ryther, "I shall, I promise you."

He seized her hair, pulled her face close, and kissed her.

And something dark and cold forced its way between her lips and into her throat. It had no weight, no substance, but Caina still felt it crawling down her throat and reaching for her heart. The guard's body collapsed to the floor, and Caina stumbled back, gagging, as cold fingers dug into her chest.

Ryther's soul. His corrupted, rotting soul.

His voice whispered inside her head.

I haven't decided yet how I'm going to kill you. Or, rather, how you're going to kill yourself. Perhaps you'll douse yourself with oil and set yourself aflame. Or perhaps you'll surrender to the guards and confess to Anabas's murder. They'll crucify you, you know, and you'll hang for days as the birds peck at your . . .

"Get out!" screamed Caina, and her words dissolved into an incoherent snarl. She felt Ryther's will tightening around her muscles, seizing control of her limbs. Desperate, she pawed at her belt. Her shaking hand curled around the dagger she had stolen from Nicorus.

Silver. Nicorus had said silver brought agony to the undead.

Can you stab the immaterial? Ryther's laughter echoed inside her skull. *Your flesh is mine, wretched little Ghost, and you will curse your mother's name before I finish with . . .*

Caina slammed the silver dagger into her left palm. The pain was blinding, but nothing compared to agony of Ryther's will forcing itself into her muscles. The wound sizzled, and black smoke rose from her skin.

And Ryther's gloating dissolved into a wail of surprised pain.

Again Caina stabbed herself, the blade sinking into her forearm, and hissing black smoke rose from the cut. Ryther's mental shriek seemed to split the world, and suddenly Caina was on her knees, gagging. The cold, invisible thing erupted from her lips, fleeing the pain, and Ryther's voice vanished from her skull. Caina blinked, her arm wet with blood, the world spinning around her.

The guard groaned and began to twitch.

Caina staggered to her feet, reeling. The heart, she had to find the heart. But where? Ryther could have hidden it in a thousand places down here. The guard sat up, and Caina saw the crimson glitter in his eyes, the lips twisted in a snarl of fury.

The cell. Ryther had come out of the leftmost cell.

Caina half-ran, half-hobbled towards it, the silver blade dangling from her right hand. She heard Ryther screaming curses at her, heard him stand and retrieve the discarded sword. Caina stumbled through the cell door. A stone coffer sat against one wall, a pulsing red glow flickering from within.

Inside lay Ryther's dead heart. It rested motionless on its side, but it throbbed with a bloody radiance. Ryther came at her, howling curses, and Caina ducked. The sword ripped at her stolen cloak and clanged off the wall.

She fell to her knees and drove the silver dagger into the glowing heart.

The dagger burst into raging white flames. The heart shuddered, the crimson glow winking out. Ryther froze, his eyes bulging. The dagger melted into an arc of molten white, and the dead heart erupted into crackling flames.

Ryther screamed, once, and fell against the wall. His face went slack, the mad glitter fading from his eyes, and Caina felt something cold and invisible erupt from his lips, something that dissolved into nothingness.

"I told you," rasped Caina, leaning on the stone coffer, "that you deserved to die twice."

The guard's eyes focused on her.

"Who . . . who are you?" he said. His voice had changed, and now he looked and sounded like a terrified young man. "I . . . I had the most horrible dream, there was a terrible voice in my head . . ."

Caina said nothing and limped away, and the guard made no attempt to stop her.

ⳤⲢ℥Ⲟ℘

Two days later, Caina burned Halfdan's pawnshop to the ground.

The guards still searched the city, seeking Anna Callenius, but no one thought to stop a tired beggar woman in a ragged cloak, her mangled left arm wrapped tight in bandages.

From the safety of an alley, Caina watched Halfdan's pyre, watched the guardsmen scramble with buckets to put out the flames. She touched one of the daggers hidden beneath her cloak, Halfdan's dagger, taken in his memory. Her teacher was dead, but she was still a Ghost of the Empire. There were still men like Ryther in the Empire.

And in Halfdan's memory she would stop them.

Caina turned and disappeared into the crowds.

THE FROG'S PRINCESS

by Kristin Noone

This story is an interesting twist on "The Princess and the Frog" by the Brothers Grimm. Kristin's not the only one playing with the story this year; Disney's December 2009 release is currently called *The Princess and the Frog*, although last year's press release called it *The Frog Princess*, and the heroine's name appears to have changed at least once so far. I don't know why changing humans into frogs (and vice versa) is such a frequent theme in stories—despite the fact I've done it once or twice (it was two stories, in different worlds, but the same frog/prince). Why frogs? Admittedly, there appears to be a belief that frogs can sound like humans, running from Aristophanes' play *The Frogs* (405 BC) to the Budweiser television commercial (1995), but is that enough to explain it?

Kristin Noone is a graduate student at the University of California, Riverside, where she is studying the interactions of medieval literature, fantasy, and science fiction. Her academic writing has covered ghosts, Robin Hood, Beowulf, and medieval romance, and her previous short story "Stitches" appears in the anthology *Strange Worlds of Lunacy*. She lives in Riverside, California, with a black cat named Percival and a houseful of books, and is currently working on a novel, especially when she needs a break from doing research. To the best of her knowledge, her boyfriend has never been a frog.

The princess Andrina Elisabetta Gwenelyn sat in the long weeds next to the moat, heedless of her elaborate gown, and wished that she might never be found.

The moat was overgrown, choked with water-rushes and dark swampy plants. The water lurked, sullen and black and ominous, around them. It refused, contrary to all logic, to catch even the faintest hints of the setting sun.

The setting suited her mood, just then. She had fled the glittering dining hall earlier, the place filled with servants in their best livery and silver bearing only a touch of tarnish, and her father's plaintive calls of "Andrina!" had chased her out into the grounds.

Andrie curled her feet up in the damp grass, and rested her head on her arms. She missed her mother—not because Signy had been a particularly loving parent, but because she never would have arranged a marriage for her daughter, without her consent, to the prince of some foreign country. And Signy would have argued to keep her child at home for reasons of her own.

Home, Andrie thought. Home was a lie. The brilliant facade her father had devised to impress the foreign prince would fool no one. King Therin had lost all interest in running the estate—much less the kingdom—after losing his queen, and the servants had responded accordingly. The sorry state of the moat was only the most external of the signs.

Perhaps, she thought, without much hope, the prince would simply arrive, take one look at the crumbling kingdom, and run off into the night. That would be a happier ending.

But it was unlikely. Her father wanted the match, and the young man came from a large and extremely powerful country. If he'd chosen Andrie as his bride, no one would wish to try to dissuade him.

Except Andrie herself, whose objections to her rushed engagement with a stranger had been brushed aside "for the good of the kingdom." The worst part of it was that she knew it was true. The marriage would help her decrepit home, bringing it a powerful ally. Young Prince Nial was not only the heir to the throne of the neighboring kingdom, but an impressive magician in his own right. He'd been trained by Andrie's own mother, after all.

She wondered why he'd been so insistent on wedding her. She was no great beauty or wit; her brown-gold hair and gray-blue eyes were pretty enough, but no one had ever been moved to write poetry in her honor. While she was fairly intelligent, a near-encyclopedic knowledge of literature and philosophy was not the kind of thing one married for. And if he expected her to live up to Signy's legendary scintillating wit, he'd be sadly disappointed.

Of course, there were other things he might be expecting from Signy's daughter, but that story at least was well known. Everyone had heard what a pity it was, that the beautiful, brilliant, magical queen had produced a child with next to no trace of her sorceress blood.

Andrie, thinking about her mother, slipped one hand into her pocket, and pulled out the small golden ball she carried. It had been the last thing Signy had given to her. Supposedly it had magical powers—Signy had never given up on her hopes for her daughter—but Andrie had never been able to make it work. She had never been able to make a single spell work, really, and she kept the little golden ball mostly as a reminder, a memento of her mother.

Signy, she suspected, had been baffled by her daughter, that strange plain unmagical creature, and though she had loved her child, it had been across a distance that neither of them knew how to bridge. Andrie had mourned her mother, but more in the way of a distant aunt or grandparent; someone she'd never really known, who'd never quite known her.

Idly, she began to toss the golden ball from hand to hand over the murky water. It wasn't so much that she missed her mother; she missed the way the world had been with her mother around.

Signy had been able to charm birds from the trees, to calm a raging wildfire, to change her own shape and wear animals' skins. That was how Therin had first seen her: a stunningly lovely golden doe, running through the woods. He had fallen in love with her the moment she stopped and spoke to him, her shape transforming with her passions, into a perfect woman. And Signy had loved him in return, seeing in him the perfect partner, the young and handsome king of a wild forest country. Their courtship and wedding had been the stuff of fairy tales, and the court for years afterward had been a center of magic and lore. Men and women came to study with the sorceress-queen, or to exchange knowledge, or simply to say that they had been there when they returned home. The palace had been a whirl of scholars, of magic, of the lore and art and imagination of all the kingdoms. It had been beautiful.

The whole kingdom—indeed, all of the ten kingdoms—had rejoiced when Signy had given birth to a child. Surely this was cause for great celebration. Surely the daughter would prove herself worthy of such outstanding parentage. Even when those hopes had proved false, the child's lack of aptitude for magic hadn't dulled the brightness of those days. And Andrie herself had enjoyed it, watching from the sidelines like an audience for the world's most luminous pageant. The knowledge of her own deficiency had stung a bit, as if she'd been born with no voice to the world's greatest minstrel. But she'd always found a sort of bright-eyed consolation in her place beside the epicenter of magic and brilliance that was her mother's life, the view from inside that charmed circle.

Andrie sighed, and flipped the ball into her other hand. The small solid weight of it was reassuring somehow.

She had wanted for nothing; both her parents loved her, in their different ways. Therin adored her because she was a reflection of his bride, his queen, and because she shared his interest in ancient books and scholars' lore. Sometimes he seemed to forget that she was only a child, speaking to her with all the animated passion of one of his philosophers. Sometimes he seemed not to realize that she was *his* child; she knew that he cared for her, but suspected from a young age that he did not understand who or what she was. Signy had loved her daughter instinctively, like a real mother; but that gulf of ability had stretched between them like a chasm neither of them could cross. Signy had always believed that her daughter must be like her; she had believed it so strongly that there was no room in her mind for any other conception. But she had been as fiercely possessive of her child as a mother wolf, and never, Andrie thought, would have allowed a foreign prince—even one of her own students—to take that child away.

It hadn't been a perfect existence; Andrie knew that much. She had known it at the time. But it had been lovely nonetheless.

She gazed at the perfectly polished golden surface of the ball as it sat in her palm, smooth and blank and revealing nothing, and tossed it into the air.

That glittering, enticing life had vanished, like enchanted smoke, when Signy had died.

Therin had secluded himself for weeks in his apartments, and refused to see anyone, even his child; when he had emerged, he was a changed man. He took no interest in anything; he had to be reminded to eat, to bathe. The running of the kingdom was left to ministers, some good, some bad, who let the orderly nation fall into disarray. The salons and scholars and students trickled away, not all at once, but slowly, over the years. The few servants that remained did so out of compassion, or misplaced loyalty, or simply because they had nowhere else to go; but they were not enough to prevent the slow decay of time. The castle, like everything else, suffered now from years of neglect.

She had fled the dinner tonight because she couldn't bear to smile and see her father pretend that everything was well, ignoring or refusing to see the tarnish all around him.

Unthinkingly, Andrie tossed her ball a little too hard, and missed the catch. It bounced off her fingertips, hit the bank, and splashed down into the moat.

"Oh, *drat*," she said out loud, with feeling, and glared at the disgusting water. "Oh, no . . ."

As she sat contemplating the relative merits of removing her shoes and stockings and wading into the muck, a sudden voice from the reeds said, "Don't worry, princess," and Andrie jumped.

"Who's there?"

"Only me, I'm afraid." A small frog, bright green and slimy with the moat-water, hopped up on the bank beside her, and blinked wide frog eyes at her.

Andrie stared. Surely not. Perhaps she had dozed off and was dreaming. Things like that never happened to her. To Signy, maybe; surely in a sorceress's world animals spoke all the time. But not to her mundane little daughter.

"I didn't mean to startle you." The frog looked sheepish, if such a word could be applied to an amphibian.

"I—er—it's all right," Andrie managed, years of courtly politeness coming to her aid. *Always be elegant*, Signy had said, *and mysterious if you can. If you cannot, you can at least be courteous.* Andrie was not elegant and would certainly never manage mysterious, but courtesy she could offer. "I was just surprised. I've never spoken to a frog before."

"For the most part, it's terribly boring," the frog said politely. "Flies, flies, and more flies . . . would you like your ball back?"

"Yes, please." Andrie watched as the frog launched itself off the bank, doing a neat little leap into the water; it was out of sight shortly, obscured by darkness. After a few moments, it reappeared, the shining gold of her ball stretching its wide mouth.

It dropped the ball into her outstretched hand, and sighed. "Ah, much better."

"Thank you," Andrie said, and added, a bit timidly, "is there anything I can do for you?" She hadn't spent years at her mother's court for nothing; magical creatures could be tricky or easily offended, and she wanted to be on good terms with this one.

Besides, it might be the only magical encounter she would ever have: she wanted it to last.

"Actually, there is." The frog blinked at her. "I would like to return to the palace with you, if I might."

Andrie couldn't for a moment imagine why a frog would want to see the crumbling palace; she gazed at it for a minute, astonished. There was an odd twinge of emotion beneath the surprise, something that it took her a minute to recognize as embarrassment. She had loved her home once; the thought of showing it as it was now to anyone, even an enchanted frog, sent a small pain into her heart. She said, stalling for time, "Why?" and then, thinking that perhaps that had come out a bit rude, added, "I mean, there's not—there's no magic left—" realizing that an enchanted creature might have heard of the sparkling heyday of Signy's court as a place to find refuge.

"My own reasons," the frog said. "Don't worry, princess. I know."

But you're only a frog, Andrie thought. A magical frog, who seemed to know a great deal about the state of her family and her home, and it was just a bit suspect that a magical helper would turn up at the moment when she needed one anyway. What reasons would a frog have for coming to her home?

But she had offered, so she nodded and agreed. In all of Signy's stories, it was never wise to offend a magical creature; they were notoriously capricious, and after all, this one had done her a favor. She couldn't very well deny it one simple request. And surely if it meant her harm, it would not have helped her or spoken so politely.

Besides, Andrie thought with a flash of inner cynicism, just about anything it could do to her would be a welcome alternative to her looming wedding plans.

She sighed. More than likely no one would notice her carrying a frog into the palace anyway; she was mostly left to her own devices, except when her father wanted her, as he had tonight. Even when her old governess had left, no one had bothered about finding a replacement.

She looked up at the setting sun and shivered. Suddenly, the edge of the dark water felt a lot colder.

She held out her hand and said, "Shall we?"

ങ‍റ‍ള‍ൊ‍ഞ

A‍ndrie carried the frog up to the castle nestled in her pocket, against the cool round curve of the golden ball. It remained quiet and quiescent the whole way, and she might have started to wonder whether she'd dreamt the whole conversation if not for the indubitable presence of Signy's ball, returned to her, a solid shape brushing against her leg through the fabric of her skirt.

She let herself in through a side door, avoiding the great portraits of Signy that gazed down at her with painted eyes, and drifted, like a ghost in the palace byways, up through the cold stone corridors. The few servants that had stayed were all downstairs, clustered by the lingering warmth of the kitchen ovens; she passed no one, only cobwebs and dried candle wicks, leaning drunkenly in their settings. Her shoes made small puffs of dust as she walked. No one bothered to clean anymore; there was no pride left in the castle. No pride left in her father.

Andrie followed her own footprints up to her room, and closed the door behind her with a sigh of relief. Here, at least, the tarnish hadn't yet reached: the whitewashed walls were still bright and clean, and the tapestries that adorned them glittered with warm color. It was not a large room, but it was cozy, thick rugs warming her feet and walls lined with leather-bound books.

She kept it neat herself; the maid whose job it was to wait on her princess could barely be bothered to light the fire in the mornings. Compared to the rest of the castle, it felt like heaven.

She fished the frog out of her pocket, and set it on the burgundy counterpane covering her bed. It blinked at her; the bright green of its skin showed up absurdly against the silk. It said nothing.

Andrie sat down next to it, thinking that perhaps she had just temporarily taken leave of her senses. She certainly felt foolish.

The frog said, quite suddenly, "You have a very nice room," and Andrie jumped.

"My apologies," the frog said. "Forgive the social awkwardness, princess. It has been . . . a long time since I've had a conversation with anyone human."

"You weren't always a frog, then?" Andrie tucked her feet up under herself, getting comfortable. It was a horribly unladylike posture, but she doubted the frog would care. Besides, her toes were cold.

"No," said the frog and then was silent for a minute. Andrie wondered if perhaps she had offended it. She was unsure how one expressed sympathy for an enchanted creature; should she offer to help, or simply apologize? Signy, she thought, would have known. But this was her adventure.

"Tell me," the frog said, "about your prince. The one who's coming tomorrow to marry you: what's he like?"

"He's not *my* prince," Andrie said and scowled. "And how did you know about that, anyway?"

"One hears things," the frog said vaguely. "Do you dislike him?"

"I don't dislike him. I don't *like* him. But I certainly dislike the idea of marrying him."

The frog made what might have been a small amused amphibian noise, but remained silent when Andrie glanced at it. "He's not objectionable personally," she went on. "He's young, handsome, a magician . . . he used to come to Mother's salons when we were younger. Arrogant, though. As if he always knew he would be a great sorcerer." She thought about Prince Nial for a minute. She hadn't seen him for years, but she remembered that aura of haughtiness he wore like a cloak, shielding him from the world. He had always been polite to her, but never friendly. Charitably, she'd hoped that perhaps he was just uncomfortable with strangers.

"He became the heir to his kingdom when his brother vanished last year," she went on. "Everyone looked for Prince Colin; even Father managed to send a few scouts out to help. I remember hoping for word—I always liked Colin." Actually, she had more than liked Colin; the times she'd met him, coming to visit his younger brother in Signy's court, he'd been kind to her. He'd been one of the few people she'd ever met who saw her as an interesting person simply because she was herself, not because she was the child of the most famous sorceress in ten kingdoms. She'd thought Colin had understood; after all, it was his younger sibling who garnered all the praise for his magical abilities, while the heir to the throne, like Andrie, could barely light a candle.

She had even hoped that someday, perhaps, their parents might see the benefits of a betrothal. It would have been a great alliance, uniting two of the largest and most powerful kingdoms.

Now, when it had finally come to pass, the wrong prince would be standing beside her.

Lots of things had gone wrong, it seemed, in the last few years.

She got up, distracting herself, and slipped out of the muddied gown, changing into one of the thick warm nightdresses from her closet. They were all a few years out of date; no one was left in the palace who cared about such things.

The frog said, interrupting her thoughts with surprising interest in its voice, "So you *don't* wish to marry your prince?"

Andrie scowled at it. "Didn't I already answer that?"

The frog blinked at her.

She sighed. "No, I don't." Andrie should have felt uncomfortable confiding her personal secrets to an amphibious creature, but somehow she didn't. The frog was surprisingly easy to talk to. Besides, it had been a very long time since she'd had a friend.

"Most princesses would jump at the offer," she said, "for the chance to marry a magician, to be a queen, to have everything we're told we should want. But no one ever asked me whether I wanted to marry him. No one asked me anything at all."

"Perhaps your father thinks he's providing for you."

"I'm sure he does," Andrie agreed, "but he doesn't know what I want. He barely knows I'm here, half the time." And she remembered, like a ghost rising palely out of memory, the long silent banquet earlier that evening, with no conversation but the clink of tarnished silver until King Therin had announced the arrival of her bridegroom the next day.

"What *do* you want?" the frog asked her, not flippantly, but seriously, as if it really wanted to know.

Andrie started to answer and then stopped and thought. It was a question she hadn't quite considered, except in abstract terms of nameless longing for things to be different.

"I want," she said finally, "to be wanted for myself, not because I'm a princess or a sorceress's daughter. If I have to get married, I want it to be to someone who cares enough to speak to me before announcing our betrothal. I want my father to be my father again and a king again." She stopped. "I wish I could fix things."

"Hmmm," said the frog.

Andrie looked at it, but it volunteered nothing more.

After a minute, she asked, "What do *you* want?" rather timidly, realizing that maybe she had been selfish in whining about her palace life to an enchanted creature trapped in a green body.

The frog blinked at her again. "Bring me to the hall tomorrow," it requested, "when your bridegroom arrives."

Andrie wasn't sure what she had been expecting, but that certainly wasn't it. "Why?" she said before she could stop herself.

"I think perhaps I can help both of us," the frog said mysteriously. "Trust me, princess." And it refused to say any more, hopping over to her dresser and settling down on the cool marble. She offered it a blanket, and it thanked her politely but absently and then lapsed back into silence.

Eventually, Andrie gave up on it and tried to go to sleep. Tomorrow, she thought, would be an eventful day, one way or another. She fully expected to remain awake all night worrying about her arriving bridegroom and whatever the ensorcelled amphibian was planning, but to her surprise she found herself oddly relaxed. It was almost comforting to have some other presence in the room, as there hadn't been since she was a small child. It felt like having a friend.

Andrie curled into her warm blankets—the tower room was drafty—and drifted off, watching the gleam of the frog's dark eyes from atop her dressing table.

ය‌ⲢⳞⲞ‌ⅇ

Surprised whispers spread across the hall as she entered the next morning. Andrie had dressed carefully for the occasion, in her favorite color, a gown somewhere between silver and periwinkle, almost the shade of her eyes. The clothing was a kind of armor; she knew that she looked more mature, almost elegant, a real princess. She needed that strength.

The eyes weren't on her, but on the creature she held, its bright green skin displayed ludicrously against her pale dress as it peeked out from her pocket. At least, Andrie thought, amused, they had noticed her this time.

The servants muttered in the background, hovering boldly around to watch the spectacle. The foreign prince's retinue looked at them a bit askance, no doubt troubled by the lack of discipline, but they stared at the princess as well. Andrie guessed that they must be wondering why their lord would be interested in such a strange, plain girl. She was a bit curious about that herself.

Her father eyed her with startled dismay as she stopped and curtseyed. "Andrina," he said faintly, "why do you have that . . . *thing?*"

Andrie looked back at him, hesitated, and finally just shrugged. She did not want to try to explain; she doubted he would understand. Besides, he would give way in the face of her silence. He no longer cared enough to argue with her.

Therin swallowed a little uncomfortably, and she pitied him. But just as she might have spoken, he seemed to decide that it did not matter, and turned, holding out his hand to the young man at his side.

"Prince Nial, my daughter Andrina. Andrina, this is Nial, your betrothed." The words hung oddly in the air, like a portent of some unimaginable event to come.

The young man took a step forward and bowed to her gracefully, like a tawny lion; but his eyes remained strangely fixed on her the entire time, sweeping over her face and form. Andrie had the uncomfortable sensation that she was being measured.

She curtseyed again, because she did not know what else to do, and murmured, "Prince Nial."

One of his hands flickered out, and caught her chin, raising it so that she was forced to look him in the eyes. Andrie wanted to shiver at the touch—his hands were cold—but his fingers were also strong, and she had the impression that they would be capable of enormous cruelty if he chose.

She looked into his eyes, dark as night, cold as sin, like bottomless pools in contrast with the bright gold of his hair.

They remained opaque and unreadable to her, and she felt a shudder of aversion. She could see nothing in those eyes, no love, no compassion, no humanity. He looked at her as he would contemplate any new possession.

Deliberately, she took a step back, freeing herself from his influence. Unexpectedly, he laughed, like a man amused by childish defiance.

"Signy's daughter in spirit, if not in power," he said. "You may do after all." It was the first time she had heard his voice, and the edge of self-satisfied arrogance to it made Andrie sure, if she had had any doubt, that she would never marry him.

Aware of her father hovering like a distracted mother hen around the edges of the conflict, she asked sweetly, "Where is your brother, Prince Nial? Did he not come to see us wed?" It was a shot not quite in the dark; surely Nial at least felt guilty over inheriting in his brother's absence, and surely he also had known of the affection between his brother and his betrothed. It had been an open secret, all those years ago at Signy's court. But Nial had insulted her; she felt the need to fire a return shot.

But she hadn't expected the reaction she received.

His face twisted, growing ugly, something warped shining past the fine features; one of those raptor-quick hands snatched at her arm, fingers pinching, and he whispered, "*My brother was not meant to be king.*"

Andrie jerked herself free of him, and her father took a small hesitant step towards her. The servants, behind them, rustled and murmured uneasily.

With a visible effort, Nial released her, calming himself. "It is a tragedy, of course," he said softly. "But it may after all be better this way. Where should the magicians of the world be, if not in charge? Who better to decide the fate of the world?"

"Anyone would be better than you," Andrie said bluntly, and this time he did not laugh, but took a step toward her, and suddenly seemed to grow in stature, wielding an aura of menace that made her shrink back. She could almost feel the power eddying around him.

Suddenly, perhaps for the first time, she was afraid.

Andrie slipped one hand into her pocket as Nial advanced, and brought it up between them, like a talisman.

The frog hopped out onto her palm, and said calmly, "Hello, Nial."

The prince stared at it. His face changed again, eyes growing wide and black; he whispered, "*Colin,*" and his right hand came up and swept the frog from Andrie's hand, sending it flying across the room.

Andrie screamed.

The frog struck the wall with a violent splat, and Andrie closed her eyes, but opened them again, and caught her breath in shock.

There was no blood, no frog's-skin; the body of the creature seemed to burst open, and a young man, perhaps a bit older than Andrie herself, fell to the floor. He sat up slowly, and the marks of the stone burned brightly against his light skin. He moved gingerly, and Andrie guessed that the impact had been more painful than his stoic expression revealed.

"Colin," Nial whispered again and advanced toward the helpless figure. "Why did you come back? You never should have come here."

Colin, Andrie thought, and remembered the boy she had once known, tall and blond and already showing traces of the king he would be. The boy she had once cared for.

He looked thin and pale next to Nial's blazing fury, white-blond hair falling in his eyes, long after months of enchanted imprisonment. But he was alive. She thought: he came to help me. He had cared for her, and he had come to save her. No one else had.

But it had gone wrong; they were in his brother's power now. Neither of them could fight a magician.

"Why did you come here?" Nial demanded once more, standing over his brother. The power gathering around him was almost palpable. "You were safely out of the way. I would have had the kingdom—both kingdoms—and Signy's daughter— everything a mage should have, everything I've deserved—"

From the floor, Colin met his brother's crazed glare calmly. "None of those things were ever yours to take, Nial."

"*You want the girl for yourself!*" Nial shrieked. "You want me to have nothing!"

"That isn't true." Colin shifted position, moving as if it hurt; his brother twitched, ready to act, ready to be provoked. Colin stopped trying to stand up, and remained still.

"You have always stood in my way," Nial breathed. "I thought I had disposed of you. I thought I had been *kind*. But," he added, expression turning satisfied, "not this time. I will kill you, this time. That way you can never interfere with me again, *brother*."

He lifted his hands, and Andrie could *see* the magic swirling and eddying around them, dark red and vicious. Colin remained focused on his brother, as if he could make the younger man sane by will alone.

He put out a hand, perhaps to plead with his brother, or to restrain him; Nial stiffened and drew a breath, preparing to fling his spell of death.

Without thinking, without considering, Andrie grabbed her mother's golden ball from her pocket, where she had held the frog, and flung it at his head.

Her aim was poor, from anger or fear or simple shock; the throw missed, and the ball struck near Nial's feet. He looked her way, and laughed.

But the ball had cracked against the solid flagstones, and a sort of shimmering golden vapor was rising from it, swirling and solidifying, wrapping itself around Nial. His expression went from amused triumph to astonishment, and he brushed at the clinging mist futilely.

A serving girl, in the background, gasped and dropped a tray of bread. The clatter was oddly muted in the sudden silence.

The otherworldly shimmer wound its way up towards his head, and in the changing hues of the mist Andrie thought she saw a familiar face.

Nial saw it too; he went white, as though seeing a ghost, and tried to step backward in horror, but the strange golden fog held him fast. He could no longer move, not even his arms; his eyes darted, seeking some escape, and his lips moved as if attempting a spell, but nothing happened.

Signy's voice filled the room, cool and clear as ever. "My greatest student," she said simply, and then the moving gold crept over Nial's face, obscuring him.

When it thinned and faded, there was nothing left of the man.

The beautiful face of Signy, limned eerily in the shimmering gold, turned toward Andrie, who stood frozen in place. Watching her, Colin slowly pushed himself to his feet, and limped to her side.

"Daughter," Signy whispered, and small drifting tendrils of gold reached out for her child.

But Andrie shrank back, like an animal frightened by a trap, and felt the reassuring human warmth of Colin's hands on her shoulders. "No," she whispered to those inviting hands.

"My daughter," the ghost of Signy said again, and Andrie understood that it was offering her all the power at its disposal, all the bright magic she had once coveted and always lacked. She could step into that shining mist, and not be consumed by it. She would come out a magician, as her mother had been. As Nial had been. It was what her mother had always wanted for her; it was all the power and glory Andrie should have had. Signy would protect her and guide her as the magic entered into her, filling her up like light, like wine. She could at last be a sorceress; she could have all the magic she had never known.

But she saw again, clearly, the man fading into nothingness before her eyes, and she sensed Colin's presence at her back, and her father, gazing spellbound at the illusion of his dead wife across the hall.

She straightened and said again, "No. I'm not you, mother."

And Signy smiled, but it was the same smile she had always used on her daughter in life: fond, but baffled, exasperated, uncomprehending. She truly couldn't understand.

For the first time in her life, Andrie felt a small pang of pity for her mother.

She started to speak, but the image of Signy turned insubstantial, flickering, and disappeared into the gold. The swirling eddies collapsed inward, falling into a tiny heap of aureate sand on the floor. Even that slowly trickled away, into the cracks between the stones. Finally, there was nothing left but silence.

Andrie looked up and saw her father moving forward blindly, groping after the vanished image. His face was blank, save for a desperate yearning.

Gently, she put out a hand to restrain him and said, "Father. Let her go."

Therin blinked at her touch, as if waking from a dream, and focused on his daughter, perhaps for the first time in years. "Andrina?"

"Yes," Andrie told him, and saw some measure of comprehension in his eyes.

Therin looked past his daughter to the tall fair-haired young man who stood beside her. "I know you," he said, and Colin nodded.

"I used to visit my—my brother, here. Sir. When we were young."

Andrie saw the faint shadow that crossed his face at the word, and slipped her hand into his.

Therin glanced at the two hands, and said, surprisingly wryly, "It seems you now have an interest in my daughter instead." It wasn't quite the voice of the king he had been, but it might have been the voice of a man who remembered being a king. "Will you be staying here for a while?"

Colin looked over at her, and smiled a little, hesitant and warm. "If you would like that," he said. "There will be things to do, first—I'll have to go home; the kingdom needs someone who can start fixing all the problems Nial left behind. But I'll come as soon as I can." *Sooner*, his tone promised, and Andrie had the feeling that he meant it. His eyes were the same bright green as the frog's skin, she noticed, beneath his pale hair.

Andrie considered this for a minute. She felt an odd sense of lightness, suddenly, as if the weight of the past had finally been lifted: from her home, from her father, even from herself. She might not be a sorceress, but she thought that she could see, looking ahead, a dizzying number of possible futures.

She looked back at Colin. "Yes," she told him. "I would like that."

SHALOTT'S INN

by Leah Cypess

MZB used to say that the Arthurian legends are the mythos of the English language, the way *The Iliad* and *The Odyssey* are for the Greeks, or El Cid is for the Spanish. Given the large cast of characters surrounding Arthur, and the variety of roles many of them play in different versions of the story, there's certainly a lot of material to work with. This story uses familiar elements: Lancelot, Excalibur, and Elaine—but it adds yet another twist to the legends.

Leah Cypess used to be a practicing attorney in New York and is now a full-time writer in Boston. She much prefers her current situation. She writes adult and young adult fantasy, and enjoys traveling, hiking, and spending time with her husband and daughter. You can learn more about her at www.leahcypess.com.

The rain streamed slantwise across the windy plain, sending thousands of tiny ripples across the black surface of the river. It slashed at the bearded face of the traveler riding the dirt road and ran in quick streams over the crumbling bridge that arched over the frothing water. On the bridge, a girl was crying.

The traveler reined in his horse. From this distance, in the dark, the girl on the bridge looked like a misshapen statue, but he could make out black hair plastered to her head and shoulders. He couldn't see her face, and couldn't have separated tears from raindrops even if he had, but the way she was hunched over told him she was sobbing.

Everything about his training pulled at him to care, to go find out why. But his mare snorted and twisted her neck, and he forced himself to loosen the reins. The fate of his liege far outweighed some country lass's forced marriage or low-born beau.

So he told himself, as sternly as possible, and nudged his horse into a walk.

ଽଌଋଈଔଏ

Elaine showed up at the kitchen right before dinner, her wet hair bound in a neat braid and her cheeks scrubbed clean of tears. She couldn't scrub away the longing in her eyes, but her eyes wouldn't give her away. No one was going to look into them.

She took the loaf of bread the cook gave her and maneuvered her way into the common room, her mind far away—as far as the endless purple mountains she could see through the windows during the day. The mountains of Faerie, where the river with its clear, bright water originated, looked closer than they were. For her they might as well be half a world away. But at least she could see them.

Usually it was enough. When she was younger, it had never been enough; she had spent her time spinning impossible dreams of following the river upward, growing wings and leaving the dingy inn behind her. Now she was older, and tried to focus on the possible, but sometimes she looked at the possible too closely and her focus exploded. It had happened just an hour ago, and she had been unable to stop herself from running out onto the old bridge, in the rain, like a crazy girl, crying and crying for something she could never have. At times she thought her father was right, and she really was crazy.

The common room was even emptier than usual, which mattered not at all. Her father based his rates on the number of guests available to pay them. Since his was the only inn this close to Faerie, his guests had no choice but to pay.

Today there was only one guest: a tall, husky man with a scruffy black beard and very blue eyes. Elaine didn't even try to guess his age. To her, anyone older than twenty was unimaginably ancient. She curtsied and put the loaf of bread on his table.

"Ale, sir?" she said.

Instead of replying, the man leaned back and regarded her steadily. Elaine stared back with frank interest. He had a light, almost invisible scar along the left side of his nose. "What is your name, child?" he asked finally.

"Elaine." She made her voice pleasant, beginning to regain her interest in the here-and-now. He seemed friendly enough, and his scar bespoke previous quests. When he got drunk, he might tell her about them, and she would hear things she wasn't supposed to know about yet. "I'm the innkeeper's daughter."

"Oh, you are, are you? Your father's a highwayman, did you know that? The prices he charges for a meal would bankrupt a baron."

Elaine dimpled at him and said nothing.

"He should be more charitable to me." The man narrowed his eyes at her. "I am a knight."

Elaine was unimpressed. Everyone who stayed at Shalott's Inn was either a knight or a madman; no one else would venture this close to Faerie. Knights were usually more courteous than madmen, though there were exceptions.

The knight eyed her for a moment longer. Then he reached out and broke a chunk of bread off the loaf, crumbling it between his blunt fingers as he brought it to his mouth. He swallowed it in one gulp. "Sir Lancelot," he said. "I follow the boy-king—Arthur. He's only a few years older than you are."

"Oh!" Elaine gasped. "You're the one who—"

"Elaine!" a gravelly voice snapped, and she whirled. Her father was striding across the stone floor. "Are you bothering the good knight? I apologize, sir. Get away now, child—you're needed in the kitchen."

"She isn't bothering me at all," Lancelot said. "I'm enjoying her company. The naivete of a child can be very refreshing after the politics at court." Her father continued scowling, and Lancelot added, "I'll pay you for her time."

"Very well," the innkeeper said grudgingly. Only Elaine saw the tiny smile on his face as he turned away. She wasn't needed in the kitchen, and he wasn't at all annoyed to have her out of the way. It was a ploy they used often.

"That's your father?" Lancelot asked. Elaine nodded. "Does he treat you well?"

"Well enough," Elaine shrugged. Her father didn't have much to do with her, as long as she stayed out of his way. "What kind of quest are you on?"

Lancelot smiled. "I'm going to get a sword."

Elaine blinked. "Already?"

He stared at her. "What do you mean?"

"Nothing." She had seen the sword in her mirror, so vaguely that she had been sure it wasn't coming for years. Of course, it might take the knight years to retrieve it from the lake; time ran strangely in Faerie. "Did you meet the queen yet?"

"What queen?"

"The one King Arthur will marry. Isn't she beautiful?"

He was staring at her oddly, and Elaine realized that, in her eagerness to learn where events stood, she had revealed too much. She flushed and looked down.

Instead of questioning her, Lancelot looked away, toward the rippled-glass window nearest them. The rain was still coming down like a dark waterfall, occasionally pierced by lightning. "Were you born here?" he asked.

Elaine blinked, surprised. "Yes."

"I've never met anyone born so close to Faerie. Is it strange here?"

"I don't know," Elaine said. "I've never been anywhere else."

He grinned at her. "Never? Wouldn't you like to see Camelot?"

"No," Elaine said. She had heard much about Camelot, city of towers and royalty, from all the knights and princes. Some of them, after a few cups of ale, could wax quite poetic about the famous city. If she saw it, she might be impressed . . . and if she was impressed by its purely human elegance, she would lose something. She wasn't sure what, but she knew instinctively that Camelot was not for her.

"You don't know what you're missing," Lancelot said. "I know many ladies-in-waiting who could use a smart, pretty girl like you as a maidservant. You'd have an easier life there, and a future, too. I'll speak to your father about it."

Elaine saw that he would, and that she would be the recipient of his goodwill whether she liked it or not. She didn't argue, just lowered her eyes and said, "Thank you. You should probably wait until you've finished your quest and are on your way back to Camelot."

"May as well." Lancelot leaned back and yawned. He had finished the entire loaf of bread. "Will you be serving breakfast tomorrow?"

"Maybe."

"If so, I'll see you then. If not, I'll speak to your father when I return from my quest."

Elaine nodded, noting that he'd said "when." Most knights, venturing into Faerie, said "if." But of course, Lancelot was a great knight, famed for his dashing exploits and stunning victories. She just didn't know whether or not they had happened yet.

কেওগভে৪০

That night, she looked into her mirror and thought about Excalibur. The sword appeared instantly, straight and powerful, and she saw that it wasn't vague at all. It was just covered by a thin, fine film of mist that blurred its edges.

The mist was Faerie, which meant the sword was in that shadowy realm, its essence not human. It must have been human-made—faeries didn't mine metal or fashion swords. But Faerie's influence descended through proximity, not through origin. Her mirror had been fashioned in Camelot, but purely human mirrors did not show visions of far-away lands and distant futures. Elaine's mother had been human, but Elaine had lived close to Faerie since the day she was born, and the wild magic that frightened travelers had seeped into her bones.

She saw the sword in the boy-king's hands, covered with bright blood, defending him from his enemies. She saw him wielding it as a man; and as the king grew older, the sword's outlines grew more distinct. Finally the mist was gone, and with it the faerie magic, and then it failed him. . . .

But she never liked to think about that, so she made her mind blank. A skein of thread appeared in the mirror, so large and clear she knew she would see it soon. It shimmered with a color no human had ever put a name to.

Elaine turned from the mirror and went to bed.

ଔଓଃ୬ଠ୫

The next morning, she watched from the window as Lancelot rode away on his white horse, blurred by the drearily persistent drizzle. Then she dressed quickly and ran down to the river that ran from Faerie to Camelot.

It was there on the bank, caught in some jutting tree roots: a skein of fine linen thread, thoroughly soaked. She caught it up with a kind of ecstasy. Two years ago, the cook had promised to teach her to weave, but Elaine hadn't been interested. She hoped the offer was still good.

She looked down at the limp wet bundle in her hand, and knew that—for whatever reason—she had been offered a key.

ଔଔଔଔ

It was a year before she saw Lancelot again.

During that year the wars drew many recruits, and there were fewer knights passing by on the road to Faerie. Elaine worked steadily on her weaving, using threads of every color she could find to produce a vibrant, shapeless web that could never become a wearable garment. The cook despaired of her.

One sunny morning, she looked into her mirror and saw Lancelot, clear and distinct, with a sheathed sword strapped to his back. She knew she didn't have much time.

Her weaving became the center of her life. The faerie skein was almost finished; she worked ceaselessly, knowing now that what she wove was a web to trap souls and take them to Faerie, where they could form whatever bodies they pleased. Her serving became messy and she never helped with the cooking. Her father swore at her often.

And it wasn't enough. Two weeks later Lancelot rode up to the inn, and there were still two handfuls of faerie thread left.

She was in the common room, serving, when he entered. He started to smile, then stopped and stared at her in bewilderment. Elaine froze, a bowl of stew in one hand, as he looked her up and down.

"How old are you?" he demanded.

"Fourteen," Elaine said.

His brow furrowed. "How long have I been gone?"

Then Elaine understood, and felt sudden sympathy. "A year. How long did you think you were gone?"

"Two days," Lancelot muttered, and shuddered. "I was warned, and yet. . . . Faerie is too twisted for me. But it was worth it. For Arthur. I have the sword that will make him a great king."

"Did you see the Lady of the Lake, or just her hand?" Elaine asked curiously. She had never been able to tell; mist shrouded the mirror when she focused on Faerie.

Lancelot looked at her sharply, but all he said was, "Where's your father? I want to discuss taking you to Camelot."

"He'll make you pay a lot," Elaine said, knowing the ploy wouldn't work even as she said it.

Lancelot smiled thinly. "I can handle him."

She pointed him to the kitchen, where her father was annoying the cook, and fled upstairs. The loom was waiting for her. She pushed her chest of clothes against her door and began to weave.

The sun brightened into noon and faded into dusk, and still she wove. The moon faded in and out of wispy clouds. She worked feverishly, eyes bright, feeling wrapped in a dream. She had to finish before morning, before Camelot. No amount of magic thread would help her once her soul had felt the touch of purely human splendor.

She finished as the sun was rising, a faded pink above the river. What she had woven was uneven and haphazard, ends unraveling already. But the faerie thread ran through it.

She stood, and uncertainty hit her.

She moved to the mirror and stared into it, looking for a reason . . . and it came. She saw herself riding with Lancelot to Camelot, gaping with childlike awe at its magnificence. A beautiful lady with ice-blonde hair took her as a maidservant, and she learned to love the feel of silk and velvet. She grew up beautiful—and Lancelot, watching her grow up, fell in love with her.

They would be happy forever. Happy and utterly human. Lancelot would never cast a longing glance in the direction of his liege's queen. And without the first spark of discord that cracked Arthur's utopia, his kingdom would last forever.

Then Elaine knew what it was the faeries wanted to prevent—why they had sent a colorful skein floating down the river. Why they had handed her soul an escape, and a key. She was fated to go to Camelot, but fate could cut two ways.

She saw herself and Lancelot, utterly content, and still she didn't move. It would mean the end of Faerie, for Arthur's peace and tolerance seduced the humans away from the worship of Faerie as no persecution ever could. It would mean the loss of something precious deep within her. But she would forget. And she would live the type of life she had never even dared dream about.

She looked away from the mirror, and when she looked back she saw only her own face staring back at her. But her face was dim and blurry . . . as if covered with a fine film of mist.

Elaine draped the web over one arm, pulled the wardrobe away from the door, and crept quietly down the stairs.

CB CR SO BO

He found her almost by accident, after five days of hard riding, when he took his horse to the river to drink. The little wooden rowboat had drifted onto the banks, just within the city borders; she lay in it so pale and silent he knew she was dead. An ugly, gaudy blanket was wrapped around her, and her lips were curved in a smile.

Lancelot fought against irrational tears. He had only spoken to her twice, after all. He had taken an interest in her, but she hadn't been his responsibility. It had been chivalrous but foolish to concern himself with a girl he hardly knew, and it wasn't his fault he had failed to protect her from her father. Or the faeries. Or herself.

The sword was heavy on his back, reminding him of his true mission: to make sure Arthur's kingdom would last forever. After Excalibur was delivered, he could return and make sure the girl was properly buried.

It's a shame, he thought, looking at her still face. *She would have been a real beauty when she grew up.*

Then he swung back onto his horse and rode into Camelot.

WOLF MAIDEN

by Linda L. Donahue

Another animal popular in fantasy is the wolf. They also appear in other genres such as mystery and romance. Sometimes I think if I see one more romance novel where the hero is a werewolf I'm going to throw it across the room. I lived with a dog who was a wolf/malamute/shepherd mix, and she was a wonderful companion, but she shed enough hair each week to make a duplicate of her. (It's a good thing we had hardwood floors; we would never have gotten all the fur out of carpeting.) But there are wolves, and then there are Wolves.

Linda Donahue, an Air Force brat, spent much of her childhood traveling. For 18 years, she taught computer science, mathematics, and aviation. She's earned a pilot's certification, a SCUBA certification, and a driver's license. As such, she has been a threat by land, air, and sea. When not writing, she teaches tai chi and belly dancing. Linda's stories can be found in various anthologies. She also coauthored a story with Mike Resnick for *Future Americas*. In non-fiction, her article on rabbit chiropractics appears in the 2007 *Rabbits USA* annual. She and her husband live in Texas and keep rabbits, sugar gliders and a cat for pets. Though she had once had a long-haired German Shepherd that looked like a wolf, she's never kept a wolf as a pet.

Asdis carried the ale-horn reverently, without losing a drop of froth. Tonight Wolf's Head village celebrated a new alliance. The fair Ilsa had married Dreng, son of a powerful jarl from an affluent village. For a bride price, Dreng had promised a dozen warriors to defend the village.

Yet a dozen dozen wouldn't replace the men killed or captured by sea ogres. Whenever the wind howled, *they* came in hordes aboard ships of human bones.

Asdis carried the ale, remembering the dead. Among the wolf pelts covering the longhouse's walls hung the helmets of those who had died defending the village. So their ghosts might enjoy the celebration, Asdis poured ale over their helms.

She had lost her father and three brothers to the ogres. Of the youngest, Ulfar, nothing had ever been found. For him, she poured ale on the wooden planks.

Onund grabbed the ale-horn. Drink had given him a complexion to match his bright red beard. "What are you thinking, Wolf Maiden? That's no way to treat Storr's good ale!"

With the men of her family all dead, Asdis and her mother lived in the longhouse. They'd come to be known as Wolf Maiden and Wolf Matron.

"It's for Ulfar," Asdis explained.

Onund sobered and handed back the horn. "Though unseasoned, he was a good man. May his death have been honorable." He wiped his mouth against the back of his three-fingered hand, the thumb and forefinger bit off by an ogre.

"I heard you compliment my ale," Storr said, stroking his braided, blond beard.

"I was lying. It's worse than ox-piss."

Laughing, Storr dragged Onund away for a game of axe throwing.

Asdis considered grabbing an axe and showing them she could throw just as well. Out of necessity women had taken over many a man's chore. Asdis, stoutly built and strong as an ox, had hands better suited to chopping firewood than embroidery. She took on the longhouse's heavy chores while her mother cooked and cleaned.

Storr waved an arm. "Eh, Wolf Maiden? What about you? Care to wager your skills?"

His offer brought a smile, her first since the last storm. Asdis strode towards them until noticing the stranger.

She'd first spotted him after she and her mother had moved into the longhouse. She never knew when he would appear, but every now and again he sat quietly in the corner, eating and drinking his fill. No one but her ever paid him any mind.

"Wolf Maiden? You coming, woman, or aren't you?" Onund called.

Asdis tried not to stare overtly. She waved at Storr and Onund. "Another time." She forced a merry laugh and added, "It wouldn't be a fair contest until I've caught up to you in ale!"

"There's a sensible-speaking woman," Storr said. "Have three and we'll call it even!"

"You've had six," Asdis's mother said, pouring him a seventh.

The stranger's smooth and pretty face made him seem harmless. So perhaps no one cared to notice him.

"Seeing as your daughter's a woman, three should be fair," Storr argued.

"I won't argue my daughter's gender but she's easily a stone heavier than you and on her it's all muscle!" Asdis's mother jabbed Storr's soft gut with her finger.

"You foul-tongued she-wolf, how you wound me." Storr staggered, feigning insult. With six ales sloshing inside him, his staggers were quite authentic. And he managed not to spill a drop of ale.

"Play your game," Asdis said. "I'll challenge the winner."

In the meanwhile, she filled her ale-horn and pretended to drink while gazing over the rim at the pretty stranger.

Never had he boasted with the men or competed in axe throwing. He caused no fights and joined none—not even wrestling matches. No wonder no one noticed him.

The longhouse door opened. Old Vorbrynja entered. A gust seemed to carry her old bones across the floor more so than the strength of her skinny legs. She sat at the wedding table and took Ilsa's and Dreng's hands.

The longhouse fell silent and still. Ale-horns remained in tight grips. No more sounds of an axe splintering wood as it struck a post. Not even whispers disturbed the smoky air.

Vorbrynja threw back her white mane of hair and announced, "They shall have nine strong children! Three daughters and six sons."

The parents of the newlyweds roared with approval and offered toasts to their new kinsman. The merriment resumed, and Storr, even with one half-blind eye, won the match against three-fingered Onund . . . as expected.

Vorbrynja laid a hand on Asdis's arm. "The Wolf Maiden shall save the village with her cubs. When he without a tongue leaves, follow him."

Before Asdis could ask why the Norn seer would shape such a fate for her, Vorbrynja had been spirited away as if carried off by a breeze. One moment Asdis stared into Vorbrynja's cloudy eyes. The next, she stared at the Norn seer's back.

Seers, truly weavers of fate, were chosen by Norns to become Norns themselves. As they aged they grew more powerful until they were no longer mortal, but goddesses.

Saving the village was good . . . yet Asdis had no cubs. She raised no animals whatsoever. If 'cubs' were meant to imply children because she was called 'Wolf Maiden,' then first she needed to marry. Given the lack of prospects, that seemed an unlikely fate for a Norn seer to shape.

As for the man without a tongue . . . Asdis glanced at the quiet stranger. Was that the reason for his silence?

He raised his ale-horn to her then stood, leaving his place neat, as always. He headed for the side door where Asdis carried in firewood. Never before had she seen him leave. Nor had she ever seen him enter. He was simply there.

Asdis ran outside and followed him into the forest.

Though he didn't walk fast, she couldn't catch up. She lengthened her stride. Though his appeared unchanged, the distance between them remained constant. She hurried her steps. Again, he walked at the same rate, and still she grew no closer.

Until suddenly she was beside him. She stopped abruptly, startled and disorientated.

"From here," he said, "the way is mist and rainbows."

So he did have a tongue. Perhaps Old Vorbrynja's words weren't meant to be taken literally.

"Will you walk with me? I wish to show you something."

She'd been told to follow him, so nodding, she stepped with him into the dense fog.

They walked in silence. Tiny rainbows danced within the mist like faerie-lights.

Though she spoke softly, her words reverberated loudly. "Who are you?"

"Forseti."

The god of justice. Had he ever behaved like a mortal man, she might have thought him merely named after the god. "Have I offended the gods?"

Forseti pointed towards a clearing in the mist. A full moon lit the glen, though Asdis was certain the moon was in quarter phase. In traversing the misty trail, they had left the world. It was the only possible explanation.

A pitiful, mangy dog was tied to a stake.

"Will you feed and care for him?" Forseti asked.

"If you wish." Asdis approached the poor animal.

The dog snarled and snapped. His ribs showed through his matted, thinning fur. He strained, pulling at his bonds, yet the flimsy cord bound him.

Forseti was gone.

"How do I get back and can I return on my own?" she called.

Forseti's gentle voice answered, "You know the way. Follow your feet."

Asdis knelt outside the dog's reach, hoping he would calm. So long starved, so long neglected, the dog was now beast, no longer possessing domestic qualities.

She returned through the mist, feeling the path with her feet, stepping where it 'felt' right. Suddenly she stood in the forest at the edge of the vanishing mist.

She ran to the longhouse, gathered a platter of venison, and ran back up the path. The mist reappeared.

Still the dog snarled. She set the platter on the ground and, using a stick, pushed it within reach. Squatting, she watched the malnourished beast eat. He devoured the meal then picked up the platter with his teeth and flung it outward.

⋘⋙

For a week, Asdis slipped away nightly to feed the mangy mutt. His fur grew in rapidly, and flesh filled out his bones. Still he snarled whenever she approached.

Two weeks passed. The dog was beautiful now, his coat thick and grey-black. His eyes, burning with wildness, glowed in the moonlight like yellow suns. His teeth gleamed white. But he was no friendlier.

She squatted, staring at the dog. "I mean you no harm."

"Then free me," the dog answered.

Asdis jumped and ran back through the mist.

The next night, for the first time, she didn't feed the dog. Dogs couldn't speak. Therefore, he was some monster, probably deserving of his fate. Yet she had agreed to care for him. But not tonight.

The next night, her debate continued. Then she saw Forseti sitting in his usual corner.

Asdis strode up boldly. "Why is the dog tied up?"

"Fenris is not my *dog*."

The god of wolves. The god to destroy other gods. So why did the god of justice wish health upon this unnatural creature? Why not let him suffer and starve? But she didn't ask. It wasn't wise to question a god's judgment.

Instead, her heart racing, she asked, "Am I to feed him forever?"

"Do what you believe is right." Forseti raised his empty ale-horn and vanished. "But the storm is coming fast."

Outside, the winds carried a howl, a warning that sea ogres were on the hunt. The wail's pitch told how many ships sailed, for the eerie sound came from wind rushing through skulls. It carried the moaning cries of warriors whose bodies had not been given the proper rites, warriors unable to move into the Halls of the Gods. From the sound, at least three ships traveled towards their shores.

Storr laid a hand on Asdis's shoulder. "They'll be landing soon. Best you and your mother go to my house. You can hide with my family."

"I can wield an axe as well as any man," she said.

Storr grinned broadly. "If my sons grow up to be half the man as you, Asdis, I'll be content."

"You need all the help you can get."

Onund joined them, shaking his head. "It's not in a woman's heart to battle. I'll have no arguments either, even if it is a woman's mind to start them. Chopping wood is easier than hacking off a limb. Wood doesn't fight back." He wiggled his mauled hand. "And it doesn't hunger for human flesh."

Asdis scoffed. "You think I fear for my beauty? I fear more we'll lose the best carpenter in the village."

Onund laughed heartily. "Have no fears for me. You can count on my return. After all, you still owe me a match."

Asdis grinned. "But Storr won the contest."

"Only because he cheated. He used all five of his fingers for gripping the handle."

"I didn't cheat!" Storr handed Onund an axe, adding, "I even used my left hand!"

"But you are left-handed," Onund roared.

They clasped arms and laughed, encouraging the land's spirits to fill their breasts with strength and to steady their hands.

"Go on, girl," Storr said. "My wife's expecting you."

"He's right, Asdis," her mother said, wrapping an arm around her. "I've lost my husband and sons. I'll not lose my daughter too."

A howl rattled the longhouse's timbers.

"Go with your mother, Asdis," Onund said, using her name, meaning he was serious. "If you are killed or taken, who will skin venison and fish or cut wood? The village would be lost without your help."

His words brought to mind those of the old seer, promising that Asdis would save Wolf's Head. But had she meant them the way Onund had?

"Come along, Asdis," her mother urged.

Storr pushed Asdis towards the door.

Wind whipped through her hair as she and her mother leaned into the gusts, heading towards Storr's home.

"I forgot something, mother. Go on ahead. I'll be right behind."

As the howls grew louder, fearful tears glistened in her mother's eyes. Then she nodded. "You are your father's daughter. I will pray to the gods that they do not take you from me as well."

Asdis ran behind the longhouse, grabbed the wood axe, then headed into the forest and mist.

The wolf Fenris sat waiting. "Where were you last night?"

Asdis raised her head, feeling the hairs on her neck prickle. "You're no dog."

"I never said I was. Why did you run?"

"I didn't expect you to speak."

"For that you let me starve a night? That seems hardly just. And you've brought no venison tonight either, but an axe. Do you think to kill me?"

"Are you hungry?"

"I could eat you."

Asdis shivered as if the surrounding mist were of ice crystals. "Is that just repayment for coming to free you?"

"True. It seems unfair, but I might nonetheless."

"Then I won't free you to feast on the most succulent meat you could ever taste."

Fenris's eyes narrowed. "What meat is that?"

"Sea ogre. Why else do you suppose my village hasn't moved when the ogres raid so frequently. Those we kill, we feast upon." None of this was true, but neither did she know for fact that sea ogres tasted bad.

Asdis cocked her head to appear thoughtful and uncertain. "I should leave you bound. It's for the best. If a cord can hold you, you'll fare poorly against ogres, and I would hate to see you harmed. Though you've shown me nothing but aggression, I've grown fond of you."

"Free me and I shall repay your kindness by ridding your village of sea ogres."

"Have I your solemn oath?"

"You do."

Asdis approached slowly. Instead of pulling against his bonds, snarling and baring fangs, Fenris sat patiently, deceptively docile, she was sure.

Tentatively, she stepped across that 'line' that had always separated them, that distance which lay at the end of Fenris's leash. Yet the wolf god sat without a ripple to his lips.

Asdis raised the axe.

It felt suddenly lighter. The blade's golden gleam cast rainbows into the mist. Knowing the gods, or that Forseti approved, Asdis severed the cord.

The wolf swelled to four times his previous size.

"Your legs cannot keep up with me," Fenris said. "Ride upon me so we can save your village and I can snack on ogre flesh."

Asdis climbed astride, his back wider than an ox's.

Fenris ran hard. As he leapt over unseen obstacles, small branches tugged at Asdis's hair and the hem of her plain skirt.

Suddenly they were out of the mist and on the forest trail. Then Fenris stopped.

"The ogres come up from the sea," Asdis said, pointing.

The sounds of fighting, of screams and death's last cry rang out in the distance.

Fenris howled, the sound long and eerie. From all sides, howls answered in return. "My children will help. In return, you must swear an oath that no man, woman or child of your village will ever again hunt my children."

Asdis agreed, knowing she would force the men to honor her word if she had to beat them fair and square in hand-to-hand combat. The villagers could fish and hunt wild boars and deer. Bearskins were as thick and warm as wolf hides.

With one hand holding tight in the dense grey fur and her other gripping the golden axe, Asdis rode Fenris into battle. Scores of wolves trailed in their wake.

Ships made from human bones had run aground. Sea ogres, armed with tridents, daggers of barbed coral, and clubs embedded with shark teeth battled the villagers. Even disarmed, an ogre had sharp teeth, long claws and scaly hide stronger than armor.

Though Dreng had brought a dozen of the finest warriors from his village, already five lay dead, their heavy, ring mail rent as easily as a poor villager's coarse cloth shirt. Of the villagers, another twenty had been slain, including Wolf Head's jarl, Ilsa's father.

Fenris's great jaws closed around an ogre and devoured him whole. As Fenris swung his head to tear apart an ogre, Asdis leaned opposite, cleaving the head off another.

Salty ogre blood sprayed the air.

Asdis and Fenris fought in rhythm, attacking from side to side. While he ate his fill of the sea monsters, she swung the golden axe, cutting head from neck, limb from torso. Those her blow didn't kill outright, the wolves fell upon and finished.

By the end of the battle, Asdis felt as if she'd chopped enough wood to last the whole village a long winter. And Fenris's stomach bulged so much it nearly dragged the ground.

Exhausted, she slid off Fenris and sat on her knees. Blood and mud soaked her skirt. She lacked even the strength to see if Storr or Onund had survived.

Fenris swung his head towards her, his twin-sun eyes burning. "I thank you for my freedom." He bit her arm. "Remember our bargain."

Asdis grabbed the wound which oozed surprisingly little blood given how her heart pounded. Yet Fenris hadn't bitten deeply, only enough to leave a scar. A reminder.

"I would not have forgotten," she said.

"The bite is my gift," Fenris said. "Lift your head and howl."

Suspicious and curious both, Asdis howled. The wolves howled in return. Laughing, she howled louder. Her bloodlust rose. She could see better in the dark. She felt stronger and . . . furry. As she talked, her words were mangled. "What have you done?"

"Now you may speak with my children. Whenever you wish, you may run with them, for their spirit lives in you, as does my child." Fenris bound off, vanishing in the first shadow, his children loping after him.

As she thought on his words, her heartbeat slowed and she felt herself return to normal. She rubbed her stomach. Perhaps it was her imagination, but she felt the stirring of a wolf-god 'cub' inside her.

Vorbrynja's whisper rode the wind. "The first of many great shape-shifting warriors."

Storr approached, hauling a badly wounded Onund. From the gash in Onund's thigh, he would lose the leg.

Dreng dropped to a knee. "Indeed you are the Wolf Maiden, guardian of Wolf's Head."

A cheer rose up, weak in sound, but strong in heart.

"Though you are now jarl, I demand a vow that every villager alive and those not yet born shall never hunt another wolf."

∽❀❀❀❀∾

A sdis hung her golden axe on the longhouse wall above her father's helmet.

Months had passed along with many storms and the ogres hadn't returned. Their bone ships had been dismantled and the remains given proper rites.

Though Asdis sat near the corner nightly, cradling her son with yellow eyes, never again did Forseti return. But sometimes she heard Fenris howl. And some nights, she ran with him.

BLACK MAGIC

by Resa Nelson

This story starts with two classic plot devices: a girl disguising herself as a boy, and a youngster running away to sea. (Is it just a coincidence that the author shares a last name with one of England's greatest naval heroes?) Everyday life at sea is eventful—and dangerous—enough without additional complications. In a story, however, you want complications, and this story certainly has them.

Resa Nelson is the author of *The Dragonslayer's Sword,* a novel about a young female blacksmith who makes swords for dragonslayers, despite her distaste for violence. Nelson is a Clarion graduate and has sold 20 stories to magazines and anthologies. Visit her website at http://resanelson.com.

The 22-year-old woman who called herself George Hall chased the last sheep on the poop deck. George was steady on her feet, despite the ship's pitch. Her recent meal of dry biscuit, pork boiled in salt water, and vinegar-like wine had left a sour taste in her mouth, but the meal held firmly in her belly. She didn't mind chasing sheep or choppy waves. She was just glad to be onboard the *Crown* instead of running a London household.

Last year she'd run away from her father's posh home and the pressure to marry. At that time, she'd already refused six proposals, and her father's patience had grown short. She was expected to bear a huge brood of children and raise them in a well appointed and supervised house, but the thought of such an orderly and predictable future turned her stomach. One day, she'd dressed in the shirt, breeches, and jacket of a seaman (as well as a long strip of muslin to wrap and flatten her chest), slipped away, and never looked back.

She believed she'd been right to run away from her father, but she often missed him, nonetheless.

George was surprised that everyone she met assumed she was a boy. Maybe none of them expected to see a woman dressed this way. She'd been hired to sail on the *Crown*, a merchant ship known as an "Indiaman" of the United East India companies. The *Crown* was a frigate carrying a 500-ton load, 156 men, and a constant fear of pirates, reflected by the fact it was armed with 56 guns. It also bore a mermaid figurehead, believed to house the soul of the ship.

George's heels clattered against the ship's floorboards as she cornered the sheep, then pounced on it. The animal bleated as if being murdered.

"None of that, Sally," George said to the sheep. As the surgeon's assistant, George's job was to help the surgeon when needed and act as barber every eighth day to the crew. Otherwise, she did whatever needed to be done.

Digging her fingers deep into its wool, George dragged Sally the sheep back to her tether. After tying the animal back up, George rubbed her hands together. One of the few things she missed about London was the perfumed oils she'd used to keep her skin soft and supple. The oil that rubbed off Sally's wool was a poor and smelly substitute, but it was better than nothing for her rough, red hands.

"George!"

She spun around to see Mr. Mungo, the first mate, eyeballing her. "Yes, Sir?"

Sporting a stubble-haired face and blonde hair tied back in a ponytail, the corners of Mr. Mungo's mouth curved up in a perpetual smirk. His eyes pierced her soul every time he looked at her. But the only time he'd ever truly frightened her was during her first week on board. It happened when he'd sent for her to report to his cabin late one night. She'd entered to find the bosun's mate naked and snoring in Mr. Mungo's bed. George had averted her eyes. Mr. Mungo had stood quietly, measuring her reaction. Finally, he'd said, "I know your secret. I know who your father is and how much he'd likely pay to get you back home, safe and sound. I reckon he'd give a fortune just to find out you're still alive." He'd paused long enough to let George absorb what he was saying, then added, "Obviously, you'd rather be here than home, so I expect no less of you than any man on the *Crown*." Mr. Mungo had laughed and nodded toward the sleeping boatswain. "Any man excepting him, of course."

Stunned, George had managed to say, "How do you know—"

Instead of answering, Mr. Mungo had smacked her bottom playfully, sending her away with a smirk.

Since that night, George had considered Mr. Mungo a secret friend, even though she never dared tell him so. Instead of telling him about her gratitude, she worked her fingers to the bone to show it.

Now, she stood at attention, ready to obey any command.

"Listen close, Bo Peep," Mr. Mungo said. "There's washing and cooking and mending to be done."

George's heart sank. Back in London, those were tasks she'd set the servants on doing. "Yes, Sir. Right away, Sir."

Just remember, she told herself, if you were in London right now, there'd be no adventure.

She'd longed for adventure since childhood. Her father was a famous London architect and her mother a distant memory. The house George had grown up in was a wonder. In the heart of London, it was a narrow townhouse with five stories.

The main and lower floors were a maze of narrow hallways and tiny rooms, while the upper floors had larger and more conventional rooms. Still, the house was like a rolltop desk, full of secrets. Even better, her father loved all the cultures of the world and was a collector of antiquities, which were stuffed in every nook and cranny.

He'd let George play with most of them when she was a child, and she'd spent hours stalking around the enormous sarcophagus that dominated a tiny room on the main floor, which opened up to several hidden courtyards. She'd pretended to be an Egyptian princess captured by ancient Greeks, whose vases lined the niches above the doorway to the next room. Sometimes she climbed the obelisk in one of the courtyards, believing she could catch the seductive scent of the open sea. George didn't know why the sea called to her. For as long as she could remember, her favorite place was the bathtub, where she'd spend hours pretending she was lounging in the lagoons of Bora Bora or drifting with the tides kissing Sicily.

George had soon learned her romantic notions of sailing the seas were just a fantasy. The work was hard, and the men were crude and stank horribly. Most were treated as little more than property and had to abide to the strict discipline of the Ship's Articles. One day, Erich Sixtus had called Jorgen Jacobsen a Swedish blockhead, and the two pummeled each other until Mr. Mungo stopped them. According to the Ship's Articles, Sixtus was docked a month's wages and given 150 lashes with the cat-o-nine-tail.

That had been a rude awakening, but George had adjusted. This was the second leg of her first journey on the *Crown* between England and India. Her ports of call ranged from Lisbon to Capetown to Ethiopia to Bombay to Calcutta. Once in port, she helped load and unload the most exotic and famous goods of trade in all the world: frankincense, salt-peter, indigo, sugar, pepper, and other spices from India. Then there was ivory and gold from the Dark Continent. And Europe's favorite shipment of all: coffee beans from Persia.

Even on days when George had nothing more exciting to do than clean and sew, her life was still far more exciting than anything she'd ever dreamed it could be.

As she turned, she thought she saw something flash across the vast Atlantic Ocean. She'd gained a reputation for having sharp eyesight. She curled her fingers around the railing, leaning over as if the few inches could give her a closer look.

"George!" Mr. Mungo stomped toward her. "Get to work!"

She pointed toward the horizon. "There's something out there, Mr. Mungo. What if it's pirates?"

"Tell the gunner and take your post," Mr. Mungo said. "We're not far from New Calabar. I'll let the Captain know this may be a good time to change course and replenish supplies."

George nodded, casting one last glance toward the horizon.

രു⊂ഃ൦ഃ൦ഃ

Sailing toward New Calabar, they came across another ship, dead in the water. It was a small ship with three masts. There were no signs of movement, no sound of human voices on the wind.

"I know that ship," Captain Garcia said. He wore a black dress coat and a silk embroidered vest. His white silk stockings and knee breeches were fastened together with silver buckles. "I served on it once."

"The sails," George said softly as she sidled next to Mr. Mungo. "They're pale green." She gasped. "And look—those are stacks made of sailcloth!" As green as the sails, the three columns standing on the other ship's deck served to bring fresh air to the cargo hold at the bottom of the ship.

Worried, George peeked at the captain, who stood on the other side of Mr. Mungo. She'd heard tales that Captain Garcia had been a pirate himself in his young and rowdy days. Everyone knew he might as well have eyes in the back of his head, because he always knew exactly what cargo he had on board and where it was at any given moment. He brooked excuses from no one, and his reputation as a man who protected his shipment was well earned.

Mr. Mungo snorted. "That ship's been vanished for 10 years now. Everyone says, if there's an end to the Earth, that ship fell over it a long time ago." He spat overboard. "Looks like everyone guessed wrong."

Captain Garcia's eyes glazed over like a boy staring through the window of a candy store.

Mr. Mungo waved one hand across the captain's face. "Don't be tempted! It's a ghost ship!"

"Precisely." Captain Garcia grinned, pushing Mr. Mungo's waving hand aside. "Whatever crew sets foot on board first has right to claim it and its shipment."

As the ship drifted closer, George saw the name painted on its side: it was the *Black Magic*, all right. She could also make out its figurehead, a 15-foot tall genii.

Strange, George thought. She'd been startled by the nudity of the *Crown*'s mermaid figurehead at first, but she soon learned that most ships had figureheads of naked women. She also learned that women were bad luck on ship—unless they bared their breasts, which would appease the gods of the sea, especially during storms.

But the *Black Magic*'s figurehead had a dark face framed by a red turban. He was a bare-chested man wearing billowy red pants. His arms were crossed, as if ready to nod his head and grant any wish.

A chill ran down the back of George's throat. What was it about the genii that seemed so familiar to her? Suddenly, she wished she were back in London, curled up in front of the fireplace with a cup of tea.

"Mr. Mungo," George whispered. "Please tell the captain we should continue to New Calabar."

But Mr. Mungo didn't hear her.

Three small boats rowed from the *Crown* to the *Black Magic*. As they drew close, George noticed moss had grown on the ghost ship's masts and sails. That's why they'd looked green from a distance.

The *Black Magic*'s upper deck ran the length of the ship, and its gun deck had five four-pound cannons on each side. Three hatches led from the gun deck down to the 'tween deck and the seamen's quarters. The ship's wheel spun lazily by itself on the quarterdeck, which was built up over the gun deck. The forecastle deck was higher still, with the galley underneath. Two narrow catwalks ran between the forecastle and quarterdeck.

As her shipmates spread out to search the *Black Magic*, George ducked under the quarterdeck and went all the way aft to discover what looked to be the captain's quarters, judging from the fold-up writing desk made of mahogany and the red silk curtains covering the window.

The captain's log was on the floor, its pages open. George scanned it as she picked it up. Judging by the dates, the entry had been made 10 years ago, the time when the ship had vanished. Flipping through the pages, she frowned as she read one of the last entries, written in a hand that didn't match the captain's handwriting. "Ancker's hearing voices again. He says they tell him to stick the daggers he found into the eyes. No one's let him, all knowing the folly of it." Wrinkling her nose in distaste, George put the book on the desk and that's when she discovered a Latin and Algerian Sea Pass. George caught her breath. She'd heard of them but never seen one until now. The pass was proof that the *Black Magic* was Danish property. Written in Danish, English, French, and Latin letters, the paper was a permit that guaranteed safe passage through pirate waters. That way, no seamen from the *Black Magic* could be captured as slaves along the Barbary Coast. All the captain had to do was show the Latin and Algerian Sea Pass, and every pirate ship was obligated to let the *Black Magic* sail through its territory in peace.

She tucked the pass into her waistband. He'd want to see this. And perhaps do a bit of forgery so the *Crown* could use it.

A simple curtain separated the sleeping bunk from the rest of the room. When George pulled it back, her eyes widened and she yelled, "Captain Garcia! Mr. Mungo!"

Moments later, their sharp heels clattered down the hallway, and they squeezed into the room alongside George. She pointed at the pile of human bones on the mattress.

"No good ever comes when you're greeted by death," Mr. Mungo said. Sweat beaded his forehead, and his voice trembled. "I say we're looking at more than a ghost ship. This here's a dead-sure sign of a curse. It's bound to rub off unless we leave right—"

Captain Garcia fished out the skull and examined it. Several back teeth were missing, but the front were made of gold. "Meet Joseph Fetch. We sailed together more than 15 years ago."

Fifteen years, George thought. That's when they say Garcia was a pirate.

Captain Garcia withdrew a sword from his side. Gripping the gold teeth between one thumb and forefinger, he smashed the jaw of the skull with the pommel in his other hand. Pocketing the gold, Captain Garcia smiled and said, "I never liked him much."

A man's scream echoed down the hallway.

George scrambled to keep up with the captain and Mr. Mungo as they headed back down the hallway.

Arno Jansen, the Danish cooper's mate, stumbled out of the mess, pale as sugar.

Plates, silverware, jugs and bottles lay in a heap next to the table dominating the room, which was also full of bones, as if everyone on board had died here.

"If it's not a curse, it could be disease," Mr. Mungo said as he slapped Jansen awake. "We should leave this ship before it's too late."

"We'll check every deck first," Captain Garcia said. "And leave nothing of value behind."

Mr. Mungo caught Arno Jansen as he fainted.

ᘓᘓᘓᘓ

The wooden steps creaked and groaned with every step that George took to the cargo hold below deck. Despite the sailcloth stacks that were supposed to bring in fresh air, the atmosphere was dense and smelled of rust and mold. But when she saw its cargo, she stared in shock. She'd never been onboard a ship like this before. Nothing could have prepared her. Like an anchor being dropped, she sank on a ladder step, too stunned to continue.

The cargo hold was a field of bones and foot irons, below two tiers of wooden shelves that stretched across the hold. Thousands of yellowed bones carpeted the floorboards, squeaking as the motion of the sea made them rub against each other. They gleamed eerily in the dim light filtered through the small inverted glass pyramids embedded in the deck above, designed to carry light down below. With nothing left to bind each skeleton together, the bones were loose and scattered. Woven among the bones were chains and shackles.

The *Black Magic* was a slave ship.

George swallowed hard. She'd heard stories from other seamen about how they crammed human cargo into a ship's depths, chaining them together and making them lie down, shoulder to shoulder, in rows and on shelves stacked only 18 inches high. She'd heard when one came down ill, that illness spread so fast that by the time the ship arrived at port, the captain was happy if a third of his cargo and crew was still alive. Assuming the captain himself was still alive, as well.

Was that what had happened here? Had all these people died and the crew along with them, leaving the *Black Magic* to drift for ten years at sea?

She jumped at a deafening crack from high above.

George froze, craning her neck to catch a glimpse of anything through the open steps to the next deck up. It couldn't have been lightning. Just moments ago, the sea had been calm and the sky clear.

Then something boomed as it crashed into the ocean, and waves rocked the ship. Heavy footsteps rained from high above, and men cried unintelligible commands.

George jumped to her feet and raced upward until she reached the top deck. "What happened?" She panted. "What's wrong?"

Her shipmates were scattered across the deck, inspecting every final nook and cranny. Only Mr. Mungo took the time to give her a quizzical look.

George ran up to him. "That sound . . . what was it?"

Mr. Mungo looked at her blankly. "What sound?"

George checked the skies. They were still clear and blue. She glanced around the deck. The masts were still in place, as were the sails and the sailcloth stacks. Nothing seemed out of order. "I heard something heavy fall into the sea."

"No one dropped anchor."

"I know what an anchor sounds like. It wasn't metal—it was larger and heavier. Almost like the sound of a figurehead falling." Automatically, George turned to check the ship's bow.

One of the men had climbed onto the figurehead. Like a boy riding his father's shoulders, the seaman straddled the wooden genii's neck, holding onto his painted turban with one hand while reaching around to the figurehead's face with the other. The seaman yelped with joy as his hand yanked away something that gleamed. As he clambered back on board from the figurehead, Mr. Mungo called out to him. "What have you got?"

It was Jansen, the same man who'd fainted after finding the skeletons. Now his face was flush with excitement. He grinned as he strode proudly toward them, holding up a pair of daggers with gems embedded in their hilts. "Some real beauties!"

The sight of the daggers unnerved George. Only kings could afford such extravagance. "Where did you find them?" she said.

Jansen grinned wider. "One was stuck in each eye."

George gasped. "That's a bad omen!"

Everyone knew the figurehead symbolized the heart and spirit of the ship. All seamen treated the figurehead with reverence and respect. She'd once heard tell of a captain who threatened to paint his own ship's figurehead with tar in a last-ditch effort to keep his crew in line, and it worked when all other forms of punishment had failed. Sticking daggers in the eyes of a figurehead was the same as blinding it. And how could any ship see where it was going if it had no eyes?

But Mr. Mungo simply wrote another line on the list he was keeping, and Jansen walked away, clutching the prize daggers to his chest.

Then she remembered what she'd read in the captain's log. Something about a crewman hearing voices telling him to stick the daggers he found into the eyes. Had the captain meant the eyes of the figurehead? How could the crewman have done it when everyone was against it?

Unless the crewman was the last one alive and was making a last-ditch effort to save himself.

"He should put those daggers back in its eyes, and we should get off this evil ship at once!" George said.

Without looking at her, Mr. Mungo muttered, "People are evil. Not ships."

A loud moan drifted up from the depths of the *Black Magic*.

On the other side of the deck, the captain called out, "Who's missing?"

George counted everyone in sight. "We're all here," she called out, but no one listened. Mr. Mungo and her shipmates were already following the captain down below.

Get out, a voice inside her said.

George wanted to climb down to one of the small boats and row herself back to her own ship, the *Crown*. She wanted to be back on board a ship that smelled like frankincense and coffee, not mold, death, and must. Every moment she spent on the slave ship was a moment too long.

But if she dared to go back to the *Crown* alone, she'd be disobeying her captain's orders, which could cost her plenty, including her career at sea.

I'm just spooked, that's all, George thought. I'll go back to the *Crown* and send someone else back with the rowboat.

But what if there was real danger? Could she live with herself if she ran away when Captain Garcia, Mr. Mungo and her shipmates were at risk?

George raced to follow them below.

ఴᏯᏠᎶᏫᏋᏏ

W hen she reached the cargo hold, they were already picking their way through the field of bones and iron shackles toward a bare-chested man with long black hair who sat on the far end of the deck, chained by his wrists and ankles.

George hesitated, staring in disbelief. "He wasn't here before."

His skin was as brown as any seaman's, but his nose was large and hooked. Even though he was sitting and covered in bones and chains, there was enough light to see that he wore red pants. He looked like the *Black Magic*'s figurehead come to life.

George's eyes narrowed. "I know this man," she said, although no one seemed to hear her. "I remember him."

Her father was a collector, and men often came to sell him artifacts from around the world. Her father also collected models of ships and never hesitated to invest in a real one. As a child, she'd been reading in an alcove when she'd overheard her father talking with a visitor.

At first, she'd paid no attention. It was only when she realized they were discussing her that she'd closed her book and crept toward the railing that surrounded the square open space that let her see them on the floor below. Her father had been nestled in his favorite leather chair, smoking a pipe. His visitor had sported a red silk turban, embroidered ivory robes, and a flash of red silk pants beneath those robes.

The visitor had argued, "She will simply follow where the rest of your continent has led for centuries. There are fortunes to be made. She will travel the world—"

"I will let no child of mine near you," her father had answered.

"Please, Sir, hear me out," the visitor had said smoothly. "She will be in good hands."

"That's what I was told when I first agreed. And I was lied to!"

Please, George had thought hard and fast. It's what I've dreamed of. Please let me go see the world!

At the same time, she'd heard father's voice say something else to the stranger, even though his lips never moved.

May the same happen to you as you wish upon others.

She'd let out a little sigh, and that's when the visitor had looked up sharply at George. She'd ducked back into the shadows upstairs, but not before his eyes had met hers.

The visitor's voice and manner had changed then. "You have something very precious inside this house," he'd said, turning back toward George's father. "Something I would like to borrow, perhaps."

"Sir," her father had replied. "Our business is done."

She'd slipped away into the depths of the house, and her father had never spoken about that visitor.

But for many years that followed, she'd wake up in a cold sweat from having nightmares about the man wearing the red silk turban.

George comforted herself with the words her father had spoken to him: I will let no child of mine near you. Perhaps her father's intent would be enough to protect her.

"Stop!" George shouted.

This time they heard her, stopping short and looking back in surprise.

"I recognize this man," George said. "He is no friend to us."

With all backs except hers turned to him, the man with the long black hair shot the same look at her that her father's visitor had given her years ago. One corner of his mouth lifted into a brief smile. Then he turned gaunt and ashen-skinned before her eyes. He moaned loudly.

The captain's face sagged with disappointment as he faced George. "Have mercy on this man. It's only by the grace of Jesus Christ that he survived when all others died. You see a miracle before you." To the others, the captain said, "Has anyone tools that would free this man?"

Jansen called out, "I saw hammer and chisel by the carpenter's bunk."

The daggers, George thought. They were stuck in the figurehead when I was here the first time. When Jansen pulled the daggers out of the eyes of the figurehead, did he release a genii?

"Jansen!" she called. "Give me your daggers!"

Jansen was already halfway across the hold. He shook his head without bothering to turn and look at her.

Still perched on the last rung of the ladder, George began to hop off in order to run and stop him, but the hundreds of bones covering the deck suddenly turned into squirming white snakes. Yelling out in fear, she shrank back, clinging to the ladder.

Standing nearby, Mr. Mungo cocked his head. "What's troubling you?"

"Those!" George's hand trembled as she pointed at the hissing snakes between them. "Snakes!"

Worry clouded Mr. Mungo's eyes. "There's no snakes anywhere on board this ship." He leaned down and picked one up while keeping his gaze on her the way he'd watch a rabid dog. The snake in his hand wound itself around his forearm, then displayed its fangs. "See?" Mr. Mungo said evenly. "It's just a bone."

George looked past Mr. Mungo to see the dark-haired man—the genii—collapse. When the genii moaned, George could hear him laughing at the same time.

Suddenly, she remembered her father's words, which had drifted into her head the day the genii had visited.

May the same happen to you as you wish upon others.

Now she remembered—her father had also been drawing. The following day she'd snooped in his home office and found a drawing of a figurehead: a genii that looked like her father's visitor.

Her father had always referred to the buildings he designed as his children. When invested with new business partners, he referred to their joint projects as his children, too.

For the first time, George realized she'd left home because she thought her father had denied her the opportunity to sail away with the stranger and find adventure. But that wasn't what had happened. Her father must have discovered the genii was a slaver. The "child" her father had said he'd not let near the stranger wasn't George—it was the *Black Magic*.

Jansen returned to the dark-haired man and took a hammer and chisel to the first of four shackles chaining him to the slave deck.

Her father had always warned her to be careful of what she wished, because wishes had a way of coming true. Had the act of putting daggers into the figurehead's eyes shackled and imprisoned the genii inside? And had removing them set the genii free from the figurehead but still shackled?

"No!" Terrified but determined, George ran onto the floor covered in snakes. Several pounced upon her legs, binding them like ropes until she tripped and fell on her knees.

The metallic ring of cleaved shackles echoed across the cargo hold.

George cried out as she struggled to free herself from the snakes.

"Ah . . . " the genii said as Jansen broke off the last shackle from his body. His voice boomed like a war drum. "That's better."

The snakes wiggled apart to create a path for the genii as he rose to his feet, suddenly blossoming from a weak and gaunt man into a healthy and robust one. As the captain, Mr. Mungo, and George's shipmates gaped in astonishment, the genii said, "Where is the architect's little girl?"

When the snakes tried to tug her forward, they created enough slack for George to slam her heels down on them. Hissing and writhing in pain, the snakes released her. George raced up the ladder, through the narrow passageways, and up the stairways to the top decks.

The figurehead was gone!

The clear skies suddenly blackened with clouds and dumped icy rain upon her. Her feet slipped beneath her, and her face slammed hard against the floorboards. Dazed, she struggled to her knees.

His breath warmed her face. "Hello, little one."

George stared into the genii's face.

Kneeling in front of her, he took her head in his hands. "Why worry about your friends and the Barbary Coast?" he whispered. "Why should you care if I sell them? My business is with you."

Thunder roared above, and the ship trembled.

Women were bad luck at sea—everyone knew it. That's why George had pretended to be a boy. She'd never have been able to get a job on a ship otherwise. It was only when a woman bared her breasts that she had the power to appease the gods and calm the seas. The rest of the time, women were magnets for trouble.

George slammed her fist into the genii's eyes, startling him enough that he let go of her.

Racing toward the bow, George pulled off her shirt, then released the muslin she wound around her chest to flatten it. She called out to the gods of the sea. "Help us!"

Lightning struck the tallest mast of the *Black Magic*, and thunder boomed like cannons.

A wall of white mist rose between George and the genii.

As the men came up from below, George pulled her shirt back on and called out to them. "Quickly! To the row boats! We must get back to the *Crown*!"

Mr. Mungo sprang into action, leading the way toward the row boats, but no one followed. "Captain!" he called. "Quickly now!"

But Captain Garcia and the others stared at the genii.

"Don't leave now," the genii told them. "There are hidden treasure chests throughout the ship. I can show you."

George and Mr. Mungo climbed down to the boats below and rowed back toward the *Crown*.

"Why won't they come?" George shouted.

Looking back, Mr. Mungo stopped rowing. His stubbled jaw went slack.

George turned to see the *Black Magic* turn into the misty white outline of a ship before it evaporated.

ඏᘓᕝᘰඏ

Months later, George wore a new dress for the first time in years. On one hand, she felt so restricted by the tight waist and bodice that she could barely breathe. On the other hand, she liked feeling like a woman again.

As she walked down the London streets, George sometimes stumbled as if the ground had unexpectedly pitched beneath her feet. That was normal. It always took a few days for her to get her land legs back.

Mr. Mungo had taken command of the *Crown*. Privately, he'd told her that ghost ships should be left alone, and he'd never make the mistake of going near one again. He also advised her to keep her shirt on if she wanted to keep working on the *Crown*.

Maybe she did want to keep working on an Indiaman merchant ship. Maybe she didn't. Once the *Crown* landed in London, George decided to take some time to think before signing up for another voyage.

All those years ago, she thought her father had been trying to control her life, and to a certain extent that was exactly what he'd done, whether it was something he intended or not. Regardless, that was no excuse for George to run away without letting him know where she was or even that she was still alive.

Now, facing his strange and clever house, George was terrified. What if he was angry with her? What if he refused to see her out of spite? Or what if he was sick and had wasted away so that she wouldn't recognize him when she saw him?

Just as she'd done when she stepped onto the slave deck covered with white snakes, George pushed through her fear and rang the bell. She was startled when a new girl answered.

What if he's died? George thought, panicking. Or moved away?

"Yes?" the servant girl said, eyeing George suspiciously.

George glanced at the name plate by the front door. It was her father's name. She pointed at the plate. "Is this correct?"

The servant girl nodded. "Who shall I say is calling?"

"His daughter," George said, breathing a sigh of relief that was as refreshing as the cool, crisp air that powered Indiamen, slave ships, and every wonderful vessel at sea. "Tell him it's Sally."

REMEMBERING

by Deborah J. Ross

From scientific debate about "nature versus nurture" and "the search for identity" to fairy tales such as "The Ugly Duckling" the same questions arise: "Who am I?" and "Why do I feel so different from everyone around me?"—the latter being particularly noticeable during one's teens. For many people, identity comes from the memories of their ancestors. Eliane, having no memory of her own family, risked everything to save the memories and children of her foster family.

Deborah J. Ross began her writing career as Deborah Wheeler, so her early stories in the *Sword & Sorceress* series are under that name, as are her Darkover short stories. Her story "Imperatrix" in the first *Sword & Sorceress* was her first professional sale, making her one of "MZB's writers." As Deborah Wheeler she also sold two science-fiction novels: *Jaydium* and *Northlight*, as well as 50 short stories—Marion alone bought a couple dozen of them. Deborah was the person Marion chose to continue the Darkover series; she's done four novels so far, and is working on the fifth. It doesn't have a final title yet—MZB's working title was *The Reluctant King*, but that will change before it sees print. Check www.mzbworks.com for the new title; it will be posted there when it's decided.

Deborah lives in the redwood forests near Santa Cruz with her husband, writer Dave Trowbridge, two cats, and a German Shepherd Dog. In between writing, she has worked as a medical assistant to a cardiologist, lived in France—which she describes as an "alien-encounter"—and revived an elementary school library. She has been active in the women's martial arts network and has spent over 25 years studying *kung fu san soo*. In her spare time, she knits for "afghans for Afghans" and the Mother Bear Project (teddy bears for children in Africa orphaned by AIDS).

Fire raced through the streets of Yvarath. The old city, where the Bharim, the People of the Remembering, huddled behind their wooden gates, had gone up like a torch. Greasy smoke smeared the night sky, blurring the moon. The stench of burning pitch mingled with the reek of charred flesh. Screams pierced the roar of the flames.

A figure darted from one shadowed alley to the next, tracing an oblique path away from the wharves. Eliane was so slender, her movements so quick and light, that only a careful observer would have seen anything in the shifting darkness but an adolescent boy. Loose pants, shapeless tunic and sandals identified her as Bharim.

She halted under the eaves of a dilapidated tavern. Two patrons tumbled through the doors and into the darkness. In the street beyond, white-robed Hounds raced by.

"Kill the accursed ones!" the Hounds chanted. "Kill them all!"

Eliane half-closed her eyes, questing outward with her mind, knowing that in doing so, she took a terrible risk. The amulets of the Hounds rendered them sensitive to the use of magic. She prayed that in the confusion, they would not be able to track her.

Matthias . . . Eliane sent her silent call into the night. There was no answer. Bharim magic was personal, limited in range. Of all of them, only Eliane could reach halfway across the city.

She had separated from her foster father when the first of the riots began. The speed and viciousness of the attacks left them stunned. Friends had sent word of the impending arrival of Hound and Questioner, but time had run out before ships could be found, captains bribed, families taken by circuitous routes to the harbor. Matthias led the first group and Eliane another, all children. Eliane had expected to find Matthias at the ship before her and when he was not, had returned to the old city, now ablaze, to find him.

In the little courtyard before the Bharim temple, bodies lashed to a row of upright stakes twisted and screamed as they blackened. At the far end, soldiers in the Duke's gold and red stood guard.

Eliane pushed through the crowd. She did not recognize any of the burning bodies. She did not want to. Beside the splintered temple doors, a single soldier stood over a knot of children. Their heads and shoulders had been smeared with ashes, and their hands bound and linked together, but they appeared otherwise unharmed. There were four of them, two stripling boys, one of them naked, a girl, and a boy of six or seven. She knew all of them, had sung their intertwined lineages on many midnight gatherings.

The children looked so frightened, they might not run when she called them. Then, as if the Mother of Blessings had heard her prayer, an explosion rocked the courtyard. Stones and slate shingles from surrounding buildings clattered to the pavement. Gouts of brilliance erupted above the roofline, from the direction of the Duke's armory. The soldiers abandoned the stakes and hurried toward the citadel. Only the one holding the tether of the children remained.

Eliane wavered, but for only an instant. Calm settled over her. The crowd dispersed, opening a path.

The soldier saw her coming. When he lunged, Eliane pivoted out of the direct path of his sword and glided past him. She moved without thinking, in that quicksilver flow of speed and wiry strength that marked her difference from the stolid, scholarly Bharim. All the care her foster family had lavished on her could not make her one of them.

The soldier, overbalanced, tripped on an uneven stone. Catching himself, he whirled to stare at her. Firelight licked his eyes. Then he fled, leaving his sword behind.

Eliane picked it up, though she had no training in how to use it. A lump of sea-silver had been set like a talisman into the hilt. When she touched the metal, it hummed against her skin.

She hurried toward the children, but an old man and a woman in a charred dress were already slicing the ropes that bound them together. She called their names, but they ignored her. The woman spirited her charges away without a backward glance.

The man hesitated. "Scatter and hide!"

"The Hounds are on the loose!" she cried. "We must leave the city!"

In response, he melted into the flame-churned night.

One boy remained, gazing at her as if entranced. Eliane remembered him from the long afternoons he came to study the Book of Remembering with Matthias. His name was Doveth. She led him, too stunned to protest, down the alleys toward the sea.

More shouting came from further up the street, toward north pier. Their brief respite was over. Eliane tightened her grip on Doveth's hand and broke from their meager cover. The boy tumbled along at her side. By some miracle, as if the Mother of Blessings truly held them in divine safety, they came unscathed to the harbor.

A skirmish had broken out on the pier where *Seawind*, the ship they had hired at an evening's notice, lay moored. A single swordsman, his back to the waves, held off a handful of soldiers.

Khalden, the mercenary Captain Horos had insisted on hiring, placed himself so that the Duke's men must come at him single file along the pier. When he spotted Eliane, his face lit, gleeful. He shouted, "Aha!" and redoubled the attack. The middle soldier toppled into the water. Another jumped over the side. The rest made a rush for land.

Only a single soldier remained, holding a stubbornly defensive posture. Eliane caught a wash of the man's desperate courage. He was alone, his companions fled, with an armed lunatic before him and another enemy—herself—behind him. Eliane lifted her sword so that it might be even more visible. She hoped her own inexperience might not manifest in that small movement. The sea-silver flared hot and tingling in her hand.

The soldier's nerve broke. He threw down his sword and raised his hands. Eliane stepped back, opening an escape. He sped past without a backward glance.

"You make a grand entrance." Khalden's eyes glittered, the battle-fever fading. "This all?" He jerked his chin in the boy's direction.

"So far. What of the others?" Eliane asked.

"Best get onboard. The safest place for you now is out to sea."

"We must wait—"

"You don't ever understand, you people. You keep trying to save everyone, as if that mattered. There aren't going to *be* any others, and if you keep dawdling, there aren't going to be even the ones you've got."

Eliane suppressed a surge of anger. The mercenary had been hired to protect *Seawind*, after all, and he had done just that. But it was Matthias's coin that had paid the captain's fee, and Matthias—

Sweet Mother of Blessings. The armory! Dragon-powder, as well as ordinary weapons—swords, crossbows, spears and body armor—was stored there. It could be detonated by magic, but that required physical proximity—

Hoof-beats clattered behind Eliane, pierced by shouting. She whirled to see torches blazing off armor and spear points. In the forefront, a rider in soldier's tunic pointed in their direction.

"That's them!" he yelled. "Don't let them get away!"

Khalden grabbed Eliane's sleeve. "Go!"

Doveth sprinted for the looming bulk of the ship. Eliane ran after him. The weathered planking creaked beneath her feet.

One of the sailors, a lanky hill-man, his bald head covered in blue tattoos, stood ready to throw off the mooring ropes. Ghostly sails caught the wind, straining. Captain Horos, his hair a gleam of golden silk against the dark water, had just helped Doveth over the gap. He held out one hand to Eliane.

Eliane threw the sword into the water and jumped. As the ship shifted, she landed off-balance on the deck. Khalden raced down the pier with a line of horsemen on his heels. Torchlight gleamed on the crossbow in the hands of the leading rider.

Khalden raced to the very edge, gathered his legs under him, and hurled himself over the water. His body thudded against the wooden side of the ship, then slipped from view. Horos dashed to the rail and leaned over.

Something hissed through the air beside Eliane's face. She turned to see a stubby crossbow quarrel quivering in the mast.

A sliver of darkness slipped from the lee of the next pier. Eliane made out an oarsman and a second man in the boat's prow. Thoughts brushed hers with the clear deep tone like polished bronze. She cried aloud in gladness. Somehow, against all chance, Matthias had made it alive out of the inferno. Clutching a bundle to his chest, he crouched in the tiny craft. A renewed battery of shouts arose from the horsemen.

There was only one thing so precious that Matthias would risk the gauntlet of soldiers to preserve and bring safely to whatever sanctuary they might find beyond the sea—the Bharim-a, the Book of Remembering, the written lineage of the People.

A howl burst from the foremost rider. In the moment of confusion on the pier, the rowboat drew alongside the ship.

Horos cursed as he hauled Khalden, dripping, on to the deck. "Go! Go!" he shouted to his crew.

"No, wait!" Eliane screamed.

Matthias rose to his knees in the tiny boat, lifting the wrapped book.

Thwap! Thwap! The horsemen quickly rearmed their crossbows. Fire exploded in Eliane's mind, shredding vision, lacing her lungs with acid.

"There he is!" Khalden's voice broke the lapping darkness.

Horos threw a rope overboard. He drew it up, empty, and cast it again.

"I can't see him—"

Eliane couldn't hear Khalden's answer.

More crossbow bolts peppered the ship. A man's voice shrieked from the rowboat.

The wharf, the city, everything Eliane had known, slipped into the distance. Her mind reeled with emptiness. Matthias was gone. The Book was gone.

Horos shouted commands at his crew. The wind strengthened, rounding the sails, and *Seawind* leapt into the night.

കരുമ

Blackness washed the deck as the last of the city lights faded. Once they passed beyond the smoke, stars glinted overhead.

Eliane went below, where the children waited. Blindly she touched the hands of the children she had brought from the city. A dozen remained, no more, out of all those Matthias had planned to save. So few, so few. They rushed into her arms. She rocked them to sleep.

കരുമ

In the darkness of the hold, Eliane flexed stiff arms and legs, and wished it were not so very difficult to pray. The words would have come more easily to Matthias, who had taught them to her. Pain rose up behind her heart like a tide and then subsided.

Noises reached her from above. The world shifted and rolled in a way that was strangely comforting, and yet she had no recollection of ever setting foot on a seagoing vessel.

As she climbed the ladder, the breeze shivered against her flesh. Voices reached her, shredded in the splash and surge of the ocean.

Eliane emerged into the brightness of the deck. She recognized the tattooed crewman and the rawboned man in a gray turban. Khalden.

This was the first time Eliane had seen Captain Horos in broad daylight, for their passage had been arranged, quickly and in darkness, by Matthias. She had glimpsed the captain only as a shadow among shadows, a gleam of shoulder-length golden hair.

"I see you're with us," the captain said. "A bit late and a bit green around the gills, but you'll do."

"Do?" Her throat felt parched, rusty with unshed tears.

"You are now crew. We're well away for the moment, with an easy wind, but that could change." He squinted up at the sky. "We'll need every able hand for the journey. We don't have supplies to reach the eastern shores, but we can resupply at Pirion."

The haunted isles, where only madmen and pirates put in.

"The way I see it," Horos continued, "you have two choices: work or swim. Look, less than half my people made it onboard. The rest are stranded back there, along with the second half of the gold for your passage."

"Matthias was bringing it in the boat," Eliane said numbly.

"There's no way we can go back," Horos continued. "We'd all be hanged, every one of us, the moment we set foot in the damned city."

"And the children—what of them?"

"They stay below, as cargo, where they can't get into any trouble."

"Let them work as well," Khalden spoke up suddenly. "Sun and exercise will be far better for them than the hold. They will be needed, not just useless puking baggage."

Images burst across Eliane's mind like flashes of fire. Waking in the dark—alone—the alarum of flight, the smell of ashes and terror, the shudders down to the very marrow of her bones—shouting, a blow to her temple, staggering in the rubble, the ground shifting—her body curled hard on itself like a shell—screams that went on and on until her throat turned raw and her heart burst, unable to hold the pain—

I will not let that happen to these children.

She turned to Horos. "We will all work. No one gets left behind in the darkness."

ೞೞೞೞ

The children took on their tasks, and the ship settled into a routine. During the first difficult days, Khalden proved an unexpected ally, offering his own rough comfort.

"I had three younger brothers," the swordsman explained. "If the work doesn't wear them out, I'll put them to whacking one another with wooden swords."

Days stretched into weeks of a sweet running wind. As Khalden predicted, the journey took on the aspect of an adventure. The children emerged from their shock and grew brown under clear skies. True to his word, Khalden invented games for them, contests from which they emerged sweating and laughing. Even Captain Horos chuckled at their antics.

When it was her time to sleep, Eliane lay with open eyes in her hammock, wondering why she could not mourn. Matthias had been the only family she could remember. Why could she not grieve for him? She whispered aloud the prayer for the dead, and felt nothing. Only when she chanted the ancient lineage did she feel some stirring of emotion and that was oddly muted, as if it were happening to someone far away.

ೞ೧೪ಌ೦

The moon passed through its changes and the small stores of food and water dwindled. The tattooed crewman cast his nets, but brought them up empty. No rain fell to replenish their supplies. Horos ordered rationing.

"If the winds hold," Khalden told Eliane as they rested together, staring out across the ship's prow at the expanse of shifting water, "we will reach Pirion in two days."

"I have heard it's a perilous harbor," Eliane said.

Khalden nodded. "Pirion sits upon the slopes of a fire-mountain, a volcano. Five years ago, it belched forth enough hot ash to set half the ships in port afire."

Fire at sea must be terrifying, Eliane thought. Sailors often had a superstitious dread of drowning. Yet to remain onboard, with the flames licking ever closer . . .

She remembered the plaza in Yvarath, and the greasy, foul-smelling smoke. To drown—to plunge into the cool refuge of the waves, to sink into their secret depths—no, she did not fear that fate.

Late one morning, the sea grew calm. Brightness seeped across the sky until not a tinge of blue remained. Huge slow swells rose and fell. Eliane finished her shift and stood against the rails, cradling her half-cup of water.

She thought of unnamed beasts in the lightless waters, mute and vast, inhaling darkness and breathing it out. The last few nights, she had dreamed of those depths, passing through them with a sense of inexplicable joy. Waking, she ran her fingertips over the palm of her hand where it had pressed against the sea-silver in the hilt of the soldier's sword.

Now, in the flat bright day, sweat trickled down Eliane's face and neck. She downed the last of the water, despite the brackish taste, and found Horos standing at the prow. He held a seeing glass.

"Nothing yet," the captain said. "Not that you could see through this muck."

Squinting into the glare, Eliane could barely make out the line between water and air. They should have already glimpsed the coastline, had the day been clear.

Eliane glanced up at the mast, where one of the middle children clung to the topmost rigging, peering outward. By the boy's posture, he could see nothing more from his vantage.

She opened her mind to the invisible horizon. Behind her eyes, she saw steam rising in billows, bubbles appearing on the surface of the water. Heat rose up before her. She reeled with it. The air seethed, glowing. She envisioned ashes crisping, a storm of tiny cinders. Brightness parted—

She hovered on the edge of an inferno. Red-orange flames erupted skyward, filling the horizon. Her vision faltered.

"Eliane!"

Khalden's voice jerked her back to her own body. Pain ran in jagged bands up her forearms from clenching the topmost railing. Her vision cleared. A puff of humid air brushed her face.

Ahead, white mist rose from the water.

"This is no natural fog," Horos told Eliane. "I've never seen its like. Can you not magick a way through it?"

Eliane frowned. "Whatever you have heard of the Bharim, we have no power over the weather."

They were out of food, almost out of water. They had to reach land within the next day or two.

"Look! Look there!" Khalden cried.

The glare off the water blinded Eliane for an instant. Then the mist lifted from sea. With every passing heartbeat, more was revealed, flecks and bubbles of foam, the broken surface of the water. A line of darkness appeared on the horizon.

Horos lowered the seeing glass, his face waxen.

Eliane took the glass and scanned the island, beginning at the line of white foam that marked the beach and then upwards. From one end to the other, from the sawtooth mountain to the empty shoreline, stretched ash and rock, blackness veined in glowing red. Once or twice, she caught a spray of pin-point embers erupting upwards. Not a trace of human habitation, or of life of any kind, showed anywhere.

Eliane directed the seeing glass toward the center of the island, where a cone of cinder-gray rock rose above the shattered slopes. Red light glimmered at the top. Even as she watched, the slopes trembled.

A moment later sound reached her, a rumbling at the very edge of hearing. On the mountain, the glow intensified, brighter with every passing minute. It shifted from ruby to gold and then white. Through the glass, Eliane saw chunks of rock, some of them immense, plunge down the sides of the cone. Fissures opened, spewing forth more embers.

A deafening crack rolled out from the island. Dense gray clouds billowed from the mountaintop and blotted the horizon. The rumbling built in waves.

"This—this can't be Pirion. We must have gotten off course," Eliane stammered.

"Not unless the stars themselves have deceived us," Horos answered in a hollow voice. He began shouting orders to bring the ship about.

Around the ship, the waters crashed and rose. The deck heaved under Eliane's feet. She caught the rail for balance.

Eliane raced to her place, hauling on the ropes. Across the towering blackness of the island, she glimpsed rivers of yellow-white. Molten rock, she thought, from the very heart of the mountain. When it reached the shore—

Seawind rocked madly. Wind-whipped spray blanketed the view. With agonizing slowness, the ship turned. A rain of hot ash pummeled the deck.

Horos screamed for more canvas. Eyes and throat burning, Eliane bent to her task. Everyone but the youngest children took their turn. More than once, several had to pull together, for the winds grew every moment in strength. The ship, under full sail now, plunged and bucked like a wild beast.

Then the rain came, pelting them from behind. Waves surged higher, the fresh water mixing with the salt. The sea was rising to meet the fury of the heavens.

Within minutes, the deck was awash. Horos shouted more orders, his voice torn by the gale.

The day, which had begun so warm and still, grew colder by the minute. Horos sent the drenched, shivering children below. Everyone else hauled and climbed and spliced and cut.

Eliane ceased to feel hunger, although thirst clawed at her. Sometimes she thought her hands shook, or perhaps it was the fury of the storm pounding through the ship. At one point, a child thrust a cup at her. It was rainwater, somehow gathered in the confusion. The water cooled her burning throat. Renewed strength flowed through her veins. She reached for the rigging to climb back up.

Seawind pitched wildly. Eliane, her hands clenched around the ropes, was pulled off her feet. The movement of the ship spun her around, so that she faced back in the direction they had come. Water sheeted from the sky and waves shot up to meet it.

In the howling storm, an immense shape took form. At first, she thought it a trick of the rain. Something *was* there, insubstantial and wavering, mist condensing against the maelstrom of white and gray.

The next moment, Eliane dropped to the deck and fell to her knees. Slipping, cursing, she hauled herself up by the railing. Splinters dug into her flesh, but she held on.

The water around the shape churned and boiled, adding steam to the tattered whirling whiteness of the tempest. Voices echoed on the wind. The ship's timbers groaned like beasts hamstrung and run to ground.

She felt the thing in the sea, as if some unknown part of her, some sense which had lain sleeping all these years, now stirred with memory . . . and recognition.

Only its upper part extended above the plunging waves, human and dragon and sea-beast all in one. The massive head lifted, mane like tangled kelp streaming over the shoulders. A crest of knobbed, interlaced coral sprang from the overhanging brow, arching over the domed skull and down the spine. The skin, what Eliane could see through the foam-whipped shroud, was green and mottled gray, patterned with pale incrustations and plated scales that shone, opalescent as moonstones. Its eyes were huge and lidless, made for peering through the lightless depths.

The apparition sank down, as if gathering itself. Arms— two or three or even five, Eliane couldn't tell—burst from the water, lashing it to even greater heights.

A noise like a gigantic whipcrack snapped through the air. Eliane jumped, almost losing her hold on the railing. She hazarded a glance aloft. The mainsail had ripped through. Ropes snapped, their shredded ends flapping madly. A small figure swung from one of them like a tattered rag.

"Doveth!"

Seawind shuddered. The boy's body plummeted downwards. The rigging broke his fall. He slid to the deck.

Eliane raced to Doveth's side. The deck tilted beneath her. She slipped, scrambled up, lost her footing again and slid. With the boy in her arms, she came up hard against the cabin house. She lay on her back, heart hammering against her ribs, rain streaming into her eyes. Above her, Horos and Khalden fought to cut the sail free. She couldn't see any of the other crew.

The boy whimpered. Somehow, she heard him above the howling gale. She pushed herself to sitting, cradling his body against hers. His face convulsed. His collarbone was broken, probably more.

Above her loomed the vast inhuman face. The mouth opened, its breath the bitter, numbing chill of the sea. It raised one arm and clenched its fist. She felt its utter, implacable rejection of air and land, and all the creatures that dwelled there. The mountain of Pirion had spoken with fire and ashes, and this creature had answered, catching *Seawind* in its fury.

Even if Horos and Khalden could salvage the sail, even if the boy in her arms survived, it was no use. In a moment, the gigantic fist would hammer the ship into splinters. The sea-beast would swallow them all.

In her arms, the boy cried out in terror. She felt his sobs ripple through her own body. Her arms tightened around him. She closed her eyes.

Oh sweet Mother of Blessings, if ever you loved your children, save them now!

The words poured from the innermost core of her heart. An image had sprung behind her eyes, of the dozen or so Bharim children who had been in her care since that desperate flight from Yvarath. She saw them sink beneath the water, bodies like sodden petals drifting downward, drawn into the inexorable, swirling currents. In the frozen dark, they settled among the bones of monstrous benthic creatures, where no one knew their names or sang their lineage. Bereft of light, of warmth, of memory. As if they had never existed, never been loved, never known a moment's joy.

Let it not be! Help them!

The fist descended, somehow missing *Seawind* and passing instead through the maelstrom. A wall of water slammed into the ship. Timbers shrieked. The prow lifted, gasping, shuddering, reaching for the light. Then it began to slip downwards.

Eliane scrambled to her feet on the tilting deck. With one hand, she clasped the terrified child against her body. With the other, she raised her own fist, filled her lungs with fury and hurled it out.

NO! YOU SHALL NOT HAVE THEM!

For an instant, time itself seemed to pause. Though the wind and rain continued, the sea scarcely moved, as if the waves were mere painted images. The ship hung suspended in its descent.

The immense, distorted head swung around. This time, the eyes were not blind pallid orbs, but glowing, lit from within. Eliane staggered under their weight. The apparition's watery breath surged over her. She felt its awareness of her, the leap of curiosity.

STOP IT! she cried, pressing the moment's advantage. *STOP IT NOW!*

The thing was *in* her mind, ringing through the caverns of her skull. Thoughts reverberated, overlapping, rippling, so that she could not tell which were her own and which from this strange creature. She no longer feared it, or the watery death it brought. She feared only for the others—her shipmates, her friends . . . her children.

Once she had heard from afar the pealing of bells from the Duke's palace, upon some celebration or other. She remembered the cacophony of sound and how it had fallen away at the end, leaving a single melody, so pure and clear that it stirred her to tears. Now the jumble of thoughts within her mind also faded. Even the storm quieted. She could hear the beating of her own heart.

The winds shifted and the apparition before her dwindled. She no longer looked upon a grotesque colossus, half sea-dragon, half parody of man, but upon a much smaller shape.

A whirlpool of deepest blue bore him up, covering the lower part of his naked form. It lifted him, so that his gaze was level upon hers. He seemed to be standing utterly still, yet in constant motion.

He bore the aspect of a bearded man, broad of chest and heavily muscled, yet with a sleekness that reminded her of dolphins. Seaweed twisted with strands of tiny pearls fell across his shoulders in a mane. When he lifted one hand toward her, the light around his body shimmered like mother-of-pearl.

The eyes that gazed upon hers reflected the same moony radiance, but she caught the darkness behind them, the deep slow brooding intelligence. The eldritch joy.

You have returned to us at last, he said.

Not as all things return to the sea, the answer came from within her. But as a child returns to the place of its birth, to the arms of its mother.

She heard, and recognized the truth.

How she had come to be stranded upon land so many years ago, she could not guess. Yvarath was a port city—in the shadowed corridors of her memory, she saw torchlight reflected off wet pilings, smelled the reek of heated pitch, heard the cry of gulls and creaking of ships at dock, tasted harbor-foul water, felt the thousand tiny knives of a barnacle bed along her skin.

As they gazed upon one another, Eliane and the sea king, the storm itself fell away into stillness. He shook his head, and the strands of his mane and beard undulated like sea-grass. The tiny pearls woven into his hair chimed like bells. He was ancient beyond human reckoning, as enduring and changeable as the sea.

She stretched out her hand, leaning far over the railing. The tips of his fingers brushed hers.

Deep beneath the sea, where the sun's brassy brilliance dimmed to moony shades, creatures moved within grottos fashioned of marble and whalebone. In memory she saw them, or perhaps it was imagination, for it seemed that a veil of dust had fallen from her eyes to reveal the true nature of things. Water currents swirled around her, but instead of blurring her vision, they enhanced it, bringing out hues and textures impossible in the dry stark light of land. She saw with her heart as well as her eyes, and knew she was one of them.

She was not of the Bharim, for all that they had fostered her with love. She had worn their human nature as a cloak, hiding her essence. Her bones were cages of coral, her teeth a row of glimmering pearls, her salty blood the sea.

She had only to shift her precarious balance and fall into the sea king's arms. The living waters would surge over them, leaving behind forever the hot choking hatred of men, the fires of Yvarath, the *difference* that had haunted her all her days. She would look upon others like herself and be recognized.

She who was lost has returned to us at last! At last! At last! Their jubilant cries would echo through the waves.

Yet something kept her feet upon the wooden planks, the fingers of her free hand curled around the railing. She had only to let go, and yet . . . she could not.

What held her here? she wondered. Matthias, her only family, was dead. Horos and Khalden were amiable comrades, but hardly her own kind. As for the children, the burden she had never sought—

Eliane leaned back, breaking the contact with the sea king.

The children. The Bharim children.

What had she sworn, that first night after their desperate escape from Yvarath? That they would not wake, alone in their terror, even as she had?

No one left behind in the darkness.

I was there to comfort them, she argued with herself. *I kept my promise.*

For today. What of tomorrow? What of their arrival at whatever haven they found? Horos would not deliberately abandon them, nor would Khalden. But who would sing their lineage and ensure their continuance?

They would live on, nameless and kinless, alive in body but lost to the spirit which had sustained their ancestors. They would no longer be Bharim.

Salt stung her eyes as she once more met the gaze of the sea king. "I cannot go with you." Eliane spoke the words aloud in the ancient language of the Bharim.

How could she make him understand? It was not because of the kindness of the Bharim in sheltering her. Nor was it a matter of honor or obedience to traditional law.

She and only she could give them the knowledge of who they were, what they were. If she broke faith with them, she could never keep faith with herself.

The sea king nodded, a slow dip of the head, the gaze never leaving hers.

So it is also among us, the passing of memory from one generation to the next. She heard his thoughts more clearly now. The contact, catalyzed by the water that was their shared life, had attuned their minds. For the sea people, the link was less fragile. Many of them, like the giant creatures of the depths, lived immense spans of time. Humans were transient as the sands.

Yes, they are, she responded. *Which is why they treasure writing.* She thought of the Book of Remembering, the Bharim-a, lost in the harbor at Yvarath.

Lost? the sea king repeated. *There is nothing lost in the sea, for it is all joined in a single unity. Whatever is given to one is given to all.*

The column of cerulean water which had supported the sea king receded. He sank below the surface, which had now subsided to gentle ripples. *Seawind* rode easily upon the surface.

Eliane sagged against the rails. She had not expected so abrupt a parting. If the sea king meant to hearten her, then he had failed. He brought no comfort, only longing beyond words. She had not even the breath to sob out her loss. She buried her head in her hands.

From aloft, someone called her name. Reluctantly, she raised her head, squinting against the sun that burst from the fleeing clouds. Khalden climbed down the rigging.

The column of darker water swirled upwards once again. The sea king's pale, wet skin shone like pearl. Although he did not smile, his entire countenance radiated an inner luminescence. He lifted his hands above the water, and Eliane saw what he held.

Nothing lost in the sea . . . Like an unexpected gift, his words came back to her. He placed the package into her outstretched hands.

The outer wrappings, leather and silk, still protected the precious Book within. Recognizing it, the boy at her side cried aloud.

Khalden rushed toward them. His gaze jumped from the injured boy to the dripping figure of the sea king. "I saw the boy fall."

Eliane stared at Khalden as if seeing him for the first time—not a hard-edged mercenary, but a devoted older brother. He might not be Bharim, or even care what that meant, but to save his friends, he was willing to brave a monster from the depths.

"When the children are old enough, you must give them this." Eliane handed the Book of Remembering to Khalden.

"But—but, Eliane—"

"Farewell, my friend. Love them as I have."

"Eliane, no!"

Khalden's parting cry reached Eliane as she jumped. The sea king caught her, strong as storm and soft as foam. Cradled in his embrace, she sank below the waves. Her last breath streamed upwards in a column of diminishing bubbles. She drew the salt water deep into her body. All sensation of cold, of longing, of separation, lifted from her. Instead of muted blues, she saw all the glorious hues of the depths, and the lower they went, the more complex the colors became, interwoven now with smell and taste and texture, senses she knew and others she had no names for.

Here she would need no names, for the sea itself would sing her lineage with every passing tide. Her people swam to meet her, and she felt their joy reverberate endlessly through the coral chambers of her bones.

SQUIRREL ERRANT

by Michael H. Payne

One of the things I look for most in a story is that it be memorable. During the reading period I'll often hold a story I like overnight. I often get a story that seems perfectly good at first reading, but the next morning I can't remember what it was about without rereading it. I was thinking about that phenomenon during the reading period, and for some reason I was remembering a story from *Sword & Sorceress 19*. Two days later I got this story, which is a sequel to the one I was thinking about. (No, I'm not psychic—I'm a large, not a medium.)

Michael H. Payne's life hasn't changed much since he sold Cluny's first adventure to *Sword & Sorceress 19*. He still lives and works in the coastal deserts of southern California, but now he seems to devote most of his life to writing and drawing his two webcomics—Daily Grind and Terebinth. Both are available for viewing at pandora.xepher.net.

A tiny click, and the visor of Cluny's helmet slammed shut over her snout. She dropped her lance and shoved the thing up with both paws. "Crocker, this is *not* a good idea!"

"Trust me." Crocker peered around the trunk of the tree they were crouched behind. "Just scamper up to that branch, leap into Michelle's window, and announce that you're the brave knight come to save her from the horrible homework dragon. She'll love it!"

Cluny fiddled with the visor till it clicked again, locking it—she hoped—into its open position. "Her spellbook's due tomorrow. If she's still working on it, she—"

"Michelle?" Crocker shook his head, his most recent attempt at a wizard's beard only serving to make his chin look dirty in the twilight. "I'll bet she's been done for a week; she's prob'bly just sitting up there fretting over comma placement. I mean, jeez, the way she gets into this stuff, you'd think she came to Huxley just to *study*."

"Imagine that." Cluny put her paws on her hips. "You suppose that's why she's on the Magister's List? While certain people who spend all week making squirrel-sized armor are barely scraping through Evocation 101?"

"Quiet, you." Crocker was still focused on Michelle's window, so Cluny had no trouble dodging the finger he flicked at her. "Besides," he went on, "you're my familiar, right? Supposed to help me in all my endeavors, right?"

His words made her blink, and she opened her mouth to object: as far as Master Gollantz could tell, *Cluny* was the one in their pairing with the sorcerous power while Crocker's abilities were perfectly attuned to support *her!* If anyone was the familiar here, it was—

But she stopped herself. Master Gollantz had given them quite a list of the unpleasant things he would do to them if the truth about her and Crocker ever got out, and as much as it galled Cluny, she had to admit that the world just wasn't ready for a squirrel sorcerer with a human familiar. . . .

So she sighed and hefted the lance from the ground. "This thing had better be usable, that's all I can say."

"Why? You planning a tournament?"

"If Rennie's feeling grumpy." At Crocker's blank look, Cluny added, "Renfield? Michelle's familiar, remember?"

"Yeah. So?"

"So he's a fox. I'm a squirrel. You figure it out."

He blew out a breath. "Will you just—?"

"I'm going, I'm going." Cluny rattled her armor and started up the tree, the lance clutched in her left front paw.

"Great!" she heard Crocker call from below. "I'll be out in the hallway waiting, and we can all head down to the Grotto for supper when you're done!"

Cluny looked back, watched Crocker run through the park toward Powell House, his robes grass-stained and tangling around his ankles. She shivered with the chill that came over her whenever they separated, the sick feeling of the link between them thinning to nothing, but that was normal till a sorcerous partnership matured. Not that she could imagine anyone ever using the word "mature" to describe *Crocker* . . .

Still, she couldn't stop a smile as he disappeared around the far corner of the building. He was coping pretty well with their strange situation, and Cluny guessed it wouldn't do any harm to go along with his stupid little gags once in a while. Besides, the sooner she got this over with, the sooner she could get back to studying for her metallurgy final . . .

She turned to the dorm, lights flicking on in various windows, but Michelle's only gave off a glow like the embers of a fireplace. Great. Probably wasn't even home. Still, the window stood slightly open, a jump of only a few feet, so Cluny set her jaw, scampered out along the branch, and sprang.

Too much, she realized the instant she launched; overcompensating for the armor's weight, she was going to sail right over the whole windowsill! She tried to turn in midair, struck out with her free paw, but all she managed to do was gouge a few splinters from the sill. Then she was falling, jangling, clattering into a heap on Michelle's carpet, her visor slamming shut over her snout again.

Several quick sounds: a tinkle of glass, a sharp hiss, a whispered "Oh, no." A rotten-egg stink curled her whiskers, and as Cluny sat up, blinking through the slits in her faceplate, the room before her burst into flames.

The heat hit her like a fist, made her start back; she caught a quick glimpse of cold blue light in the center of the fire before a shadow rose up in front of her and kicked her sideways. She rolled till she could stop herself, then she rattled upright and shoved the visor open.

Some sort of striped cloth hung in front of her, the pattern the same as Michelle's sofa. But before she could wonder who, why, or what, a voice above her growled, "What do you think you're doing?" Cluny turned, and there was Rennie glaring down at her, his pointed ears folded, his eyes solid black. "And what in Acheron are you dressed as??"

"Wait a minute." Cluny held up a paw, still a little shaky. "Where's Michelle? What's that smell? Why did—?"

"Shut up!" Rennie hissed. "You idiot! That's an unbound firedrake out there!"

"What?" Cluny blinked, then pushed past the fox to peer around the sofa. The light was fading from the window she had just fallen through, but in front of the now blazing fireplace, Cluny could see Michelle sprawled, a blue glow wrapped around her . . . and beside her, its wings tucked back, its long neck stretching up to sniff Michelle's face, stood a slender four-legged lizard about the same size as Rennie. Cluny forced a swallow. "What's a *firedrake* doing here?"

"Extra credit." Rennie's voice came from behind her. "You bind a guardian into your spellbook, it's just about an automatic 'A.'"

Cluny turned to stare up at him. "But a firedrake? What made you two think you could bind a firedrake?"

"Hey, squirrel, we had the thing caught, sealed, and just about set when you came crashing in! This is all *your* fault!" His voice grew softer. "I just hope that cold ward holds."

"Cold ward?"

Rennie gave her a look. "Don't they teach you frosh anything? You always have protection wards ready, especially when you're dealing with something as dangerous as—"

"OK, I knew that." Like the watery healing spell she'd come up with when she'd tried to teach Crocker how to make fireballs; a deep breath, and she forced herself to calm down. "But shouldn't we call the fire department or something?"

"Brilliant." The fox sniffed the air. "OK, here's the plan: you crawl out at the other end of the sofa and make as much noise as you can. The drake goes after you, and I go out the window to get help."

"Whoa, now: I do what?"

"You do what I say!" Rennie snatched her up between his paws, his breath against her whiskers making the hot air even hotter. "That's my Lady out there, and if she gets hurt, I swear I'll carve you up for appetizers!"

Cluny returned his glare, but she knew he was right. "Fine. Just let me skin Crocker before you eat me." She wriggled from Rennie's grip, slapped her visor down, grabbed the lance from where she'd dropped it, and started tromping along the wall for the other end of the sofa.

She reached it, stopped, looked back, and saw the fox waiting, his fur vibrating, his muscles tensed. Cluny took a breath, slipped out, scampered under the coffee table, and leaped into the room with a shout of "Ho, dragon!"

The firedrake had been tapping a claw against the glowing blue shell around Michelle's hand, but now it raised its head, its fiery eyes brightening as they fixed on Cluny. "Were you addressing me?" it asked, its voice like steam from a kettle.

Cluny leveled her lance and stepped forward. In what she hoped was a menacing voice, she said, "Begone from here, foul creature, or taste the wrath of my blade!"

The firedrake cocked its head. "Technically, a lance doesn't *have* a blade. It's more of a stabbing weapon."

She tried to keep her paws from shaking. "Just begone, or you'll taste it anyway!"

The lizard's grin showed hundreds of needle-like teeth, but Cluny's attention was caught by a white flash at the window:

the tip of Rennie's brush disappearing over the sill. The firedrake saw it, too, its head snapping over, but by then, the fox was gone.

Smoke jetted from the drake's snout, and it slowly turned back to her. "So. You were the distraction. Well played." It rubbed its chin with a claw. "But while your friend may indeed return with help in time to stop me from demonstrating the joys of immolation to anyone *else* in this realm, I shall at least introduce them to you." The firedrake spread its wings. "En garde, knight."

Its neck snapped forward, and Cluny leaped sideways. Heat prickled the fur along her tail, and she heard the crackling whoosh of wood catching fire—the coffee table, no doubt. That would expand the thing's range of motion, she found herself remembering from evocation class: unbound firedrakes didn't like getting too far from open flames.

She rolled to her paws and found that she'd managed to put Michelle's glowing legs between herself and the drake. Mind racing, she hefted the lance . . . and remembered Professor Scuttle's lecture in metallurgy class about iron and how well it conducted magical energies: "Some critters," the old gnome had said, "you just gotta wave cold iron at 'em, an' it nigh to sucks the magic right out their bodies."

Were firedrakes like that? Cluny was trying to remember when she saw the reptile's head appear around Michelle's feet. "Ah, *there* you are." Its snaky neck came next, then the rest of it. "Now, where were we? Oh, yes." And it cocked its head back for another blast.

With a cry, Cluny leaped straight for it, the lance aimed at its chest. It sidestepped just the way she'd hoped, and she let the tip of the lance drop to jab her true target: the firedrake's front paw. She felt the squish of the point penetrating the thing's scales, heard the drake scream, spitting fire wildly, and using the lance as a pole, she vaulted up over the flames to land on Michelle's leg.

She spun, hoping to see the lizard writhing in agony at the steel's touch, but it was just standing there, licking its paw. "Ouch," it said, then raised its head to her. "First touch to you, knight. My turn now, though." Its head snapped forward, and fire burst out.

Cluny ducked, knew she was too late, cringed, waiting to feel her armor melt to slag around her. But when only a hot wind flowed past, she opened her eyes, the flames turning to ash as they met the blue glow of Michelle's ward.

The ward! Of *course*! Cluny sprang up, squinted through the smoke and the faceplate to see the drake on the floor spreading its wings and cocking its head again. A quick prayer to the gods of conductivity, and Cluny jabbed the butt of her lance against the blue at Michelle's knee. Cold bit into her paws, but she managed to hang on and swing the lance toward the firedrake; the lizard's chest was ballooning out with its breath, and the lance's tip just brushed its scales.

Blue fire stroked down the metal, the cold of the ward spraying into the firedrake, and it shrieked, its neck snapping out like a whip. The frost on her paws made Cluny grit her teeth, blue dancing over the drake's scales for a long moment. Then it toppled over.

Cluny wrenched her numb paws from the lance and blew on them, rubbing them warm. The lizard's sides barely fluttered, and Cluny leaped down, eyes on the window, when—

"Michelle?" came Crocker's muffled voice from the hallway. "Cluny? You guys in there?"

"Crocker!" Cluny spun, clattered for the door. "Run!"

The doorknob rattled, and Crocker's scruffy, chubby face peered in with a grin. The smile vanished immediately, and his eyes went wide. "Hey, what—?"

Cluny leaped for his robes and clawed her way up. "No time! We've gotta get outta here before—!"

A groan from behind cut her off; a glance back saw the firedrake rising to its paws, its head swinging like a pendulum. Cluny scrambled to Crocker's shoulder. "Move, Crocker!"

"A firedrake?" she heard him mutter. "Michelle?"

"Come on, come on, come on!" Cluny pounded the side of his head. "Before it wakes up!"

"Too late," came a familiar breathy voice; Cluny looked down, saw the firedrake with wings spread, its head cocked. "I'm afraid, O knight in shining armor, that I cannot allow either you or your steed to leave this place." Fire burned at its muzzle, and the thing's head lashed forward, a ball of twisting flame bursting toward her.

No time to run, nowhere to go, nothing she could do but—

She brought her paws up, mentally wrapped Crocker's power around her shoulders like a cloak, and shouted the words for her old watery healing spell. The air went thick and damp just as the drake's fire splashed into her, and clouds of steam sizzled up to fill the room. Cluny kept chanting, kept replenishing the water till the firedrake's breath gave out, till she saw the lizard draw its head back for another blast.

A quick change of wording, certain components she knew were in every standard projectile spell, and Cluny thrust her paws forward, felt a big bubble of the water she was generating sploosh away from her, aimed it as well as she could for the startled look on the firedrake's face, and let it plop right on top of the thing.

Shouts echoed from down the hall, but Cluny was staring at the globe of water now sitting on Michelle's floor, the firedrake floating inside, its head twisting one way, then the other. She couldn't stop a little laugh from getting loose: it wouldn't even drown, she realized, what with all the healing elements she'd put into that spell . . .

Crocker's panting was the next thing she noticed; she turned on his shoulder and saw him staring with open mouth at the firedrake swimming around. Then the voices were coming up behind her, a particularly harsh one asking, "What's this?"

Cluny turned. Novices and familiars jammed the hallway, and Master Watts, the Resident Mage at Powell House, was pushing his way through them, his scowl making him look more like a scarecrow than usual. Something moved at his feet, and Cluny heard Rennie shouting, "Get out of the way, you idiots!"

Of course, Crocker was standing in the doorway, but with the sudden crowd, he couldn't move back. So he stepped in as Rennie rushed past, Master Watts dousing the burning coffee table and bringing the lights up with a snap of his fingers, then squatting to poke Michelle's foot, the blue glow around her beginning to sparkle and fade. He squinted at the globe, the firedrake blinking back, then stood and rounded on Crocker and Cluny. "You there. *You* did this?"

Crocker's breath had slowed, but Cluny knew he wasn't up to talking yet. So she bowed and said, "Yes, sir. This is Terrence Crocker, and I'm Cluny; we're at Mayfield House."

"Mayfield?" His scowl grew. "But that's a frosh dorm."

"Yes, sir; we're both—"

"Michelle!" The word burst from Crocker's mouth; Cluny had to grab hold as a shudder wracked his entire body. He blinked several times, then put his hands to his forehead. "Cluny? What just happened? I feel like a wall fell on me."

She tapped his ear. "Crocker? Open your eyes."

Crocker peered out from behind his hands, then dropped them and jerked back against the wall. "Master Watts! Where, uh, I mean, how—?"

"Back among us, eh, Crocker?" Something close to a smile creased the R.M.'s thin cheeks. "You throw an interesting ward for a frosh. I haven't seen your name on the Magister's List; where have you been hiding yourself?"

"Hiding? I, uh, I mean, I haven't, sir! I, uh, just—"

A groan from Michelle, and Master Watts turned to her. "Slowly, Steiverson: you've had a bit of a shock."

Michelle's eyes widened. "The firedrake! Where—?"

"There." Master Watts waved at the bubble, all trace of his smile gone. "I encourage experimentation here at Powell House, Steiverson, but in this profession, we must know our limitations. Firedrakes are not to be trifled with, and attempting to bind one unsupervised is nothing short of foolhardy." He shook his head. "Had Crocker here not come by, I shudder to think what might have occurred."

From the floor beside Michelle, Rennie turned and glared at Cluny. Cluny gritted her teeth. "Uh, actually, sir, Michelle and Rennie had everything pretty much in hand till I came crashing through the window."

Crocker's face went pale. "Oh, no. You mean you—"

"No, I mean *you*." Cluny reached up to jab a claw into his nose. "It was *your* stupid joke, remember?"

Crocker covered his eyes again, and Master Watts crossed his arms. "Come along," the mage said. "Out with it."

"It was . . ." Crocker stopped, cleared his throat. "I . . . I thought Michelle had been studying too hard, so I sent Cluny up here to surprise her. I didn't know she was binding a firedrake, and I . . . I . . ." His voice petered out, and he brushed at the grass stains on his robe.

"I see." Master Watts's voice seemed to echo. "Who is your advisor, Crocker?"

Crocker swallowed so hard, Cluny could feel it where she sat on his shoulder. "Master Gollantz, sir."

"The Magister himself?" Master Watts looked from Crocker to Cluny and back again, the pressure of his gaze combing through Cluny's fur like a winter wind. "There is *definitely* more to you two than meets the eye. . . ."

Cluny swallowed then, but Master Watts just turned away. "I shall speak to him on this matter, have no doubt of that. Oh, and don't forget your drake when you go." He waved, and the bubble on the floor popped; Cluny looked down to see the firedrake shaking water from its wings.

A gasp rose from the students, and what little color remained in Crocker's face drained away. "You bound it, after all," Master Watts went on, "and they *do* make fine familiars, much better then common animals: I'm sure your squirrel can find some other novice."

Cluny started to object, but she heard a hiss from the floor below. "You? My master? This cannot be!"

Panic prickling her whiskers, she leaped from Crocker's shoulder, landed with a crash of armor beside the drake, its eyes whirling and fixed on her, and crooked a claw at its face. "You will acknowledge our master, wyrm!" She swept her claw away to point at Crocker. "You've been bested and bound, and you will acknowledge him!"

The drake's power washed over her, a hot dry rush that made her head feel like an expanding balloon. It struggled against her, tried to overwhelm her, but she was still dripping with the water she'd made, the water she'd bound him in, and she smothered his rebellion—*his?* How did she suddenly know that this firedrake was a male?—with a single thought.

More hissing from the drake, then he turned and bowed his head to Crocker. "I find myself obliged to call you master."

Crocker was still staring, his mouth open, but he had regained at least enough presence of mind to bow back to the lizard. "Excellent," came Master Watts's voice from the hallway. "Back to your studies, now, the rest of you!"

A few moments of muttered voices, Michelle standing shakily and moving to the sofa, Rennie hopping into her lap. Then silence in the hall and in the room till Michelle burst out with: "Well, that's just great! *I* do all the work, and *you* end up with my firedrake!"

The lizard hissed beside Cluny. "Speak respectfully!" It snapped its head to her. "Shall I devour her, master?"

"No!" Cluny yelled at the same time as Crocker.

"Just . . ." Michelle slumped further into the sofa, her head lolling back and her eyes closing. "Just leave me alone, OK, Crocker?"

Crocker slumped, too. "I'm sorry, Michelle. I—"

Rennie's fur bristled. "She asked you to leave."

Cluny tapped Crocker's ear. "C'mon," she whispered. "We'll get this settled tomorrow."

For a moment, she wasn't sure if he'd heard. Then with a sigh, he turned and moved out into the hallway.

Wings behind her: Cluny looked back to see the drake fluttering after them. "You better carry him, Crocker. He's likely to give someone a heart attack flying like that."

Crocker gave a groan and spun around. "Like me, for instance! Cluny, what're we gonna *do* with this thing?"

"*Thing?*" The firedrake pulled up to hover in front of Crocker, its eyes swirling. "I am Shtasith the Immolator! And were it not for the sufferance of our common master, I would show you the true power of my name!"

"Shhh!" Cluny looked up and down the hall, but no one seemed to be around. "Let's just get out of here before anything else happens, OK? Shtasith, let Crocker carry you."

Steam gusted from the firedrake's snout, but he held still while Crocker took him in shaking hands and tucked him against his still-damp robes. "This is *insane*, Cluny! What . . . what . . . what're we gonna *do?*"

Cluny took a deep breath, Crocker's warm familiar scent and power mixing with the firedrake's, spicy and wild. "We're going to study hard, be very careful, and show these people magic like they've never seen before!"

HOPE FOR THE DAWN

by Catherine Soto

Catherine Soto's work first appeared in *Sword & Sorceress 21*, so this is her third appearance, as well as her third story in the Temple Cats series. She says that bronze fish, with the name of the nation and the month they were to be admitted to the capital, actually were used as tokens for diplomatic embassies during the Tang Dynasty; they were divided in half, and the halves were matched up when the embassy arrived and sought admittance.

Catherine's body may be in San Francisco, but her heart is clearly in China. When not writing or at the obligatory day job, she hangs out at the Asian Art Museum, explores sushi bars, and collects Asian art. She is also currently amassing a collection of t-shirts with Chinese characters, courtesy of the local Olympics store.

L in Mei, in that half-awake state just before waking, dreamt she was a cat. It was just before dawn, and the sound of a temple bell sounded in the distance. She blearily opened her eyes just long enough to identify the bundle of fur on her chest, her cat Twilight. Shadow, Twilight's litter-mate, slept with Lin Mei's brother Biao Mei on the other side of the room.

She closed her eyes again. She recalled the odd dream, fixing it in her memory before it faded away.

Step by step, the boards go by underfoot. Jump up on the box—intriguing smells coming from within. Cinnamon? Jump down, explore more. Coils of rope, bolts of cloth, boxes with more intriguing smells wafting out from inside.

She was walking on four feet. Scent, sound, and touch were as important as sight.

Yawn and stretch. Walk down the middle of the room, past stacks of wonderful-smelling stuff. Outside into the cold night. Almost dawn. Man and woman in shadows. Talking. A quick nod, man runs away into night, woman turns and enters. Follow, crawling through gap under gate. Find sleeping friend. Lie down on top, curl forepaws under chest, feel rise and fall of friendly breathing. Contentment. Sleep.

Lin Mei lay there quietly, enjoying the warmth of the quilt covering her body. It had been a long time since she'd enjoyed such a luxury. Wang Liu, the merchant who owned the compound and was their employer for the winter, had given his guards some old quilts. Guards worked better when they got enough food, sleep, and pay.

It was still dark, but dawn was near. She considered the dream. No doubt the presence of the cats had triggered it, but those dreams were more frequent lately. She recalled a series of similar dreams she'd had earlier that winter, which had turned out to be caused by the presence of a Stone Serpent Demoness in the rock garden in the center of the compound. Her present dreams were doubtless due to the two cats who were sleeping in her room every morning, regardless of where they had started the night. The markings on them: dark faces, paws, and tails, had prompted some people to call them "Devil Cats." Lin Mei didn't believe that; they gave her a warm feeling of comfort when they were nearby.

Biao Mei stirred and turned over under his quilt, dislodging Shadow.

"Time to rise, Sister," Biao Mei said, standing and grabbing his sword and dagger. Lin Mei mouthed a phrase she had not learned at her mother's knee and gently slid out from under the quilt, leaving Twilight undisturbed on the bedding.

Her sword and dagger were by her side also. She slid both into her sash. She and her brother were young, seventeen and fifteen years, but already tragedy and a harsh life had taught them hard lessons. They slept fully clothed and with their weapons close at hand.

Shadow had already curled up on the quilt next to Twilight. Lin Mei and her brother left them and went outside. It was still dark, but the household was already stirring. The kitchen was coming to life. Outside carts went by, the sounds of creaking wheels coming over the compound's walls. Biao Mei walked to the privy, leaving her alone on the veranda. She automatically melted back into the shadow under the eaves, her eyes adjusting to the darkness. And so she was the only one who saw the small side door of the main building open just enough to allow a slender figure to enter the women's quarters. It was one she recognized, and she realized it was also the woman in her dream.

"Too much barley bread last night?" she asked when her brother returned. He made a face. "Watch until I return," she said.

Alone in the privy, she considered her options. As a guard, she should report anything out of the ordinary. But she knew the woman, so the only question was why she had been outside. A nighttime romantic liaison? Perhaps. Something else? Also possible. Finally she decided that discretion was the wiser course. Besides, aside from one glimpse, all Lin Mei had was a dream. While it was known that the ancestors often visited in dreams to bring messages and understanding, they seldom involved cats. For now, silence was best.

After washing and eating a light breakfast, they went to the practice hall and began the day. Along with Biao Mei, she went through the eight Sword Forms, then began again. After the second round, they went out to the well for a drink.

There they met Ro Min and Kin Shin, two female bodyguards who had come from the capital last autumn with Wang Liu's new wife.

"Good morning," Ro Min greeted them.

"Good morning," Biao Mei replied. Lin Mei nodded to hide her smile. Biao had a young boy's crush on Ro Min, who was quite attractive.

"Starting early?" Kin Shin asked. Lin Mei nodded. "Good," Kin Shin replied. "Best get the routines out of the way before the day's events begin."

"What day's events?" Lin Mei asked.

The two bodyguards looked at each other. "The embassy from Tifun arrived yesterday afternoon," Ro Min replied. "The ambassador and his party are staying in the Dragon Inn. But most of the embassy is encamped outside the city walls. Later today the ambassador will present his credentials to the Magistrate." Lin Mei nodded. Kendar was a frontier outpost, albeit a wealthy one, and one of the duties of the Magistrate was to keep an eye on border traffic. Welcoming an embassy—and checking its credentials—would be one of his duties.

"How many are encamped outside?" Biao Mei asked.

"More than a thousand men," Ro Min said. "Most should return home now that they brought the ambassador this far." The embassy would need only a small guard now that they were safely in the Empire.

"I can see why they are encamped outside," Biao Mei said. "Aside from being too many to stay at the inn, letting that many inside Kendar would not be wise." The two bodyguards nodded in agreement. Tifun was a predatory empire to the south, barbaric and warlike. In the last century, it had been expanding out of the Yar Lung Valley. More than a few times, the Empire's armies and the hordes of Tifun had met in battle as they fought for control of the strategic Silk Road.

"The Dragon Inn is just down the street," Kin Shin said. "From the roof you can see in and maybe see the embassy."

She was right. The inn was two compounds over, and they were not the only ones perched on rooftops. In Kendar, far from the capital, buildings were low, one or two stories high, built of earthen walls faced with plaster or tiles to guard against rain. Wide tile roofs were supported by pillars and beams brought down from the mountains.

The Dragon Inn was a converted estate, purchased from the family of a wealthy man who had met an early and, rumor had it, richly-deserved end. It sprawled across half a block, with four main buildings and six minor ones used for storage and servants' quarters. There was generally not enough travel to need such a large establishment, so most of the year the proprietor rented out storage space. But now it was full, with the ambassador's personal guards and servants quartered there.

"There seems to be a commotion," Biao Mei noted. Lin Mei looked where he was pointing. He was right. There was a flurry of movement near the main hall, as officials ran about frantically. An armed man, the bodyguard commander from the look of his richly gilded armor, shouted orders and waved his arms as his men rushed to the inn's gates.

Suddenly he looked up and saw all the spectators. He shouted more orders in the guttural tongue of the Tifun, and his men raised bows.

"Drop!" Ro Min yelled, unnecessarily. Lin Mei and Biao Mei were already dropping to the cover provided by the slope of the roof. They all slid down to the eaves and swung to the courtyard below. Lin Mei noted that even in divided skirts the two bodyguards navigated the descent with practiced ease. Interesting.

"What's going on?" she asked.

"Not certain," Ro Min said. "Go and tell Shin Hu what has happened. We will tell Wang Liu about this." The bodyguards hurried off, while Lin Mei and Biao Mei ran to find their commander.

Shin Hu listened in attentive silence as they recounted what they had seen. When they finished, he gave them a long hard look, then nodded.

"Obviously they are disturbed," he said, pointing at the courtyard. They turned and saw three arrows sticking in the sand garden at the far end of the courtyard. With practiced eyes, they measured the trajectories and saw they intersected with the positions they had occupied on the roof. Those had not been warning shots.

Shin Hu ordered his force to barricade the gates and take up positions on the walls and rooftops, cautioning them about more arrows. "You two," he said, eyeing them with an iron-hard gaze, "see to all the buildings. Make sure there are no intruders." With quick nods they rushed off to obey.

"I know why he wants us to do this," Biao Mei commented as they prowled through the main storage building where trade goods were stacked to the rafters. "We seem to have found quite a few intruders of late."

"Pray to our ancestors we find no more," Lin Mei replied. "With Tifun warriors inside Kendar and shooting arrows at us we have enough worries."

"Truth in that," he replied, peering into a space between stacked bales of silk. "And there are a thousand more outside the walls. I wonder how many of the tales we've heard about them are true?"

"Even one is too many," she replied absently, eyeing a stack of carpets that brushed against the rafters overhead and wondering how to get up and check the space above them. Suddenly she was overtaken by vertigo, and it seemed as if she was looking down from the rafters, instead of up at them. She swayed, and trained reflexes made her drop to one knee and steady herself with one hand on the floorboards.

"Lin Mei!" her brother cried, moving quickly to her side.

"It's nothing," she said, "just a flash of dizziness." In truth the moment had passed, and she felt clear headed again.

She stood, looking about, and then looked up to see Shadow peering down at her from the rafters.

A moment of annoyance came and went, replaced by a sudden thought. With the ease of long practice, she set her mind into meditative state. Then she thought about looking around, seeing what the space above the carpets held. Shadow moved to a spot above the center of the stack and looked around.

Suddenly it came to Lin Mei, a view of the space between the carpets and the roof, enlarged to the size of a great hall, with a carpeted floor stretching to the far distance.

She shut down the vision, a cold certainty growing in her.

"Are you well?" Biao Mei asked, looking at her worriedly.

"Yes," she replied, blinking back to her normal vision.

They finished checking out the rest of the storerooms. Lin Mei noticed that Shadow kept up with them, although he managed to avoid Biao Mei's sight.

Shin Hu listened to their report almost absently. "Get some rest," he ordered brusquely in dismissal. "I suspect we'll be busy later." With that, he turned and strode away to inspect the men on the walls and rooftops, leaving Lin Mei and her brother looking at each other in wonder.

"What is going on?" he asked, in a low worried tone.

"Nothing good, I fear," she replied. She spied Ro Min and Kin Shin sitting on the veranda across the courtyard, inspecting several quivers filled with arrows. That made sense; they were superb archers. But the fact that they were inspecting their armaments was ominous.

"Can you take a walk and talk with the two archers?" she asked her brother. "I suspect they might know more than we do." He nodded and strode across the courtyard. Lin Mei smiled. He would enjoy talking with the two women, especially Ro Min, and she would have some time for an errand of her own.

"So you are here again," the old cook said as she entered the kitchen. He was slicing radishes for the midday meal. She had stopped for a cup of tea, and she brought him one. He set aside his knife and picked it up. "You want something," he said, taking a sip.

She eyed him carefully. He had been a monk in his youth, before a young man's indiscretion and the resulting scandal had sent him away from the monastery and down to the lowlands. But the mountains were the land of Tifun, and there were a hundred Tifun warriors inside Kendar, and a thousand more outside walls that would not stop them for long if they decided to enter. She would have to be careful.

"What do you know about dreams?" she asked. He took a sip of tea, eyeing her closely.

"Dreams can have meaning," he replied. "The ancestors sometimes visit us in dreams, to give warning, or advice. Spirits also can visit, as can ghosts and demons."

"What kind of spirits?" she asked, taking a sip of her tea. He smiled slightly.

"Many kinds," he replied. "The spirits of the mountains, the rivers and streams. Heaven has many, and then there are animal spirits." He saw her eyes look up at that.

"Like cat spirits?" she asked. He sat back, eyeing her with eyes that knew more than they might have wanted to.

"It has happened," he said softly.

"What has happened?" she asked. He looked at her for a long time, his wise old eyes probing her until he felt he was gazing into her soul.

"The Tao, he said slowly, "can take many forms. Like a stream that flows around boulders, over a bed of rocks, or through a bed of sand so that it is not seen from above. It can harden to ice in the winter, or vanish into the air in high summer. It can be solid and hard like a stone, or alive, like a tall tree in the mountains."

"Or something else alive?" she asked. He smiled.

"The abandoned temple you sheltered in early last winter," he began, "was once the abode of the mountain and forest spirits of these lands. When men went away and there was no one to offer the proper services and rites, some of the spirits sought other abodes. Many of the cats who used to guard the temple left. But some stayed, and perhaps there was a reason for that."

"The spirits entered the cats?" she asked.

He gestured to the stove. "If we take a burning ember from the stove and use it to light a lamp, is it the same flame, or is it a new flame that is born of the heat from the old one? If the essence of a spirit quickens a new one in another form, who is to say whether they are the same, or different?"

Something told her she had learned all she was going to, for the moment anyway. She thanked the old cook and left, taking both empty teacups back to the wash rack.

Outside her brother was still in the company of the two bodyguards. She didn't like the look on their faces.

"What's wrong?" she asked.

"The Tifun Fish is missing," Ro Min said. "The ambassador is demanding its return by dawn tomorrow or he will order the city destroyed."

୧୨୧୨ଡ଼ଓ

"When the Khan of the Tifun asked to send an embassy to the Celestial Court, he was presented with a token, a bronze fish," Ro Min explained. "On it is the name of his country and the month they are expected in Chang An. A duplicate of the fish is at the capital. When the embassy arrives the two tokens will be compared and if they match, the embassy will be received. But the embassy must arrive with its token during the month inscribed on it, or they will not be received."

"How much time is left?" Lin Mei asked.

"The embassy is due in the third month," Ro Min replied. There was silence as the news sank in. It was now the week before New Year. The journey to Chang An, the capital, would take at least two months.

"There are no suspects?" Biao Mei asked.

"Everyone in the Dragon Inn is being questioned," Kin Shin said grimly. Inwardly Lin Mei winced. "Questioning" by the Magistrate's men could be a painful business.

"The Inn compound was guarded on all sides by Tifun and Imperial troops," Shin Hu said. "It would have been difficult for thieves to enter and leave. Still, a bronze fish would be easy enough to hide under clothing."

"The embassy arrived early yesterday," Kin Shin noted. "Not much time for thieves to plan something. Most likely, it was done by someone inside."

"Why would thieves steal a bronze fish?" Biao Mei asked. "It is not something you can easily sell in the market." Ro Min gave Lin Mei a sympathetic look; Lin Mei smiled wanly. Her brother was a brave, loyal, and skillful fighter, but she often had to do the thinking for both of them. Fortunately she was up to the task.

"Perhaps the intent was to prevent the embassy from being received," Ro Min pointed out gently, as Kin Shin and the rest of the room struggled to keep their composure.

"Is the ambassador serious about destroying Kendar?" Lin Mei asked.

"With those barbarians, I would take any threats seriously," Shin Hu said.

"It would be an act of war!" Biao Mei said. "Tifun and the Empire would fight again!"

"We would not see it," Shin Hu said grimly. "Riders were seen leaving the Tifun camp just an hour ago. If they return with enough reinforcements, Kendar will be overrun in a day." There was a moment of grim silence. They all knew about barbarian ways of war. A quick death in combat was the best they could hope for.

"Kendar may be a frontier outpost," Shin Hu went on, "but we can make them pay dearly for it."

"Buy low and sell high," Wang Liu chuckled grimly from where he stood in the doorway. "You would have made a good merchant, Shin Hu." Shin Hu grunted at that while everyone else laughed.

"Is there any way to find out more?" Lin Mei asked as she walked outside next to Ro Min.

"Perhaps," the older woman replied absently. "I could inquire." With that she strode away with a swish of her divided skirts.

"What was that about?" Biao Mei asked.

"We'll find out," Lin Mei replied absently. "Can I be alone for a while? I want to get some meditating after all this excitement."

"If it helps you," her brother replied. "I'll take a walk around the city. See what the defenses look like."

"Good idea," she replied. An idea came to her. "Can you make some inquiries about the owners and history of the Dragon Inn?" she asked.

"As you ask, so it is done," her brother replied, settling his sword and dagger in his sash and sauntering off. Lin Mei watched him go off with a fond look. The task would keep him usefully occupied, and he might learn something useful. Meanwhile, she had important business.

Two hours later, she stirred from a semi-trance and opened her eyes, releasing the images in her mind. Nearby the two cats yawned in weariness, settled down on a mat, and dozed off. She didn't blame them; they had had a tiring two hours. So had she, for that matter. But she was beginning to have an idea of what was going on.

She could see with the cats' eyes, hear with their ears, smell and feel what they did. And, to some extent, she could direct their actions. At any rate, she could plant suggestions or ideas in their minds, and they might, or might not, act on them.

She looked about at the walls of their quarters. Biao Mei had not yet returned. Well and good. This was something she needed to think about for a bit. She stirred, easing cramped muscles, and stood. Shoving her sword and dagger in her sash, she went outside.

Kin Shin was at the well. Lin Mei went to stand by her in the shadow of the roof that sheltered it from the sun.

"Any news?" she asked. The older woman shook her head.

"We must wait for Ro Min to return," she said. "And your brother as well." At Lin Mei's look she smiled slightly. "He has been in the market and in the tea rooms inquiring about the Dragon Inn. I think he makes a better swordsman than a spy."

Lin Mei laughed. "He has his value, usually when swords are drawn."

"Wait for Ro Min to return," Kin Shin said soberly. "There may be more useful news then." With that she turned and went back into the women's quarters, leaving Lin Mei puzzled.

After a moment's thought, she sought out Shin Hu, and, after getting his approval, went out into the streets of Kendar, knotting her conical sun hat as she went out through the gates. A short walk later and she was in the center of town.

Normally the streets would be bustling with shoppers, people on errands, and strollers. Now the traffic was sparse, and the few people out went about their affairs hurriedly. There was an air of worry.

She stopped and bought a pair of pork buns from a vendor near the Magistrate's compound, and leaned against a wall nearby to eat them.

"Are they any good?" a voice asked. She turned her head and saw Ro Min.

"They go down and stay down," Lin Mei replied. "That will do."

Ro Min made a face. "I don't want to know where you've eaten," she said. The wall was in the shade; she took up a spot next to the younger girl. "Your brother has been asking questions," she commented. "The Dragon Inn seems to be an object of interest."

"It keeps him busy," Lin Mei replied. "I had some things to consider." Ro Min looked at her for a moment before nodding.

"The interest is not misplaced. The owner of the inn, Chin Ma, is no one I want to see unless it is his turn at the execution grounds."

"He is that bad?" Lin Mei asked, looking at the archer, who nodded.

"He was a business partner of the prior owner, Feng Ha, with caravans going as far as Samarkand and Khoand. People say they did more than trade, often arriving at destinations with more goods than they started out with. Others say they knew routes not on the Imperial census, with profits not listed or taxed."

"Bandits and smugglers," Lin Mei translated.

Ro Min nodded. "Their dealings with people in this city were just as bad, and no one was sad when Feng Ha was found dead, drowned in his own blood, after a late night of wine and singing girls. The doctors said it was a ruptured liver, after all the wine, but some suspect he drank more than wine."

"His partner took over the business?" Lin Mei said.

"He paid a small price for it, and the compound as well, but the family did not contest the offer. They took the money and left for the South. Chin Ma's son runs the caravan business now, and he is more of the same."

"Does his bad character affect business at the Dragon Inn?"

"He has few lodgers, and people wonder why he keeps up the pretense of running an inn."

"Perhaps he has other business an innkeeper's trade will hide," Lin Mei said. Ro Min looked at her for a moment.

"You know more than your years should allow," she said. Lin Mei just looked back.

"The Empire has an interest in his dealings with the lands beyond our borders," the archer went on after a moment. "Gold from Tifun is rumored to rest in Chin Ma's treasure room. His ambitions exceed those of an honest merchant." Lin Mei pondered that for a moment, and then it dawned on her. The furtive pre-dawn meeting, and Kin Shin's cryptic comment by the well.

"Chin Ma is suspected of being a traitor," Lin Mei said, "and you are not *just* a bodyguard." Ro Min looked sideways at her for a moment, as if considering something.

"The game of shadows requires discretion," she said. "Do not say more than needed. Come with me."

Lin Mei followed her into a maze of alleys and short narrow streets. Kendar had grown from a small frontier outpost into a moderately large city, and the inner city reflected its modest origins.

After a while, Ro Min stopped at a seedy noodle and tea shop and entered, Lin Mei behind her. It was empty, and the wizened shopkeeper bowed low in greeting. Ro Min ordered tea, and they sat down at a small table, quietly sipping their tea, until a young man entered. Lin Mei recognized him. She had seen him meeting Ro Min, but that was in her dream.

"Xi An, the shopkeeper's son, and one of our men," Ro Min introduced him. "Xi An, Lin Mei, a trusted friend." Lin Mei and the young man bowed in greeting.

"Did you learn anything?" Ro Min asked.

"Only that there appears to be a lack of cooperation with the Magistrate on the part of Chin Ma," Xi An replied. "He has allowed his servants to be questioned, but is slow to allow a search of his compound."

"Odd," Ro Min said, "considering that there are a hundred Tifun warriors in his compound and a thousand more outside the city, and the ambassador has threatened to destroy the city at dawn if the Bronze Fish medallion is not found."

"The ambassador does not seem concerned," Xi An went on. "He spent the morning with a cool jar of wine and two of his favorite singing girls." Lin Mei wondered how he knew all this. She began to suspect that there were more young men like Xi An in Kendar, and that Ro Min and Kin Shin were much more than they seemed. The hair on the back of her neck prickled. She was swimming in deep water here. But as she listened an idea began to percolate in the back of her mind.

"Is there some way we can get in and do a search of our own?" she asked. "Perhaps the Bronze Fish is in Chin Ma's treasure room."

"There may be," Ro Min said slowly. "Men like Chin Ma avoid the light for their own reasons. So do we. But it is only in poems of the heroic age that heroes sneak into heavily guarded compounds and carry out daring feats."

"We may have a slight advantage," Lin Mei said. "And with the death of Kendar as the alternative, what is there to lose?"

There was no arguing with that, and after a few quiet instructions to Xi An the meeting broke up, and she and Ro Min returned to Wang Liu's compound.

Later, after a short demonstration, Ro Min looked at Lin Mei with a look akin to one who has seen a ghost. The cats were in a corner, lapping up some mare's milk from a bowl.

"You can see with their eyes?" she asked.

"And hear with their ears, and smell with their noses," Lin Mei replied.

"And they will take your orders?"

"As much as cats will," Lin Mei replied. Ro Min looked aside for a moment, as if forming a plan in her mind.

"Get some rest," she said. "I will make some arrangements and talk to some people. We will say nothing about the cats for now." Lin Mei nodded, and the older woman left.

Biao Mei arrived soon after, with very much the same information as Ro Min had given her. "Get some rest," she told him. "Ro Min and Kin Shin may be planning something for later and may need our help."

"Planning what?" he asked, clearly excited.

"She didn't say, but whatever it is, we should be ready and rested." To emphasize the point, she retreated to her sleeping mat and lay down, her blades by her side. After a short while, Biao Mei followed her lead.

Kin Shin came for them just after sunset. Biao Mei and Lin Mei were armed and ready in dark clothing, and their blades were freshly honed. They joined Ro Min, Shin Hu, and three of his men. No one said anything about the pack Lin Mei had slung on her back with two small heads sticking out of the top. They went over the plan, leaving out only a small portion that Ro Min and Lin Mei had worked out earlier.

The streets were already dark, with only a few people out. They were not the only armed groups out, but everyone seemed to have a mission, and, except for the night watch, who let them pass when Ro Min showed them a placard from the Magistrate, no one stopped them. For a moment, Lin Mei wondered what was on the placard and how it had been obtained. Then she decided she didn't want to know.

They passed the Dragon Inn and two more compounds before turning into a narrow alley that wound around an attempt at a garden and ended at the Red Carp, one of Kendar's less reputable establishments. They all stopped to wind black silk scarves around their heads, hiding their faces but for their eyes. Kin Shin knocked on a side door, three quick taps, and it was opened by a middle-aged woman in heavy make-up and an elaborate brocaded gown. Silently she led them down a hallway to a door at the end.

Even with impending doom hanging over the city at dawn, there appeared to be a lively amount of activity in that place, if the sounds from some of the rooms were any indication.

The door at the end of the hallway opened onto a stairway going down into darkness. Torches were lit, and the party went down, hands on the hilts of their weapons. Lin Mei noted that Ro Min and Kin Shin had left behind their long bows in favor of short nomad-style bows.

A door waited at the bottom that opened onto a tunnel cut into the hard soil. They made their way through the tunnel, lit only by the light of their torches. It was a long tunnel, and she noted that there were two side tunnels that led off in opposite directions. So there were ways for patrons to enter the Red Carp without being seen. Interesting. They went to the end of the main tunnel and found a stairway.

"This leads up into the shrine to Chin Ma's ancestors," Ro Min whispered. "It can be locked from within and allow him to be undisturbed after he enters."

"He uses the shrine to his ancestors as a means to visit a brothel?!" Biao Mei asked.

"Not all are as filial as you," Kin Shin said wryly. Ro Min suppressed a smile as Shin Hu led the party upstairs.

The shrine was a small building in the standard design, with an altar to Chin Ma's ancestors at one wall. It was bare save for some candle sconces and a mat on which Chin Ma would presumably kneel and pray to the spirits of his ancestors. A double door at the other end was closed, with a beam of wood that could be used to bolt it shut leaning against the wall next to it. With a few gestures Shin Hu posted his men next to the door.

"Chin Ma's treasure room is in the large building next to this one." Ro Min whispered, unfolding a map she took out from beneath her jacket. "The veranda is screened by Red Flower vines, so once we reach the veranda we will be hidden from view. The treasure room is at the end of the main hallway. A double door opens on the hallway. The treasure room is strongly built, and the walls and the door are of double thickness with a brass lock. This may help us open the door." She took a pouch on her belt. Inside were various hooks and thin pointed rods which Lin Mei recognized as lock-picking tools used by thieves. Merely possessing them was taken as proof of evil intent by most courts.

Shin Hu nodded and went to the small window, peering out. "There are still a hundred men in the courtyard," he reported back.

"We have made arrangements," Ro Min said with a slight smile. "For the moment, we wait."

They settled down on the floor, Shin Hu and his men resting against the wall with the stoicism of veterans. Ro Min and Kin Shin settled into lotus position, their bows and quivers by their sides. Biao Mei imitated them while Lin Mei let Shadow and Twilight loose, letting them roam about and stretch after the confinement in her pack.

"I think they are ready," she said in a low voice after a while. Ro Min nodded and went to the door, opening it just enough to peer out. Lin Mei settled into lotus position, resting her hands on her thighs and closing her eyes. After a few moments, she was in a trance.

Suddenly she was in a large, brightly lit room, which she recognized as the shrine room, only larger. Scents were sharper, the slightest sounds now seemed louder, and she could feel the grain of the wood underfoot.

She thought about going out, and Shadow and Twilight slipped out the door. Outside it was bright with moonlight. A crowd of men sat about fires in the courtyard, drinking and talking. The two cats jumped up on a rock near an ornamental pond and watched, Lin Mei seeing the scene through their eyes. She thought about looking around and the cats swiveled their heads, taking in the whole courtyard.

"No one is looking this way," she said quietly, still in half-trance. Shin Hu nodded.

"We go now!" he said. Lin Mei nodded, calling the cats to her, and stood, breaking the connection. Quickly she followed the rest out the door and through the darkness to the veranda next door, taking the stairs two at a time to end up crouching next to her brother. Shadow and Twilight came scampering up the steps after them.

Ro Min had her lock picks out, and she made quick work of the lock while Kin Shin covered her, an arrow nocked on her bow. With a soft click, the door came unlocked, and she teased it open barely a hand's width. She looked at Lin Mei and nodded.

Lin Mei relaxed against the wall and made contact with the cats, who quickly slipped through the slender gap in the door. By now, Lin Mei was getting the knack of seeing through their eyes and had no difficulty in adjusting to their viewpoint. She was in a large hallway, brightly lit, with two men who stood as the two cats entered.

"Guards," she whispered. "Two, at the end!" Ro Min grabbed her bow, nocked an arrow, and nodded to Shin Hu, who grabbed one of the doors while one of his men took the other. Ro Min stood to shoot while Kin Shin knelt. The doors were barely opened when the arrows were let loose, speeding through the gap.

They heard a sound of impact and then two bodies falling. They all entered quickly, closing the door behind them. Ro Min took a moment to lock it.

Lin Mei scooped up the cats and followed the rest. In moments they were at the treasure room door. Shin Hu's men dragged the dead guards out of the way. Interestingly enough, they were Tifun warriors.

Then they heard the faint sound of splashing water, and voices. Ro Min and Kin Shin looked at Shin Hu, who nodded. The archers nocked fresh arrows, and the rest drew their swords.

The sounds were coming from the door next to the treasure room.

Lin Mei slid to the door, twisted the knob, and pushed it in. Ro Min and Kin Shin stepped to cover it, bows ready, while Shin Hu and his men rushed it.

It was a bath, ornate and redolent with the scents of sandalwood, aloes, and incense. In it were a man, corpulent, with an elaborate topknot, and two pretty girls, who seemed as if they would scream until Shin Hu made a suggestive movement with his sword.

"Who are you?" the man asked angrily, starting to rise until Kin Shin's bow motioned him back down.

"Servants of the Empire," Ro Min said from behind her mask. "And you must be Chin Ma, traitor."

"Bind them," Shin Hu commanded. In moments they were all bound and covered with robes taken from racks at one end of the room.

"We have come for something that is not yours," Ro Min said. "It belongs to the Empire, and will be returned to Chang An."

"Fool!" Chin Ma spat. "The Emperor came to power by the assassin's knife, and so will I."

"Installed by the hordes of Tifun," Shin Hu said. "You will let barbarians sack and loot the capital? And divide the empire?"

"It has happened before," Chin Ma said, "and the empire has recovered. Tifun will get the Western lands, and be a shield against the Turks, and the Empire will be reborn."

"The man is mad," Biao Mei said, wonderingly.

"These types always are," Ro Min said. "We came here to recover a bronze fish. Let's get to work."

It took a bit longer to pick the lock of the treasure room, but eventually they were inside, gazing at stacks of gold bars, copper cash, and jade and silver scroll rollers.

"Enough to pay a rebel army," Sin Hu breathed. "Chin Ma has been planning this for a long time."

"If we do not recover the bronze fish, the empire may fall anyway," Ro Min said. "Let's search."

They found it at the bottom of a stack of scrolls of Sung Poetry, wrapped in a bolt of heavy silk. On one side was the name of Tifun and the sign for the third moon. After ensuring that Chin Ma and his friends were securely bound, they headed back to the door.

࿇ৠৠ৹

Dawn broke soon after the first temple bells finished ringing. The city rose, a sense of dread hanging over it like a heavy fog. Lin Mei and her brother dressed in clean clothes and joined Ro Min and Kin Shin in the courtyard. They were armed with their regular longbows. Shin Hu and his men were arrayed behind them, armed and armored. Wang Liu's regular guards, also armed and armored, ringed the courtyard. He nodded.

"Let's go," he said quietly. They all turned and, in double file, went out through the main gate and into the street, where they met the Magistrate and his guard. They turned and marched down to the Dragon Inn, the Magistrate leading the way.

At the gate of the Dragon Inn, they stopped, and the Magistrate addressed the guards in a loud voice.

"I, Sin Wai, Magistrate, arrive to see the master of this house." Slowly the main gate opened, and Chin Ma, surrounded by guards, came out.

"I, Chin Ma, will see the Magistrate," he said. Lin Mei looked at the guards, saw they were all Tifun, and a chill ran down her back.

"I request the presence of the Ambassador of the Khan of Tifun, who is the guest of this Inn."

"I will see the Magistrate," a loud voice said from within the compound. A tall, lean man strode out, clad in gold-chased robes and a turban.

"Yesterday something was taken that is the Empire's," Sin Wai began. "In the Empire we have justice. We have found the thief and recovered that which was taken." He motioned, and one of his clerks came forward, bearing a box. He opened it and took out an object wrapped in heavy silk. Slowly, ever so slowly, he unwrapped it to reveal the bronze fish.

"You may now continue on your travels into the Empire," Sin Wai said. He motioned, and the clerk stepped forward to present the bronze fish to the ambassador, who took the fish with a placid face, with not a hint of what he was feeling.

"And the thief?" he asked. Slowly Sin Wai raised a hand to point a finger at Chin Ma.

"That is the thief," he said.

"No!" Chin Ma said suddenly. "No!" He drew a dagger from within his robes and lunged at Sin Wai.

Lin Mei had never seen her brother move so fast. With a blur he stepped forward while drawing his sword and slashing down, severing Chin Ma's arm. At the same moment two arrows sped by him, one entering Chin Ma's neck and the other piercing an eye and lodging deep in the skull. Lin Mei looked back, and saw both Ro Min and Kin Shin had arrows already nocked and ready for a second shot, should one be needed.

In an instant swords were drawn by all who had them, Lin Mei among them. She feared there would be a battle. But Sin Wai and the Ambassador both stepped forward, arms raised.

"Cease!" Sin Wai yelled. "Cease! There will be no more blood. This is Imperial business." Slowly swords were lowered.

"I thank you for your efforts," the Tifun ambassador said. "I am pleased at this demonstration of the righteousness of Imperial Justice," he added solemnly.

"We are pleased also," Sin Wai said. "I wish you a safe and pleasant journey." With that he turned and walked away, his entourage following, leaving Chin Ma—and his ambitions—dead.

SCAM ARTISTRY

by Mercedes Lackey & Elisabeth Waters

The most useful friend an editor can have is a writer who, when you call and say "I need something funny, less than 1000 words long, with a strong female character," will produce exactly what you need by the end of the week. This is not, of course, the only—or the most important—reason I value my friendship with Misty, but it certainly doesn't hurt.

Mercedes Lackey made her first sale to *Sword & Sorceress 3* and *4* (she gave Marion Zimmer Bradley two stories that were so good that Marion couldn't bear to part with either of them). She has sold so many stories and novels since then that I can't keep track of them all. At the moment, I think she has at least five different series going at once—and that's just the novels. Her latest book in the Godmother series, *The Snow Queen*, came out in May of this year, the new Valdemar novel, *Foundation,* in October, and she's edited a new Valdemar anthology, *Moving Targets And Other Tales Of Valdemar,* which is due out in December. She's so busy, in fact, that we've been trying to collaborate on a sequel to "Dragon in Distress" (S&S 12, ebook available at Fictionwise.com) for two years now and haven't finished it. To get "Scam Artistry" I had to beg, plead, and write the first draft. I'm really impressed with what she did with it, and I hope that you will be as well. There's just one thing bothering me now: the raven I keep seeing outside my window.

Quoth perched on a cornice above the street and waited for Agatha to catch up with him. She was punctual; he was just early. Having wings helped in getting around the city, especially when there was a Marathon in progress.

Quoth was a familiar; his job was to train young witches. He'd first taken this form about 1910, when, after centuries of being a cat, he'd had enough and decided to go with something with wings. Unfortunately his first young witch had had a penchant for Poe and puns, and had immediately labeled him with the name of "Quoth." Quoth, the raven, could only reflect that at least he hadn't been plastered with the moniker of "Nevermore."

He seemed to attract or be attracted to the odd ones. Not that most witches were anything other than odd but . . . he got the oddest of an odd lot. Take Agatha. Most witches discovered their powers in their teens. Not Agatha. Menopause kicked her witchy ways into high gear. And having been a Flower Child in the 60s who had never quite gotten over it . . . well he was afraid he was going to end up constantly saving her from herself.

Like now. Here came trouble. On an intersection course with Agatha who was jingling her way up the street, patchwork skirt, India blouse, backpack, long braids, love beads and all.

"Can you help me?" the burly man dressed in jeans and a plaid flannel shirt asked. "My truck got towed, and I need bus fare to get back to the office. I'm the construction supervisor— I'm working on a job over there—" he gestured to a building in the next block. "If you give me money for bus fare, I'll meet you back here on Monday and pay you a hundred dollars."

There was certainly a good deal of construction going on in the neighborhood, but most of it was not taking place on Sunday afternoon, and the building he indicated did not show any visible signs of work. Nevertheless, to Quoth's dismay, Agatha dug into her pocket and produced a ten-dollar bill.

"You don't have to pay me back," she said smiling. "You know that sharing is caring, right? And you care about your fellow man and know you need to help?"

The man nodded. From here Quoth could tell he was repressing a smug smile, probably thinking the dippy hippy had done way too many drugs 40 years ago.

Agatha grinned. "Then when you encounter someone in need, give them what you have."

"You sweet child!" the man took the money and gave her a big hug. "Thank you!"

"You're welcome," she said. "Good luck." She smiled again, turned, and continued on her way.

'Sweet child?' A pigeon swooped down to land on the sidewalk in front of her. The face of a pigeon is not well-equipped to express incredulity, but it did its best.

The woman laughed softly and turned into a nearby alley. The pigeon flew after her, landed on her shoulder, and changed to Quoth. 'If he only knew!'

"So I'm older than I look."

'Only by a few decades,' her familiar retorted. 'And might I question the adjective *sweet* as well?'

"He's running a scam," the mage pointed out. "He's not limiting himself to truth."

Quoth did a little hop of surprise. 'If you know it's a scam, why did you give him money?'

"Did you miss the *geas*? 'Then when you encounter someone in need, give them what you have.' He took the money *after* I said that, which means he consented to the terms." She grinned. "He doesn't know it yet, but he just became a generous friend to the poor and needy."

Quoth snapped his beak in shock. "You're not as—"

"—dumb as you thought?" Agatha chuckled. "Welcome to the club. The first thing I did when the Power knocked me over was read everything I could get my hands on about it. You're not dealing with just anyone here, bird. I am a *librarian*."

Quoth gulped. In the world of magic, words were power, and in the world of words, the people who held all the keys—

"Now, shall we get on our way? You were going to show me the little shop where I could get supplies. They'd better not overcharge me. I've been comparison shopping on the net."

"Oh. Right." Quoth flapped heavily into the air.

This was going to be . . . interesting.

൬൬൬൬൬

Books in beautiful packages...

Norilana Books
Classics

www.norilana.com

Publishing some of the best, rare, and precious classics of world literature in trade hardcover and paperback editions.

Printed in the United States
134935LV00011B/8/P

9 781934 648780